Don't Look Back

Amanda Quick

BANTAM BOOKS

NEW YORK TORONTO LONDON SYDNEY AUCKLAND

DON'T LOOK BACK

A Bantam Book / June 2002

Book design by Rachel Reiss

Library of Congress Cataloging-in-Publication Data

Quick, Amanda.
Don't look back / Amanda Quick.
p.   cm.
ISBN 0-553-80200-3 (alk. paper)
1. Gems—Collectors and collecting—Fiction.   I. Title.

PS3561.R44 D66 2002
813'.54—dc21
2001049960

Published simultaneously in the United States and Canada

PRINTED IN THE UNITED STATES OF AMERICA

RRH   10 9 8 7 6 5 4 3 2 1

For Catherine Johns:
What a joy is friendship.

❦

And to Riley and Ferd—both gone but
not forgotten—and all of the other
creatures, large and small, who add an extra
dimension to our lives while they are with us.

Acknowledgments

MY MOST SINCERE THANKS TO CATHERINE JOHNS, CURATOR, Romano-British Collections at The British Museum, for the insights and background on Roman Britain and ancient jewelry. Her personal, professional guidance, together with the wealth of information provided in her many publications, including *The Jewellery of Roman Britain, Celtic and Classical Traditions,* were invaluable. I am even more grateful for the friendship that we forged during the time it took me to write this book.

I also want to thank her for introducing me to Mr. Samuel Lysons, one of the founders of archaeology in Britain. The standards he set in his excavations and the beautifully illustrated reports he created in the late eighteenth and early nineteenth centuries are still admired today by professionals in the field.

I am, of course, solely responsible for any errors.

And, as always, my thanks to Frank, whose support and understanding are matched only by his uncanny ability to rescue me from computer disasters and rolling blackouts. I love you, sweetheart.

Don't
Look Back

Prologue

THE KEEPER SET ASIDE THE CANDLE AND OPENED THE OLD, leather-bound volume. He turned the aged pages carefully until he found the passage he sought.

> ... It is said they meet in secret in the dead of night to conduct their strange ceremonies. There are rumors that the initiates worship the snake-haired Gorgon. Others claim that they gather in obedience to their master, who commands Medusa's power to turn men to stone.
>
> The master's talent is said to be a strange and terrible sort of magic. After inducing a deep trance in his victims, he issues orders to them. When he releases them from their thrall, they execute those commands without question.
>
> The great mystery is that those upon whom the art is practiced have no memory of the instructions they were given while they were entranced.
>
> It is believed that the master's power is greatly enhanced by the forces of the strange gem he wears.

The stone is carved with the fearsome image of Medusa. A wand is cut into the gem below the creature's severed neck. This device is said to be a representation of the magical rod used by the cult's master to effect a trance.

The carved gem is similar to an onyx, save that its alternating bands of colors are rare and exceedingly strange shades of blue, instead of black and white. The dark outer layer is so deep in hue as to be almost black. It frames the image of Medusa, which is cut into the light-colored layer of the stone. This second layer is a shade of blue reminiscent of fine, pale sapphires.

The gold bracelet in which the stone is set is worked with many small piercings to create a pattern of entwined snakes.

The master is greatly dreaded in these parts. His identity is always concealed by a hooded cloak during the cult's ceremonies. None knows his name, but the gem carved with the Gorgon's head and the wand is his emblem and seal. It is also believed to be the source of his power.

I am told that the stone is known as the Blue Medusa.

One

TOBIAS WATCHED LAVINIA WALK UP THE STEPS OF NUMBER 7 Claremont Lane and knew at once that something was very wrong. Beneath the deep brim of her stylish bonnet, her face, always a source of intense fascination for him, showed signs of an odd, brooding tension.

In his admittedly limited experience, Lavinia rarely brooded over a problem or a setback. She was more inclined to take immediate action. *Much* too inclined to do so, in his considered opinion. *Reckless* and *rash* were words that came to mind.

He watched her from the window of the cozy little parlor, every muscle in his body tightening with a battle-ready tension. He had no patience with premonitions and other such metaphysical nonsense, but he trusted his own hunches, especially when it came to matters concerning his new partner and lover. Lavinia looked nothing short of shaken. He knew better than most that it took a great deal to rattle her composure.

"Mrs. Lake is home," he said, glancing at the housekeeper over his shoulder.

"About time." Mrs. Chilton set down the tea tray with an air of enormous relief and bustled toward the door. "Thought she'd never get here. I'll just go and help her with her coat and gloves. She'll be wanting to pour the tea for her guests, I'm sure. Likely be looking forward to a cup herself."

From what he could see of her face in the shadow of the bonnet, Tobias had a feeling that Lavinia was more in need of a healthy dose of some of the sherry she kept in her study. But the medicinal dose of spirits would have to wait.

The guests waiting for her here in the parlor had to be dealt with first.

Lavinia paused at the front door, searching through her large reticule for her key. He could read the signs of strain around her fine eyes quite clearly now.

What the devil had happened?

During the affair of the waxwork murders a few weeks ago, he thought that he had come to know Lavinia rather well. She was not easily flustered, overset, or frightened. Indeed, in the course of his own occasionally dangerous career as an investigator, he had met very few people of either sex who were as cool in threatening circumstances as Lavinia Lake.

It would require something quite dramatic to put that grim expression in her eyes. The prickle of unease that drifted through him had a chilling effect on both his patience and his temper, neither of which was in especially good condition at the moment. He would look into this new situation just as soon as he could get Lavinia alone.

Unfortunately, that would not be for some time. Her guests appeared prepared to converse at some length. Tobias did not care for either of them. The tall, elegantly lean, fashionably attired gentleman, Dr. Howard Hudson, had introduced himself as an old friend of the family.

His wife, Celeste, was one of those extraordinarily attractive females who are only too well aware of their effect on the male of the species and not the least hesitant to use their gifts to manipulate men. Her shining blond hair was piled high on her head, and her eyes were the color of a summer sky. She wore a gossamer-thin muslin gown patterned with tiny pink roses and trimmed with pink and green ribbons. There was a small fan attached to her reticule. Tobias considered that the dress was cut quite low for such a brisk day in early spring, but he was almost certain that the deep neckline was a carefully calculated decision on Celeste's part.

In the twenty minutes he had spent with the pair, he had reached two unshakable conclusions. The first was that Dr. Howard Hudson was a charlatan. The second was that Celeste was an out-and-out adventuress. But he suspected he would do well to keep his opinions to himself. He doubted that Lavinia would welcome them.

"I am so looking forward to seeing Lavinia again," Hudson said from the chair where he reclined with languid ease. "It has been several years since we last met. I am eager to introduce her to my dear Celeste."

Hudson possessed the rich, resonant voice of a trained actor. It had a deep, vibrant quality that one associated with well-tuned instruments. The sound grated on Tobias's nerve endings, but he had to admit that it commanded attention in an almost uncanny fashion.

Hudson cut a decidedly fashionable figure in an excellently tailored dark blue coat, striped waistcoat, and pleated trousers. His neckcloth was tied in an elaborate and unusual manner that Tobias thought his brother-in-law, Anthony, would have admired. At one-and-twenty, Anthony was at the age when young men paid acute attention to such things. He would no doubt also approve of the unusual gold seals that decorated Hudson's watch.

Tobias mentally calculated that the doctor was somewhere in the middle of his forties. Hudson was endowed with the distinguished, well-modeled features of a man who would no doubt always turn ladies' heads, regardless of his age. His wealth of dark brown hair was silvered in a striking manner, and he wore his clothes with an authority and aplomb that would have done credit to Brummell himself in the heyday of his social reign.

"Howard." The strain evaporated from Lavinia's green eyes as she swept into the parlor. She held out both hands in unmistakable and enthusiastic welcome. "Forgive me for being late. I went shopping in Pall Mall and misjudged the time and the traffic."

Tobias was fascinated by the change that had come over her in the past few minutes. If he had not caught that brief glimpse of her expression when she came up the steps, he would never have guessed now that she had been troubled.

It annoyed him that the mere sight of Dr. Howard Hudson had had such an uplifting effect on her mood.

"Lavinia, my dear." Howard rose and took both her hands in his long, well-groomed fingers, squeezing gently. "Words cannot express how wonderful it is to see you again after all this time."

Another wave of disturbing, albeit inexplicable, unease washed through Tobias. Hudson's most arresting features, aside from his riveting voice, were his eyes. An unusual combination of brown and gold in color, they had a compelling effect.

Both voice and gaze were no doubt extremely useful in his profession, Tobias thought. Dr. Howard Hudson was a practitioner of the so-called science of mesmerism.

"I was so very pleased to receive your note yesterday," Lavinia said. "I had no notion that you were in London."

Hudson smiled. "I was the one who was delighted to discover that you were in Town. Imagine my surprise, my dear. The last I heard, you and your niece had gone off to Italy as companions to a lady named Mrs. Underwood."

"Our plans changed quite unexpectedly," Lavinia said smoothly. "Emeline and I were obliged by circumstances to return to England sooner than we had anticipated."

Tobias raised his brows at that understatement, but he wisely kept silent.

"Well, that is certainly fortunate as far as I am concerned." Howard gave her hands another little familiar squeeze and released her. "Allow me to introduce my wife, Celeste."

"How do you do, Mrs. Lake," Celeste murmured in dulcet tones. "Howard has told me so much about you."

Tobias was briefly amused by her manner. The almost theatrically gracious inclination of Celeste's head did not conceal the cold assessment in her pretty eyes. He could see her measuring, weighing, and passing judgment. It was obvious that she immediately dismissed Lavinia as no threat and of no consequence.

He was amused for the first time that afternoon. Dismissing Lavinia was always a mistake.

"This is, indeed, a pleasure." Lavinia sat down on the sofa, arranged the skirts of her plum-colored gown, and picked up the teapot. "I had no notion that Howard had married, but I am delighted to hear it. He has been alone much too long."

"I had no choice in the matter," Howard assured her. "One look at my beautiful Celeste a year ago and my fate was sealed. In addition to making me a lovely wife and companion, she has proven herself quite adept at handling my business accounts and appointment book. Indeed, I do not know how I would get by without her now."

"You flatter me, sir." Celeste lowered her lashes and smiled at Lavinia. "Howard has attempted to teach me some of his skills with mesmerism, but I fear that I have no great talent for the science." She accepted the cup and saucer. "I understand my husband was a dear friend of your parents?"

"He was, indeed." A wistful expression crossed Lavinia's face. "He was a frequent visitor in our home in the old days. My parents were not only exceedingly fond of him, they counted themselves among his greatest admirers. My father told me on several occasions that he considered Howard to be the most accomplished practitioner of mesmerism he had ever met."

"I take that as a very great compliment," Howard said modestly. "Your parents were both extremely skilled in the art themselves. I found it fascinating to watch them work. Each had a unique style, but each achieved amazing results."

"My husband tells me that your parents were lost at sea nearly a decade ago," Celeste murmured. "And that you lost your husband that same year. It must have been an extremely trying time for you."

"Yes." Lavinia poured tea into two more cups. "But my niece, Emeline, came to live with me some six years ago and we do very nicely together. I am sorry that she is not here to meet you this afternoon. She is with friends attending a lecture on the monuments and fountains of Rome."

Celeste managed an expression of polite sympathy. "You and your niece are alone in the world?"

"I do not think of it as being alone," Lavinia said crisply. "We have each other, you see."

"Nevertheless, there are only the two of you. Two women alone in the world." Celeste gave Tobias a veiled glance. "In my experience, being on one's own without the advice and strength of a man to lean upon is always a difficult and unhappy situation for a woman."

Tobias nearly fumbled the cup and saucer that Lavinia had just thrust into his fingers. It was not Celeste's completely inaccurate assessment of Lavinia's and Emeline's personal resources and abilities that jolted him. It was the fact that, for a few seconds there, he could have sworn that the woman was deliberately flirting with him.

"Emeline and I manage very well, thank you," Lavinia said, an unexpected edge on her words. "Pray, have a care, Tobias, or you will spill your tea."

He caught her eye and realized that beneath her drawing-room manners, she was irritated. He wondered what he'd done this time. Their relationship seemed to lurch from the prickly to the passionate with jolting force and very little middle ground, as far as he could determine. Neither of them was entirely comfortable yet with the fiery affair that had blossomed between them. But he could certainly say one thing about their liaison: It was never dull.

That was unfortunate, to his way of thinking. There were times when he would have given a great deal for a few dull moments with Lavinia. The time might provide him with an opportunity to catch his breath.

"Forgive me, Lavinia," Howard said with the air of a man who is about to broach a delicate subject. "I cannot help but notice that you are not practicing your profession. Did you abandon the science of mesmerism because you found the market weak here in London? I know that it is difficult to attract the proper sort of clientele when one lacks social connections."

To Tobias's surprise, the question seemed to catch Lavinia off guard. She gave a tiny start that caused the teacup in her hand to tremble. But she recovered swiftly.

"I have embarked upon another career for a number of reasons," she said crisply. "While the demand for mesmeric therapies appears to be as strong as ever, the competition is extremely fierce in that line and, as you noted, it is not easy to attract an exclusive sort of clientele unless one has connections and references in Society."

"I understand." Howard nodded somberly. "Celeste and I will have our work cut out for us, in that case. It will not be a simple matter for me to establish a new practice here."

"Where have you been practicing until now?" Tobias asked.

"I spent several years in America, traveling and lecturing on the science of mesmerism. A little over a year ago, however, I grew homesick and returned to England."

Celeste sparkled at him. "I met Howard in Bath last year. He had established a flourishing practice there, but he felt it was time to come to London."

"I hope to discover a greater variety of interesting and unusual cases here in Town," Howard explained very seriously. "The vast majority of my clients in Bath, as in America, sought treatments for rather ordinary afflictions. Rheumatism, female hysteria, difficulty with sleeping, that sort of thing. All worrisome enough for the patients, of course, but rather boring for me."

"Howard intends to conduct research and perform experiments in the field of mesmerism." Celeste gave her husband an adoring look. "Indeed, he is dedicated to discovering all of the uses and applications of the science. He hopes to write a book on the subject."

"And to do that successfully, I must be able to examine clients with more exotic nervous disorders than one generally encounters in the country," Howard concluded.

Lavinia's eyes lit with enthusiasm. "That is a very exciting and admirable goal. It is high time that the science of mesmerism was accorded its proper due." She shot a speaking glance in Tobias's direction. "I vow, a great many ill-informed people still persist in believing that mesmerists are all quacks and charlatans of the worst order."

Tobias ignored the barb and swallowed some tea.

Hudson exhaled heavily and shook his head with a grave air. "Unfortunately, I must admit that there are far too many fraudulent practitioners in our profession."

"Only advancements in the science will discourage that sort," Lavinia declared. "Research and experiments are precisely what is needed."

Celeste gave her an inquiring look. "I am curious to know the nature of your new career, Mrs. Lake. There are so few professions open to a lady."

"I am in the business of taking commissions from persons who wish to employ me to make private inquiries." She put her cup down on the saucer. "I believe I have some of my cards around here somewhere." She leaned across the arm of the sofa and opened a small drawer in a table. "Ah, yes, here we are."

She removed two small white cards from the drawer and handed one each to Howard and Celeste.

Tobias knew exactly what was engraved on the little white rectangles.

PRIVATE INQUIRIES
DISCRETION ASSURED

"Most unusual," Celeste said, looking rather baffled.

"Fascinating." Howard pocketed the card and frowned in evident concern. "But I must tell you that I am sorry to learn that you have given up your practice. You had a great gift for mesmerism, my dear. Your decision to change careers is a loss to the profession."

Celeste eyed Lavinia with a considering expression. "Was it only the fear of competition that made you abandon the science?"

If he had not been watching Lavinia, Tobias thought, he would have missed the shuttered expression that came and went very quickly in her eyes. Nor would he have noticed the tightening of the little muscles in her throat. He could have sworn she swallowed before she answered the question.

"There was an . . . unpleasant incident involving a client," Lavinia said neutrally. "And the income was not what one might wish. It is difficult to charge high fees in the country, as I'm sure you know. In addition, I had Emeline's future to consider. She was out of the schoolroom and I thought it time that she acquired a polish. There is nothing like travel abroad to give one some elegance and refinement, I always say. So, what with one thing and another, when Mrs. Underwood's offer of a Season in Rome arrived, I thought it best to accept."

"I see." Howard did not take his eyes off her slightly averted face. "I must admit that I did hear rumors of the unpleasantness in that little village in the North. I trust you did not let it affect you unduly?"

"No, no, of course not," Lavinia said a bit too quickly. "It is just that by the time Emeline and I returned from Italy, I was inspired to try my hand at this new venture and I have found it very much to my taste."

"It is certainly an odd occupation for a lady." Celeste gave Tobias a speculative look. "I assume that you do not disapprove of Mrs. Lake's new profession, sir?"

"I assure you I have moments of extreme doubt and deep uncertainties about it," Tobias said dryly. "Not to mention any number of sleepless nights."

"Mr. March is teasing you." Lavinia gave Tobias a repressive glare. "He is in no position to disapprove. In fact, upon occasion, he undertakes to act as my assistant."

"Your *assistant*?" Celeste's eyes widened in genuine shock. "Do you mean to tell me that you *employ* him?"

"Not quite," Tobias said mildly. "I'm more in the way of being her partner."

Neither Celeste nor Howard appeared to hear his small correction. They were both staring at him, astonished.

Howard blinked his eyes. "Assistant, you say?"

"*Partner*," Tobias repeated very deliberately.

"I engage Tobias's services on the odd case now and again." Lavinia moved one hand in an airy gesture. "Whenever I have need of his particular expertise." She smiled very sweetly at him. "I believe he is only too pleased to have the additional income. Is that not so, sir?"

He was growing impatient with this conversation. It was time to remind her that she was not the only one with teeth.

"It is not just the money that attracts me to our *partnership*," he assured her. "I must admit that I have discovered several additional, extremely pleasant benefits on the side."

She had the grace to blush, but predictably enough, she refused to give ground. She turned back to her guests with a benign smile.

"Our arrangement affords Mr. March the opportunity to exercise his powers of logic and deductive reasoning. He finds the business of being my assistant quite stimulating. Is that not correct, sir?"

"Indeed," Tobias said. "In fact, I think it is safe to say that our association has afforded me some of the most stimulating exercise I've had in years, Mrs. Lake."

Lavinia slitted her eyes in silent warning. He smiled, satisfied, and ate one of the tiny currant-jam pastries Mrs. Chilton had placed on the tea tray. Mrs. Chilton did wonders with currants, he reflected.

"This is all quite fascinating." Celeste examined Tobias over the rim of her teacup. "And just what is the nature of your particular expertise, Mr. March?"

"Mr. March is very good at ferreting out information from certain sources that are not readily available to me," Lavinia said before Tobias could respond. "A gentleman is free to make inquiries in certain places where a lady would not be welcomed, if you see what I mean."

Understanding lit Howard's expression. "What an extraordinary arrangement. I take it this new line has proven more lucrative than your old one, Lavinia?"

"It can be quite profitable." Lavinia paused delicately. "On occasion. But I must admit that in terms of financial remuneration it is a trifle unpredictable."

"I see." Howard looked concerned again.

"But enough about my new career," she said briskly. "Tell me, when do you expect to begin giving therapeutic treatments at your new address, Howard?"

"It will take at least a month or more to make all the final arrangements regarding the furnishings," he said. "Then, too, I must put the word out in the proper quarters to the effect that I will be accepting clients and that I am interested only in the more unusual afflictions of the nerves. If one is not careful, one can find oneself overwhelmed with ladies seeking therapy for female hysteria, and as I mentioned, I do not want to spend my time treating such a mundane disorder."

"I see." Lavinia fixed him with an expression of surprisingly keen interest. "Will you be placing advertisements in the newspapers? I have been considering doing that myself."

Tobias paused in mid-munch and lowered the remains of the currant pastry. "What the devil? You never mentioned any such scheme to me."

"Never mind." She waved away his inquiry with a small sweep of her hand. "I will explain the details later. It is just a notion that I have been toying with lately."

"Toy with something else," he advised. He popped the last bit of pastry into his mouth.

Lavinia shot him a repressive glare.

He pretended not to notice.

Howard cleared his throat. "In truth, I probably will not put notices in the papers because I fear it will only attract the usual assortment of ordinary clients with ordinary nervous problems."

"Yes, I suppose there is some risk of that." Lavinia looked pensive. "Nevertheless, business is business."

The conversation veered off into the arcane and the highly technical aspects of mesmerism. Tobias wandered back to the window and listened to the lively discourse, but he took no part in it.

He had serious misgivings about the entire business of mesmerism. The truth was, until he encountered Lavinia, he had been convinced that the results of the French inquiries into the subject were correct. The investigations had been led by such esteemed scientists as Dr. Franklin and Lavoisier. The conclusions were simple and straightforward: There was no such thing as animal magnetism and therefore mesmerism had no scientific basis. The practice was nothing short of fraud.

He had readily accepted the proposition that the ability to induce a deep trance was a charlatan's act suited only for entertaining the gullible. At most he would have conceded that a skilled mesmerist might possibly be able to exert influence over certain weak-minded individuals, but that only made the business all the more suspect in his opinion.

Nevertheless, there was no denying that the public interest in mesmerism was strong and showed no signs of abating, in spite of the views of many medical doctors and serious scientists. He sometimes found it disquieting that Lavinia was trained in the art.

The Hudsons took their leave half an hour later. Lavinia went to the front door to see them off. Tobias remained at his post at the window and watched Howard hand his wife up into a hackney.

Lavinia waited until the coach had set off before closing the front door. When she walked back into the parlor a moment later, she appeared far more at ease than she had when she had arrived home. The visit with her old family friend had evidently eased some of the tension. Tobias was not certain how he felt about Hudson's power to elevate her mood.

"Would you care for another cup of tea, Tobias?" Lavinia reseated herself on the sofa and picked up the pot. "I am going to have some more."

"No, thank you." He clasped his hands behind his back and looked at her. "What the bloody hell happened while you were out this afternoon?"

She flinched at the question. Tea splashed on the table.

"Good heavens, see what you made me do." She seized a small napkin and went to work blotting up the drops. "What on earth makes you think that something happened to me?"

"You knew that you had guests waiting for you. You had invited them yourself."

She concentrated fiercely on wiping up the small spill. "I told you, I lost track of time and the traffic was terrible."

"Lavinia, I am not a complete idiot, you know."

"Enough, sir." She tossed the napkin aside and fixed him with a dark look. "I am in no mood to be put through one of your inquisitions. Indeed, you have no right to press me about my private affairs. I vow, lately you have begun to sound altogether too much like a husband."

An acute silence fell. The word *husband* hung in the air between them, written in letters of fire.

"When, in fact," Tobias said eventually and very evenly, "I am merely your occasional partner and sometimes lover. Your point, madam?"

A rosy flush colored her cheeks. "Forgive me, sir, I do not know what came over me. That was uncalled for. My only excuse is that I am somewhat vexed at the moment."

"I can see that. Speaking as your concerned, occasional partner, may I ask why?"

Her mouth tightened. "She was flirting with you."

"I beg your pardon?"

"Celeste. She flirted with you. Do not deny it. I saw her. She was not particularly subtle about it, was she?"

He was so astonished that it took him a few seconds to comprehend what she was talking about.

"Celeste Hudson?" he repeated. The implications of the accusation reverberated in his head. "Well, yes, I did notice that she made a few dilatory efforts in that direction, but—"

She sat very straight, her spine rigid. "It was disgusting."

Was Lavinia actually jealous? The dazzling possibility sent a pleasant euphoria through his veins.

He risked a small smile. "It was rather practiced and therefore not particularly flattering, but I would not call it disgusting."

"I would. She is a married woman. She had no business batting those lashes at you the way she did."

"It has been my experience that women who are inclined to flirt do so whether or not they happen to be married. Some sort of inborn compulsion, I suspect."

"How awkward for poor, dear Howard. If she carries on like that with every man in sight, he must be humiliated and unhappy a great deal of the time."

"I doubt that."

"What do you mean?"

"I have a hunch that poor, dear Howard finds his wife's gift for flirtation extremely useful." Tobias crossed to the tea tray and helped himself to another pastry. "In fact, it would not surprise me to learn that he married her precisely for her talents in that line."

"Really, Tobias."

"I am serious. I have no doubt but that she attracted any number of gentlemen clients to his practice in Bath."

Lavinia appeared quite struck by that observation. "I had not thought of that possibility. Do you suppose she was merely attempting to interest you in a series of therapeutic treatments?"

"I think it's safe to say that Mrs. Hudson's eyelash-batting amounted to nothing more than a form of advertisement for Hudson's mesmeric therapy."

"Hmm."

"Now that we have settled that matter," he continued, "let us return to my small inquisition. What the devil happened today while you were out shopping?"

She hesitated and then gave a small sigh. "Nothing significant. I thought I saw someone in the street I once knew." She paused to take a sip of tea. "Someone I did not expect to see here in London."

"Who?"

She wrinkled her nose. "I vow, I have never met anyone who can manage to return so repeatedly to a subject that a person has made very clear that she does not wish to discuss."

"One of my many talents. And no doubt one of the reasons why you continue to employ me as your assistant now and again on the odd case."

She said nothing. Not mutinous or stubborn, he thought. She was deeply uneasy and perhaps not certain where to start her story.

He got to his feet. "Come, my sweet. Let us collect our coats and gloves and take a walk in the park."

Two

"Well, Howard?" Celeste looked at him across the small space that separated them in the hackney. "You said that you were driven by curiosity to see how your old family friend had done in the world. Are you satisfied?"

He contemplated the view of the street, his handsome profile at an oblique angle. "I suppose so. But I confess I find it absolutely extraordinary that Lavinia would abandon a career in mesmerism for such an odd business."

"Perhaps Mr. March is the lure that drew her into this other career. It is obvious that they are lovers."

"Perhaps." Howard paused. "But it is difficult to credit that she would give up the practice for any reason, including a lover. She truly did have a talent for the art. I suspected for some time that she would make a more accomplished practitioner than either of her parents. And they were both very skilled, indeed."

"Passion is a very powerful force." She gave him a knowing smile. "It can cause a woman to alter the course of her life. Only consider our own connection and how my life has changed because of it."

Howard's expression softened. He reached out to pat her gloved hand with his long, elegant fingers. His brilliant eyes darkened.

"It is you who changed my life, my dear," he said in his rich, velvety voice. "I shall be forever grateful that you chose to join your fate with mine."

They were both lying through their teeth, she thought. But they each did it very well.

Howard returned to his study of the busy street. "What do you think of Lavinia's associate, Mr. March?"

She gave herself a moment to ponder the subject of Tobias March. She considered herself something of an authority on the male of the species. For most of her life her fortunes had depended on the accuracy with which she could assess men and the skill she could bring to the task of manipulating them.

She had always possessed an aptitude for the business, but she considered that her serious study of the subject had begun with her first husband. She had been sixteen years old. He had been a widowed shopkeeper in his seventies who had conveniently expired in the middle of an unsuccessful attempt to fulfill his marital duties. She had inherited the shop, but having no intention of spending her life behind a counter, she had immediately sold it for a rather nice sum.

The money from the sale of the small business had enabled her to purchase the gowns and fripperies required to move up a couple of rungs on the social ladder. Her next conquest was a dull-witted son of a member of the local gentry, who had paid her rent for four months before his family discovered the affair and cut off his allowance. There had been others after that, including a man of the cloth who had insisted that she wear the garments of his calling while he made love to her on top of the altar.

The affair had ended when they were discovered by an elderly member of the congregation. The woman had promptly succumbed to a fit of the vapors at the sight of what was happening on the altar. All had not been lost, Celeste reflected. While her lover waved a vinaigrette under the nose of the stricken member of his flock, Celeste had slipped away through a side door, taking with her a very fine pair of candlesticks that she was certain would never be missed from the church's large collection of silver.

The candlesticks had sustained her financially until she met Howard. He had proved to be her greatest triumph to date. She had known the moment she met him that he had unique possibilities. The fact that he was not only personally attracted to her but also appreciated her clever nature had simplified matters. When all was said and done, she was in his debt. He had taught her a great deal.

She sorted through her impressions of Tobias March. Her first observation was that, although he was endowed with excellent shoulders and a very fine physique, he appeared to have little interest in fashion. His coat and trousers had been cut for comfort and ease of movement, not style. The knot in his cravat had been simple and severe, not fashionably intricate.

But she considered herself an astute student of men, one who was accustomed to looking past such superficial elements. She had known immediately that March was very different from the other gentlemen she had encountered in her life. It was obvious to her that he possessed a steel core at the center of his being that had nothing to do with physical prowess. She had seen it in the veiled depths of his cool, enigmatic gaze.

"In spite of Mrs. Lake's comments to the contrary, I do not think that he is merely her assistant," she said finally. "I very much doubt that Mr. March would take orders from anyone, man or woman, unless it suited him to do so."

"I am inclined to agree," Howard said. "When he maintained that he was Lavinia's occasional partner, he did so with the easy air of a man who is merely sparring with his opponent for his own entertainment."

"Yes. He was certainly not enraged or humiliated by Mrs. Lake's claim that he was in her employ. In fact, I gained the distinct impression that the subject of which of them is in command is something of a private joke between them."

Which, in turn, suggested a very intimate connection indeed between Lavinia and Tobias, she thought. She had tried to test that relationship with a bit of flirting, but the results had been inconclusive. March had regarded her with those cold, unreadable eyes and given nothing away.

All in all, Tobias March was a very interesting and no doubt rather dangerous gentleman. He might well prove useful in the new future that she was planning. She would first have to lure him away from Lavinia Lake, of course, but surely that would present little challenge to her unique talents. Mrs. Lake offered little in the way of serious competition, as far as she could see.

Celeste toyed with the little fan that dangled from her reticule and smiled slightly. In her entire life she had never met a man she could not handle.

"What is it that intrigues you so about Mrs. Lake, Howard?" she asked. "I vow, if you continue to carry on like this I shall start to wonder if I ought to be jealous."

"Never that, my dear." He turned his head and transfixed her with the full power of his amazing eyes for a few seconds. His voice deepened. "I promise you, you command all of my passions."

Her breath caught in her throat. This was not a rush of longing or excitement, she knew. It was fear that made her suddenly breathless. But she managed to cover the reaction with another smile and lowered lashes.

"I am relieved to hear that," she said lightly.

She was certain that her voice sounded normal, but her pulse was still beating too heavily. With an effort of will she contrived not to clench her gloved hands.

Howard pinned her with his fascinating gaze for a moment longer. Then he smiled and looked away. "Enough of Lavinia and Mr. March. They are, indeed, an unusual pair, but their odd business is none of our concern."

When his attention shifted back to the street scene, she drew a deep breath. It was as if she had been released from an invisible snare. She collected her scattered thoughts and steadied herself.

In spite of Howard's seemingly casual attitude, she did not entirely trust his careless dismissal of the curiosity that had led him to inform Lavinia of his presence here in Town.

Howard was most definitely intrigued by Mrs. Lake. She told herself that she should welcome the distraction. If nothing else, his interest in his old acquaintance would serve to divert his attention at this critical juncture in her plans. Nevertheless, she had the uneasy feeling that she was missing something.

She watched him closely, studying the distant, contemplative expression on his face. It worried her. These strange periods of withdrawal and silence were becoming more frequent of late. They had begun when he had been seized with the compulsion to go beyond the mere practice of mesmerism and had plunged into extensive research of the subject.

And quite suddenly her well-honed intuitive understanding of the male sex stumbled upon the truth. She saw it all with dazzling clarity.

"You accepted Mrs. Lake's invitation to tea because you wished to discover whether or not she had become as skilled in the practice of mesmerism as yourself," she said quietly. "That is what this is all about, is it not? You had to know if, after all these years, she presented a challenge to your own great talents or if she had somehow learned more than you have discovered."

Howard stiffened ever so slightly. The slight physical reaction confirmed her conclusions. He turned toward her with startling speed and she found herself plunging into the fathomless depths of his eyes.

He said nothing. But she felt as if she were frozen in her seat. She did not think she could have moved even if the carriage had burst into flames. Panic swept through her. He could not possibly know about her plans, she thought frantically. There was no way he could have uncovered her scheme. She had been very, very careful.

Howard smiled, breaking the small spell. The mesmerizing intensity of his gaze faded.

"I congratulate you, my dear," he said. "You are, as always, most insightful. Do you know, I had not fully comprehended my own curiosity about Lavinia until I saw her today for the first time after all these years. It was only then that I realized I had, indeed, been driven to discover whether or not she had fulfilled her potential as a mesmerist. She had such an incredible natural gift for the art, you see. I recognized it years ago when she was but a young girl. I was certain that all she required was time and practice to perfect her skills."

Celeste breathed deeply and recovered her nerve. "Did you perhaps wonder if she had surpassed even your skills, Howard?"

He hesitated. "Perhaps."

"That would be an impossibility." She spoke with absolute, unfeigned conviction. "There is no one more adept. Even the great Mesmer himself must be in awe of your talents."

Howard chuckled. "I thank you for the sentiments, my dear, but under the circumstances, I fear that we are highly unlikely to discover the truth of Mr. Mesmer's degree of admiration for my skills."

"It is unfortunate that he died a few years ago and was never able to see you work. But I assure you that he would have been impressed. No, more likely extremely envious of you, sir. And as for Mrs. Lake, you need not concern yourself with her. She presents absolutely no challenge to you whatsoever. She has obviously chosen to ignore whatever natural aptitude she may have had in favor of another career."

"So it would seem." He patted her gloved hand. "You never fail to lift my spirits, my dear. I vow, I do not know what I would do without you."

She smiled and allowed herself to relax slightly. But she dared not let down her guard entirely. The business that lay ahead of her was too important to be handled carelessly. She had taken risks before, but this affair was far and away the most dangerous scheme upon which she had ever embarked.

It would be worth it, she assured herself. If all went as planned, the profits from the venture would enable her to alter her destiny yet again. She would be in a position to move into Society and at last obtain everything that she had craved so long.

The only obstacle in her path was Howard. She must not underestimate him, she thought.

Three

"THIS HAS CERTAINLY BEEN MY DAY TO COME FACE-TO-FACE WITH persons from my past," Lavinia said. "First my encounter in Pall Mall, and then the visit with Howard Hudson. I hasten to assure you that the two men occupy entirely different positions in my esteem."

They sat together on the stone bench in the artful and quite artificial Gothic ruin that Tobias had discovered years ago. The architect had no doubt intended the graceful structure, with its elegant pillars and charmingly decayed walls, to be used as a place of quiet contemplation. But he had made the mistake of situating it deep in a remote, overgrown section of the large park, and as a result, the public had never taken an interest in it. The fashionable world, after all, came to the park to see and be seen. They did not come in search of privacy and seclusion.

Tobias had come across the ruin in the course of a long walk and had adopted it as his own private retreat. Lavinia knew that she was the only other person he had ever brought here to share it with him.

He had made love to her here. The memory swept through her, stirring a volatile brew of emotions that she had never even dreamed she was capable of experiencing until she met Tobias. Nothing about her association with him was simple or straightforward, she thought. On the one hand, he was the most infuriating man she knew. He was also the most exciting gentleman of her acquaintance. Just the act of sitting here close to him sent little whispers of intense awareness through her.

She did not know yet what to make of their unusual association, with its complicated mix of business and passion. But she did know that life would never again be the same now that she had formed a connection with Tobias March.

"Who was he?" Tobias asked.

She fussed for a moment with the skirts of her gown, purchasing some time to pull her thoughts together.

"It is a long story," she said eventually.

"I am in no hurry."

There was no delicate place to begin. And she knew Tobias well enough by now to realize that he would not give up until he had his answers. In addition to being the most infuriating and most exciting man she had ever met, he was also the most single-minded, persistent, and stubborn.

She may as well get on with the explanations. It was the only way either of them would get home before dark.

"You may recall that I mentioned an unfortunate incident in the North."

"Yes."

"The gentleman I glimpsed in Pall Mall this morning is connected to the incident. His name is Oscar Pelling. The reason I was late arriving home was that I was somewhat rattled by the sight of that dreadful man. I stopped in a tea shop to fortify myself and settle my nerves."

"Tell me about this Oscar Pelling."

"The long and the short of it is that he accused me of being responsible for his wife's death." She paused. "He may well be correct."

There was a short silence while Tobias dealt with that blunt statement. He leaned forward, rested his forearms on his thighs, and loosely clasped his big hands together between his knees. He studied the tall weeds that formed a green screen around the ruin.

"He blamed your mesmeric treatments?" he asked.

"Yes."

"Ah."

She stiffened. "Pray, what does that comment signify, sir?"

"It tells me why you gave up the profession two years ago and turned to a variety of other careers to support yourself and Emeline. You feared that you might have wrought some harm with your art."

There was another silence. A lengthier spell this time.

Lavinia exhaled deeply. "It is no wonder you embarked upon a career in the private-inquiry business, sir. You have a distinct talent for deductive logic."

"Tell me the whole tale," he said.

"Oscar Pelling's wife, Jessica, was one of my clients for a short time. She came to me for treatment of a nervous disorder." She hesitated. "Jessica seemed a very pleasant woman. Pretty. Somewhat taller than average. Elegant. Wealthy, refined ladies of her station frequently possess very sensitive nerves. They are prone to attacks of the vapors and mild bouts of female hysteria."

He nodded. "I've heard that."

"But it was obvious at once that Jessica's condition was much worse than I would have expected. She was, however, very reluctant to allow me to put her into a trance."

"Why did she come to you for treatments if she did not wish to undergo a trance?"

"Perhaps because she felt that she had nowhere else to turn. She came to me only three times. On each of those occasions she was extremely agitated. In the course of the first two visits she questioned me quite closely on the precise nature of a mesmeric trance."

"Did she fear being under someone else's control?"

"Not exactly. Mrs. Pelling seemed more concerned with the possibility that she might unwittingly confide private, personal information in the course of the trance and not recall later just what she had said. I assured her that I would repeat to her precisely whatever words she spoke while in the trance, but I don't think she felt entirely confident of my discretion."

"She did not know you well."

Lavinia smiled briefly. "Thank you for the compliment, Tobias."

He shrugged. "It is nothing short of the truth. I would trust you with my deepest secrets. In fact, I have done so on more than one occasion."

"And I would trust you with mine, sir." She studied the line of his broad shoulders. Tobias could be stubborn and arrogant beyond belief, but one could entrust him with one's life. "I believe we are even now establishing that fact."

He nodded. "Proceed."

"Yes, well, as I said, I got the impression that, although Jessica Pelling was extremely anxious about undergoing the experience, she also felt that she had little choice."

"A desperate woman."

"Yes." Lavinia paused, recalling the events of that last session. "But not, I would have said, a despondent woman."

Tobias glanced at her, surprise glinting in his intelligent eyes. "She was not suffering from melancholia, then?"

"I did not believe so at the time. As I said, during the first two visits we discussed the therapeutic nature of mesmerism. I described it to her as precisely as possible while she paced back and forth in front of my desk."

Tobias unclasped his hands, straightened, and began to massage his left thigh with an absent air. "Mrs. Pelling sounds as if she was serious about seeking a cure for her nervous condition, but she no doubt distrusted the entire business of mesmerism. I can certainly comprehend the dilemma."

"I am well aware that you have no use for the science. You believe that those who give therapeutic treatments with it are all charlatans and quacks, do you not?"

"That is not entirely true," he said evenly. "I believe that some feeble-minded persons may be susceptible to a mesmeric trance. But I do not think that a practitioner would be able to impose his or her will on a man of my nature."

She watched him massage his thigh and thought about the bullet he had taken in his leg several months ago. He had steadfastly refused her offer to use a mesmeric trance to ease the ache he frequently endured.

"Rubbish," she said briskly. "The truth is that the thought of being put into a trance by me unnerves you so that you would prefer to suffer the discomfort of your wound rather than experiment with the procedure. Admit it, sir."

"When I am around you, my dear, I always feel as though I am in a trance."

"Bah. Do not try to fob off such uninspired compliments on me."

"Uninspired?" He abruptly ceased rubbing his thigh. "I am crushed, madam. I thought it a rather charming riposte under the circumstances. In any event, my wound has healed quite nicely without the aid of mesmerism."

"It pains you frequently, especially when the weather turns damp. It is giving you some trouble even as we speak, is it not?"

"I find a glass or two of brandy does wonders," he said. "I shall have some as soon as I get home. Enough on that subject. Pray, continue with your tale."

She switched her attention to the overgrown greenery in front of her. "When Jessica Pelling came to my rooms on the third and last occasion, I could see that she was distraught. She asked no more questions, but simply instructed me to put her directly into a therapeutic trance. I experienced no difficulty in doing so. Indeed, she was an excellent subject. I began to question her in an attempt to discover the source of her anxiety. To my great shock, she revealed that she was in mortal fear of her husband."

"Oscar Pelling?"

"Yes." Lavinia shuddered. "They had been wed for only a year, but she described a nightmarish existence."

She summoned up the details of the last session with Jessica Pelling:

". . . . Oscar is angry again tonight." Jessica *spoke with the unnatural calm of the entranced. "He says that I selected the wrong dishes for the evening meal. He claims that I did it deliberately to flout his*

authority as the master of the house. He tells me that I am defiant. He will have to punish me again. . . ."

Lavinia felt a cold chill in the pit of her stomach. "Did he hurt you last night, Jessica?"

"Yes. He always hurts me when he punishes me. He says it is my fault that he is forced to administer the blows."

"What happened, Jessica?"

"He sends the servants to their quarters. Then he seizes me by the arm. He drags me to the bedchamber and he . . . he hurts me. He strikes me again and again."

Lavinia searched Jessica's attractive face. There was no sign of marks or bruises.

"Where does he strike you, Jessica?"

"My breasts. My stomach. Everywhere but my face. He is always very careful not to bruise my face. He says he does not want anyone to feel sorry for me. I am such a poor wife that I would surely take advantage of a black eye or a cut lip to try to elicit sympathy from those who do not know that I deserved to be punished."

Lavinia stared at her, horrified. "Does he hurt you often?"

"The rages are becoming more frequent. It is as though he is coming closer and closer to losing control altogether. It is clear that he married me only to secure my inheritance. I think that soon now he will kill me."

Lavinia pulled herself out of the memory of the dreadful session.

"I vow, I could not bear to hear any more of her sad tale," Lavinia said. "I cut short the trance and told her what she had said to me."

"How did she respond?"

"She was humiliated. At first she denied it. But I could see from the way she held herself that she was in pain that was of both a psychic and physical nature. When I confronted her with that observation, she broke down and wept."

"What can I do?" Jessica said through her tears.

"Do?" Lavinia was stunned by the simple question. "Why, you must leave him at once, of course."

"I have dreamed of leaving him." Jessica dried her eyes with the handkerchief Lavinia gave her. "But he controls my fortune. I have no close family left to call upon for assistance. I cannot even afford a ticket for the stage to London. And what would I do if I did manage to escape? I have no way to make a living. I would end up on the streets. And I fear that Oscar would come after me. He cannot abide a defiant woman. He would punish me terribly when he found me. He might well kill me."

"You must hide. You could take a new name. Declare yourself to be a widow."

"Not without money." Jessica clutched her reticule very tightly. "I am trapped."

Lavinia looked at the ring that Jessica wore. "Perhaps there is a way . . ."

"It certainly does not surprise me that you got involved in the affair," Tobias said dryly. "What did you do?"

"Jessica wore a very unusual ring. It was gold and set with colored stones and tiny, sparkling diamonds in the shape of a flower. I asked her about it. She told me that it had come down through her family and that she had worn it since she had left the schoolroom. It looked at least somewhat valuable."

Tobias nodded matter-of-factly. "You urged Jessica to use the ring to finance her new life."

Lavinia shrugged. "It seemed the obvious course of action. The only other solution to her problem that I could see was that she contrive to poison Oscar Pelling. Something told me that she would falter at the notion of murdering her husband."

Tobias's mouth edged upward slightly at one corner. "Unlike you?"

"Only as a last resort," she assured him. "In any event, I thought the ring plan was the best. I knew that if she could get to London with it, she would be able to sell it for a reasonable sum. Not enough to allow her to live in luxury for any length of time, of course, but sufficient to give her a means to survive until she could establish herself in a career."

"My sweet, you have reinvented yourself so many times that I fear

you overlook the fact that not everyone is as resourceful and determined as you are."

She sighed. "You may be right. I must say that even though I thought
my plan was splendid, Jessica looked appalled when I outlined it. She
appeared quite daunted by the notion of taking on a new identity and
finding a way to support herself. She had always had money, you see.
The idea of getting by without her fortune terrified her."

"Damned unfair, too," Tobias mused. "After all, the money was
hers."

"Well, yes, of course. I sympathized entirely on that point. But in
my opinion, it was either turn her back on her fortune and take a new
name or start research on the fine art of preparing poison. As I said, I
did not believe that she would be enthusiastic about the latter course
of action."

"Sometimes you send a bit of a chill through me, Lavinia."

"Nonsense. I'm certain that had you been in my shoes, you would
have given her the same advice."

He shrugged and offered no comment.

She frowned, rethinking her remark. "I take that back. You
wouldn't have advised her to go to the trouble of establishing a new
identity. You would have arranged for Pelling to meet with a nasty accident."

"As I was not in your shoes, there is no point speculating."

"Sometimes you send a bit of a chill through me, sir."

He smiled at the echo of his own words, no doubt concluding that
she was making a small joke. But she was not joking, she thought.
Sometimes he did send a small chill through her. There were some
shadowy places deep inside Tobias. Occasionally it struck her quite
forcibly that there was still a great deal that she did not know
about him.

"What happened to Jessica Pelling?" he asked.

"I never saw her again," Lavinia whispered. "She committed suicide
the following day."

"How? An overdose of laudanum? Did she drink too much of the
milk of the poppy?"

"No. She chose a more dramatic means. She went out riding in the midst of a violent storm and cast herself into the swollen river. Her horse returned without her. Later a maid found a note in Mrs. Pelling's bedchamber declaring her intention to drown herself."

"Hmm."

There was a short silence.

"They never found her body."

"Hmm."

"It happened from time to time." Lavinia clasped her hands very tightly in her lap. The memories of that awful day were so fresh and vivid now that she had to fight to draw air into her lungs. "The river was very deep and treacherous in places. It was not unheard of for some unfortunate soul to fall in when it was in flood and never be seen again."

"Oscar Pelling blamed you for his wife's death?"

"Yes. He confronted me in the street immediately after the searchers had abandoned all hope. He was in a state of such rage that I...I was almost afraid for my own safety."

A great stillness came over Tobias. "Did he touch you? Put his hands on you? Hurt you in any way?"

The implacable expression that had appeared in his eyes nearly took her breath away. She swallowed and hurried on with her tale.

"No," she said quickly. "No, indeed. He would hardly have dared to attack me in front of so many witnesses. But he accused me of driving Jessica to her death with my mesmeric treatments."

"I see."

"He made certain that the rumors of my incompetence spread quickly throughout the countryside. Within a very short time Oscar Pelling had utterly destroyed my reputation in the region. I lost all of my clients." She hesitated. "In truth, I was no longer certain that I wanted to continue in the profession."

"Because you feared that Pelling was correct. That your therapy had played some role in Jessica's death."

"Yes."

There it was, she thought: Her darkest secret had now been revealed to Tobias. It suddenly dawned on her that this was the real reason she had been so shaken by the sight of Oscar Pelling. Her intuition had told her that it would somehow lead to this terrible moment when Tobias would discover that she had been involved in the death of an innocent woman. She knew all too well how much he distrusted the science of mesmerism and what he thought of those who practiced the art. She braced herself for his reaction, even as a part of her wondered when and how his opinion of her character had become so important. Why did she care so much what he thought of her?

"Pay close attention to me, Lavinia." Tobias reached out and covered her tightly knit fingers with his own large, powerful hand. "You bear no guilt in the matter. You only tried to help her. It was a desperate situation and it called for desperate measures. Your plan for Jessica to use her ring to pay for her new life under a new name was an excellent scheme. It is not your fault that she lacked the nerve and the will to carry it out."

At first she thought she had not heard him aright. *Tobias was not blaming her*. The world seemed to brighten a bit, the air becoming clearer and more fragrant. She allowed herself to breathe again.

"But perhaps by encouraging her to take such a risk, I forced her to confront her own helplessness and cast her into the depths of despair." Lavinia squeezed her fingers into her palms. "Perhaps I made her feel that it was all hopeless and that the only way out was suicide."

"You showed her a possible escape route. It was up to Jessica to use it." Tobias pulled her snugly against his side and wrapped his arm around her. "You did all that you could."

It was odd how pleasant it was to nestle against him, she thought. He was an exceedingly difficult man, but on occasion, Tobias's solid, unwavering strength had a decidedly soothing effect on her senses.

He did not blame her for what had happened.

"I should not have let that brief glimpse of Pelling upset me so today," she said after a while. "It is perfectly reasonable that a gentleman of his wealth and position would come to Town occasionally to shop and to tend to his business affairs."

"Very true."

"And it is not at all strange that I chanced to see him in Pall Mall. After all, London is a small world in many ways, especially when it comes to shopping."

"It was not the surprise of seeing a familiar face in Pall Mall that unsettled your nerves," Tobias said. "It was that spotting Pelling brought back memories of the incident that destroyed your career as a mesmerist."

"In part." But mostly it was because I sensed that I would have to confess it all to you, she added silently. That was why I had to stop for that cup of tea. That was why I was late. I did not want to face you with this tale.

But it was done. The truth had come out and Tobias did not hold it against her. Indeed, he painted her as something of a heroine in the drama. Astonishing.

"You have a new career now, Lavinia," he said bracingly. "What happened in the past no longer matters."

She relaxed a little more, savoring the heat of his body.

After a while he cradled her head in the crook of his arm and lowered his mouth to hers.

"It is a little chilly out here for this sort of thing," she mumbled against his lips.

"I will warm you," he promised.

$\mathcal{F}$our

THE SMALL GROUP OF EAGER YOUNG GALLANTS THAT HAD ENCIR-cled Emeline on the front steps of the institute made Anthony uneasy. They all professed a great interest in discussing the lecture they had just attended, but he suspected most of them had ulterior motives. Emeline, however, appeared unaware of that possibility. She was busily holding forth with her opinion of the talk.

"I fear that Mr. Lexington has not spent much time, if any, in Italy," Emeline declared. "He gave a very poor description of Roman monuments and fountains. As it happens, my aunt and I had an opportunity to spend some time in that city recently, and I—"

"That no doubt accounts for your brilliant sense of fashion," one gentleman declared fervently. "I vow, that gown you are wearing is a most exquisite shade of amber gold. The color of the sky at sunset. It is surpassed only by the brilliant glow of your eyes, Miss Emeline."

There were several murmurs of agreement.

Emeline never faltered. "Thank you, sir. Now, as I was saying, my aunt and I were fortunate enough to be able to stay for some months in Rome, and I can assure you, Mr. Lexington did not do justice to his subject. He failed to convey the true elegance of the standing monuments. As it happens, while in Italy, I was able to make several sketches and some drawings—"

"I would very much enjoy viewing your sketches, Miss Emeline," said a voice at the edge of the crowd.

"As would I, Miss Emeline."

"No monument, no matter how spectacular, could compare to your own elegance, Miss Emeline," someone else vouchsafed.

He'd had quite enough, Anthony thought. He made a show of removing his watch from his pocket. "I'm afraid I must interrupt, Miss Emeline. The hour grows late. I promised your aunt that you would be home by five o'clock. We will have to hurry."

"Yes, of course." Emeline bestowed a charming smile on the small group. "Mr. Sinclair is quite correct. We must be off. But I have very much enjoyed our conversation. It is quite amazing, really. I had no notion that so many of you were interested in Roman fountains and monuments."

"Fascinated, Miss Emeline." A gentleman dressed in a coat that was cut so snugly Anthony wondered how he could move his arms swept her a deep bow. "I assure you, I am absolutely entranced by the subject and by your remarks on it."

"Transfixed," another assured her.

That started a heated competition in which every man in the group sought to convince Emeline that his own intellectual interests were more elevated than those of anyone else in the crowd.

It was all Anthony could do to avoid baring his teeth. He tucked Emeline's arm in his and drew her swiftly down the steps. A chorus of farewells drifted after them.

"I did not realize that we were so pressed for time," Emeline murmured.

"Have no fear," Anthony said. "We will be home before your aunt begins to fret."

"What did you think of Mr. Lexington's lecture?" she asked.

He hesitated and then shrugged. "To be perfectly blunt, I found it quite dull."

She gave her warm laugh. "We are in agreement on that point. Nevertheless, I very much enjoyed the afternoon."

"As did I."

He would have enjoyed it far more, he thought, had he not been obliged to wade through the herd of dandies gathered inside the lecture hall. He was quite certain they had not been drawn there by an interest in Roman monuments and fountains. Emeline was the lure. She had come into a mild sort of fashion lately after a number of successful appearances in some of the most important ballrooms of the ton.

He was well aware that Emeline's lack of an inheritance and family connections would not allow her to swim in exalted social circles for long, in spite of Lavinia's machinations. Furthermore, prudent matchmaking mamas would work hard to ensure that their sons did not look too seriously in Emeline's direction.

Unfortunately, that did not prevent many of the young bloods of Society from being intrigued by a lovely and unusual Original. Nor would it stop heartless rakes and debauchers from attempting to seduce her as a form of perverted sport.

He had appointed himself Emeline's guardian, and he considered it his duty to protect her from unwanted attentions. But what worried him the most these days was that she might decide to sample some of those attentions.

It would all be so much simpler if he was in a position to declare his affections and make an offer for her hand. But the long and the short of it was that he could not afford to keep her in the style to which she deserved to become accustomed.

He had spent a great deal of time lately pondering his problems and concocting various possible solutions. It all came down to one key point: He had to find a way to make a decent living and he had to do so quickly, before one of the men hanging around Emeline defied his parents and convinced her to run off with him.

The walk home to the little house in Claremont Lane was a brisk one, due not only to the fact that the afternoon was coming to a close but because the threat of rain dampened the air.

"Is something wrong?" Emeline asked when they reached the little park and turned the corner. "Are you ill?"

That startled him out of his reverie. It annoyed him that she thought him sickly. "No, I am not ill. I am thinking."

"Oh. I thought, perhaps, from your expression that the ice cream we had earlier did not sit well."

"I assure you, I am in excellent health, Emeline."

"I was merely concerned."

"Emeline, your aunt has made it clear that she wishes you to enjoy another Season before you even think of accepting an offer of marriage."

"What on earth does marriage have to do with this?"

He braced himself. "It is quite likely that at any moment one of those...those *gentlemen* who accosted you after the lecture today might decide to offer for your hand."

"Oh, I doubt that. None of their mamas or papas would approve. They can all look a good deal higher for wives and I'm sure they will do precisely that when the time comes."

"It is not unheard of for a reckless man to...to elope with someone whom his parents might not deem suitable," Anthony said darkly.

"As gentlemen are forever doing in those books of poetry that Aunt Lavinia loves to read?" Emeline chuckled. "How very romantic. But I very much doubt that I am the type to inspire a runaway marriage."

"You are *precisely* the type." Anthony came to a sudden halt and turned to face her. "You must be on your guard, Emeline. There is no telling when some rake may show up at your bedroom window in the middle of the night and beg you to join him in the carriage he has waiting in the street." Just as he had envisioned himself doing in certain fevered fantasies, he thought.

"A Gretna Green marriage?" Emeline's eyes widened. "Nonsense. I cannot imagine any of those gentlemen having the spirit to do anything so thrilling."

Anthony felt his stomach clench. "You mean that you would consider it *exciting* to run off with one of those empty-headed dandies?"

"Yes, indeed."

His blood ran cold.

And then she smiled. "Quite impossible, of course."

"Impossible." He seized on that. "Yes, of course. Absolutely impossible."

"Indeed."

But it was not impossible and well he knew it. It had happened on at least one occasion last Season that he was aware of, and it would no doubt happen again this Season. Sooner or later, a young couple who had been forbidden to wed would run off to Gretna Green in the middle of the night. If their frantic papas did not catch up with them before the deed was done, the pair would return as newlyweds. Their parents would be forced to accept the fait accompli. And Society would have yet another tidbit of gossip to savor over tea.

If he had an ounce of common sense he would keep silent, Anthony thought. Instead, he cleared his throat.

"Uh, why precisely do you say it would be *impossible* to make a runaway marriage with one of those gentlemen?" he asked carefully.

"Because I am not in love with any of them, of course." She glanced at the tiny watch pinned to the front of her pelisse. "Come along, Anthony, we must hurry. We do not want to get caught in the rain. Aunt Lavinia will have an attack of the vapors if I ruin this new gown."

She was not in love with any of them.

It did not follow, he reminded himself, that she loved *him*, but at least she had not developed a tendre for anyone else.

His spirits revived miraculously. He grinned. "Calm yourself, Emeline. Any lady who can take Tobias on as a business partner is hardly likely to faint dead away at the notion of a ruined gown."

Emeline laughed. "You do not know how much stock Aunt Lavinia places in Madam Francesca's gowns. She considers them investments."

Unfortunately, he knew precisely why Lavinia was investing heavily in gowns from the exclusive dressmaker these days, he thought. She still entertained visions of marrying Emeline off into the ton.

Halfway along Claremont Lane, he saw Tobias and Lavinia going up the front steps of Number 7.

"It looks as though we are not the only ones who are late arriving home today," Emeline said cheerfully. "Lavinia and Mr. March must have gone out for some exercise."

Anthony studied Tobias lounging against the iron railing while he waited for Lavinia to retrieve her key from her reticule. Even from this distance he could detect his brother-in-law's air of deep satisfaction. Tobias looked very much like a large beast relaxing after a successful hunt.

"A rather lively bit of exercise, if I am not mistaken," Anthony muttered.

"I beg your pardon?" She gave him a curious look.

Fortunately he did not have to come up with an explanation for the remark. At that moment Tobias turned his head and saw them coming toward the steps.

"Good afternoon, Miss Emeline." Tobias nodded at her. "How was the lecture?"

"Not as learned as one might have hoped, but Anthony and I had a pleasant day nonetheless," Emeline said easily.

Mrs. Chilton got the door open just as Lavinia found her key.

"Would you care to come in for some tea?" Lavinia asked Anthony.

"Thank you, no." He looked pointedly at Tobias. "I wish to speak with you, if you don't mind."

Tobias elevated one brow and straightened away from the iron railing. "Can it wait?"

"I'm afraid not. It is a matter of some importance."

"Very well. We can discuss it on the way to my club." Tobias turned to Lavinia. "I will bid you good day, madam."

"Good day, sir."

Anthony was somewhat surprised by the uncharacteristically soft nature of her farewell, but Tobias did not appear to find it odd.

They waited until the ladies were safely inside their own front hall before heading toward the corner to find a hackney.

They managed to hail a carriage without difficulty and got into the cab.

Tobias settled onto one of the seats and gave Anthony a considering look.

"Is there something amiss? You look as if you have swallowed a spoonful of unpleasant medicine."

This was the second time in the past hour that someone had assumed him to be ill from his expression, he realized. It was annoying.

"I am in need of a fortune," he announced.

"Aren't we all?" Tobias stretched out his left leg. "If you find one, let me know. I will be delighted to share it with you."

"I am serious. I wish to acquire a sum of money that will enable me to support a wife in a proper style."

"Bloody hell." Tobias met his eyes. "You're in love with Miss Emeline, aren't you?"

"Yes."

"Damnation, I was afraid of this. Have you declared your affections to her?"

"Of course not. I am in no position to do so, because I cannot ask her to marry me."

Tobias nodded in resigned comprehension. "Because you lack a fortune."

Anthony drummed his fingers on the window ledge. "I have been giving the matter some thought."

"Lord save us from young men who think too much."

"I am very determined about this."

"Yes, I can see that. I collect that you have concocted a plan to acquire this fortune you feel you need?"

"I have a good head for cards. With a bit of practice—"

"No."

"Granted, I have never played them for high stakes because you have always been so opposed to the notion of gambling, but I believe that I could do quite well at the tables."

"No."

"Hear me out." Anthony leaned forward, intent on pressing his point. "The vast majority of gamesters do not approach their play in a logical manner. Indeed, they usually sit down to their cards after they are well into their cups. It is no wonder that most gentlemen lose heavily. I, however, intend to treat gaming from the standpoint of a mathematical problem."

"Your sister would come back to haunt me if I were to allow you to go into the hells. You know as well as I do that her greatest fear was that you would become a gamester."

"I know that Ann feared I would end up destitute, as our father did. But I assure you, that would not be the case."

"Hell's teeth, it is not the fact that your father lost everything he possessed because he could not resist the damned gaming tables that worried her so greatly. It is that he got himself killed over a disputed hand of cards while trying to recover his losses. In the long run, there is no winning in that career."

"I am not my father."

"I know that."

Anthony stiffened. He had dreaded this conflict, well aware from the moment he had hatched his scheme that it loomed in front of him. The strategy was complicated, but he told himself he had to stick with it.

"I do not wish to argue with you over this matter," he said. "We both know that you cannot stop me. I am no longer a boy. This is my decision to make."

Tobias's eyes darkened to the shade of a storm at sea. In all the years he had lived with this man who had been more of a father to him than his own parent, Anthony thought, he had rarely seen such cold and implacable promise in his gaze. A chill went through him.

"Let us be clear on this," Tobias said in his softest, most dangerous voice. "If you insist upon going into the hells, you can expect the devil's own quarrel with me. You may believe that I cannot stop you, but you can count on finding me in your path every time you turn around. I have an obligation to Ann's memory. Do not think that I will ignore my promise to her."

He had known this would be difficult, Anthony reminded himself. He drew a deep breath and straightened his shoulders.

"I have no wish to be at odds with you over this," he said. "You know full well that I respect you and your loyalty to your oath. But I am quite desperate and I do not see that I have any great choice in the matter."

Instead of launching into another lecture, Tobias turned his attention to the darkening street outside the window. He sank into a deep, brooding silence.

Anthony endured it as long as he could. Then he made a stab at trying to lighten the grim atmosphere inside the carriage.

"Tobias? Do you intend to cease speaking to me altogether?" He forced a small smile. "That is not like you. I expected something a bit more forceful. A threat to cut off my quarterly allowance, such as it is, perhaps."

"I told you a moment ago that you are not the only one who would very much like to get his hands on a fortune."

Anthony was bemused by the sudden change in the direction of the discussion. "I assumed you were joking."

"I assure you, I am not joking."

Comprehension struck with the force of summer lightning. "Good God, this is about Mrs. Lake, is it not? Are you thinking of asking her to marry you?"

Tobias turned his head very slightly. "I am in no more of a position to ask her to marry me than you are in a position to ask Miss Emeline for her hand."

He would never get a better opening, Anthony thought. It was time to shift to the second phase of his carefully calculated plan.

"On the contrary," he said smoothly. "You are not in such dire straits. In fact, I envy you. After all, it is not as if you are totally lacking in resources. You make fat commissions from time to time in the course of your career as an investigator."

"My profession is a highly erratic and unpredictable means of making a living and well you know it."

"Mrs. Dove certainly paid you handsomely for the inquiries you made on her behalf in the affair of the waxwork murders. You came away with sufficient funds to enable you to invest in one of Crackenburne's ships, did you not?"

"I was able to afford only a single share in that venture. Furthermore, I will have no way of knowing whether or not it will be successful, let alone to what extent, until the bloody ship returns from the East. That will not happen for several months."

"And in the meantime, you must bide your time and hope that Mrs. Lake does not get swept off her feet by some other gentleman who can afford to support a wife," Anthony said.

"As you can see, I am not unsympathetic to your plight."

Anthony shrugged. "If it is any comfort, I very much doubt that Mrs. Lake would ever marry for money."

Tobias said nothing. He went back to gazing out the window.

"Emeline has discussed her aunt's feelings on the subject of marriage with me," Anthony said.

That information got Tobias's attention. "What did Miss Emeline tell you?"

"She is quite certain that, although Mrs. Lake is always going on about the importance of finances, she secretly possesses a deeply romantic nature."

"Lavinia? Romantic? Where in Hades did Emeline get that notion?"

"I expect it is Mrs. Lake's taste for romantic poetry that gave her the notion."

Tobias brooded on that for a moment. Then he shook his head. "Devil take it, there is no denying that Lavinia is very fond of poetry. But she is far too pragmatic to allow it to influence her personal decisions."

Anthony sighed inwardly. He reminded himself that, while Tobias possessed any number of excellent qualities, his brother-in-law had no patience with romantic or sentimental gestures, nor had he ever bothered to hone the fine art of charming the ladies.

"Emeline seems absolutely certain that, because of her romantical sensibilities, Mrs. Lake would never be able to give herself in a loveless marriage," he said patiently. "No matter how financially secure the arrangement promised to be."

"Hmm."

Tobias's air of gloom would have been almost humorous under

other circumstances, Anthony thought. But in truth, he actually felt rather sorry for his brother-in-law.

Tobias had indulged in occasional affairs in the past, Anthony reflected, but since they had lost Ann and the babe all those years ago, he had never known his brother-in-law to care enough about a lady to allow himself to be brought to this sort of impasse. The business with Mrs. Lake was serious. Tobias required guidance.

Anthony cleared his throat. "It strikes me that you would do well to take a more romantical approach with Mrs. Lake. I cannot help but notice that you seem to be quite brusque with her on occasion."

"No doubt because she insists upon arguing with me at every turn. I have never met a more stubborn female."

"I expect she grows weary of listening to you issue orders."

Tobias's jaw clenched. "Bloody hell. I can hardly be expected to transform myself into an imitation of Byron and his ilk. For one thing, I am too old to play the romantic poet. For another, I cannot write verse worth a damn."

"I am not suggesting that you become a poet. Just that you might try the odd poetical turn of phrase."

Tobias narrowed his eyes. "Such as?"

"Well, upon first greeting her in the morning, you could compare her to a goddess."

"A *goddess*? Have you gone mad?"

"Just a suggestion."

Tobias started to massage his left thigh. He fell silent for a long moment.

"Which goddess?" he asked eventually.

"Well, one can never go wrong likening a lady to Venus."

"Venus. That is absolute rubbish. Lavinia would laugh in my face."

"I don't think so," Anthony said softly. "I do not think that any lady would laugh at finding herself compared to Venus in the morning."

"Huh."

He had done all he could for the moment, Anthony thought. It was time to shift the subject back to the more pressing topic.

"If I could come up with the necessary blunt," he said casually, "perhaps Crackenburne would allow me to purchase a share in one of his shipping ventures also."

"You will not find the money you need for an investment in those infernal clubs where fools seek their fortunes with hazard and cards," Tobias said. "There is a reason they call them hells."

The somber shadows lengthened in the carriage.

Tobias's mouth thinned. "I have told you often enough that you could make an excellent career as a man of business. You have a head for figures and details. Crackenburne would be happy to recommend you to one of his friends."

"I have no interest in that profession."

Silence fell.

"I do have another suggestion," Anthony said. He was cautious now, feeling his way as he slipped closer to his ultimate goal.

Tobias looked wary. "What is it?"

"You could take me on as your assistant."

"You already perform that function on occasion."

"But only in the most informal manner." Anthony warmed to his topic. The notion had been brewing in the back of his mind all afternoon. "I mean to assume a post as your official assistant. A sort of man of affairs for you, as it were. In return, you will teach me the fine points of making private inquiries and conducting investigations."

"And what do you expect to gain?"

"An income," Anthony said.

"Instead of an allowance, do you mean?" Tobias asked dryly.

"Precisely. And occasional bonuses would be nice."

"Wouldn't they, though? Nothing like an occasional bonus, I always say."

Anthony sucked in a deep breath. "Will you at least think about my proposition?"

Tobias met his eyes. "You're serious, are you not?"

"Never more so. I believe that I have a flair for the profession."

"I'm not sure that there is any such thing as a *flair* for this line of work," Tobias said. "In my experience, one falls into this business when other, more respectable alternatives fail to produce an income that is sufficient to keep one out of the workhouse. Rather like the career of streetwalking."

Five

EMELINE LOOKED AT LAVINIA ACROSS THE WIDTH OF THE BREAK-fast table. "You are quite certain that this business of seeing Oscar Pelling in the street yesterday has not disturbed you unduly?"

"I admit I was somewhat jolted initially by the sight of him." Lavinia opened her newspaper. "But I have recovered nicely, thank you."

Thanks to the fact that she no longer had to conceal her dark secret from Tobias, she added silently.

"You always do."

"Always do what?"

Emeline smiled. "Recover nicely. Indeed, you have a talent for bouncing back, my dear aunt."

"Yes, well, one really has no alternative, does one?" Lavinia took a sip of coffee. "And as I said, it was likely that sooner or later I would come across Pelling now that we are back in London. Even gentlemen who prefer their estates, as Pelling does, must come to Town once in a while to tend to their business affairs. At least he did not appear to notice me."

"I suppose so." Emeline made a face. "Dreadful man. I trust he will soon return to his estates."

"I'm sure he will. He was not one to enjoy the pleasures of Society, as I recall." Lavinia turned a page of the newspaper. And who cared a fig about Pelling, anyway, now that Tobias knew the truth and did not count it against her? Life certainly seemed a good bit lighter and brighter this morning.

Emeline helped herself to some jam from the little pot in the center of the table. "I want to talk to you, if you don't mind."

"You are talking to me."

"I mean, I want to discuss something important. I have been thinking about my career."

"What career? You don't have one."

Lavinia did not look up from the newspaper. A sheet of paper and a pencil lay on the table next to her coffee cup. After much thought, she had concluded that before undertaking the task of writing an advertisement for the newspapers, it would be instructive to study the subject.

To that end, she had decided to make a list of especially effective words and phrases that appeared in the most attractive advertisements. Her goal was to develop a riveting vocabulary that could be employed in the notices that she herself eventually would write to advertise her services as an investigator.

The notices in this morning's paper were a varied lot. Most were not particularly arresting, in Lavinia's opinion. There was an announcement of rooms available to let *with a pleasant view of the park,* and another alerting *gentlemen of fashion to the arrival of superior cotton shirting guaranteed to prevent profuse perspiration.*

Far and away the most interesting notice had been placed by a Dr. G. A. Darfield, who offered treatments for *widows and married ladies who suffer from delicate nerves and female hysteria.* He promised *singularly effective remedies especially suited to the female constitution.*

"That is precisely my point," Emeline said. "I do not have a career."

"Of course you don't." Lavinia pondered the advertisement that offered treatments for female hysteria. "What do you think of the phrase *singularly effective remedies?*"

"It sounds too medicinal in nature. Lavinia, you are not listening to me. I am attempting to discuss my future."

"What is the problem with your future?" Lavinia picked up the pencil and jotted down the words *singularly* and *effective*. "I thought it was shaping up rather nicely. Thanks to Joan Dove, we have invitations to two of the most important social events of the Season—the Stillwater ball and the one Joan herself is planning. Which reminds me, we have appointments with Madam Francesca for fittings for our gowns."

"Yes, I know. But I do not want to talk about balls and fashions." Emeline paused. "I mean to establish myself in a profession, Lavinia."

"Nonsense." Lavinia frowned at a milliner's advertisement: *An excellent selection for discerning persons who are interested only in the most fashionable bonnets and hats.* "No gentleman of the ton wants a wife who has established herself in a career. Do you think I should describe my services as *fashionable?*"

"I don't see how one can describe the business of making confidential inquiries as *fashionable*."

"On the contrary. It is obvious that if one wishes to attract an exclusive clientele one must contrive to appear fashionable, regardless of the services one offers. No member of the ton can abide the notion of being unfashionable."

"Lavinia, I do not intend to marry any gentleman who moves in the ton. Indeed, I cannot imagine a more dreadful fate."

Lavinia wrote down the word *fashionable*. "Surely you do not intend to marry a farmer. Neither of us was excessively fond of rusticating, as I recall."

"I have no intention of wedding a farmer. I have decided that I would like to become your associate."

"What do you mean? You already are my associate. Indeed, we associate daily. What do you think about the phrase *effective devices for gentlemen of intrigue, offered in a confidential and discreet manner?* That has an interesting ring to it, don't you agree?"

"Yes." Emeline frowned delicately. "But I have no notion of what it means."

"Neither do I." Lavinia pursed her lips. "That is a bit of a problem, is it not? Perhaps if I altered the vocabulary somewhat—" She broke off at the muffled sound of the front door opening. "It appears we have a visitor. It is much too early for a social call. Perhaps it is a new client."

"More likely it is Mr. March." Emeline helped herself to another warm biscuit. "I have noticed that he no longer stands on formality when he calls upon you."

"He never did stand on it," Lavinia muttered. "If you will recall, he was busily smashing the statuary in our little shop in Rome the first time he introduced himself. His social graces have not improved a great deal since that first meeting, in my opinion."

Emeline smiled and took a dainty bite of her biscuit.

Lavinia listened warily to the sound of bootsteps coming down the hall. "You may be right in that he seems to be getting worse, however. This is the second time this week that he has paid a call at breakfast."

Emeline's eyes brightened. "Mayhap Anthony will have accompanied him."

"*Do not go to any trouble, Mrs. Chilton.*" Tobias's voice reverberated through the paneling of the breakfast room. "*Some of the eggs and your excellent potatoes will do nicely.*"

In spite of her irritation, Lavinia found herself listening intently, as she always did, to the slight hitch in his stride as he approached. Some part of her relaxed when she noted that he did not appear to be favoring his left leg unduly today. That was no doubt because the morning had dawned clear. She knew that the wound bothered him most when it rained or when a damp fog clung to the city.

Tobias appeared in the doorway and came to a halt. "Good day to you, ladies."

"Mr. March." Emeline beamed. "How lovely to see you. Is Mr. Sinclair with you?"

"No. He wanted to accompany me, but I dispatched him on some business." Tobias looked at Lavinia, a determined glint in his eyes. "I vow, you are looking lovely today, madam. The very incarnation of Venus rising from the sea. Indeed, the sight of you aglow in the morning light elevates my spirits, clarifies my thoughts, and inspires me to metaphysical contemplation."

"Incarnation of Venus?" Lavinia paused, her cup halfway to her mouth, and frowned in concern. "Are you feeling ill, Tobias? You do not sound yourself."

"I am in excellent health, thank you." He glanced expectantly at the enameled pot. "Any coffee left?"

Emeline responded before Lavinia could question his uncharacteristic greeting further.

"Of course." Emeline picked up the pot. "Please sit down. I shall be delighted to pour some for you. Perhaps Mr. Sinclair will pay us a call after he has finished with his business affairs?"

"I doubt it. He will be occupied for most of the day." Tobias took a chair without further ado and helped himself to the last biscuit.

Emeline poured coffee. "Mr. Sinclair did not mention that he had plans for today."

"Very likely because he did not have any plans until he took a notion to engage himself as my assistant."

Emeline looked up sharply and set down the pot with a small thud. "Assistant?"

Tobias shrugged and reached for the butter and the jam pot. "He tells me that he wishes to embark upon a career as an investigator. Says he wants me to teach him the business."

Emeline was riveted. "Indeed. That is amazing."

"Personally, I found it decidedly depressing." Tobias finished spreading butter and jam on his biscuit and took a large bite out of it. "As you know, I have been urging him toward a more stable profession. I envisioned him becoming a man of business. But according to Anthony, the only other career that interests him is that of professional gamester."

"What a coincidence," Emeline said.

Tobias regarded her with dry disbelief. "I hope you are not going to say that you are also inclined in that direction, Miss Emeline."

"I have no interest in becoming a gamester, of course." Emeline cast a quick look at Lavinia and delicately cleared her throat. "But I was just explaining to Aunt Lavinia that I have decided to embark upon a career myself. I would like to begin training for my new profession immediately."

"And I was just telling Emeline that she need not even consider such a course of action." Lavinia refolded her newspaper. "Her social calendar is quite full these days. She has no time to study a profession."

"That is not true," Emeline said. "I intend to follow in your footsteps, Lavinia."

There was a short, extremely heavy silence.

Lavinia finally realized that her mouth had fallen open in a most unattractive fashion. She managed to get it closed.

"Ridiculous," she said.

"I want to become your assistant, just as Anthony is doing with Mr. March."

Lavinia stared at her, frozen in her chair by the sheer horror of it all.

"Ridiculous," she said again. "Your parents would be shocked at the very notion of their dear daughter going into trade."

"My parents are dead, Aunt Lavinia. Their feelings need not be considered in this matter."

"But you know perfectly well how they would feel about it. When you came into my care I assumed a certain responsibility to establish you in the world as they would have wished. A lady does not go into this sort of business."

Emeline smiled. "You are in the business and I consider you a lady." She looked at Tobias. "Don't you consider Aunt Lavinia a lady, sir?"

"Absolutely," Tobias said easily. "I will call out any man who says otherwise."

Lavinia rounded on him. "This is your doing, sir. You have put this crazed notion into Emeline's head as well as Anthony's."

"I fear you cannot blame Mr. March," Emeline said.

Tobias swallowed some of the biscuit and held up both hands, palms out. "I assure you, I gave neither of them any encouragement."

Emeline smiled across the rim of her coffee cup. "If you must blame someone, blame yourself, Aunt Lavinia. You have been my greatest inspiration since the day I came to live with you."

"*Me?*" Lavinia was stunned into momentary speechlessness a second time. She wondered if she was on the verge of swooning. She had never actually experienced a fainting spell, but surely this sensation of breathless dread was a prelude to such an event.

"Indeed," Emeline continued firmly. "You have impressed me greatly with your astonishing ability to come about after the most devastating reversals of fortune. Reversals that would have crushed most people, male or female. I do so admire your extraordinary resilience and cleverness."

Tobias's mouth twitched. "Not to mention your ingenious ability to garner invitations to some of the most important and exclusive social affairs of the Season, Lavinia. No one else of my acquaintance could have managed to combine an investigation into murder with the successful launch of a young lady into Society as you did a few weeks ago, madam. It was a truly astonishing feat."

Lavinia propped her elbows on the table and dropped her face into her hands. "This is a disaster."

"Emeline is quite right to hold you up as a paragon and model of female behavior." Tobias picked up his coffee cup. "Indeed, I do not see how she could do better than to look to you for inspiration."

Lavinia raised her head and glared at him. "Kindly cease your teasing, sir. I am not in the mood for it."

Before Tobias could respond, Mrs. Chilton walked into the breakfast room bearing a heavily laden dish. "Here ye are, sir. Eggs and potatoes."

"Thank you, Mrs. Chilton. Your talents in the kitchen are really quite remarkable. If you ever take a notion to leave your present employer, I hope you will apply for a position in my household."

Mrs. Chilton chuckled. "Doubt that'll happen, sir. But I thank you for the offer. Will there be anything else?"

Tobias tilted the small jam pot to examine the interior. "I believe that we are out of your excellent currant jam, Mrs. Chilton. I vow, it is far and away the best I have ever tasted."

"I'll fetch some more."

Mrs. Chilton vanished back through the door that led to the kitchen.

Lavinia gave Tobias a repressive look. He gave no indication that he noticed. He was too busy with his eggs and potatoes.

"I'll thank you not to try to steal my staff, sir," she said.

Emeline uttered a tiny, dramatic little exclamation and made a show of glancing at the watch pinned to her bodice. "Oh, dear, you will have to excuse me." She folded her napkin and rose lightly to her feet. "I must go and dress. Priscilla and her mama will be here shortly. I promised that I would accompany them on a shopping expedition this morning."

"Emeline, wait," Lavinia said quickly. "About this notion of a career—"

"I will discuss it with you later." Emeline gave her a jaunty wave from the doorway. "I must hurry. Wouldn't want to keep Lady Wortham waiting."

She disappeared down the hall before Lavinia could argue the matter.

Silence descended on the breakfast room.

Left with no other target, Lavinia turned back to Tobias. She pushed aside her plate and folded her arms on the table.

"This business of Anthony wanting to follow in your footsteps has obviously put some extremely misguided notions into Emeline's head."

Tobias set down his knife and fork and looked at her. The amusement was gone from his eyes, she noticed. It had been replaced by a far more serious expression, one that was not devoid of sympathy and understanding.

"Believe it or not, Lavinia, I comprehend your concerns more deeply than you can imagine. I am no more eager for Anthony to pursue a career as an investigator than you are for Emeline to do so."

"What are we to do to change their minds?"

"I haven't the foggiest notion." Tobias swallowed some coffee. "And I am rapidly coming to the conclusion that the matter is out of our hands, in any event. We can guide but we cannot control them."

"This is dreadful. Just dreadful. She will ruin herself if she is not careful."

"Come now, Lavinia. You overstate the case. This situation may not be to your liking, but there is no need to resort to theatrics. It is hardly a tragedy."

"Perhaps not in your opinion, but it certainly is in mine. I had so hoped to see Emeline safely established in a home of her own with a husband who cared for her, one who could support her in a suitable fashion. No gentleman of the ton will even consider marrying a lady who works at this investigation business."

Tobias watched her with enigmatic eyes. "Do you dream of such a fine marriage for yourself also, madam?"

She was utterly floored by that wholly unexpected question. For a second or two, she could not think of what to say.

"Of course not," she finally got out quite brusquely. "I have no interest whatsoever in marrying again."

"Is it because you loved your first husband so deeply that you cannot bring yourself to even consider a second marriage?"

An odd panic assailed her. This was a truly dangerous topic of discussion. She did not want to even start down this road, she thought, because it would inevitably lead to painful speculation on the depth of Tobias's love for the wife he had lost in childbirth. She doubted very much that she would ever be able to compete with Ann's beautiful, gentle ghost. Anthony had described his sister as an angel.

Whatever else I am, Lavinia thought, including a so-called paragon of the sort of female who can live by her wits, I am no angel.

"Really, sir," she said briskly, "it is not my opinions of marriage that we are discussing. This is about Emeline's future."

"And Anthony's as well."

She sighed. "I know. They have developed a tendre for each other, haven't they?"

"Yes."

"Emeline is so young."

"So is Anthony."

"I fear neither of them can possibly know their own heart at such a tender age."

"You could not have been any older than Emeline when you married. Did you know your own heart?"

She straightened in her chair. "Of course I did. I wouldn't have married John if I had been the least uncertain of my feelings on the matter."

She had, indeed, been sure of herself, but looking back she knew that her feelings for John had been the sweet, pale sentiments of an innocent and very romantic young woman. If John had lived, no doubt their love would have matured into something stronger and deeper and more substantial. But as it was, her memories of her gentle husband were wispy, thin mementos that she kept tucked away in a pink-and-white keepsake box somewhere near her heart.

Tobias's mouth curved in a wry smile. "You are nothing if not strong-minded and extremely certain of all your opinions, regardless of the subject, are you not?"

"Mine is a decisive and forceful personality, sir. Perhaps that is due to my early training as a mesmerist."

"More likely you were born with a strong will, madam."

She narrowed her eyes. "I suspect the same could be said of you, sir."

"Isn't it interesting to discover how much we have in common?" he asked pleasantly.

Six

THE FOLLOWING AFTERNOON, TOBIAS EMERGED FROM HIS CLUB and pulled his watch out of his pocket to check the time. It was only just going on two. He was in no hurry and it was a fine day to walk.

He ignored a passing hackney, and with the ease of long familiarity, he made his way through a maze of lanes and streets. His goal was the bookshop where he had made arrangements to meet Lavinia. He planned to treat her to a dish of ice cream and then, if luck was with him, to persuade her to retreat to the crumbling ruin in the park for some extended lovemaking in the spring sunshine.

With that last thought in mind, he cast a wary eye on the heavens. The sun was indeed shining, but there was a nip in the air and he sensed clouds gathering in the distance. He could only hope that the rain would hold off until he could complete the interlude with Lavinia in the park. A fortnight ago they had been interrupted at the crucial moment by a cold shower from the heavens that had done nothing to enhance the romantic ambience.

The business of having to search out suitable locations for their trysts was fast becoming a nuisance, he reflected. A man of his years was not supposed to have to steal away to remote sections of the park or fumble in a closed carriage in order to enjoy his lady's affections. He ought to be able to enjoy said affections in a proper bed.

But beds were extremely hard to come by when one was engaged in an affair.

He was a block away from the bookshop, toying with the notion of taking Lavinia off to a country inn for a day or two, when a vision in spring pink stepped out of a milliner's shop and nearly collided with him.

"Mr. March." Celeste Hudson smiled brilliantly at him from beneath the brim of a charming confection fashioned of palest pink straw and intricately laced ribbons. "How delightful to see you again so soon."

"Mrs. Hudson." He grasped her elbow to steady her. "A pleasure. Is your husband about?"

"Heavens, no. Howard has no patience with a lady's shopping."

Her laughter was light, almost bubbling. Damned near a rippling brook, he thought. But it had a brittle, false quality that made him think of brightly colored artificial flowers and the pleasure-garden mirrors that reflected distorted images. He was profoundly grateful that Lavinia never laughed like that.

"I cannot say that shopping is one of my favorite sports," he said.

Celeste opened her little fan and looked at him over the edge in a flirtatious manner that he knew she must have practiced.

The leaf of the fan, Tobias noticed, was exquisitely painted in an unusual and quite dazzling pattern. There were a number of bright, shiny beads attached to it. The sparkling bits and bobs were arranged in an intriguing pattern that caught the light and attracted his eye. The thing appeared more suited to the ballroom than the street, he thought. But, then, he was hardly an expert on matters of female style.

"Where is Mrs. Lake?" Celeste asked in throaty tones. "Or are you alone this afternoon?"

"I'm on my way to meet Lavinia, as it happens." The manner in which Celeste manipulated the fan annoyed him. He looked away from it. "She is picking up a new volume of poetry at a bookshop not far from here."

"Poetry. How nice. I am rather fond of that sort of literature myself." Celeste twirled the fan in a clever movement that made the sunlight bounce on the glittering ornaments. "I have been meaning to pay a visit to a bookshop. Do you mind if I walk with you, Mr. March?"

"Of course not."

She slipped her gloved fingers under his arm with a graceful expertise that he could only admire, and continued to make the light dance on her fan.

"A lovely day, is it not?" she murmured.

"The good weather won't last long."

"Come now, don't be so pessimistic, Mr. March."

"It's not pessimism." It was difficult to avoid the damned fan, he discovered. Celeste managed to angle the thing in such a way that it kept snagging his gaze. He had a sudden urge to snatch the thing out of her hand and toss it into the gutter. "It's a statement of fact."

She tilted her head so that the pink straw bonnet framed her pretty features to excellent advantage. "I collect that you are a man who prefers to deal with the hard realities of life. Not one who allows himself to enjoy fantasies and dreams."

"Fantasies and dreams are for those who wish to delude themselves."

"I disagree, sir." She looked at him over the top of her fan again, her eyes as bright and intriguing as the shiny beads. "Some fantasies and dreams can come true. But only for those who are willing to pay the price."

"I think it far more likely that after handing over the required fee, one would find oneself left holding only a handful of sparkling bubbles that would soon burst and disappear."

Sparkling bubbles that would look very much like the glittering beads on the fan, he thought.

She smiled at him and, with a quick twist of her hand, made the fan dip and swoop. "Perhaps your problem is that you have never had the good fortune to actually encounter a fantasy or a dream. My advice is not to judge the value of the goods until you have had a chance to sample them."

"As I am not likely to be offered free samples, I doubt I shall have the opportunity to form any judgments concerning the wares."

"Ah, now, in that you are seriously mistaken." Celeste laughed again and squeezed his arm lightly, intimately. "I can assure you that there are free samples to be had if one happens to know the right place in which to shop."

"As I just told you, I am not particularly keen on shopping."

The fan fluttered in her hand. The tiny lights flashed.

"I can show you where to find some very excellent free samples, Mr. March," she said softly. "What is more, I can promise you that when you have had a taste of the wares you will be *completely* satisfied."

He looked down into her glowing eyes. "Would you mind putting that bloody fan away, Mrs. Hudson? I find it irritating."

She blinked, clearly startled. The fan stilled abruptly in her hand. The invitation and the promise faded in her eyes.

"Of course, Mr. March." She snapped the fan closed. "Forgive me, I had no idea that it bothered you."

"*Mrs. Hudson,*" Lavinia called loudly from halfway down the block. "This is a surprise. Imagine meeting up with you and Mr. March here in the middle of the street."

Tobias smiled at the sound of her voice. It was a crisp, bracing tonic, a strong antidote to Celeste's cloying sweetness.

He watched Lavinia stride purposefully toward them, a small bundle that no doubt contained a newly purchased volume of poetry in one hand, a perky green-and-white parasol in the other. She was dressed in a deep emerald green gown and a striped-green pelisse.

Another one of Madam Francesca's creations, he thought. The gemlike hues set off Lavinia's red hair, which was bound up beneath a clever little green hat.

She came to a halt in front of him and gave him a steely smile.

"You're late," she announced.

She was not in a good mood, he realized. Beneath the wispy veil of the hat, her eyes glinted in a dangerous fashion.

"My fault, I'm afraid," Celeste murmured. She did not take her hand away from Tobias's arm. "We bumped into each other here on the street and fell to chatting. I trust you will forgive me for distracting your Mr. March for a moment or two?"

"In my experience, Mr. March is rarely distracted unless he wishes to be distracted." Lavinia gave Tobias another icy little smile. "I collect that the subject you were discussing was quite riveting?"

"I believe we were conversing about the pleasures of shopping," Tobias said. With a small but determined movement of his arm, he succeeded in dislodging Celeste's dainty little claws.

"Shopping?" Lavinia raised her brows. "Not one of your favorite subjects, as I recall." She turned back to Celeste. "Speaking of shopping, I saw your fan just as you were folding it, Mrs. Hudson. Most unusual. May I ask where you purchased it? I should like to find a similar one."

"I'm afraid that won't be possible." Celeste dropped the fan into her reticule. "I made it myself."

"You don't say." Lavinia's eyes widened admiringly. "I am extremely impressed. Unfortunately, I possess no artistic talents whatsoever."

"I'm sure you have other talents, Mrs. Lake."

There was a distinct edge to Celeste's voice now, Tobias noticed. The rippling-brook effect had vanished entirely.

"I like to think that I do have one or two humble skills," Lavinia said with patently false modesty. "Take shopping, for instance. I consider that I have a distinct talent for being able to spot cheap, shoddy goods at a glance."

"Indeed." Celeste stiffened, but her condescending smile remained firmly fixed. "I, on the other hand, have always had a knack for identifying frauds and charlatans. I suspect such individuals are something of a problem in your new line, are they not?"

"Whatever do you mean?"

Celeste raised one shoulder in a delicate shrug. "Evidently just *anyone* can set herself up as an investigator and make claims of expertise that cannot possibly be verified."

"I beg your pardon?"

"How on earth is a potential client to know whether or not he or she is dealing with an individual who is actually qualified to make private inquiries?" Celeste asked innocently.

"If one is wise, one selects an investigator the same way one selects a practitioner of mesmerism," Lavinia shot back smoothly. "One relies upon references."

"You can provide references, Mrs. Lake? I am astonished to hear that."

It was time to intervene, Tobias decided. He did not relish the notion of stepping into the middle of this skirmish, but his duty as Lavinia's occasional partner was clear. He dared not stand by and watch her get drawn into a loud and embarrassing scene right here in the middle of the street. She would never forgive him for allowing her to humiliate herself in such a public fashion.

"Speaking of business matters, Mrs. Hudson," he said just as Lavinia opened her mouth to respond to Celeste's latest goad, "I assume that you and Dr. Hudson have several excellent references from your time in Bath."

"Yes, of course we do." Celeste glared at Lavinia. "Howard gave therapeutic treatments to only the most exclusive sort. I made certain of it."

"I doubt if your clientele was any more exclusive than ours," Lavinia shot back.

"Indeed?" Celeste gave her a pitying look. "I think it is highly unlikely that you can count such distinguished gentlemen as Lords Gunning and Northampton on your list of clients."

Lavinia opened her mouth to retaliate. Tobias took her arm in a firm grip and squeezed just hard enough to get her attention. She shot him a disgruntled look, but she closed her mouth.

"Impressive," he said quickly. "Unfortunately, Mrs. Lake has not yet acquired any titled clients, but perhaps she will be lucky enough to do so one of these days. Meanwhile, you must excuse us. We have an appointment."

"We do not have an appointment," Lavinia said.

"Yes, we do," he said. "You have obviously forgotten it." He smiled at Celeste. "Good day, madam."

Celeste switched her attention back to him. The sparkling look returned to her eyes, and her voice became warm and husky once more. "Good day, Mr. March. It was a pleasure meeting up with you. I trust that we shall bump into each other again in the very near future. I would very much like to continue our discussion of how one may obtain free samples of certain very special wares."

"Indeed," he said.

He turned, and dragging Lavinia with him, walked swiftly away.

There was a short moment of silence. He could feel Lavinia vibrating with outrage on his arm.

"You do realize," Lavinia said, "that she was attempting to put you into a trance with that silly fan."

"It occurred to me, yes. It was an interesting experience. Especially in light of the fact that she made a point of telling us the other day that she had no talent for the art of mesmerism."

Lavinia sniffed with undisguised disdain. "I doubt if she does have much genuine ability. But she has been working with Howard for a year, so it is possible that she has picked up a few rudimentary skills."

"And chose to practice them on me? I wonder why she went to the trouble."

"Don't be ridiculous. The answer is perfectly obvious, if you ask me. She intended to seduce you and thought to use her poor mesmeric techniques to accomplish her goal."

He smiled. "Do you really believe that was her objective?"

"I am quite certain of it. It is clear to me that she finds you fascinating, intriguing, and something of a challenge."

"I would be flattered were it not for the fact that I have the distinct impression that Celeste places all men into one of two categories. Useful and Not Useful. I have a nasty suspicion that she has decided that I fit into the former."

Lavinia tilted the parasol to get a better look at him. "You believe that she thinks she can somehow use you?"

"It is a blow to my pride, of course. Nevertheless, I am forced to conclude that it is the most likely explanation for her interest in me."

"And just how do you imagine that she might use you, sir?"

"Damned if I know," he admitted.

"Rubbish." Lavinia's hand tightened around his arm. "I think she is madly attracted to you and thinks it would be amusing to indulge in an affair."

He grinned. "As I am not the sort of man who can be put into a trance by just *any* passing mesmerist, we are unlikely to ever discover the truth of her intentions."

"I trust not."

"Are you by any chance jealous, Lavinia?"

"Of her extremely limited mesmeric skills? Certainly not."

"Not of Celeste's mesmeric talents." He lowered his voice. "Of her interest in me."

She gazed straight ahead. "Is there any reason why I should feel the pangs of jealousy?"

"No."

She brightened. "Then the subject does not arise."

"The subject has arisen. You're avoiding it."

"Really, Tobias. You are a man of honor. Your word is your bond. Of course I trust you."

"That is not quite the question I am asking."

"That nonsense about free samples." Lavinia gave him a suspicious look. "She was offering herself to you, wasn't she?"

"You know me, my dear. I have never taken the trouble to master the fine arts of flirtation and innuendo, so I cannot say for certain what she was about with that chatter."

"Bloody hell." Lavinia came to a halt and spun around to face him. "That is precisely what she was doing. That hussy as much as offered you a free sample of the extremely cheap goods she is selling. What nerve."

"You *are* jealous." For some reason he felt quite cheerful.

"Let's just say that I do not trust that woman any farther than I could throw that hackney over there."

"On that point, we are in complete agreement." Tobias looked back over his shoulder to where Celeste had been standing a few minutes ago. "The goods may be cheap, but I very much doubt that anything Mrs. Hudson offers—including samples—would prove to be free."

 Seven

THE SIGHT OF THE UNLIT WAREHOUSE LOOMING IN THE DARKNESS near the river gave her a moment of nervous dread. For the first time in this endeavor she experienced true fear. It started in her palms, an icy, prickling sensation that climbed up her arms and spread through her chest. Suddenly she found it hard to breathe.

What was the matter with her? It was almost finished. She had come too far to lose her courage at this juncture.

She took a deep breath, and the disturbing sensation passed. She was in command of herself once more. Her brilliant future lay before her. All she had to do was complete this night's work and she would be on her way into the ton's glittering ballrooms and elegant drawing rooms at last.

Hoisting the lantern, she went to the door of the warehouse and opened it carefully. The rusty hinges groaned in protest.

Inside, she paused again on the threshold and surveyed the cavernous interior of the building. The flaring light from her lantern splashed sharp shadows across a jumble of empty packing crates and shipping casks. For a terrible instant they looked like so many monuments and headstones scattered about in an abandoned grave-yard. She shuddered.

It is too late to turn back now. You've come too far. All the way from that dreadful little shop. Soon you will move in Society.

A rapid skittering sound emanated from a corner between two large crates. She flinched.

Rats, she thought. Just rats, fleeing from the light.

She heard the bootsteps behind her, and another cold wave of fear flashed through her. It was all right, she assured herself. He had received her message and had come to meet her, just as she had instructed. They would conduct their business and that would be the end of it. When it was over, she would be poised to move into her golden future.

"My dear Celeste," the killer said in a voice as soft and low as a lover's. "I have been waiting for you."

She knew then that something had gone terribly wrong. Another lightning bolt of freezing horror flashed through her. She started to turn, fumbling frantically with the little fan. She opened her mouth to speak so that she could bargain for her life. This was why she had not brought the bracelet with her. Her plan had held an element of risk, so she had left the Blue Medusa in safekeeping as surety for her own life while she negotiated the new price.

But it was too late to bargain. He already had the cravat around her throat, silencing her so that she could not use her skills to save her own life. In those last moments when the red darkness clouded her brain, she knew with horrifying clarity that she had made a fatal mistake. She had known he could be ruthless, understood that he was obsessed. But she had not recognized the madness in him until now.

When it was finished, he looked down at the results of his handiwork and was quietly satisfied. The creature would never again play her tricks on him or any other man.

He picked up her reticule, opened it, and poured out the contents. It contained the usual paraphernalia one expected to find. There was a handkerchief and some coins for the hackney she would not be hailing. But what he sought was not inside.

The first stirrings of alarm went through him. He went back to the body and knelt to check the folds and pockets of the cloak.

Not there either.

A feeling uncomfortably akin to panic swept over him. He suppressed it and quickly patted down her clothing.

Still nothing.

He yanked up her skirts to see if she had concealed it between her thighs.

But there was no sign of it.

Desperate now, he rose and hoisted the lantern to check the surrounding floor. Perhaps she had dropped it during her death struggle.

But a few minutes later he was forced to confront the terrible truth. The Blue Medusa was gone. And he had just murdered the only person who could have told him where it was hidden.

Eight

"ARE THERE ANY MORE OF THOSE CURRIED EGGS, MRS. CHILTON?" Tobias turned a page of the morning newspaper he had brought with him. "They are excellent."

"I'll bring some out, sir." Mrs. Chilton chuckled as she backed through the door that led to the kitchen.

"And another currant biscuit would go very nicely with the eggs," he added. "You do have a way with currants, Mrs. Chilton."

"I made plenty of extra," she assured him. "Had a hunch you'd be here this morning."

The door swung shut behind her.

"Indeed." Lavinia looked up from her own newspaper and eyed Tobias across the width of the table. "This is the third time in a week that you have appeared at breakfast. You are becoming predictable in your habits, sir. I vow, it has reached the point where we could set our clock by your arrival here in the mornings."

"I have reached the age at which a man must look after his constitution. They say that regular habits and a properly cooked breakfast are essential to good health."

"So you've decided to combine both vital principles of health and eat here every morning, is that it?"

"The routine also provides me with a daily walk, another extremely healthful activity."

"You did not walk here this morning. You arrived in a hackney. I saw you."

"Watching for me, were you?" He put down the paper, looking pleased. "I used a hack because it rained last night, in case you did not notice. The air is still somewhat damp."

"Oh, dear." She bit her lip, concern temporarily swamping her irritable mood. "Is your leg aching badly today?"

"Nothing a good breakfast cannot remedy." He drank some coffee with the air of a man settling in to savor the first meal of the day with hearty relish. "By the way, did I mention that you look like a sea nymph playing in the waves of a southern sea with the sunlight on your hair this morning?"

She gave him a frosty glare. "It is far too early for such poor humor, sir."

The breakfast-room door opened again. Mrs. Chilton bustled in with a dish of curried eggs and two currant biscuits. "Here you are, sir. Help yerself."

"Ah, Mrs. Chilton, your cooking is just what a man needs to fortify himself to face the day."

The heavy door knocker clanged in the distance.

Lavinia frowned. "Probably one of Emeline's friends. Mrs. Chilton, please inform whomever it is that she went out walking with Mr. Sinclair."

"Aye, madam."

Mrs. Chilton disappeared down the hall. But a moment later when the front door opened, it was not the voice of one of Emeline's many acquaintances that Lavinia heard. It was Howard Hudson's low, rich tones that echoed in the corridor.

"Hudson." Tobias did not look pleased. "What the devil is he doing here at such an uncivil hour?"

"I might remind you, sir, that you chose to visit at a rather early hour yourself." Lavinia crumpled her napkin and rose quickly. "If you will excuse me, I shall go and see what he wants."

"I'll come with you."

"That is not necessary."

Tobias ignored that comment. He was already on his feet. She knew from the look in his eyes that he was not going to allow her to banish him to the breakfast room while she greeted Howard.

"Correct me if I am mistaken," she said as she led the way out the door, "but I have the impression that you are not overfond of Dr. Hudson."

"The man is a mesmerist. I do not trust the members of his profession."

"I am a mesmerist, sir."

"A *former* mesmerist," he said as he followed her down the hall. "You have embarked upon a new career, if you will recall."

"Yes, indeed, and I also seem to recall that you are not particularly approving of my new profession either."

"That is another matter entirely."

She arrived at the entrance of the parlor at that moment and was thus saved from having to respond to his remark.

Howard paced in front of the window, his shoulders tight and hunched with tension. His clothes were rumpled. He had not bothered with a stylish knot in his neckcloth. His boots were unpolished.

Although he had his face averted so that she could not see his expression, she knew at once that something terrible had occurred.

"Howard?" She went forward quickly, conscious of Tobias behind her. "What is it? What has happened?"

Howard spun around and fixed her with his fathomless gaze. For an instant it seemed to her that she had been transported to an odd metaphysical plane. The atmosphere around her was suddenly too still. The rattle of a carriage in the street was abruptly muted, as though the sound came from a vast distance.

With a small, determined effort, she mentally shook off the strange sensation. Normal noises returned and the disturbing feeling passed. Howard's gaze appeared normal once more.

She glanced at Tobias and saw that he was studying Howard closely, but otherwise he appeared completely unaware of the brief, very curious alteration in the atmosphere. Perhaps it had all been a product of her imagination, she thought.

"Celeste is dead," Howard said heavily. "Murdered the night before last by a footpad. Or so they tell me." He put his fingers to his temples. "I still cannot bring myself to believe it. If I had not seen her body myself yesterday morning when the authorities came to inform me, I vow I would..."

"Dear God." Lavinia went forward swiftly. "You must sit, Howard. I'll have Mrs. Chilton bring in some tea."

"No." He sank down onto the edge of the sofa, looking bemused. "Please, do not go to the trouble. I could not possibly drink it."

Lavinia sat beside him. "I have some sherry. It is excellent for overcoming the effects of shock."

"No, thank you," he whispered. "You must help me, Lavinia. I am really quite desperate, you see."

Tobias went to stand in front of the window and turned so that the morning sun was at his back. Lavinia was familiar with this habit of his. She knew he chose the position because it put his own face in shadow and served to give him a better view of Howard.

"Tell us what happened," Tobias said without inflection. "Start at the beginning."

"Yes. Yes, of course." Howard massaged his temples with his fingertips, as if attempting to bring order to his troubled thoughts. Dread and despair darkened his gaze. "It is all still somewhat muddled, you see. One shock after another. I fear that I am still reeling from the blows. First the news of her death and now this other information."

Lavinia touched his sleeve. "Calm yourself, Howard. Do as Tobias suggested. Start at the very beginning of the thing."

"The beginning." Howard slowly lowered his hand and stared blankly at the carpet. "That would be a fortnight ago when I first realized that Celeste was having an affair."

"Oh, Howard," Lavinia said softly.

She glanced at Tobias. He was watching Howard with that de-tached studiousness that she had learned meant that he was assessing the situation and weighing the information with icy calculation. His ability to step into that remote realm both intrigued and irritated her. When he was in this mood he was oblivious to emotion and the dic-tates of the sensibilities that would seem natural to the situation.

"She is—was—so young and so beautiful," Howard said after a moment. "I could scarcely believe my good fortune when she con-sented to marry me in Bath. I think that a part of me always knew that there was a grave risk that someday I would lose her. It was only a mat-ter of time, I suppose. But I was in love. What choice did I have?"

"You're certain that she was involved in an affair?" Tobias asked neutrally.

Howard nodded bleakly. "I cannot be certain how long it had been going on, but once I tumbled to the truth, there was no way I could deny it. Believe me, I made every effort."

"Did you confront her?" Tobias asked.

Lavinia winced at the relentless manner in which Tobias was press-ing Howard. She tried to signal him silently to soften his attitude, but he apparently did not notice.

Howard shook his head. "I could not bear to do so. I told myself that she was young, that the liaison was nothing more than a brief ad-venture. I hoped that she would eventually grow bored with the other man."

Tobias watched him. "Do you know the identity of her lover?"

"No."

"You must have been curious, to say the least," Tobias said.

The very flatness of his words made Lavinia tense. His tone might have been perfectly even and uninflected, but the bone-deep chill in his eyes made her catch her breath. She suddenly understood. If Tobias ever found himself in Howard's position, he would move heaven and earth to learn the identity of the lover. She did not want to think about what he would do after that.

"I suspect that she went to meet him the night before last," Howard whispered. "I had learned her small habits and ways well. I sensed her excitement and anticipation on those occasions when she planned to slip away to be with him. We were to attend a demonstration of animal magnetism performed by a gentleman named Cosgrove, who claims to be able to effect amazing cures with his mesmeric skills. But at the last moment she feigned an indisposition and declared that she would stay home. She insisted that I go. She was well aware that I had very much looked forward to witnessing Cosgrove at work."

"So you did attend the demonstration?" Lavinia asked. She kept her voice soothing and gentle in an attempt to compensate for Tobias's interrogation.

"Yes. The man proved to be a complete charlatan and I was vastly disappointed. When I returned home, I discovered that Celeste was gone. I knew then that she was with him, whoever he is. I lay awake all night waiting for her to return. She never came home. The next morning the authorities informed me that her body had been found inside a warehouse near the river. I have spent the past day and a half in a haze, dealing with the funeral arrangements."

"Was she stabbed?" Tobias asked almost casually. "Or shot?"

"Strangled, they said." Howard gazed bleakly at the wall. "I'm told the cravat the bastard used was still around her throat when she was found."

"My God." Unconsciously, Lavinia raised a hand to her own throat and swallowed.

"Any witnesses?" Tobias asked.

"None that I know of," Howard whispered. "No one has come forward and I have no hope that any will. As I said, the authorities believe that she was the victim of a footpad."

"Very few footpads use cravats as murder weapons," Tobias said evenly. "Generally speaking, they don't even wear them. Footpads are not much interested in fashion, in my experience."

"I was told they suspect that the cravat was stolen earlier in the evening from some gentleman the killer robbed," Howard explained.

"A bit of a stretch," Tobias muttered.

He sounded exceedingly callous, Lavinia thought. "That is quite enough, sir."

There was a short pause.

Howard and Tobias met each other's eyes for that moment. Lavinia recognized the look as one of those silent, extremely irritating, man-to-man exchanges that completely excluded women.

"Who found the body?" Tobias asked.

Howard shook his head. "Does it matter?"

"It might," Tobias said.

Howard rubbed his temples again, concentrating. "I believe the man who came to inform me of Celeste's death mentioned that one of the street lads who sleep in the abandoned buildings near the river led the authorities to her. But there is more to this. Something else has happened that I must tell you about, Lavinia. Something very odd."

She touched his shoulder. "What is it?"

"I received a caller late last night." Howard gave her a stark look through a fan of spread fingers. "Indeed, it was nearly dawn when he arrived. I had sent the housekeeper away because I could not bear to have anyone else around while I came to terms with my grief. The stranger pounded until I awoke and went downstairs to open the door."

"Who was he?" Lavinia asked.

"A most unpleasant little man who wouldn't step into the light, so I never got a good look at him." Howard slowly lowered his hands to his thighs. "He called himself Mr. Nightingale. Said he was in the business of arranging certain types of transactions."

"What sort of transactions?" Tobias asked.

"He told me that he acts as a go-between for those who wish to buy and sell antiquities in what he called an *extremely discreet* manner. Apparently he guarantees anonymity for both buyer and seller."

"In other words the transactions are not always of a legal nature," Tobias said.

"I got that impression, yes." Howard sighed heavily. "This man, Mr. Nightingale, told me that he had heard rumors to the effect that a very valuable antiquity had recently been stolen and that Celeste had been involved in the theft."

Lavinia was dumbfounded. "Celeste stole a relic?"

"I do not believe that for a moment." Howard waved the possibility aside with an impatient movement of one long-fingered hand. "My Celeste was no thief. Nevertheless, Nightingale claimed that word had gone out in the underworld to the effect that she was murdered for the damned thing."

"What was the nature of this antiquity?" Tobias asked, showing the first signs of genuine interest in the proceedings.

Howard's brows bunched together in a line above his patrician nose. "Nightingale described it as an ancient gold bracelet of Roman design. It was originally discovered here in England, a remnant of the days when this country was a province of the Roman Empire. It is set with a strange blue cameo carved with the image of Medusa."

"What did Mr. Nightingale want from you?" Lavinia asked.

"Apparently the bloody thing is most unusual and is considered quite valuable to a certain sort of collector."

"And Nightingale makes his living off unusual collectors who favor odd antiquities?" Tobias concluded.

"So he claimed." Howard did not look at him. He focused his attention entirely on Lavinia. "Nightingale assumes that I know something concerning the whereabouts of the missing cameo. He made it clear that he can arrange to sell it for a fortune. He offered to pay me a fee if I will turn it over to him."

"What did you tell him?" Tobias asked.

"What could I say?" Howard spread his hands. "I explained that I knew nothing about the Medusa. I don't think that he believed me, but he warned me that I am in grave danger, regardless of whether or not I told him the truth."

"Why are you in danger?" Lavinia asked.

"Nightingale said now that word has gone out that the cameo is floating around somewhere in the underworld, any number of collectors will be searching for it. Some, he says, are extremely dangerous men who will stop at nothing to obtain what they desire. He...he likened them to sharks in the water circling a sinking ship. He said that I was in the position of the sole survivor clinging to the wreckage."

"He tried to frighten you," Lavinia said.

"And succeeded rather well, I must tell you." Howard seemed to fall into himself. "Nightingale claimed that the only safe course of action was to deliver the relic to him immediately. He promised to make it worth my while. But I cannot possibly do that because I do not have it."

There was a short silence while they all contemplated that news.

Tobias shifted position a little, propping one shoulder against the windowsill and folding his arms. "What else do you know about this antiquity?"

Howard did not look at him. He continued to focus his gaze on Lavinia. She did her best to appear encouraging and sympathetic.

"I've never seen the damned thing," Howard said. "I can only tell you what Nightingale told me. He referred to it as the Blue Medusa. The name is no doubt due to the peculiar color of the stone."

"Medusa," Tobias repeated thoughtfully. "A once beautiful woman with glorious hair who managed to offend Athena and got herself turned into a hideous monster for her efforts. She became one of the three Gorgons."

"The one whose gaze turned men to stone," Lavinia said.

"No man could slay her because to look at her was to die. She was eventually killed by Perseus, who—rather cleverly, I always thought—backed toward her while she slept, using his shield as a mirror to reflect her image. That way he did not have to look directly at her while he hacked off her head."

"Not what one would consider a particularly charming image for an item of fashionable jewelry," Howard muttered.

"Actually, Medusa was a very common theme for ancient jewelers," Lavinia said. "I saw any number of old rings and pendants set with Medusa-head cameos while I was in Italy. Her image was believed to be able to ward off evil."

"Turn your enemy or the source of a threat to stone, hmm?" Tobias shrugged. "There is a certain logic to that thinking."

Howard cleared his throat. "Mr. Nightingale told me that the cameo in this particular bracelet is a unique version of Medusa. It is believed to be the emblem of some ancient, obscure cult that flourished in secret for a time here in England. In addition to the familiar figure of a woman's head with staring eyes and snakes twisting in her hair, there is a small rod or wand carved into the stone beneath the severed throat."

"Did Mr. Nightingale tell you anything else about the relic?" Lavinia asked.

Howard furrowed his brow. "I believe he said that the bracelet itself is fashioned of gold of a very pure and excellent quality that has been pierced in any number of places to create a distinctive pattern of intertwined snakes."

"Pierced work," Lavinia said softly.

Tobias glanced at her. "You have seen such antiquities?"

"Yes. I saw a pair of gold bracelets in Italy that had been worked in such a fashion. Several gemstones of various colors were set into them. They had been discovered in a tomb, together with some coins from the fourth century. Quite incredibly beautiful, I must say. The piercing created a pattern of twisting leaves that was so fine and delicate it looked like so much gold lace."

Howard continued to watch her as though she was his only source of hope. "I can tell you nothing more about the Blue Medusa. Nightingale claims Celeste was killed because of it. But I do not believe that. At least, not entirely."

"What do you think happened?" Tobias asked.

"I have spent hours pondering the circumstances of her death," Howard admitted sadly. "I have come to the reluctant conclusion that, although my Celeste was, by nature, no thief, she was young and impulsive. She may have been led astray by her lover."

Lavinia stilled. "Are you saying that you think her lover persuaded her to steal the bracelet for him and then murdered her?"

"It is the only explanation that makes any sense to me." Howard clenched one hand into a fist and rested it on his thigh. "I believe that the bastard arranged to meet Celeste the night before last. He no doubt instructed her to bring the bracelet to the rendezvous. My sweet, innocent Celeste went to meet him in the middle of the night, and the monster strangled her with his cravat and stole the bracelet."

Lavinia glanced at Tobias to see how he was reacting to the theory. He appeared lost in thought. Or perhaps that was boredom she saw on his hard face. With him, one could not always be certain of the distinction, she reflected.

She turned back to Howard. "I am so terribly sorry for your loss."

"Lavinia, you must help me." Howard reached out abruptly and took her hands in his. "I do not know where else to turn. You say that you are in the business of making private inquiries. I wish to employ you to find the man who killed my Celeste."

"Howard—"

"Please, my dear friend. Nightingale warned me that I myself am in danger, but I care nothing for my own safety in this matter. I seek justice for my dear wife. You cannot deny me. I beg you to help me find her murderer."

"Yes, of course, we will help you, my friend," Lavinia said.

Tobias's expression sharpened without warning. He dropped his arms and straightened away from the windowsill. "Lavinia, we must discuss this matter before we accept the commission."

"Rubbish," she said. "I have already decided to accept it. You may join me as my partner in the affair or you may decline. That is your choice, naturally."

"Bloody hell," Tobias said.

"Thank you, my dear." Howard raised Lavinia's hands and kissed them. "Words cannot express my gratitude."

Tobias watched him in the manner of a hawk watching a mouse. "Speaking of expressing your gratitude, Hudson, there is the small matter of our fee."

"Money is no obstacle," Howard assured him.

"Always nice to hear that," Tobias said.

$\mathcal{N}$ine

"I don't like this case, Lavinia."

"Yes, I can see that you do not approve, sir. Indeed, you have already made your feelings on the subject abundantly clear. You were nothing short of rude to Howard."

She swept into the small study, went directly behind her desk, and sat down. For some odd reason that she had yet to fathom, it was always easier to discuss unpleasant topics with Tobias when she put the large block of mahogany between them.

She refused to admit to herself that he could be *intimidating*, but there was no getting around the fact that he was quite capable of exhibiting a formidable strength of will and a certain forcefulness of mind that would make any prudent person cautious.

Here in her study, enthroned behind the big desk, she was in command, she told herself. Most of the time.

"I will be blunt." He gripped the edge of the mantel and used it to lower himself down into a crouch in front of the hearth. "I don't trust Hudson."

She watched him light the fire, aware that he always favored his left leg, even on good days, when he undertook the small task. She opened her mouth to inquire about the old wound but managed to swallow the words before they could escape. He would not thank her for the sympathy, especially not while he was in this mood.

She folded her hands on top of the desk. "You have allowed your negative feelings concerning mesmerists in general to influence your opinion of Howard. It is really very closed-minded of you, sir."

He concentrated on the flames he had coaxed forth. "Hudson did not tell us the whole truth."

She raised her eyes to the ceiling in silent entreaty. There was no help from above, however.

"Yes, yes," she said, not bothering to conceal her impatience. "I am very well aware that, in your professional opinion, the client *always* lies, but I do not see why you should apply that narrow and somewhat misguided theory to Howard. He is obviously a desperate and distraught man whose only wish is to find his wife's killer."

"I do not think that we can assume for one moment that he wants her murderer found."

She stared at him, shocked. "What on earth do you mean? Of course he wants the villain discovered."

"I think it is far more likely that what Hudson wants is the missing bracelet."

Her first thought was that she had not heard him aright. "*I beg your pardon?* Are you saying that you do not believe that Howard wants his wife's killer found?"

"I do not doubt but that he wants us to find her lover." Tobias tightened his grip on the mantel and levered himself upright. "Because he believes that the lover has the bracelet."

"Tobias, you are not making sense. The lover is also the murderer."

"Not necessarily."

He went to the window and stood looking into the tiny garden behind the house. "In my *professional* opinion, I believe that it is quite likely that Dr. Howard Hudson is the person who murdered Celeste."

She was stunned by the certainty of his words. It took her a few seconds to find her voice.

"Are you mad, sir?" she finally managed in a whisper.

"I know that you consider him an old friend of the family. But put aside your personal feelings and consider another possible version of events."

"What version is that?"

"Mine." Tobias did not turn around. "It goes like this. Hudson learns that his much younger and extremely attractive wife has betrayed him with another man. He cannot rest until he knows the identity of her lover. One evening he makes an excuse to attend a demonstration of mesmerism given by a competitor, but he leaves early. He returns to the house and follows his wife to her rendezvous. He finds her alone, perhaps waiting for her lover. In a rage, he confronts her. There is a terrible quarrel. He strangles her with his own cravat."

She drew a deep breath. "What of the lover?"

Tobias shrugged. "Perhaps he arrives at the scene in the midst of the quarrel, realizes that something has gone wrong, and flees before Hudson sees him. Perhaps he never shows up at all."

"But why would Howard murder Celeste? He loved her."

"We both know that love can turn to hate in a crucible that is heated with the fires of betrayal and rage."

She started to argue the point, but the memories of what she had learned in the course of their last case made her hesitate.

The tall clock ticked in the silence.

"I understand your concerns," she said at last. "Mind you, I do not believe for a moment that Howard killed Celeste, but I can see where a professional investigator who did not know him personally might consider the possibility."

"And I can comprehend your desire to believe that Hudson is honest and sincere. I know how much it means to you to reestablish your acquaintance with him. He is, after all, someone whom your parents considered a friend. He shares some of your own memories of happier days. He reminds you of a time when you were not so alone in the world."

Reluctantly, she admitted to herself that he had a point. It had been good to see her old family friend again, in large part because Howard was a link to her past. His presence brought back lingering traces of the warmth and the quiet security of the close-knit family life she had known when her parents had been alive. The world had seemed so much simpler in those days. The future had looked rosy and bright and free of dark clouds.

"It was certainly good to see Howard again after all these years," she said briskly. "But I do not think that the pleasure of renewing our acquaintance has blinded me to the facts. I know Howard better than you do, Tobias. He was never a man given to rages or fits of strong passion. Indeed, he was always a model of self-control. His is a scholarly nature. I never saw him exhibit any inclination toward violence."

"You knew him as a visitor in your parents' home. In my experience, people are generally on their best behavior under such circumstances." He did not take his eyes off the small garden. "You cannot possibly know his innermost thoughts. You cannot know him the way a wife would have known him."

She thought about that. "You have logic on your side."

He looked at her over his shoulder, one brow raised in mocking surprise. "You astound me, madam. I did not expect you to accept my opinions so readily."

"I did not say that I accepted them. In point of fact I disagree with them entirely. But I can now comprehend why you hold those views. Let us get to the meat of the matter. Would you prefer not to assist me in solving this case, Tobias?"

"Bloody hell."

He swung around with a suddenness that caused her to sit back very quickly in her chair.

"The only way I would abandon this investigation," he said, "would be if I could convince you to give it up. And I can see that is highly unlikely."

"Impossible, actually."

He covered the small space in less than a couple of heartbeats, leaned across the desk, and planted his big hands on top of some papers that cluttered the surface.

"Let us have one thing understood between us, Lavinia. I have no intention of allowing you to make inquiries on your own into a situation that involves murder."

"It is not your place to determine the sort of cases I choose to investigate."

"Damnation, if you think that I will let you risk your neck—"

"That is quite enough, sir." She shot to her feet. "You have always had the most annoying tendency to issue orders, but you have grown decidedly worse in that regard since the business of the waxwork murders. Indeed, you have become extremely overbearing of late, and I must tell you that it is not an attractive quality in a man."

"I am not overbearing," he said through his teeth.

"Yes, you are. Indeed, it is no doubt such a natural condition for you that you do not even notice when you slip into that mode."

"I am merely attempting to instill some common sense into this situation."

"You are attempting to give me orders and I do not like it. Hear me well, sir." She leaned forward a little, putting her face close to his. "We are either equal partners in this venture or else I shall solve the case on my own. The choice is yours."

"You are, without a doubt, the most infuriatingly stubborn, willful woman I have ever met."

"And you, sir, are the most arrogant, dictatorial man of my acquaintance."

They glared at each other across the width of the desk for a long moment.

"Hell's teeth." Tobias straightened abruptly. An edgy expression simmered in his eyes. "You leave me no alternative. I am not about to let you take this case on your own."

She concealed a small sigh of relief. The unfortunate truth was that she had had only limited experience investigating murder. One case of it, to be precise, hardly sufficient to make her an authority in the field. She had a great deal yet to learn about her new profession, and Tobias was the only one who could instruct her in the fine points.

"It is settled, then," she said. "We are agreed that we will be partners in this affair."

"Yes."

"Excellent." She sat down quickly. "I believe the first step is to make a plan, is it not? As I recall, you are very fond of plans."

He did not move. "I am. I only wish that I had a plan that enabled me to deal more effectively with you, Lavinia."

She gave him a cool smile. "My, my. And here it was not long ago that you were holding me up as a paragon of female behavior suitable for Emeline to emulate."

"I cannot think what made me say such a thing. I must have taken temporary leave of my senses." He shoved a hand through his hair. "I find that happens frequently when I am in your vicinity."

She chose to ignore that. "About our plan, sir. It occurs to me that we must approach this puzzle from several different angles."

He rubbed his jaw, thinking. "You are right. There is the antiquity itself to be investigated. We must also try to discover the identity of the owner, the person from whom it was stolen."

"I have had some experience with the antiquities trade. I am acquainted with a number of persons who deal in relics. Rumors of the theft of an item as unusual as the Blue Medusa will no doubt be rampant by now. Why don't I make the inquiries in that direction?"

"Very well. You see to the legitimate shops and dealers. I will deal with the other sort." He started to pace. "Smiling Jack has any number of contacts among the criminal class. He will likely know this mysterious person who calls himself Mr. Nightingale. I shall ask him to arrange a meeting."

This was, she decided, the perfect opportunity to bring up a matter that she had been mulling over for several days. She cleared her throat delicately.

"Now that you raise the subject of your criminal connections," she murmured, "I may as well tell you that I have decided that it would be very helpful for me to become acquainted with your friend Smiling Jack."

"Out of the question. One does not take a lady into the Gryphon."

She had anticipated resistance, she reminded herself. "I could go in disguise, as you do, sir."

"And just how do you plan to disguise yourself?" His mouth curved grimly. "As a tavern wench?"

"Why not?"

"Absolutely not." He stopped smiling and gave her a narrow-eyed look. "I have absolutely no intention of introducing you to Smiling Jack."

"But I might need his connections myself one day. Only consider how efficient it would be if we were both able to contact him. It would not be necessary for you to be inconvenienced whenever the need to consult with him arose."

"Save your breath, Lavinia. There will be no introductions." He must have noticed her mouth opening again to further her argument, because he immediately raised his hand for silence. "I suggest we get back to business. If you are determined to pursue this new venture, we don't have time for one of our more spirited discussions."

"You are attempting to change the subject, sir."

"Not attempting, madam, I *am* changing it."

Much as she disliked admitting it, he was right. They did not have time for a quarrel. She subsided reluctantly, propped her elbows on the desk, and rested her chin on the heels of her palms.

"We could use some assistance," she mused. "I hesitate to say this, but I feel obliged to point out that this case provides both of us with an ideal opportunity to give our would-be apprentices a taste of this work."

Tobias came to a halt in front of her desk and met her eyes. Neither of them spoke for a moment, but she was quite certain she knew precisely what he was thinking. This deep sense of responsibility they had each assumed for the younger people who had been left in their care was something they had in common, she thought.

She smiled wryly. "You are no more eager to teach Anthony your trade than I am to instruct Emeline in the business, are you?"

He exhaled deeply. "This is not the career Ann would have chosen for him."

"But it was never Ann's decision to make, was it?" she said gently. "It is Anthony's choice."

"The same can be said of you and Emeline. Her choice of a profession is not yours to make."

"I know. It is just that I had hoped to establish her in the sort of life her parents wanted her to have. They naturally wished to see her safely and securely wed." She frowned. "Although I must admit that the sight of Oscar Pelling on the street the other day was a sad reminder that marriage is not always a safe, secure institution for a woman."

Tobias fixed her with a steady look. He said nothing.

His unwavering gaze made her uncomfortable for some reason. "Well, that is neither here nor there, is it?" She sat forward determinedly and pushed aside the piece of paper on which she had been making notes for the advertisement she planned to write. She reached for a pen and a fresh sheet of foolscap. "Please sit down, sir. It will be helpful if we outline our plan, will it not?"

"Perhaps." He sat down across from her. "In addition to determining the identity of the bracelet's owner, we need to learn more about Celeste Hudson."

She tapped the tip of the quill against the inkwell. "We can ask Howard some questions."

"No offense, Lavinia, but I'm not at all certain one could rely upon his answers."

"Are you implying that he would lie about her? Why would he do that?"

"If he is not a murderer, as you insist, then the best that can be said is that he was blind to his wife's true nature."

"You may be right on that last point," she said, "but he would certainly not be unique, would he?"

"No," Tobias admitted. "I doubt if most of the men in the ton know their wives any better. And vice versa."

"How do you propose to learn more about Celeste, in that case?"

He smiled thinly. "I shall do precisely what you suggested one ought to do when one sets about selecting a competent mesmerist or investigator. I shall consult her references."

"What references?" She suddenly recalled the conversation in the street two days earlier. "Oh, you mean the ones she mentioned in Bath? Lord Gunning and Lord Northampton?"

"Yes."

"Are you acquainted with them?"

"No. But Crackenburne will no doubt be familiar with them. If he is not, he will know someone who is acquainted with them."

"That reminds me. You have mentioned Lord Crackenburne on several occasions. He seems to be very useful to you."

"He knows virtually every gentleman in Society and a sizable number of those who hang around the fringes."

"I should like to make his acquaintance." She gave him her sweetest smile. "Surely you can have no objection to introducing me to him. As you just pointed out, he is a gentleman."

"I have no objection," Tobias said. "But it is unlikely to happen."

She stopped smiling. "Why not?"

"Since the death of his wife, Crackenburne hardly ever leaves his club. Which is what makes him so useful, of course. He hears rumors and gossip before anyone else does."

She glared. "He must go home sometime."

"Not that I've noticed."

"Really, Tobias, a man cannot *live* at his club."

"He can if he wishes. A club is a gentleman's home away from home."

"But—"

He glanced pointedly at the tall clock. "I do not believe that we have time for any more digressions, do you?"

She felt her jaw tighten but she knew that he was right. Reluctantly, she returned her attention to the piece of paper in front of her.

"Very well, sir," she said. "If you insist upon being rude."

"Of course I insist upon being rude. I have a talent for it." He sat forward and glanced absently at one of the papers she had moved aside. His eyes narrowed in a faintly puzzled expression.

"What's this?" he said, reading aloud. "*Superior and exclusive services provided to persons of quality who wish to commission private inquiries?*"

"Hmm? Oh, yes, I believe I mentioned that I intend to put a notice of my professional services into the papers. I am making a list of striking words and phrases that appear in advertisements." She reached for the sheet of paper he was examining. "That reminds me, there was a particularly effective bit of writing in this morning's paper. I had best jot it down before I forget it."

He frowned at what she had written on the sheet of foolscap. "I thought I made it clear that I do not recommend putting an advertisement in the papers. You will likely attract all sorts of odd clients. In our line we are better off relying upon word of mouth."

"You are free to operate your business in an old-fashioned manner if you wish, but I am determined to try a more modern approach to obtaining clients. One must do something to attract attention."

He angled his head to read another line. "*Confidential and effective devices for gentlemen of intrigue?*"

She studied the words with a sense of satisfaction. "I thought it had a very attractive ring to it. I especially like the phrase *gentlemen of intrigue*. It is very . . . well, *intriguing*, don't you think?"

"Very intriguing, indeed."

"Naturally, I do not wish to imply that I provide services only for gentlemen of intrigue."

"Naturally."

"I want to appeal to ladies also. I am thinking of substituting the phrase *persons of intrigue*." She paused as another notion occurred to her. "How does this sound? *Private and confidential services provided for ladies and gentlemen of intrigue.*"

There was an acute silence from the other side of the desk. She looked up sharply. The corner of Tobias's mouth was twitching. She knew that twitch, she thought. She did not trust it for a moment.

"Well?" she challenged. "What do you think of it?"

"I believe that I can almost guarantee that any advertisement patterned after the one in the morning paper aimed at *gentlemen of intrigue* will bring an extremely interesting assortment of clients to your doorstep," Tobias said.

"You have seen the notice?"

"Yes, I have, as a matter of fact. I paid close attention to it."

"Which only goes to prove that the wording is quite eye-catching."
She hesitated. "Although I must admit that, in spite of the interesting
turn of phrase, it is a bit difficult to determine the precise nature of the
devices that the firm offers for sale, isn't it?"

"It is an advertisement for condoms, Lavinia."

Ten

LAVINIA WALKED INTO THE ANTIQUITIES SHOP SHORTLY AFTER
two o'clock that afternoon. Emeline was right behind her, brimming
with enthusiasm for the task ahead.

Edmund Tredlow, a rumpled little man in wrinkled breeches and a
poorly tied, unstarched neckcloth, paused in the act of dusting a
statue of a lascivious-looking Pan and peered at them through the
lenses of his spectacles.

"Mrs. Lake. Miss Emeline. How nice to see you both." He set aside
the duster and hurried forward to bend over Lavinia's gloved hand.
When he looked up, squinting slightly, there was a familiar gleam in
his eye. Lavinia knew that the expression did not indicate admiration
for her person, or even raw lust. It was the possibility of a spirited
bout of bargaining that excited Tredlow.

"Good day to you, Mr. Tredlow." Lavinia retrieved her hand.
"Emeline and I have stopped in to have a quick word with you, if you
have the time."

"Have you got another antiquity to sell, then? I must confess, in
spite of my misgivings, I was able to obtain a rather nice price for the

Apollo you brought in a few weeks ago. The collector I managed to interest in the statue was extremely pleased with the quality."

"Fortunately, I do not, at present, find it necessary to sell any more of the excellent antiquities we brought back from Italy," Lavinia said smoothly. "But I would be grateful if you could give me the benefit of your considerable professional experience."

Tredlow looked immediately wary. "What, precisely, do you wish to know?"

Emeline gave him a stunningly brilliant smile. "My aunt has told me on several occasions that she is aware of no other dealer of antiquities in all of London who possesses as much knowledge of the market as yourself, sir."

Tredlow turned an odd shade of red. Lavinia's first horrified thought was that he had been struck by a fit of apoplexy. Then she realized that he was *blushing*. She stared in amazement, unable to take her eyes off the extraordinary sight.

"I have been in this line for a good many years," Tredlow stammered. "I like to think that I have learned a few things about the business."

"Indeed, that is obvious." Emeline looked around the shop with an expression of glowing admiration. "Such wonderful pieces you have for sale, sir. I vow, I haven't seen anything as nice as that collection of Greek vases in any other shop in Town."

"Only the finest here at Tredlow's." Tredlow fairly simpered. "I have a reputation to uphold, you know."

He had the look of a man who has just received a visitation from a siren, Lavinia thought. Tredlow was entranced.

Emeline blinked her eyes at him. "I only wish I had the time to spare for a complete tour of your collection today, sir. I know that you could teach me so much about antiquities."

"Any time, Miss Emeline." He rubbed his hands together. "I assure you it would be my privilege to instruct you in the subject. Speaking of Greek vases, I must tell you that I have an especially interesting assortment in my back room. The subject matter of the designs is most unusual. I sell them only to the most discerning connoisseurs. Perhaps you would like to make an appointment to view them?"

Lavinia had had enough. She had seen some of the Greek vases that Tredlow kept in the vast, overcrowded storage room at the rear of his shop. The subject matter of the designs was not at all suitable for young, unmarried ladies.

She cleared her throat quite forcefully. "About my questions, Mr. Tredlow."

He ignored her, evidently unable to take his eyes off Emeline.

Emeline smiled at him. "My aunt truly does have need of your professional expertise, sir. I would be very grateful if you could assist her."

"What's that? Oh, yes." Tredlow gave himself a small shake, managed to tear his gaze away from Emeline, and turned reluctantly to Lavinia. "How can I help you, Mrs. Lake?"

"As you may have heard, sir, I occasionally conduct discreet inquiries on behalf of certain persons of quality."

The last remnants of the moonstruck look vanished from Tredlow's expression. Acute disapproval replaced the lascivious warmth that had been there a moment ago. "I believe you did mention that you were attempting to make a living in that rather odd fashion."

"My aunt has taken me on as her assistant," Emeline confided. "She is teaching me the business."

Tredlow looked deeply concerned. "Not a proper occupation for a young lady, if you ask me."

"A good deal more proper than your offer to show her your private collection of Greek vases," Lavinia snapped. "Now, then, shall we get down to business, sir?"

His bushy whiskers bounced in an agitated manner. "I presume that, as you are here on *business*, you are prepared to pay for my advice and expertise?"

"Of course." Lavinia paused meaningfully. "If it proves helpful."

Tredlow rocked on his heels. "Of course, of course. Well, then, what is it you wish to know?"

"We have reason to believe that within the past few days, an ancient Roman bracelet was stolen. The antiquity was apparently discovered here in England, not brought from Italy. It is said to be a gold, pierced-work relic set with an unusual blue stone carved with the head of

Medusa. There is a tiny wand cut into the stone. Have you heard about the theft?"

Tredlow's wildly overgrown whiskers jumped again as he pursed his lips in a frown of acute interest.

"You refer to the Blue Medusa?" he asked sharply.

"Yes, do you know it?"

"I have heard of it." A crafty gleam lit his eyes. "But I was not aware that it had been stolen. Are you quite certain of that?"

"That appears to be the case, yes."

"The Blue Medusa," Tredlow repeated softly, as if speaking to himself. "Stolen. Interesting. Word will no doubt spread quickly."

Lavinia did not care for the new tone in his voice any more than she had for the one he had employed with Emeline. "Mr. Tredlow, we wish to know the identity of the owner of the bracelet."

He squinted at her through his spectacles. "Obviously, as you do not know him, I must assume that you are not making these inquiries on his behalf."

"No. My associate and I have been engaged by another concerned party."

"I see. Well, now. If it has been stolen, one can assume that the thief will likely be looking for an expert in antiquities. He will need to consult with one who can properly evaluate the relic and, perhaps, assist him in arranging a discreet sale."

Sudden alarm swept through Lavinia. She exchanged a glance with Emeline and saw that she, too, had grasped the nature of this new problem.

She turned back to Tredlow. "I would strongly advise you, sir, not to contemplate for even a single second getting involved with the thief. He has already committed murder once, and I doubt very much if he would hesitate to kill again."

"*Murder.*" Tredlow's eyes widened. He flung out a hand and fell back a step. "Surely you are mistaken?"

"He killed a woman, apparently to silence her."

"Dear me, dear me. How dreadful." Tredlow hesitated hopefully. "I don't suppose it might have been an accident of some sort?"

"Hardly. He strangled her with a cravat."

"I see." Tredlow heaved a deep sigh. "How unfortunate. Not the sort of thing that is generally good for business."

"Unless one is in my line, of course," Lavinia said. "Now, then, concerning the name of the owner of the Medusa bracelet. You were about to mention it, I believe."

"Not before we mention my fee."

Lavinia recalled Howard's anguished words: *Money is no obstacle.* "How much do you want for this tiny snippet of information that I can no doubt obtain elsewhere without too much trouble, Mr. Tredlow?"

Tredlow fell to haggling with his customary enthusiasm. It was, after collecting erotic Greek vases, his favorite sport. Fortunately, Lavinia thought, she'd had some experience in that line herself. The enforced stay in Rome a few months back had been instructive in many respects.

"Lord Banks owns the Medusa, I believe," Tredlow said when the bargain was struck. "The only reason I know that is because the relic found its way into Prendergast's shop about a year and a half ago. Prendergast very wisely consulted with me to determine a price. He is extremely weak in the field of British-Roman antiquities, you know."

"I see." Lavinia kept her voice noncommittal. She was well aware of the long-standing rivalry between Prendergast and Tredlow.

"I saw Prendergast later and asked what had become of the bracelet. He mentioned that he had sold it to Banks. I was somewhat surprised. At one time Banks was quite an active collector of antiquities, but he got rid of the vast majority of his best pieces a few years ago after his wife died. Don't know why he wanted the Blue Medusa, but there you have it."

"I wonder why Lord Banks hasn't sent word around concerning the theft," Emeline said with a puzzled air.

Tredlow snorted. "His lordship is quite elderly, you know. Both feet in the grave, as it were. I'm told he has a bad heart and in recent months his mind has become a sieve. Probably can't recall what he had for breakfast, much less whether or not he owns the Blue Medusa. I doubt that he even knows he's been robbed."

"That would certainly explain why he has not made the theft public." Lavinia tapped the toe of her kid half boot and pondered that information. "What better victim than one who isn't even aware of his loss?"

"But surely there is someone in his household who would be aware that the bracelet has gone missing," Emeline said.

Tredlow shrugged. "As far as I know, his only relation is his niece. A Mrs. Rushton, I believe. She came to live with Banks a few months ago after she learned that he was on his deathbed. Probably didn't expect him to hang on this long."

Excitement brushed across Lavinia's nerves. Tobias had told her that an impatient heir made a lovely suspect.

"This Mrs. Rushton is in line to inherit Banks's fortune?"

"So I'm told."

"Is she a collector?" Lavinia asked, trying not to give away her growing anticipation.

Tredlow grunted. "If the lady had a serious interest in antiquities, I would have seen her in my shop by now. As I have not made her acquaintance, I think it's safe to say that she is no collector and would have no notion at all of the value of an item such as the Blue Medusa." His brows rose in speculation. "I wouldn't be surprised to hear that she is still unaware of the fact that the bracelet has been stolen."

"Yet the rumors are out in the underworld," Emeline observed.

Tredlow dismissed that with a shrug. "Probably initiated by the thief in his efforts to attract a potential purchaser for the relic."

"Do you happen to know Banks's address?" Lavinia asked quickly.

"His lordship has got a crumbling old mansion in Edgemere Square, I believe."

"Thank you, Mr. Tredlow." She retied her bonnet strings. "You've been very helpful." She swung around and made for the door. "Come, Emeline, we must be off."

Tredlow scurried after them and politely opened the door. He swept a deep bow and then fixed Lavinia with a darkling gaze. "When should I expect my fee, Mrs. Lake?"

"Don't worry." Lavinia lifted one gloved hand in airy farewell. "You shall receive it just as soon as my client pays me for my services."

"Now, see here—"

Lavinia went smartly through the opening, forestalling further conversation. Emeline gave Tredlow a sweet smile and followed. The door closed behind them.

Out on the street in front of the shop, Emeline looked at Lavinia. "I saw a certain shrewd gleam in your eyes when Tredlow mentioned Banks's niece, Mrs. Rushton. I am coming to recognize that expression. What were you thinking?"

"It occurred to me that, as Banks's heir, Mrs. Rushton may be involved in this affair in one of two ways. Either she had some part in the theft—"

"That seems unlikely, if you ask me. After all, she was set to inherit the bracelet, together with the rest of Banks's fortune."

"Or she is every bit as much a victim as Banks himself. As you just pointed out, she was due to inherit. His loss is her loss."

"Which means?"

"That she may well be a potential client for Lake and March."

Emeline looked at her with gratifying admiration. "Aunt Lavinia, that is positively brilliant. You may well have uncovered a second client in this affair."

"Indeed." Lavinia tried to remain modest. It was not an easy matter. Two clients would mean double the fees.

"Mr. March will be very pleased," Emeline said.

"It will be interesting to see if he is properly appreciative of my initiative." Lavinia frowned. "Lately he has begun to take a distinctly proprietary air toward my business."

"Proprietary?"

"Yes." Lavinia paused in the street to wait for a farmer's wagon to move past. "One might even call him dictatorial. He is forever telling me what I should and should not do. He even had the nerve to tell me that I had no business placing an advertisement in the newspapers."

"Oh, dear."

"As if it was any of his concern how I choose to advertise my business."

"I'm sure he means well."

"Rubbish. He means to discourage me from pursuing a career as an investigator. If you ask me, he does not like the fact that, when we are not working together as partners on a case, I am, in effect, his competition."

"Come now, Aunt Lavinia, it is natural that he feels a duty to advise you in matters pertaining to your business. After all, he has had a great deal more experience than you have had."

"He is doing his best to keep my experience quite limited."

"Why do you say that?"

"As an example, he refuses to introduce me to his connections in the criminal underworld. Just this morning, I suggested that he introduce me to that tavern owner he calls Smiling Jack. He refused."

"I see what you mean," Emeline said. "I suppose Mr. March feels that it would be inappropriate for you to consult with the owner of a tavern."

"In my experience, Mr. March has never been overly concerned with the niceties of propriety," Lavinia declared. "I do not believe for one moment that he is attempting to protect me from unsuitable connections. It is far more likely that he wishes to keep Smiling Jack to himself."

"Do you really think so?"

"Yes, I do. As proof of that conclusion, I must tell you that he also made excuses not to introduce me to Lord Crackenburne."

"Hmm."

"Some nonsense about Crackenburne never leaving his club."

"Well, that does seem a bit strange."

"In addition to offering opinions regardless of whether or not I have requested them and refusing to introduce me to some of his acquaintances, you will also note that Mr. March has taken to appearing quite regularly at breakfast."

Emeline nodded. "We do seem to see a lot of him in the mornings."

"It is exceedingly expensive to feed a man of his size and appetite on a regular basis."

"Mr. March does enjoy his food, does he not?"

"It is not his food, Emeline," Lavinia said with grave precision. "It is *our* food."

"I think I understand what is going on here," Emeline said gently. "You feel that Mr. March is crowding you."

"On the contrary. Mr. March is not content to merely crowd one. His ambition is to trample one into the dust and leave one lying flattened on the roadway."

"Lavinia, I hardly think——"

"All in all, it is imperative that I show him that I am perfectly capable of handling my own business affairs without his constant supervision, and that I can come up with clues and suspects without his assistance. Which brings us back to Mrs. Rushton."

Emeline looked intrigued. "What do you mean?"

"Edgemere Square is not far from here. We shall pay a call on her on our way home."

"Excellent. I shall look forward to watching your interrogation techniques."

"Speaking of techniques," Lavinia said.

"Yes?"

"I must tell you that I was impressed with the manner in which you employed that extremely syrupy smile and that blatant flattery to Mr. Tredlow. Your approach rendered him quite cooperative. Very efficient work."

"Thank you." Emeline was pleased. "My particular method of conducting inquiries may be somewhat different from your own, but I feel it has possibilities."

"Indeed, especially when one is interrogating gentlemen. Is it a difficult technique to master?"

"It comes quite naturally to me."

TOBIAS STRETCHED OUT HIS LEGS, STEEPLED HIS FINGERS, AND REgarded Crackenburne. The club was quiet at this hour. The only sounds were the snapping of the flames in the fireplace, the clink of coffee cups on saucers, and the crackle of newspapers.

"Another case?" Crackenburne asked without looking up from his newspaper.

"Mrs. Lake and I are conducting an inquiry on behalf of an old friend of hers, Dr. Howard Hudson."

"Ah, yes, the mesmerist whose wife was found strangled."

"I never fail to be astonished by your remarkable ability to keep up with the latest gossip." Tobias turned his attention to the flames. "Apparently Mrs. Hudson was murdered by her lover for an ancient bracelet that she evidently stole."

"You sound doubtful."

"Celeste Hudson was quite beautiful, much younger than her husband, inclined to flirt, and may have been involved in an illicit love affair."

"I see. In other words, you suspect that her husband killed her."

"I think it is an extremely likely possibility, yes. To be sure, I do not doubt the whole tale. It is quite probable that Celeste Hudson had a lover and that the pair of them contrived to steal the antiquity. But Lavinia is convinced that Hudson is innocent of both murder and theft and only seeks justice for his dead wife. I, on the other hand, think what he really wants is to recover the antiquity that went missing that night."

Crackenburne grunted. "I don't wish to dampen your enthusiasm, but I must point out a potential drawback to this particular case."

"Save your breath, I have already spotted it. If it turns out that I'm right and that Hudson did murder his wife, Lavinia and I are highly unlikely to collect our fee."

"Um, yes." Crackenburne folded the newspaper and peered over the rims of his spectacles. "Anything I can do for you?"

"What can you tell me about Lords Gunning and Northampton? All I know is that they reside in or near Bath and may have been clients of Hudson's."

Crackenburne gave the matter some thought and then shrugged. "Not much, I'm afraid. If they are the gentlemen I am thinking of, both are elderly. Both are in ill health. Both are wealthy. They have memberships in this club, but I haven't seen them here in years."

"That's all?"

"I'm afraid so. But I'll see if I can turn up more information, if you like."

"I'd appreciate it," Tobias said.

"I must say, I rather enjoy this detecting business of yours." Crackenburne picked up his coffee cup. "Almost as interesting as the old days during the war when you conducted your clandestine inquiries on behalf of the Crown."

"I'm glad that you are amused," Tobias said. "Personally, I have concluded that my career as a spy afforded me a far simpler and more restful life and put considerably less strain on my nerves than my present occupation as Mrs. Lake's occasional partner."

THE BANKS MANSION WAS A VAST, GLOOMY PILE OF STONE IN THE Gothic style. Tucked away in a remote neighborhood, it rose several stories above a large, high-walled garden. The narrow windows on the upper floors were shrouded with dark drapes. In Lavinia's opinion, the structure would have been well suited to a horrid novel featuring specters and the odd skeleton.

"Even if one did not know that the master of the house was slowly decaying inside, one could guess as much from the street," Emeline said.

"It is a somewhat depressing place, is it not?" Lavinia banged the brass knocker. "But I suppose that is only to be expected under the circumstances. His lordship is dying, after all. And taking his time about it too."

The housekeeper opened the door and peered out, blinking, as if the sunlight on the doorstep was unexpected and unwelcome.

"We wish to speak to Mrs. Rushton." Lavinia put her card into the woman's gnarled hand. "Please give her this and tell her that it is very important."

The housekeeper stared at the card, as though puzzled by the printing, and then scowled. "Mrs. Rushton isn't in this afternoon. She's off getting one of her treatments."

"Treatments?" Lavinia repeated. "What sort of treatments?"

"Got weak nerves. Started going to one of those mesmerists a few weeks ago. Does wonders for her, she says. Can't tell the difference, if ye ask me, but the long and the short of it is, she ain't home today."

The housekeeper closed the door in Lavinia's face.

Emeline's eyes were alight with excitement. "Mrs. Rushton goes to a mesmerist."

"Indeed." Lavinia led the way down the steps. She did not trouble to conceal her satisfaction. "A very interesting bit of news, is it not?"

"But what does it imply?"

"I do not know where it will take us, but there is no getting around the fact that it is a connection of some sort."

Emeline hurried after her. "When will you tell Mr. March about this latest development?"

Lavinia pondered that for a few seconds. "Tonight when I see him at the Stillwater ball. He may well turn up this information on his own. I want to be certain he knows that I got here first. I have no wish to listen to him take the credit. Quite intolerable."

Eleven

"I FOUND OSCAR PELLING." ANTHONY'S VOICE WAS STRAINED with the effort to conceal his pride and excitement. "It wasn't easy. I had to make inquiries at a number of inns before I discovered that he is staying at the Bear's Head in Shuttle Lane."

"Excellent work." Tobias eased aside the carriage curtain and checked the night-shrouded street. It was shortly after nine. The unmistakable stench of the river told him that they were nearing their destination. "Did you learn anything of his business in Town?"

"I spoke with one of the stable lads at the inn."

Tobias glanced at him, frowning slightly. "I trust you didn't give yourself away? I do not want Pelling to know that we are making inquiries."

"Of course I was careful to act very casual." Anthony looked offended. "Just a bit of conversation about horses and the departure times of the coaches and the quality of the out-of-town gentry who selected that establishment when they came to London. That sort of thing."

"Well, then? What did you discover?"

"Nothing alarming. As Mrs. Lake guessed, Pelling is here for the usual reasons. He is a man of some substance, after all. He has business with his bankers. The stable lad said he heard him talk about paying a visit to his tailor and boot-maker. Just the customary routine of a wealthy gentleman who does not come to London frequently."

"Hmm." Tobias contemplated that information. "The stable lad knew nothing of Pelling's business affairs, I assume?"

"No, of course not. He's a stable lad, after all." Anthony paused a beat. "In terms of personal information, the only thing he volunteered was that Pelling was amusing himself in the evenings with one of the prostitutes who does business in the neighborhood near the inn."

"Find the woman," Tobias said.

Anthony swallowed and turned red. "Uh—"

"Something wrong?"

"No, not at all," Anthony said quickly. "I'll, uh, pursue that line of inquiry immediately." He coughed once and cleared his throat. "I'd rather you, uh, did not mention this aspect of the investigation to Mrs. Lake or Miss Emeline, if you don't mind."

It dawned on Tobias that Anthony would be mortified if Emeline discovered he was interviewing prostitutes.

"No need to be concerned on that front," he said. "I haven't told either of them that we are looking into Pelling's activities. I do not want to alarm them."

"Mrs. Lake may not thank you for keeping this from her," Anthony warned.

"If we discover nothing to concern us, she need not know about these particular inquiries. In any event, when you locate the light-skirt Pelling is bedding, come to me. I'll handle the inquiry personally."

Anthony looked considerably relieved. "If you're sure."

"I'm sure." Tobias glanced out the window. "We have arrived." He rapped on the roof of the hackney, signaling the coachman to stop.

The vehicle clattered to a halt. Tobias opened the door, gripped the edge of the cab, and eased himself down onto the pavement. It was no longer raining, and his leg was in better form today than it had been yesterday, but even on good days he had no great inclination to vault in and out of carriages the way he once had. He told himself that it was the effects of the wound he had suffered in Italy, not the fact that he was perilously close to forty, that caused him to exit vehicles with considerably more dignity than he had employed in his younger years.

"Don't forget to instruct the coachman to wait for us," Anthony said. "We don't want to find ourselves without transportation in this neighborhood. Not at this hour of the night."

He jumped lightly down to the pavement with a careless ease that made Tobias sigh inwardly.

"We will be only a few minutes." He tossed some coins to the man on the box. "Be so good as to wait for us."

"Aye, sir." The coachman made the coins disappear and reached for his bottle of gin. "I'll be here when ye've finished yer business."

Tobias walked toward the glowing yellow windows of the tavern. He sensed Anthony's anticipation.

"Remember, say nothing at all until we are in Smiling Jack's office," he said. "Your manner of speaking will give you away instantly in this crowd. Is that quite clear?"

Anthony grimaced. "I assure you, your instructions in the fine art of disguise are as plain this time as they were the other ten times you gave them to me this evening."

"If I tend to repeat myself, it is because I have good reason. The last thing we need tonight is a brawl with one of the patrons inside."

"I promise you, I will not say a word."

Tobias looked at the evil amber glow of the tavern windows and shook his head. "You will never believe it, but Lavinia actually asked me to bring her here to introduce her to Smiling Jack. She planned to disguise herself as a tavern wench."

Anthony was startled. "Hell's teeth. I assume you refused?"

Tobias smiled humorlessly. "One does not bring a lady to this sort of establishment. But I believe she was annoyed with me. Seemed to feel that I was trying to keep her from consulting with my contacts."

"Which is precisely the case, is it not?"

"Yes. But it is for her own good. I cannot have her traipsing about in this part of town. She is too inclined toward reckless behavior as it is. I certainly do not want to encourage her in that direction."

Tobias halted in front of the door of the Gryphon and gave his companion one last survey.

Anthony was garbed in the rough attire of a dockside laborer. In his heavy boots and ill-fitting trousers and coat, he looked as if he had just finished a long day unloading cargo from one of the ships moored at the nearby wharves. The shapeless hat pulled down low over his head concealed his fashionably cut hair and shielded his features from curious eyes.

Tobias had donned a similar costume for the evening's outing. In addition to the laborer's clothing, his slight limp added a distinct touch of authenticity to his appearance. The patrons of the Gryphon made their livings in a variety of dangerous occupations, some legal and some quite illegal. Wooden legs, missing fingers, eye patches, and scars were common among them.

"You'll do." Tobias pushed open the door of the smoky tavern. "Do not look anyone directly in the eye. Such an act may be taken as a rude insult."

"I believe you mentioned that instruction several times also." Anthony's grin came and went in the dark shadow of his low hat. "Calm yourself. There is no need to be anxious. I will not fail you."

"It is the possibility that I am failing you that makes me uneasy tonight," Tobias said quietly.

Anthony turned his head sharply. "You must not think of it that way. This is my choice."

"Enough," Tobias said. "Let us get this business done."

He opened the door and walked into the busy tavern, deliberately accentuating his limp. Anthony followed.

The roaring fire on the massive hearth infused the crowded room with a hellish light that suited the surroundings. The wooden benches and booths were crammed with men who had come here to drink, play cards, and flirt with the sturdily constructed serving maids.

Tobias made his way through the throng. He glanced back at one point to make sure that Anthony was close behind and saw that his companion was riveted by the sight of one of the bosomy maids. The woman's large, swelling breasts threatened to spill out of her bodice as she bent over to serve three tankards of ale.

"They are all fashioned in a statuesque manner," Tobias muttered. "Smiling Jack likes them that way."

Anthony grinned.

They went down a hall and stopped at the door to Smiling Jack's office. It stood ajar. Tobias rapped once and pushed it open.

"Good evening to you, Jack."

Tobias did not bother to roughen his words. There was no need for pretense here in this room. He and Jack knew each other well from the old days when they had associated as spies. In his former profession as a smuggler, Jack had frequently been in a position to obtain information that had been quite useful to the Crown.

Jack had turned to a new career as a tavern owner in recent years, but his talent for collecting useful bits and pieces of gossip and rumors had not changed. He operated in this world very much as Crackenburne did in the world of a gentleman's club.

Jack looked up from the act of pouring a brandy. He smiled broadly at the sight of Tobias and Anthony in the doorway. The expression twisted the long scar that ran from mouth to ear into a ghastly death's head grin.

"Right on time, I see, March. As usual." Jack squinted at Anthony with great interest. "And who's this you've brought with you?"

"My brother-in-law, Anthony Sinclair." Tobias shut the door. "You've heard me speak of him. I'm in the way of teaching him the business."

"A pleasure to meet you at last, young Sinclair." Jack chuckled. "Going into the same trade, are ye?"

"Yes, sir," Anthony said proudly.

Jack nodded. "I like to see a business stay in the family. And you'll not find a more skilled instructor in the art of investigatin' than March here. Never knew anyone better at prying into other folks' secrets. The fact that he hasn't had his throat slit for his efforts in all these years is proof that he's got a talent for the profession, if ye ask me."

"Thank you for the excellent references," Tobias muttered. "If you don't mind I'd like to move on to a more pressing topic. I received your message this afternoon. What is it you have to tell me about Nightingale?"

"I will explain in due time. But first sit down and let me pour you both a brandy."

Tobias took one of the unyielding straight-back chairs near the hearth. He reversed it, as was his custom, and sat astride. Anthony watched him and then quickly went through the same routine with the other chair. He folded his arms along the back, just as Tobias did, and took the glass of brandy Smiling Jack handed to him.

"I'll admit that I've not had a lot of contact with Mr. Nightingale." Smiling Jack went behind his broad desk and lowered his massive bulk into the oversize chair. "He trades in stolen antiquities, jewelry, and art. Only the finest and most valuable items. Boasts a very exclusive clientele, I'm told. An altogether higher class of business than my own humble line, I fear."

"Nonsense." Tobias sipped the brandy. "In my opinion there is not a great deal of difference between smuggling and tavern-keeping and the trade in stolen antiquities and art. And I'll match you against Nightingale any day when it comes to exclusive clientele."

Smiling Jack chuckled. "I appreciate your kind remarks, my friend. Now, then, as to Nightingale, he specializes in handling transactions between clients who prefer not to meet face-to-face for various reasons. He sets up auctions and sales for such persons."

Anthony frowned. "How does an illegal auction work?"

Smiling Jack settled into his chair and assumed a lecturing air. "Nightingale acts as a go-between for his clients. He notifies interested parties of the item that is on the block and solicits bids. He guarantees anonymity to all concerned. Takes a plump commission and appears to manage a decent livelihood."

Tobias drummed his fingers on the wood chair back, thinking. "Does he ever commission thefts?"

Jack rested one hand on his large belly and pondered that. "I cannot say. But I certainly wouldn't put it past him to take advantage of an opportunity if there was enough blunt in it."

"You mentioned his exclusive clientele," Tobias said. "Do you know the names of any who have done business with him?"

"No. As I said, part of what they pay for is a guarantee of absolute discretion. Nightingale provides it. His stock-in-trade is his reputation, after all. He is very careful to preserve it."

Tobias thought of the words Lavinia had printed on her business cards: *Discretion Assured.* "It seems that my associate, Mrs. Lake, is not the only one who attempts to lure the more exclusive sort with a promise of discretion."

Jack raised his beefy shoulders in a great shrug. "The proprietor of a business must do what he or she can to ensure a profit. Now, then, as you requested, I sent word to Nightingale that you wished to meet with him. He responded with such speed that I think it is safe to say he is as eager to discuss this business of the missing antiquity as you are yourself."

"When and where?"

"I'm afraid that will be up to Nightingale. You need not concern yourself with locating him. He will find you."

"I do not have a lot of time to waste."

Jack grimaced. "I got the impression that you will see him soon. Very soon."

Tobias took another swallow of brandy and lowered the glass. "What else can you tell me about Nightingale? Can you describe him?"

"We've met on one or two occasions, but to tell you the truth, I wouldn't recognize him on the street if he walked up to me and offered a civil greeting. Nightingale makes it a point not to be seen in the light of day by any of his clients or business associates."

Anthony looked intrigued. "How does he make his, uh, arrangements?"

"He works only at night and he's careful to stay in the shadows. Uses a couple of street lads to deliver his messages." Jack rolled his brandy glass between his wide palms. "From what little I've seen of him, I can tell you that he's a small man. Judging from the sound of his voice, I'd say he's not young. But not old and frail either. Caught a glimpse of him moving off down a foggy lane once. He's got an odd way of walking."

"How is that?" Tobias asked.

"A sort of a twist and a slide to his gait, if you know what I mean. I'll wager he suffered an unfortunate accident at one time or another and the bones never healed properly."

"An accident of that sort would not be surprising, given his line of work," Tobias said. "Probably ran afoul of a dissatisfied client."

"Aye."

Anthony glanced at Tobias, as if asking permission to put forth a notion of his own.

"What is it?" Tobias asked.

"It merely occurred to me that mayhap Mr. Nightingale effects a severe limp as a part of his disguise."

Tobias chuckled. "An excellent point. It is, indeed, a distinct possibility."

Jack glanced at Tobias and closed one eye in a knowing wink. "I'd say your new assistant has a knack for the trade."

"I've been afraid of that," Tobias said.

Anthony smiled, clearly pleased with himself.

Jack turned back to Tobias. "So, then, ye've taken on another case with your occasional partner, eh?"

"Our client claims that his wife was murdered by whoever convinced her to steal the antiquity," Tobias said neutrally.

"Ah, yes, the mesmerist's wife."

Anthony straightened. "You've heard about the affair?"

"Aye." Jack took a swallow of brandy. "Sooner or later that sort of news generally makes its way to the Gryphon." He studied Tobias. "You're searching for a killer again, my friend?"

"So it would seem."

Anthony glanced at Tobias in surprise. "What do you mean by that? There is no question but that Mrs. Hudson was murdered."

"The lady is dead, all right," Tobias said. "But I am not at all certain that her killer is unknown to us."

"I don't understand," Anthony said.

"The lady had arranged a meeting with her lover the night she died," Tobias said patiently. "Her husband was aware of the affair and he admits he knew about the rendezvous. He attended a demonstration of mesmerism that night. The lady was later found strangled. Those are the only real facts we have at this point."

Anthony was still baffled but Jack nodded, comprehension plain on his scarred features.

"You think Hudson followed her to the rendezvous and killed her in a jealous rage," he said.

Tobias shrugged. "I think that is the most likely explanation of events, yes."

"And then discovered too late that she had made off with a valuable antiquity and that the thing was missing." Jack snorted. "Talk about rough justice, eh?"

"Hold on here," Anthony said quickly. He turned to Tobias. "Are you saying that you believe Hudson hired you and Mrs. Lake to find Mrs. Hudson's lover, not because he wants to bring the killer to justice but because he wants to recover the bracelet?"

"In a word, yes," Tobias said.

"But if you believe that your client is lying, why did you agree to take the case?" Anthony demanded.

"I had no choice in the matter." Tobias finished his brandy. "My *partner* made it clear that she was determined to look for the lover and the bracelet with or without me."

"And you could not let her take on such a dangerous case alone," Anthony concluded.

"That sums up the situation very precisely." Tobias looked at Jack. "Have you anything else to tell us?"

"Only that I would advise a bit of caution," Jack said. "The fact that Mr. Nightingale is involved in this affair is a bit worrisome. Word has it that several of his clients are not only very rich but quite ruthless when it comes to acquiring items for their collections."

"Oddly enough, I had already reached that conclusion." Tobias stood and put down the empty brandy glass. "Come, Tony. We must be on our way if we are to arrive at the Stillwater ball before midnight.

I can only hope that Nightingale will not keep us cooling our heels for very long."

"I doubt that he will," Jack said. "But the only thing I can tell you with any great certainty is that the meeting, when it does occur, will take place at night."

Twelve

SHORTLY AFTER MIDNIGHT LAVINIA STOOD WITH TOBIAS AT THE edge of Lady Stillwater's elegantly proportioned ballroom and watched Anthony lead Emeline into the sweeping turns of a waltz. A sense of inevitability descended on her.

"They do look very well together, don't they?" she said.

"Yes, they do." There was no inflection in Tobias's words. "I know that you had every intention of marrying Emeline off to a wealthy man, but sometimes love gets in the way of an otherwise entirely commendable scheme."

She watched the dancers. "It might be just a passing flirtation."

"Don't sound so hopeful. I fear the worst."

She winced. "The *worst* being that they are falling in love?"

"That is your view of the matter, is it not?" he said in that same, too-even voice.

For some odd reason the casual manner in which he agreed that *falling in love* was, indeed, the worst possible outcome flattened her spirits. She wondered morosely if Tobias would consider the possibility of falling in love himself an equally dreadful fate.

"Unfortunately, I feel obliged to inform you that Anthony does, indeed, seem to have a talent for the investigation business," Tobias added. "Now that he has had a taste of it, I doubt very much that I shall be able to persuade him to reconsider a more stable career."

She heard the grim resignation in his voice and understood. He had tried to do his best as a substitute father for his young brother-in-law, just as she had struggled to secure a safe future for Emeline.

"Do you think we have failed them both?" she asked quietly.

"I don't know," he said. "But I will say that when one sees them so happy together, it is difficult to feel that we are allowing them to ruin their lives entirely."

She brightened a little at that comment. "There is something to be said for love, is there not?"

"Something, yes. Precisely what, I cannot hazard a guess."

She did not know what to read into those words, so she decided to change the topic. "I must tell you that Anthony is not the only one who shows a flair for investigation. Emeline demonstrated a remarkable degree of skill with interrogation techniques this afternoon."

"The two of you did very well to get the information concerning Lord Banks's connection to the bracelet so quickly today."

"Thank you." She was briefly distracted by the praise. Then she returned to her subject. "The thing is, Tredlow practically melted into a puddle when Emeline smiled at him and complimented him on his reputation in the antiquities business. I vow, she would have got the information out of him even if I had not been there to promise him a fee for his professional services."

"Charm is always a useful talent, and Miss Emeline has a great quantity of it."

Lavinia nodded. "I have always known that she had a gracious way about her, but I admit that I had not realized until today how useful the ability to entrance gentlemen could be in the investigation business."

"Hmm."

"As a matter of fact, watching Emeline's excellent performance this afternoon gave me an idea."

There was a short, wary pause.

"What sort of idea?" Tobias asked cautiously.

"I am thinking of asking her to instruct me in the technique of employing charm to obtain information from gentlemen."

Tobias choked on the mouthful of champagne he had been in the process of swallowing. He sputtered and started to cough.

"Good heavens, sir, are you all right?" Alarmed, she reached into the little beaded reticule that Madam Francesca had insisted she purchase to go with her gown. She yanked out a handkerchief and thrust it into Tobias's hand. "Here. Use this."

"Thank you," he mumbled into the square of delicately embroidered linen. "I believe that what I really need, however, is a large glass of claret." He snagged another glass of champagne off a passing tray. "But I suppose this will have to do for now."

She frowned as she watched him down half the contents of the glass. "Is your leg bothering you again?"

"It is not my leg that is troubling me."

She did not care for the gleam in his eyes. "What is it, then?"

"My sweet, you have any number of admirable skills and talents. But as your loyal, occasional business partner, I must tell you that, in my considered opinion, any attempt on your part to study the art of charming gentlemen into giving up their secrets would be a complete waste of your time."

The fact that he assumed charm to be a skill that was beyond her struck her to the quick.

"Are you implying, sir," she said coldly, "that I lack the ability to cause gentlemen to dissolve into puddles?"

"Not at all." His teeth flashed in a wicked grin. "You certainly have a dissolving effect on me on occasion."

She glowered. "You find my notion of studying the techniques of charm quite amusing, do you not?"

"I regret to say that I do not believe that either one of us has an aptitude for charm. I speak with some authority because, as it happens, Anthony has been attempting to teach me some of the finer points of the art."

She was stunned. "He has?"

"Indeed. I have run one or two experiments on you recently, and as far as I can tell it has had no effect whatsoever."

"*You* tried to charm *me*?"

"For all the good it did. Obviously you failed to even notice my poor efforts."

"When do you ever employ charm—" She broke off, remembering his recent comments at breakfast. "Oh, yes. That business of me resembling an incarnation of Venus."

"And there was that rather nice line comparing you with a sea nymph. I practiced that one for the length of the entire distance between my house and yours this morning."

"Just because you have no gift for charm does not mean that I cannot learn the skill."

"Save your energy, my sweet. I have concluded that charm is an inborn attribute. One either possesses it naturally, from the cradle, as is the case with Miss Emeline and Anthony, or one lacks it altogether and no degree of instruction will enable one to acquire it."

"Rubbish."

"I fail to see why you are concerned with learning how to charm gentlemen," Tobias said. "You contrive to do rather well without that skill."

"I believe that is an insult, sir."

"I did not mean it as such."

She narrowed her eyes. "Perhaps I would enjoy charming certain gentlemen."

"Me, for instance?" He smiled in a kindly fashion. "It is a pretty thought, but it is not necessary, my dear. I am content with you just the way you are."

"Really, Tobias."

"Yes, really. It is apparent to me that you and I have established an understanding of each other's nature that goes beyond insincere platitudes and meaningless compliments."

"You may be correct; nevertheless, it strikes me as an extraordinarily useful inquiry technique and I am strongly inclined to perform some experiments of my own before I abandon the whole notion."

"I trust you will be cautious, madam. I am not at all certain that my nerves are strong enough to sustain the shock of a heady dose of charm delivered by you."

She had had enough of his teasing. "Do not concern yourself, sir. I was not planning to waste any such hard-won skill on you. I suspect you would be utterly impervious to charm, in any event."

"No doubt." His voice softened to that low pitch that told her he was no longer teasing her. "Nevertheless, if you choose to conduct any experiments with charm, I must insist that you confine your researches to me."

She caught a glimpse of something in his eyes that was both dangerous and exciting, but she was not certain what to make of it. There was an element of irony here, she thought. This was just the sort of situation where the ability to charm a gentleman would be quite useful.

"Why should I confine my experiments to you, sir?" she asked lightly.

"I cannot, in good conscience, allow you to put any other innocent gentlemen at risk."

"You, sir, are no innocent."

"It was a figure of speech." His gaze went past her shoulder. "Speaking of one who knows the value of charm, here is Mrs. Dove."

Lavinia was oddly disappointed that Joan had chosen this moment to seek her out in the crowded ballroom. These brisk verbal exchanges with Tobias never failed to invigorate her senses and infuse her with a certain pleasant heat.

Nevertheless, business called.

She collected herself and turned to greet the striking woman coming toward them.

Joan Dove was in her mid-forties, but her pale blond hair hid the telltale streaks of silver well. With her fine, classical features and her superb sense of style, she was frequently mistaken for a much younger woman. It was not until one drew close enough to notice the faint lines at the corners of her eyes and the worldly experience in her gaze that one got a hint of her true age.

Although she had been widowed for a full year, Joan still wore only gray and black in memory of her much-loved husband. While the gowns were limited in their colors and hues, they were inevitably in the first stare of fashion. Madam Francesca saw to that.

Tonight she was serenely elegant in silver satin trimmed with exquisite little black roses. The neckline was cut low to frame her fine shoulders and bosom. The skirts fell in perfect folds to her ankles.

"Ah, there you are, Lavinia. Tobias." Joan smiled at both of them. "A pleasure to see you this evening. I collect that Emeline and Anthony are enjoying themselves on the dance floor."

"Indeed." Lavinia smiled with satisfaction. "This is another social coup for both of them, and I cannot tell you how much I appreciate your efforts to secure the invitations for us."

"Think nothing of it. Now that I am getting out a bit more, it is in my own best interests to ensure that there will be people at these affairs with whom I can enjoy conversation. I consider you and Tobias to be not only good friends but colleagues as well."

Lavinia caught Tobias's eye. They exchanged glances of mutual understanding that needed no words. The thought of Joan as a colleague was unsettling.

It had been Joan's suggestion that they should consult with her on difficult cases where her unusual connections might prove useful. Indeed, she was quite enthusiastic about what she viewed as her new *hobby*.

Although Joan had been their first important client and Lavinia would always be grateful to her, not only for the business but for introducing her to Madam Francesca, there was good reason to have some misgivings about the notion of taking her on as a consultant. On the positive side, however, she offered her services for free.

Joan was a mysterious woman with a shadowy past. One of the few things that Lavinia knew for certain about her was that, before his untimely death, her husband, Fielding Dove, had controlled a powerful criminal organization known as the Blue Chamber. At its zenith, the ring had possessed extensive legal and illegal business interests that reached beyond England all the way to the Continent.

The Chamber had supposedly disintegrated and collapsed following Dove's death last year. But Tobias had picked up rumors in certain underworld quarters to the effect that many of the Chamber's enterprises had not been destroyed after all. They were merely under new management.

And the most likely new proprietor in sight, as far as Lavinia and Tobias could determine, was Joan Dove.

Some questions, Lavinia thought, were better left unasked.

"I am happy to tell you that I have been quite busy with my researches on behalf of Lake and March this evening," Joan said cheerfully.

The enthusiasm in her voice caught Lavinia's attention and made her look at her friend more closely. This lightness of spirit was new. Perhaps Joan was, at long last, emerging from mourning.

"Lake and March," Lavinia repeated thoughtfully. "I rather like the sound of that."

"Personally, I do not care for it," Tobias said. "If you must give our *occasional* partnership a formal designation, Joan, you may refer to the firm as March and Lake."

"Rubbish," Lavinia shot back. "Lake and March is far more appropriate."

"I disagree," Tobias said. "The senior partner always comes first."

"Age is a consideration, of course, although I would not have been so rude as to call attention to yours. Nevertheless—"

"I was referring to being the senior in terms of experience in the profession," Tobias muttered. "Not my years."

Lavinia smiled sweetly and turned back to Joan with an inquiring expression. "Now, then, you were saying, madam?"

"Before I was so rudely interrupted by your little squabble about the proper name for your business relationship with Mr. March, do you mean?" Joan's eyes glinted with a rare amusement. "Yes, well, I was about to tell you of some rumors that are circulating among certain members of the ton who take a keen interest in antiquities."

Tobias put down his champagne glass and looked at Joan with acute interest. "You have my undivided attention, madam."

"I knew it," Lavinia said, excitement bubbling inside her. "Word of the missing Medusa has begun to move through high circles, has it not? That is precisely why I contacted you earlier today and asked for your assistance, Joan. With your social connections you are in an ideal position to learn this sort of information."

"I am delighted to be able to consult on this matter." Joan kept her eyes on the crowd and lowered her voice to a confidential tone. "What I discovered is that the news of the Blue Medusa has captured the interest of a certain collector, an extremely wealthy, powerful gentleman who has a reputation for obtaining whatever he sets out to possess."

"How do you know he wants the Medusa bracelet?" Lavinia asked.

"Because he rarely deigns to appear at social affairs, even though he is on every hostess's guest list. The fact that he just walked into this ballroom is proof that he is after the bracelet. I cannot imagine anything else that would have brought him here."

Lavinia followed Joan's gaze and saw a man standing with a small group near a cluster of palms. He was well dressed, and he held himself with the cool arrogance and unmistakable assurance that came with rank and wealth. In that, he had a great deal in common with most of the other men in the room tonight. He should have been virtually indistinguishable from those around him. But he stood out in the crowd in some indefinable way, even though he was obviously making no effort to do so. If anything, given his quietly elegant appearance and manner, he was making every effort to be perceived as a part of the landscape.

Yet, Lavinia thought, her eye had gone straight to him. She had known at once which man Joan was watching. In a sea of colorful little fish, he was a poorly disguised shark.

Rather like Tobias, she thought uneasily. The realization made her take a swallow of champagne.

Physically, however, the two had little in common. For one thing, the stranger was older than Tobias—late forties, perhaps. For another, his hairline had receded in a dramatic fashion, drawing attention to a high forehead and a strong profile. He was also taller and more elegantly slender than Tobias.

"Who is he?" Lavinia asked.

"Lord Vale," Joan said softly.

There was something in her voice that made Lavinia glance quickly at her. She was startled to see an expression of interest in her friend's face. It occurred to her that she had never seen Joan regard any other man in that manner.

Joan found Vale intriguing.

"Bloody hell," Tobias muttered. "Is Vale involved in this affair?"

"So it would seem," Joan said. "What is more, I suspect that he is aware that you and Lavinia are investigating it. There simply is no other reason why he would be here tonight."

"Damnation." Tobias set down his unfinished champagne. "I could have done very nicely without this complication."

Lavinia looked at him. "Why are you concerned about Vale?"

Tobias did not take his attention off the man on the other side of the room. "As Joan just told you, Vale is a collector with very discriminating tastes. He possesses the financial resources to satisfy those tastes. It is rumored that if money alone will not help him obtain what he chooses to acquire, he is willing to employ other means and methods."

"He is the founder of a very exclusive club," Joan said. "The members call themselves the Connoisseurs. Only those who collect the most exotic and unusual antiquities are invited to join. Vacancies occur rarely. When they do, a prospective new member must present a suitable relic for the club's private collection in order to be considered for admission." She paused. "There is an opening for a new member now, as it happens."

Tobias glanced thoughtfully at Joan. "How do you know that?"

"Because the vacancy was created by my husband's death a year ago. He was a member of the Connoisseurs for many years."

"I wonder why Vale has not filled the opening in the club membership," Tobias said.

"Perhaps no suitable candidate has applied," Joan said. "Do not forget, the prospect must present not simply a very fine artifact but one that is considered unusual or extremely rare. It is not easy to find such a relic."

Lavinia caught her breath. "The Medusa bracelet would almost certainly qualify as an acceptable membership artifact."

"Indeed. The club's museum is a very *private* collection, one that is never open to public viewing. I doubt that Vale or any of the members would be inclined to question the source of a relic provided that it was suitably exotic and rare." Joan contemplated Vale. "Given his lordship's appearance here tonight, I think we must assume that he has no intention of sitting back in hopes that some other collector will find the Blue Medusa and present it to the club's museum. Vale plans to acquire it himself."

Tobias glanced at her. "Do you know him well?"

Joan hesitated. "He was a guest in our home on occasion when my husband was alive. Fielding liked him. The two respected each other. But I cannot say that I know Vale well. I do not think anyone can make that claim."

"No," Tobias agreed. "Probably not."

"Have you met him?" Joan asked.

"Crackenburne introduced us. But like you, I cannot claim a close acquaintance. We certainly do not move in the same circles."

"Look, he has left his companions," Lavinia said. "He's coming toward us."

"So he is," Tobias said quietly. "You were right, Joan. He knows about Lavinia and me."

They watched Vale glide smoothly around the edge of the dance floor, bestowing an almost imperceptible nod here and there, pausing once or twice to greet someone. But although his path appeared random, it was clear to Lavinia that he was working his way toward where the three of them stood in the alcove.

"He'll no doubt attempt to interrogate both of you," Joan warned. "He will be very polite about it, of course, but he is a very clever man. Be careful what you say if you wish to keep your secrets."

Vale materialized out of the crowd at that moment and stopped in front of them. Lavinia studied him covertly and saw that there was another way in which he differed from Tobias in terms of physical appearance.

Vale had the haunting eyes of a romantic artist.

"Joan." He bent gracefully over her gloved hand. "It is good to see that you are getting out into Society again. It has been too long."

"Good evening, Vale." She retrieved her hand with a smooth motion. "Do you know my friends? Mrs. Lake and Mr. March."

"March." Vale nodded once in Tobias's direction and then he turned to Lavinia. "A pleasure, Mrs. Lake."

When he took her hand she noticed the odd iron ring he wore. It was shaped like a small key. She tried for a truly charming smile and added a little curtsy for good measure.

"Lord Vale."

He did not look particularly dazzled, she noticed. He merely bowed briefly over her hand and turned back to Joan.

"May I have the honor of a dance, madam?" he said.

Joan stiffened ever so slightly. The tiny hesitation was almost undetectable. If Lavinia had not been watching her she would have missed it altogether.

"Yes, of course," Joan said, recovering quickly.

She flicked a puzzled glance back at Lavinia as Vale led her away.

Lavinia watched the pair move out onto the dance floor.

"Well, so much for being interrogated," she said. "It appears that the only thing Vale had in mind was a dance."

"Don't be too certain of that. As Joan said, Vale is subtle." Tobias clamped a hand under her arm. "Come, there is nothing more we can do at the moment and I find myself in need of some fresh air."

"It is a bit stuffy in here, is it not?"

She allowed him to steer her toward the French doors that opened onto the terrace. They walked out into the cool of the spring night.

Tobias did not stop at the low rock wall. He kept going, drawing her with him down the stone steps into the lantern-lit garden.

They strolled along a path toward the darkened conservatory attached to the rear of the mansion. The windows of the large greenhouse glinted in the moonlight.

Lavinia pondered the surprise and uncertainty that she had seen in Joan's eyes when Vale had led her out onto the floor. There were very few things that could fluster Joan, but Vale's invitation to dance had come close to achieving that rare state.

"I wonder if perhaps you and Joan are both wrong about the reasons for Vale's presence here tonight," she said.

"What the devil makes you think we might be wrong?"

"It is simply that I gained the distinct impression that Vale's goal was to dance with Joan, not to find out how our investigation was proceeding."

"Vale is an expert at concealing his goals. Joan is equally skilled at the business, if you ask me."

She blinked at the unmistakable thread of irritation in his voice. "You are annoyed."

"No."

"Yes, you are. I can sense it quite clearly. You are in an ill temper. What on earth is the matter? Are you irritated because Vale did not attempt to question us?"

"No."

"Tobias, really, you are being very difficult."

He came to a halt in front of the conservatory and opened the glass-paned door.

Lavinia hesitated when she saw that he intended to enter. "Do you think we should go inside?"

"If the owner had wanted no one to enter, he would have seen to it that the door was kept locked."

"Well, I suppose—"

He tugged her gently into the humid atmosphere and shut the door. The heavy scents of rich earth and growing things teased her senses. There was enough moonlight streaming through the myriad windows to reveal the ranks of palms, ferns, and other plants arrayed in neat rows. She smiled as the pleasant warmth enveloped her.

"Isn't this spectacular?" She surveyed the heavy foliage and started slowly down an aisle, pausing here and there to sample the fragrance of a flower. "I imagine that this is how it feels to stroll through a jungle. I trust we will not encounter any snakes or wild beasts."

Tobias fell into step beside her. "I would not depend on that if I were you."

"Your mood is not improving." She stroked a long, glossy leaf.

"Do not get too close to that." Tobias pulled her back from the plant. "I do not recognize the species and there is no point taking chances."

She swung around, exasperated. "I have had quite enough of your surly mood. Tell me what is wrong, Tobias."

He looked at her, eyes dark and brooding in the moonlight. "If you must know, when I watched Vale lead Joan out onto the floor, I was suddenly overtaken with an overpowering desire to ask you to dance."

She could not have been more astonished if he had suddenly announced that he could fly.

"You wished to *dance* with me?"

"I don't know what the bloody hell came over me."

"I see."

"I have never taken much interest in dancing," he continued. "And with this damned leg of mine, that sort of exercise is entirely out of the question. I would make a complete fool of myself on the floor."

In the distance she could hear the muted strains of the waltz emanating from the ballroom. A deliciously exhilarated sensation swirled through her. She smiled at him in the shadows.

"There is no one to see you make a fool of yourself in here," she said softly.

"Except you."

"Ah, but I am already well aware that you are not a fool, and there is nothing that you could say or do that would make you out to be one in my eyes."

He looked at her for a long moment. Then, very deliberately, he reached for her and drew her into his arms.

And for the first time in their tumultuous acquaintance, they danced together.

His steps were awkward and careful, as if he was afraid he would accidentally step on her toes or topple her to the floor of the greenhouse. But that did not matter, she thought. What mattered was that there was music in the distance and moonlight glinted on his dark hair. What mattered was that the air around them was heavy with the exotic fragrances of flowers that had come from far-off climes. What mattered was that she was in his arms and that time was standing still for a precious little eternity.

It was a scene of metaphysical enchantment, a scene that could have come straight from the pages of one of her precious books of poetry.

Tobias moved with her in a slow, measured tread down the aisle of tropical plants. She rested her head against his broad shoulder. The waltz was faerie music. The moonlight was liquid silver. The lush foliage that surrounded them was a magical garden.

When they reached the small bower at the far end, he stopped and tightened his hold on her. He kissed the curve of her bare shoulder.

"Tobias."

A delicious urgency swept through her. She wrapped her arms around his neck and raised her mouth to meet his.

His kiss left her breathless.

He eased the tiny sleeves of her gown down her arms, drawing the low-cut bodice to her waist. His powerful, competent hands cradled her breasts with astonishing tenderness. She felt his thumbs brush across her nipples and shivered in response.

He lowered himself onto the padded bower bench and pulled her down astride his thighs. His hands slid up her legs under the billowing satin folds of her gown. When he cupped her gently with his palm, her head fell back.

He slid one finger along her cleft, resting it against the small, tight nubbin at the top. She breathed deeply and moved against his hand.

He unfastened his trousers. She reached down and encircled him with her fingers. Her thumb glided across the broad, straining tip of his shaft.

He groaned with fierce pleasure.

"At times like this," he muttered against her throat, "I cannot doubt your powers of mesmerism. You never fail to entrance me."

"I may be a trained mesmerist, but you, sir, are nothing less than a sorcerer."

The moonlight and the magic closed in around them.

$\mathcal{T}$hirteen

IT WAS THE FIRST TIME SHE HAD DANCED SINCE FIELDING'S DEATH.

Joan felt oddly bemused as Vale guided her through the sweeping turn.

She had never thought to waltz with any man again, had never even dreamed that someday she might enjoy the music and the graceful patterns with anyone other than her beloved Fielding. Yet here she was, in the arms of one of his more dangerous friends, and it was intoxicating.

"Your gown is exquisite, madam," Vale said. "But I cannot help but notice that you still wear the colors of mourning, even though it has been a year since Fielding departed this world."

"I miss him," she said quietly.

"I understand. I miss him too. Fielding was my friend. But I must tell you that I do not believe that he would have wanted you to wear nothing but gray and black for the rest of your life."

She did not know what to say to that. The truth was that until quite recently she had not even thought about ending her period of mourning. She had had no desire to end it. Indeed, she knew that some part of her had anticipated wearing somber hues forever.

But the certainty that she was doomed to live out her days in a state of melancholia had begun to abate in recent weeks. Lavinia and Tobias had broken through the dark trance in which she had been ensnared. They had found answers to the questions surrounding Fielding's death, questions that had haunted her for months. In doing so, they had helped free her from a gloom that had seemed unrelenting.

"We shall see," she said.

Vale smiled, obviously content for now with her response. He swept her into another long, gliding turn.

He was, she thought, an excellent dancer. She relaxed and gave herself up to the glorious strains of the waltz and the sure strength of his arms.

"You have acquired some interesting new companions," Vale said after a while.

The comment brought her back to the reality of the moment with a decided jolt. This was no pleasant dream. Vale did nothing without a reason. She must be on her guard.

"You refer to Mrs. Lake and Mr. March, I believe," she said smoothly. "They are, indeed, somewhat out of the ordinary. But I find I enjoy their company."

He chuckled. "That is no doubt because you, madam, are very much out of the ordinary yourself." He paused for another turn. "I know nothing of Mrs. Lake, but there are a number of rumors about March."

"You surprise me, sir. I would not have thought you the type to give credence to gossip."

"You know very well that I pay very close attention to certain types of gossip, just as Fielding did."

"What do the rumors say of Mr. March?" she asked.

"Among other things, they tell me that he served as a spy during the war and that he continues to make a living in a rather unorthodox fashion." Vale gave her a knowing look. "I believe he accepts commissions to conduct private investigations on behalf of persons who prefer to avoid Bow Street."

"A most unusual line of work."

"Yes, it is."

"But no doubt quite an interesting occupation."

Vale's brows rose. "One hears that he and, presumably, his good friend Mrs. Lake are presently searching for a certain antiquity."

"Ah."

Vale looked amused. "What does that signify, madam?"

"Merely the fact that you mention this relic implies that you too are looking for it, sir."

He sighed mockingly. "Subtlety is lost on you, madam. You know me too well."

"On the contrary, sir. I do not know you well at all. But when it comes to the matter of rare antiquities, I am acquainted with some of your tastes."

"Yes, of course. You and I and Fielding discussed the pleasures of collecting many times over the years, did we not?" He spun her into another turn. "I believe that you are something of an authority yourself."

"I do not claim any great expertise, but I admit that I learned many things about relics while listening to you and Fielding discuss and compare your acquisitions," she said.

"And of course, you have inherited Dove's outstanding collection, have you not? Tell me, madam, do you intend to add to it?"

Keep him guessing, she thought. Give nothing away.

"If that is a subtle way of asking me whether or not I plan to acquire the Blue Medusa," she said, "I cannot give you an answer as yet. I have not made up my mind."

"I see." He brought her to a halt at the edge of the dance floor, neatly manipulating her into the seclusion of a private alcove. He did not take his hand from her arm. "I have no wish to find myself competing directly with you."

"But that wish would not stop you from doing so should the need arise, correct?"

He smiled and ignored the question. "There is another aspect of this situation that alarms me, madam."

"I am astonished, sir. I did not think anything could alarm you."

"On the contrary. You are the widow of one of the few men I have ever called friend, and I would be negligent in my responsibility to Fielding's memory if I did not try to prevent you from exposing yourself to undue risk."

"I assure you, I am not at risk in this matter."

"I am concerned about your role in this affair, Joan."

"Do not trouble yourself with any concerns on my behalf, my lord." She smiled. "I assure you, I am well able to take care of myself. My husband was an excellent instructor in many subjects, not just antiquities."

"Yes, of course." He did not look pleased with her response, but he inclined his head very civilly. "I apologize if I have intruded into your private affairs."

"You need not apologize, sir. I am happy to tell you that I am assisting Mrs. Lake and Mr. March in their investigations."

That stopped him cold. If she had not witnessed his stunned expression, she would never have believed him capable of such a degree of astonishment. A tiny thrill of triumph shot through her.

"Assisting them?" he repeated blankly. "Bloody hell, Joan. What the devil are you talking about?"

She chuckled. "Calm yourself, my lord. It is merely a hobby of mine." She was oddly pleased with having disconcerted him to such an extent. "But an amusing one, if I do say so."

"I don't understand."

"It is really quite simple. I have connections in places they do not. When those connections might prove useful, I endeavor to take advantage of them."

His mouth quirked humorlessly. "Am I one of those connections? Is that why you accepted my invitation to dance? So that you could pursue your investigations on behalf of March and Mrs. Lake?"

"Not at all, sir. I danced with you because you asked me and because it pleased me to do so."

Irritation flashed in his eyes, but he bent politely over her hand. "I trust you enjoyed yourself, madam."

"Oh, I did, indeed, sir, even though I am well aware that the only reason you are here tonight is because you are after the bracelet and you wanted to discover my role and the role of my friends in the affair. I trust you are satisfied with the results of your own inquiry."

He straightened but he did not immediately release her hand. "A word of warning, Joan. This affair of the Medusa is a dangerous business."

"I shall bear that in mind, sir."

He looked less than pleased with that, but they both knew there was nothing he could do about her involvement in the situation.

"I will bid you good night, madam," he said.

"Good night, my lord." She gave him a demure curtsy. "I am honored that you chose to renew our acquaintance this evening, even though I know you had ulterior motives."

He paused briefly in the act of turning away. "The honor was mine. Allow me to tell you that you are wrong on one point, however. I did not invite you to dance solely because I wanted to quiz you on the subject of the bracelet."

"No?"

"I asked you," he said deliberately, "because I very much wished to dance with you."

He disappeared into the crowd before she could think of a response.

She stood there for a long time and thought about how much she had enjoyed her brief moment in Vale's arms.

TOBIAS OPENED HIS EYES AND STUDIED THE GLEAM OF SILVER light on a nearby leaf. He was flat on his back on the padded bench, one booted foot on the floor. Lavinia was on top of him, her skirts tumbled across his thighs, her breasts pillowed against his chest. He looked up at the night on the other side of the conservatory windows and wished that he did not have to move.

He wondered if Lavinia found this business of conducting an affair as bloody uncomfortable at times as he did. What he would not give for a warm bed.

Lavinia stirred, started to snuggle, and then abruptly stiffened.

"Good heavens." She flattened her palms on his chest and levered herself up to a sitting position. "It is very late. We must return to the ballroom. By now Joan or Anthony or Emeline will no doubt have noticed that we have disappeared. It would be extremely awkward if someone came in search of us and found us together like this."

He sat up slowly, eyeing the position of the moon through the glass panes of the conservatory roof. "We have not been gone all that long. I doubt we've been missed."

"Well, we certainly cannot dawdle here any longer." She struggled with the bodice of her gown. "Is my hair badly mussed?"

He watched her put herself to rights. "Your hair looks fine."

"Thank heavens." She got the sleeves of the gown up over her shoulders, stood, and shook out her skirts. "I cannot imagine anything more embarrassing than walking back into Lady Stillwater's elegant ballroom looking as if ... as if—"

"As if we had been making love?" He got to his feet and shoved his shirttails back into his trousers. "Somehow, I do not think there are many who would be greatly surprised."

"What?" She swung around, her voice rising, eyes widening. "Are you saying that everyone knows that we—" She broke off and waved one of her hands wildly.

"That we are lovers?" He grinned at her expression of horror. "I suspect so."

"But how can that be? I have never told a single soul." She glared at him. "Tobias, I vow, if you have discussed the details of our personal connection with *anyone*, I shall throttle you."

"I take grave offense at that, madam." He held up both hands, palms out. "I am a gentleman. I would not dream of disclosing such intimate details to anyone. But I must tell you that our friends and relatives would have to be uncommonly stupid not to have concluded that we are engaged in an affair."

"Oh, dear." She looked nonplussed. "Do you really think so?"

"Calm yourself, Lavinia. It is not as if we are two young, inexperienced people with reputations to consider. We have both been out in the world for some time and have acquired a certain immunity. Provided we are reasonably discreet, no one will so much as blink at what we choose to do in private."

"But what of Emeline and Anthony? We really ought to set a proper example, don't you think?"

"No," he said flatly. He shrugged into his coat. "There is no call for us to set an example for them. The rules are different for people of our age and experience. Emeline and Anthony know that as well as we do."

She hesitated. "Well, yes, I suppose what you say is true. Nevertheless, discretion is required, and in future we really must take more care when it comes to this sort of thing."

"I will allow that your concerns on the subject of discretion are not entirely unfounded. In addition, I have noticed that this business of sneaking around has a few other drawbacks. One is forever searching for privacy. Indoor locations are hard to come by, and when they are not available, one is obliged to keep an eye on the weather."

"True. But I have been thinking about the matter lately and I have concluded that there are some positive aspects."

A chill of dread went through him. "Such as?"

"I do worry about being discovered and I still get a jolt of horror whenever there is a close call. And then there is the discretion issue. But when all is said and done, I must admit that it is quite thrilling at times."

"Thrilling," he repeated evenly.

"Indeed." Her voice brightened with enthusiasm. "Odd as it seems, I have begun to wonder if perhaps the very risk of being discovered is responsible for a certain sense of excitement."

"Excitement."

"Yes. And I must say that the frequent change of location endows the business with a definite touch of novelty."

"A touch of novelty."

Good God, she had grown to *enjoy* the clandestine aspects and the uncomfortable venues. This was his own fault, he thought. Like Dr. Frankenstein in that new horrid novel he had been hearing about, he had created a monster.

"How many other people do you think will have made love in a conservatory?" she continued with what sounded like genuine scholarly interest.

"I have no notion." He yanked open the door. "Nor do I care to discover the answer to that question."

"Do you know," she continued brightly, "some of our more daring trysts remind me of scenes from certain poems. Byron's writings, especially, come to mind."

"Bloody hell." He stopped and turned around to confront her. "I don't know about you, but I have no intention of spending the rest of my days hiring dirty hackneys and searching out secluded sections of the park whenever we wish to—"

The long scrape of a boot sliding on gravel stopped him cold. He turned swiftly, putting Lavinia behind him.

"Who goes there?" he said. "Show yourself."

There was movement on the other side of the hedge. A low, hulking figure slithered around the corner of the bristling greenery and came to a halt at the edge of a patch of moonlight. He wore a many-tiered greatcoat that cloaked him from neck to ankle. A shapeless hat was pulled down over his face. He stood slanted and hunched, a walking stick in one hand.

"Forgive me if I am interrupting," the stranger rasped in a bruised voice. "I assumed the two of ye had finished your business in the conservatory."

Lavinia peered at the strange little man over Tobias's shoulder. "Who are you, sir?"

"Mr. Nightingale, I presume?" Tobias did not take his eyes off the newcomer. "I was told you preferred to meet under cover of darkness."

"Aye, sir, that I do. Darkness offers a cloak of privacy that is difficult to obtain in any other way." Mr. Nightingale sketched a small bow. "A pleasure to meet ye both."

"How did you get into this garden?" Lavinia asked. "Lady Stillwater maintains a small army of servants. I cannot imagine how you managed to slip past them."

"On a night such as this, with so many people coming and going, it was quite a simple matter to get past the footmen at the front door. Rest assured, I do not intend to stay long." He chuckled hoarsely at some private joke. "I have no great interest in dancing."

"What do you want with us?" Tobias asked.

"Rumor has it that ye are looking for a certain artifact."

"To be precise, we are looking for the person who murdered a woman in order to steal the artifact," Lavinia said.

Mr. Nightingale made a lumpy movement that was no doubt intended to be a shrug. "Either way, ye're looking for the Blue Medusa, are ye not?"

"Well, yes," Lavinia agreed. "If we discover it, we'll no doubt learn the identity of the killer. Can you help us?"

"I've got no interest in murderers, although I wish ye well in your hunt," Mr. Nightingale said. "Generally speaking, murder is bad for me business. Oh, I'll admit that it does add a bit of spice now and again and sometimes drives up the prices in certain quarters. But unfortunately, it can just as often lower them. There are any number of clients who get nervous when there's murder involved, ye see."

"What is your interest in the bracelet?" Tobias asked.

"Have ye heard of a small, very exclusive club known as the Connoisseurs?" Mr. Nightingale asked softly.

Lavinia inhaled sharply, a small, startled gasp. But she kept silent.

"We know of it," Tobias said. "What does it have to do with this case?"

"The number of members is limited. Openings occur rarely. They come about only when a member dies, quits, or is tossed out of the club. Competition to join the club is fierce."

"Go on," Tobias said.

"As it happens," Mr. Nightingale continued softly, "such an opening has existed for a year now and word has gone out that it will at last be filled. Rumor has it that the Connoisseurs is accepting applications."

"Prospective members must present an artifact for the club's private museum of curiosities, I believe," Tobias said. "The person whose offering is judged the most suitable will be admitted to the club."

"You are well informed, Mr. March." Nightingale nodded approvingly. "The Keeper of the club's museum makes the final decision, and the deadline for applications is less than a fortnight away."

"You think the Blue Medusa will appeal to the Keeper, is that it?" Tobias asked.

"The Keeper is known to have a strong preference for British-Roman antiquities. They say he has a passion for 'em." Mr. Nightingale shook his head. "Don't understand it meself. Most collectors of a truly discriminating nature prefer relics from the ancient ruins abroad. Hard to compare a cameo found in some English farmer's field with a fine statue discovered in Pompeii, if you ask me. But there ye have it. Each to his own, I suppose."

"Given the Keeper's personal preference for artifacts discovered in England," Lavinia said, "the Blue Medusa would suffice nicely as a membership offering for the club's private museum."

"Aye." Mr. Nightingale's eyes gleamed briefly in the deep shadow of his shapeless hat. "I believe it's fair to say that whoever presents it to the Keeper will be admitted to the Connoisseurs."

"What precisely is your interest in the bracelet?" Tobias asked. "Thinking of applying for admission?"

"Me?" Nightingale gave his raw laugh again, as if Tobias had said something vastly entertaining. "I've no wish to join a fancy club. My interest is in the money to be made in the process. I intend to hold a very private auction, ye see. I will invite only certain exclusive persons to bid."

"Persons who are anxious to join the Connoisseurs and will pay whatever it takes to obtain the relic that will ensure admission, is that it?" Tobias asked.

"Precisely," Mr. Nightingale said.

"Assuming we find the bracelet," Tobias said, "why the devil should we turn it over to you?"

"I hear ye're a man of business, sir. I'm offering a business proposition. If ye and your associate here turn up the bracelet, I am prepared to pay ye a handsome fee."

"I'm afraid it will be quite impossible for us to turn the bracelet over to you," Lavinia said briskly.

Tobias cleared his throat. "Uh, Lavinia—"

"If we should happen to locate it," she continued, "we would be obliged to return it to its rightful owner."

"Who will soon be dead, according to the rumors I've heard." Mr. Nightingale snorted softly. "Where he's going, I doubt he'll have any need of it."

"That doesn't mean that you have any right to steal it from his estate," Lavinia snapped.

Tobias tried again. "Lavinia, I think you've said enough."

"I'm not talking about stealing the bloody bracelet," Mr. Nightingale growled. "I'm discussing a business proposition."

Lavinia raised her chin and looked down her nose at Nightingale. The little man was, Tobias thought, one of the few people in the world whom she could look down at, given her own stature.

"My associate and I do not engage in illicit bargains of the sort you are describing," she said coldly. "Is that not correct, Mr. March?"

"It might be possible to fulfill our commission and engage in a legal bargain that is profitable for all concerned," Tobias said carefully.

Lavinia and Mr. Nightingale both looked at him.

"Just how do you intend to accomplish that?" Lavinia demanded.

"I'm not certain yet," he admitted. "But given the amount of money at stake in this affair, I fully expect inspiration to strike at some point."

Mr. Nightingale gargled. "A man after me own heart, ye are, sir. Not one to let a golden opportunity slip through your fingers, are ye?"

"Not if I can help it," Tobias said. "Given that you have asked for our assistance, I have a few questions for you."

"What sort of questions?"

"Have you heard any rumors at all about the mesmerist's wife?"

"The lady who was murdered in this affair?" Mr. Nightingale moved his twisted frame in a negative motion. "They say she conspired with her lover to steal the bracelet. Some say that when the deed was done, he strangled her and took the damned thing. Others say her husband followed her to the rendezvous that night and murdered her. Either way the antiquity has vanished. That is all I know."

Tobias watched him. "But the Medusa has not come up for sale on the underworld market or else you would not be seeking our assistance."

"Ye have the right of it, sir," Mr. Nightingale said. "Been no rumors of the damned thing being offered for sale. None at all."

"Doesn't that strike you as odd?" Tobias asked.

Mr. Nightingale squinted in the shadows. "Odd?"

Lavinia glanced at Tobias. "Why do you find it strange?"

"Given the value of the Medusa in certain quarters, I would have expected the killer to contact a man of business in the antiquities line, a professional such as Mr. Nightingale here, as swiftly as possible. One would think that the villain would be anxious to turn a profit immediately."

"Perhaps the thief is waiting until the furor over the murder fades," Lavinia suggested.

"But holding on to the bracelet puts him at great risk," Tobias said. "It is dangerous to keep it in his possession, because it is evidence of a murder that could send him to the gallows."

Lavinia contemplated that briefly. "You have a point. Furthermore, the killer is no doubt aware by now that we are looking for him. One would, indeed, think that he would want to get rid of the Medusa as swiftly as possible."

Mr. Nightingale studied Tobias from beneath his slouchy cap. "The murder is your affair. I told ye, I've got no interest in it. I'm a simple man of business, and me only concern here is for the profit that's to be made if this thing is handled properly. Well, sir? Have we got a bargain?"

"Mrs. Lake is correct," Tobias said slowly. "If we recover the bracelet, it must be returned to its rightful owner."

"Now, see here," Mr. Nightingale began heatedly, "I thought ye just said—"

Tobias cut him off with a raised hand. "However, as you noted, the owner is not in the best of health, and the lady who is in line to inherit apparently has no particular interest in antiquities. For a fee, I would be willing to put your offer before her. I cannot guarantee that she will deal with you, but at least you would have a chance of obtaining the Medusa."

"Huh." Nightingale mulled that over for a long moment. "The profit would not be nearly so high if I must first purchase the Medusa from Banks's heir. I would no doubt be obliged to give her a fair price for the damned relic. And then there would be your fee on top of it, March."

"Something tells me you would do very nicely out of the arrangement," Tobias said easily. "Your clientele is not the sort to quibble over your inflated prices. All they care about is acquiring the Medusa."

"And just think of the advantages, sir," Lavinia said smoothly. "Any bargain you struck with Banks's heir would be legal and without risk."

Mr. Nightingale waved that aside with a cramped hand. "Takes some of the sport out of it, if ye ask me."

"Nevertheless," Tobias said, "that is all we are prepared to offer. Take it or leave it."

"Damn yer eyes, March, can't ye see there's more profit in this for all of us if we keep the heir out of it?"

"Unfortunately, we've got our professional reputations to consider," Tobias said. "Can't have gossip going around that March and Lake are in the habit of taking advantage of heirs. Not good for business."

"Humph." Mr. Nightingale rapped his walking stick on the ground a couple of times. "Very well, if that's your only offer, I'll accept it. Mind ye, though, if the Medusa falls into me hands from some other source, our arrangement no longer stands. I won't owe ye or Banks's heir a penny."

He turned away without another word and made to move off into the shadows, one foot dragging heavily.

"I understand," Tobias said quietly to his back. "But if matters transpire in that fashion, do not be surprised if the heir hires us to recover her stolen bracelet. In which event, we would know precisely where to look."

Mr. Nightingale halted and looked back over his hunched shoulder. "Is that a threat, March?"

"Consider it more in the nature of a bit of professional advice," Tobias said softly.

"Bah. I'll give ye some advice in return. If ye and your lady hope to make your fortunes in the investigation business, ye'd best develop a more practical attitude toward matters of a financial nature."

Nightingale slouched off around the hedge without waiting for a response.

There was a short silence. When he was certain they were alone again, Tobias took Lavinia's arm and started toward the bright lights of the ballroom.

"There is something I have been meaning to tell you," Lavinia said quietly.

"A shudder of dread passes through me whenever you say those words, madam."

"It is about Mrs. Rushton, Banks's heir."

"What about her?"

"I suspect that she may be involved in this in some manner."

He stopped and turned so that he could examine her face in the glow that spilled from the ballroom windows. "What the devil are you talking about?"

"I may have neglected to mention that after we got Banks's name from Tredlow this afternoon, Emeline and I called at the Banks mansion."

"Yes, you certainly did neglect to mention that little tidbit," he said evenly. "Why?"

She made a face. "If you must know, I was saving it for a surprise."

"Allow me to inform you, Lavinia," he said, aware of a painful tightness in his jaw, "that there is *nothing* I hate more than a surprise in the course of an investigation."

"Yes, well, it was only a small one," she muttered. "I suppose I wanted to impress you. Or maybe simply make a point."

"What the devil is your point?"

Irritation flared in her eyes. "My point is that you are forever assuming the role of instructor and expert in our partnership. Always going off to consult your private connections. Connections, I might add, that you refuse to introduce to me."

"Damn it, Lavinia—"

"I wanted to demonstrate that I was perfectly capable of conducting my share of an investigation."

He said nothing.

"You need not look at me like that, Tobias. We are equals in this partnership, and I have every right to pursue my own inquiries when the opportunities present themselves."

"Bloody hell."

"Calling at the Banks mansion was a perfectly logical thing to do. After all, Mrs. Rushton might be a suspect."

"A suspect? Mrs. Rushton?"

"You are the one who has pointed out on more than one occasion that heirs sometimes grow impatient." Triumph blazed in her eyes. "Furthermore, if she is not a suspect, she may well be a potential client. After all, as a victim of theft, she has a great interest in recovering the Medusa. She may be persuaded to pay us a fee to find it for her."

He could not quarrel with her logic, he thought. But that did nothing to improve his temper.

"Did you speak to Mrs. Rushton?" he asked.

"No. She was out for the afternoon."

"I see." He relaxed slightly.

"Taking her weekly mesmeric treatment," Lavinia added very deliberately. "It seems the lady suffers from delicate nerves."

He could see that she was extremely pleased with herself. "The news that Mrs. Rushton is taking treatments from a mesmerist is your big surprise?"

Her delight faded to a disgruntled expression. "You must admit that it is a striking connection."

"Lavinia, half of London takes mesmeric treatments for nerves or rheumatism."

"Not *half*." She glared. "You must admit that there is more than a mere hint of a coincidence here. Our case involves a dead woman who was intimately associated with the practice of mesmerism, and now we have a possible suspect who takes mesmeric treatments. I intend to investigate Mrs. Rushton more closely."

"When?"

"Tomorrow morning."

He gripped the edge of the terrace wall while he contemplated the possibilities.

"I will accompany you," he said finally.

"Thank you, but that is not necessary." She gave a disdainful little sniff. "I can handle this by myself."

"I have no doubt of that, madam." He smiled coldly. "But I cannot resist the opportunity to watch you at work. Perhaps you are right. I may have been overlooking your contributions to this partnership. It is time I paid attention to see if I can learn a few things from you."

Fourteen

LAVINIA AND TOBIAS WERE USHERED INTO LORD BANKS'S HUSHED, heavily draped drawing room shortly after two the following afternoon.

The interior of the mansion was even more depressing than the exterior, Lavinia thought. The colors were muddy and dark; the items of furniture, large, heavy, and old-fashioned.

A severe-looking woman of indeterminate years sat reading a book near the window. She was dressed in somber brown bombazine. A handsome, decorative chatelaine, with several keys attached, hung from a cord at her waist. Her hair was pulled back in a tight knot.

"Good afternoon," Mrs. Rushton said in uninviting tones.

She put down her book and peered first at Lavinia, with a distinct lack of interest. But when she switched her attention to Tobias, her expression brightened immediately.

Rather like a cat that has just spotted a bird in the garden, Lavinia thought.

"Thank you for seeing us on such short notice," Lavinia said more coldly than she had intended. "We will try not to take too much of your time, but we feel certain you will be interested in what we have to say."

"Please, sit down." Mrs. Rushton smiled very warmly at Tobias as she motioned her guests to the brown sofa.

Lavinia seated herself, but Tobias went to take up his favored position at the nearest window, putting what little light seeped into the room behind him, as was his habit.

"I shall come straight to the point," Lavinia said. "My associate, Mr. March, and I are in the business of conducting private inquiries."

That information succeeded in distracting Mrs. Rushton briefly from Tobias. She blinked a couple of times at Lavinia. "I don't understand. I thought Bow Street Runners handled that sort of thing."

"We are employed by a more exclusive sort of clientele than that which patronizes Bow Street," Lavinia said.

"I see." Mrs. Rushton looked blank.

"Persons of quality who insist upon the utmost discretion come to us," Lavinia added by way of clarification.

Out of the corner of her eye she saw Tobias's mouth twitch in that very annoying fashion that made her want to grind her teeth. She paid no attention. It was important to establish the proper impression upon a potential client. She understood such things, even if he did not.

"Indeed." Mrs. Rushton's attention drifted back toward Tobias. "How interesting."

"At the moment," Lavinia said icily, "we are searching for a killer."

"Good heavens." Mrs. Rushton put a hand to her bosom. Her eyes widened. "How very bizarre. I have never heard of ladies pursuing that sort of career."

"It is rather uncommon," Lavinia agreed. "But that is neither here nor there. Please allow me to explain our business with you. Mr. March and I have reason to believe that a woman who was murdered recently stole something of considerable value from this household shortly before her death."

"I beg your pardon?" Mrs. Rushton stared at her. "But that is impossible. I assure you that no one has broken into this house." She looked around quickly. "See for yourself. The silver is still here. Nothing is missing."

"The object in question is a very old bracelet," Tobias said.

"Nonsense," Mrs. Rushton said with great authority. "I would most certainly have noticed a bracelet missing from my jewelry box."

"This was an extremely ancient piece of jewelry known among collectors as the Blue Medusa," Lavinia said. "Do you know it?"

Mrs. Rushton grimaced. "If you refer to that old bracelet that my uncle keeps locked in a chest in his bedchamber, yes, of course I know it. It is really quite unfashionable and certainly not what one would call a particularly interesting antiquity. Found right here in England, I believe. Not as though it came from one of the classical ruins of Greece or Rome, now, is it?"

"Do you know why Banks acquired that particular relic after selling off his collection of antiquities?" Tobias asked.

Mrs. Rushton gave a soft snort. "If you ask me, an unscrupulous dealer took advantage of the fact that my uncle was starting to become quite confused in his thinking a year and a half ago. A result of several fits of apoplexy, I'm afraid."

"The Blue Medusa is considered quite valuable by some," Lavinia ventured cautiously.

"I will admit that the gold appears to be of excellent quality and it is rather nicely worked," Mrs. Rushton said. "But the stone is quite unattractive. I wouldn't dream of wearing it. I intend to sell the thing as soon as my uncle makes his transition. The doctor does not expect him to survive the month, you know."

"We have heard of his lordship's illness," Lavinia said gently. "Please accept our condolences."

"He has not been well for some time. It will be a blessing when he finally passes on to the next world."

A blessing for whom? Lavinia wondered.

"We understand that you moved in here to take care of him," Tobias said neutrally.

"One must do one's duty, of course," Mrs. Rushton said with a martyr's firm resolve. "There was no one else, you see. I am the last of the line. I have done my best, but I can tell you that the task has not been an easy one. It has put a great strain on my nerves, which, I must tell you, were never very strong."

"I understand," Lavinia murmured encouragingly.

"When I was a child my mother warned me that I would need to take care not to expose my delicate nerves to extreme strain. She was right. After the shock of my dear husband's death three years ago, I discovered that I was prone to female hysteria. It is a very distressing affliction. One which my doctor tells me requires regular treatments."

"If we might return to the subject of the Medusa," Tobias said before Lavinia could pursue that line of inquiry, "when was the last time you checked to see that it was secure in Banks's safe?"

"I beg your pardon? Oh, yes, the relic." Mrs. Rushton abandoned the topic of her nerves with obvious reluctance. "It has been some time since I opened the safe, but I'm certain everything is in order."

"I think it would be a good idea to make sure that the Medusa is still there," Tobias said.

"I don't see why I should—"

"It would set my mind at ease, Mrs. Rushton," Tobias said. "And greatly steady my nerves. Mine are a trifle delicate, just as yours are. You know how it is when one becomes anxious."

"Yes, of course I do." She rose immediately and went to stand very close to Tobias. She smiled up at him and patted his arm. "I had no notion that you suffered from poor nerves, sir. I understand completely. Indeed, only someone else who is similarly afflicted could possibly comprehend. You have my deepest and most sincere sympathies."

"Thank you," Tobias said. "About the bracelet—"

She winked at him. "If you will excuse me for a moment, I will just run upstairs and have a quick look so that I may put your mind at ease."

She hurried out of the drawing room.

Lavinia looked at Tobias.

"Delicate nerves?" She raised her brows. "You?"

"I'll wager you never even knew that I suffered from that sort of thing."

"I never *dreamed* it. Well, at least you are not likely to succumb to female hysteria."

"For which I give thanks every day. I wonder if there is a male version."

She frowned. "This is going to be somewhat awkward if the bracelet is in that safe."

His mouth twisted. "I very much doubt that it is there. Mr. Nightingale does not strike me as the type to chase after false rumors."

Mrs. Rushton swept back into the drawing room a short time later. Alarm and bewilderment were etched in her face.

"Good God, the bracelet is gone, just as you said." She came to a halt in the center of the carpet, clutching the chatelaine. "I don't understand. I told you, there is no sign that any thief entered this house. There are no broken windows or locks. The housekeeper keeps a very close eye on things. I would have been told if anything of value had gone missing."

Tobias looked at the key ring in her hand. "Was the safe locked when you went to open it just now?"

"Yes." Mrs. Rushton stared down at the keys that dangled from the chatelaine. "Just as it should be."

"Are there any other keys to the safe?" Lavinia asked.

"No, only this one. I took possession of all the keys the day I moved into this household."

"Well, there you have it, Mrs. Rushton," Lavinia said. "The bracelet has been stolen. And although you never thought highly of it, I can assure you it is worth a great deal to some people. I assume you want it found?"

"Yes, of course."

Lavinia summoned up her best professional smile. "In that case, Mr. March and I would be happy to accept a commission from you."

Mrs. Rushton hesitated, frowning warily. "Commission?"

"To conduct inquiries into the matter," Tobias explained. "On your behalf."

"You expect me to pay you a fee if you find the bracelet?"

"That is generally how it works," Lavinia said.

"I see. I'm not sure about this. It is all rather confusing, to say the least. I believe I can feel my nerves reacting to the strain of this situation already."

Tobias folded his arms. "Our understanding is that the bracelet constitutes a portion of your inheritance. But I must tell you that it can be extremely difficult for someone who is unfamiliar with the antiquities market to strike an excellent bargain with a dealer. There are any number of frauds and charlatans in the trade, to say nothing of outright criminals who will not hesitate to take advantage."

"Yes, I have heard that." Mrs. Rushton was steadier now. "My uncle always maintained that one must be extremely careful in such transactions."

"He was right," Tobias said. "But as it happens, Mrs. Lake and I have connections in that market. If we are successful in recovering the Medusa for you, we will be happy to help you make arrangements to sell the thing at a very fine price."

"For another small fee, of course," Lavinia put in quickly.

A shrewd look appeared in Mrs. Rushton's eyes. She sank down slowly onto a chair. "Naturally, I would not have to pay you this second fee until I had received my profits from the sale of the bracelet?"

"Naturally," Tobias said. "Now, then, do you wish us to pursue the matter for you?"

Mrs. Rushton devoted only two or three seconds of close consideration to the question before nodding once, decisively. "I will give you a commission provided I do not have to pay you so much as a single penny if you are unsuccessful in locating the bracelet."

"That is understood," Lavinia said. "Now, then, as we have established a business arrangement, I would like to ask you some questions, if you don't mind."

"What sort of questions?"

"You mentioned that you suffer from delicate nerves and that you are prone to bouts of female hysteria."

"Yes."

"When I called yesterday afternoon, your housekeeper remarked that you take regular treatments from a mesmerist."

"Indeed," Mrs. Rushton said. A glow of enthusiasm blazed in her eyes. "Dr. G. A. Darfield. He is excellent, I must say."

Lavinia recalled one of the advertisements she had studied. "I saw a notice of his services in a newspaper. He claims to be especially skilled at alleviating the symptoms associated with female hysteria in married women and widows."

"I can assure you that I have consulted with many doctors and various types of medical practitioners over the years, but I have never had such amazing results as those I have obtained from Dr. Darfield's therapies. I cannot begin to describe the marvelous sense of relief and well-being that descends upon me following a session with him."

"May I ask if you ever consulted Dr. Howard Hudson?" Lavinia asked, holding her breath.

"Hudson?" Mrs. Rushton's brows snapped together above her long nose. "Hudson? No. I have never even heard of him. Does he treat cases such as mine?"

Bloody hell, Lavinia thought. She had been convinced that she would uncover a link between Mrs. Rushton and Celeste Hudson.

"Dr. Hudson's wife was the lady who was murdered," Tobias said. "We have reason to believe that she may have been involved with the theft of the bracelet."

"Dear heaven." Mrs. Rushton touched her bosom again. "This entire affair is becoming odder at every turn." She gave Tobias a melting glance. "I am relieved to know that a gentleman of your obviously vigorous physique is investigating, Mr. March."

Lavinia cleared her throat. "I am also investigating the case. I assure you, I am every bit as vigorous as Mr. March."

LAVINIA WENT STRAIGHT TO THE SHERRY CABINET THE MOMENT she walked into her study. She poured two glasses, handed one to Tobias, and then threw herself down into her favorite chair.

She propped her ankles on the hassock and watched Tobias crouch carefully to light the fire. He seemed to move without obvious discomfort today, she thought, no doubt because the sun was out.

"Damnation," she said. "I was so certain that we would uncover a connection between Mrs. Rushton and Celeste Hudson."

"That would have been much too convenient." Tobias gripped the mantel and used it to haul himself to his feet. He took a long swallow of sherry. "This case does not lend itself to simple answers. But look on the bright side. We have got another client."

"Thanks to me."

"Indeed." He raised his glass in a mocking salute. "You did very well."

"Mmm." She sipped sherry. "Unfortunately, I am forced to conclude that, although approaching Mrs. Rushton was my idea, it was the sight of your *obviously vigorous physique* that secured us the commission."

"I am delighted to know that I was able to contribute in some small way."

"Not small," she mumbled into the glass.

"I beg your pardon?"

"I believe Mrs. Rushton was persuaded to employ us because she has concluded that the portion of your *obviously vigorous physique* that interests her is most assuredly not small."

He grinned. "You're jealous."

"The woman is a female version of a lecherous rake. She reminds me of my former employer, Mrs. Underwood."

"The lady's sexual proclivities aside, the fact that she hired us to find the Medusa would seem to settle the question of whether or not she might have been involved in the theft."

"So it would appear."

"Come now, Lavinia, you saw her face when she returned from checking to see if the bracelet was missing. It was obvious that until that moment she had no notion that it was gone."

"I suppose it's possible that she is a very fine actress." Lavinia leaned her head back against the cushion. "But I'm inclined to agree with you. My intuition tells me that she was not pretending her response. She truly *was* stunned by the loss of the bracelet."

"Yes." Tobias wandered over to the window and stood looking out into the small garden. "Now all we have to do is find the bloody Medusa and the killer and we can collect fees from a number of different clients. I must admit, I was not at all enthused about this case at the start, but it is beginning to show some potential for profit at last."

"What do you suggest we do next?"

"Mrs. Rushton believes that she has the only key to the safe in Banks's dressing room, but she did not take up residence in the household until a few months ago. It's quite possible that the servants know more than she realizes. Some of them would have had access to those keys for years."

"Do you think it would be a good idea to interview them?"

"It certainly cannot hurt. But the Banks household staff is large. It will take hours to talk to all of them. I believe that I shall set Anthony to the task. It will be fine training for him."

"Emeline can accompany him. As I told you, she has a certain talent for charming answers out of people."

"As does Anthony. I believe they will make an excellent team. If nothing else, the business is bound to be exceedingly boring. Perhaps it will discourage both of them from pressing on with careers in this line."

Lavinia sighed. "Do not pin your hopes on that strategy, sir."

He turned around slowly and gave her a wry smile. "You are right. One long morning of dull interviews is not likely to put either of them off, is it?"

"No. Meanwhile, what shall I tell Howard? To be honest, I am worried about his state of mind, Tobias. He is quite distraught."

"Why don't you advise him to seek treatment for his weak nerves?"

"That is not at all amusing, sir."

"Wasn't meant to be."

She eyed him closely. "You really do not care overmuch for Howard, do you?"

"I think the man very likely murdered his wife in a fit of jealous rage," Tobias said shortly. "No, I cannot say that I am fond of him."

"I would remind you that you are quite free to quit this case."

"That is impossible and well you know it." He came to stand over her, gripped the arms of her chair, and leaned down to put his face very close to hers. "I cannot walk away from it as long as you insist upon being involved in the affair."

The cold, grim determination in his eyes sent an unaccountable shiver through her. "Why are you so suspicious of Howard? You have no evidence to indicate that he murdered Celeste."

"I may lack the evidence to support my belief, but I am very sure that your old family friend has ulterior motives in this affair. I am certain that he has no interest in avenging his dead wife. He is using you to help him find that damned bracelet."

"Rubbish. You took a strong dislike to Howard even before Celeste was murdered. Admit it."

"Very well, I admit it. I did not like the man one damned bit before his wife turned up dead, and I trust him even less now."

"I knew it. I could see it in your eyes that first day when I walked into the parlor and found you with him. But for the life of me, I cannot comprehend such instant dislike on your part. What on earth set you so strongly against him right from the start?"

For an instant she thought he would not answer. She was aware of his powerful hands tightening around the arms of her chair. The fierce planes and angles of his face looked as if they had been hewn from stone. There was an implacable, immovable, unalterable quality about him that, in another man, would have sent a shock of dread through her.

But this was Tobias. She knew that he could be dangerous, but never toward her. The only threat he represented to her was the one aimed at her heart.

"Hudson wants you," Tobias said.

She stared at him in disbelief. "I beg your pardon?"

"He wants you."

"Are you mad? Good heavens, sir, the man is an old family friend. I grew up thinking of him as a . . . a sort of uncle. I'm sure he thinks of me as a niece."

"None of that changes the fact that he wants you."

"But he never . . . I never . . . I mean, there was nothing—" She broke off, sputtering, and made a bid to collect herself. "I assure you, Howard never gave any indication that he was interested in me in that way. He never said a word to me. As a matter of fact he attended my wedding and wished me happiness. I have no reason to doubt that he meant it."

"Perhaps he did at the time. Perhaps something changed when he saw you again."

"Tobias—"

"Between men, some things do not need explanation or interpretation. Hudson wants you."

"Really, sir."

"Yes, really." Tobias unclamped his hands from around the chair arms and straightened. He went back to the window and returned his attention to the garden. "He desires you intensely."

Now that he was no longer bending over her, she was finally able to catch her breath. But his absolute assurance on the point he was attempting to drive home had rattled her.

"You say that between men some things do not require explanation or interpretation," she said very steadily. "The same is true between men and women."

"What the devil do you mean by that?"

She drummed her fingers on the arm of the chair and tried to find the right words. "A woman usually knows when a man is attracted to her. She may not know his heart, let alone whether or not he is in love with her, but she knows when he feels a physical passion for her. Such things are not easy to hide."

"Your point, madam?"

"If Howard wants me, it is not because he has conceived an overwhelming romantic passion for my person," she said dryly. "I would know if that were the case."

Tobias turned back to face her, his mouth quirked in cold amusement. "You are sure of that?"

"Absolutely certain."

"I do not share your certainty. But say for the sake of argument that you are correct. That leaves us with a very interesting question."

"What question is that?"

"If he does not desire to have you in his bed, why does he want you?"

"Tobias, you are the most incredibly stubborn man I have ever met."

He ignored that. "Because I assure you, madam, Hudson most definitely wants you."

Fifteen

Tobias walked into the cheerful little breakfast room with what had lately become a familiar sense of satisfaction and anticipation. Outside, a light, misty rain was falling, but in here all was warm and cozy. The enticing aromas of hot coffee, eggs, and freshly baked muffins swirled in the air.

Emeline gave him her warm, gracious smile. "Good morning, sir. How nice to see you."

"Miss Emeline."

Her smile dimmed only slightly when she looked past him into the empty hall. "Oh, I see Mr. Sinclair did not accompany you."

"He will be along in an hour to fetch you so that the two of you may start your inquiries at the Banks mansion." He turned to Lavinia. "Good morning, madam."

Lavinia looked up from the morning paper, a decidedly frosty expression in her vivid eyes. She was dressed in a rich, dark purple-red gown that framed her elegant neck in a dainty little ruff. Her red hair was bound up in a stylish knot at the back of her nicely shaped head and set off with a lacy cap. He thought about making love to her in the

Stillwaters' conservatory and how it had felt when she had come undone in his arms. The memories heated his blood. He wondered if he would ever grow accustomed to the effect she had on him.

He smiled. "I vow, your eyes resemble emerald seas in the morning sun."

"It is raining, in case you had not noticed, sir."

Emeline gave Lavinia a troubled frown. "Aunt Lavinia, there's no need to be rude. Mr. March paid you a very pretty compliment."

"No, he did not." Lavinia turned the page in her paper. "The remark about my eyes was just another part of a diabolical experiment he is attempting to perform on me."

Emeline was clearly baffled. "An *experiment*?"

"Mr. March thinks to employ charm in an effort to influence me so that I will take his instructions and orders in regard to my business affairs."

Emeline switched her bemused eyes to Tobias, silently seeking clarification.

He pulled out a chair and winked at her. "As you can see from her gracious, welcoming manner, my cunning plan is working. She is soft clay in my hands." He reached for the coffeepot.

Lavinia folded the paper with a crisp snap. "We do not generally expect callers at breakfast, you know."

"I'm amazed to hear you say that." He slathered butter on a muffin. "I have joined you for breakfast on several occasions of late. One would have thought that you would have grown accustomed to the sight of me at your table at this hour. Mrs. Chilton certainly has. I've noticed that she has begun making extra servings of everything."

"Indeed. And I have noticed the cost of those extra servings. They have begun making a dent in the household accounts."

"Larder and pantry getting a bit bare?" He helped himself to a large spoonful of currant jam. "Don't fret. I shall have Whitby send over some supplies."

"That is not the point," Lavinia said.

He took a mouthful of muffin. "Why raise the issue if it is not the point?"

Emeline chuckled. "My aunt is in an ill temper this morning, sir. Do not pay her any heed."

"Thank you for alerting me to her foul mood." He swallowed the bite of muffin. "I might have missed it altogether if you had not called it to my attention."

Lavinia rolled her eyes and went back to reading the paper.

"Never mind," Emeline said quickly. "Please tell me more about the inquiries Anthony and I are to conduct today."

"Mrs. Rushton has agreed to allow you to question the members of her household staff," he said. "We wish to ascertain whether any of them might have had access to the key to the safe in Banks's dressing room."

"I see. You believe that one of them might have been involved in the theft of the bracelet?"

"It is a possibility that must be ruled out. But you and Anthony will need to be subtle in your questioning. None of the servants is likely to simply announce that he knows something about the affair."

"No, of course not." Emeline's enthusiasm for the project vibrated in her voice. "Anthony and I will be very cautious and circumspect."

"Remember to make notes, even if the details you learn do not sound as if they would be important. Sometimes the smallest point proves to be crucial to the solution."

"I shall keep very complete notes," Emeline assured him.

Tobias looked at Lavinia. "What are your plans for the day, madam?"

"I have a few errands to see to this afternoon," Lavinia said with a vague air as she continued to read her newspaper. "I thought that I would call upon Mrs. Dove to find out if she has had any new thoughts on the case. What about you, sir?"

"I intend to consult with Crackenburne and Smiling Jack again," he said. He could be vague, too, he thought.

She nodded without looking up. "An excellent plan."

No doubt about it, he thought. Lavinia had concocted some private scheme she intended to carry out today. He knew the signs all too well.

The great difficulty in conducting an investigation with Lavinia was that he was obliged to spend nearly as much time keeping an eye on her as he did searching for answers for the client.

The dark green door opened just as Lavinia started up the steps. A woman emerged from the front hall of Dr. Darfield's rooms. Her cheeks were flushed with the pink glow of good health and there was a cheerful expression in her lively eyes.

"Good day." The lady bestowed a friendly smile on Lavinia as she swept past. "Lovely weather, is it not?"

"Very nice," Lavinia murmured.

The lady set off with an energetic stride, a living tribute to the skills of Dr. Darfield. Lavinia watched her for a moment, thinking of Mrs. Rushton's enthusiasm for the treatments she received from the mesmerist.

Obviously the good doctor inspired a very positive reaction in his patients.

She continued up the steps and clanged the knocker, still not certain what had induced this urge to pay a call on Mrs. Rushton's mesmerist today. Perhaps it had something to do with the great disappointment she had endured yesterday. She had been so certain that Mrs. Rushton's interest in the mesmeric therapies constituted a link with Celeste. It was very hard to give up the notion that she had come across a clue.

The door opened almost at once. A very handsome young man smiled at her. He was fashionably dressed in a brown velvet coat, yellow waistcoat, pleated trousers, and an intricately tied cravat. His blond hair had been ruthlessly attacked by a curling iron. Artfully arranged curls fell forward over his eyes in a seemingly careless style that had no doubt required a great deal of time in front of a mirror.

"Good day, sir. I wish to consult with Dr. Darfield."

"Do you have an appointment?"

"No, I'm afraid not." She stepped quickly into the hall and turned to smile at him before he could figure out how to politely close the door in her face. "My case of bad nerves came upon me quite suddenly this morning and I cannot wait for professional assistance. I fear that if I do not get help immediately, I may have an attack of female hysteria. I am hoping that you will be able to fit me into Dr. Darfield's schedule."

The young man looked deeply troubled. "I'm so sorry, but Dr. Darfield is very busy today. Perhaps you could come back tomorrow?"

"I'm afraid I really must see him now. My nerves are in the most dreadful condition. They are very delicate."

"I understand, but—"

She recalled the details of Dr. Darfield's advertisement, with its emphasis on widows and married ladies. "I have been a widow for some time and I fear that the strain of being alone in the world has taken its toll." She patted her reticule. "I am, of course, prepared to pay a bit extra for the inconvenience to Dr. Darfield's schedule."

"I see." The young man glanced thoughtfully at her reticule. "In advance, as it were?"

"Yes, of course."

He gave her a winning smile. "Why don't you have a seat in the reception room and I will have a look at the appointment book. It may be possible to work you in this afternoon."

"I cannot tell you how grateful I am for your consideration."

The secretary ushered her into a room across the hall and disappeared. Lavinia sat down, removed her bonnet, and surveyed her surroundings with professional interest.

She was accustomed to the soothing, calming quality that most practitioners of mesmerism sought to effect in their reception rooms. But Dr. Darfield's decorator had chosen a more dramatic theme.

The walls were covered with large murals depicting scenes from a Roman bath. Admirably painted classical columns framed tableaux of voluptuous, scantily draped ladies disporting themselves in the waters.

There were a number of full-size statues standing in the corners of the room. She recognized them as reproductions, but they were all very nicely modeled figures of nude Greek and Roman gods. Upon closer inspection she saw that they were extremely *well-endowed*

gods. Not unlike some of the statuary that she had sold quite prof-
itably during her sojourn in Italy, she thought.

Scenes of lovers entwined in various graphic poses were depicted on
the red-figure Greek vases that flanked the windows.

There always seemed to be an inexhaustible demand for naked
Greek and Roman gods in the antiquities business, but she was somewhat startled to see such figures here in a mesmerist's waiting room.

A low, masculine voice drew her attention to the small group of
people in the corner. Three ladies, presumably patients, were gathered
around a young man who, if anything, was even more handsome than
the secretary. He read to the ladies from a leather-bound volume.

Lavinia recognized the lines. They were from one of Shakespeare's
more sensual sonnets. Pleased with the prospect of listening to
some well-read poetry, she collected her skirts, preparing to rise
and move to another chair, one that was closer to the young man with
the book.

At that moment, the door of the waiting room opened again. The
blond secretary motioned to Lavinia.

"Dr. Darfield will see you now," he said in a low voice.

"Excellent." Already out of her chair, she changed direction and
went through the door into the hall.

The secretary closed the door softly and inclined his head toward
the staircase.

"Dr. Darfield's treatment rooms are on the floor above," he said. "If
you will follow me I will show you."

"Thank you."

He gave her a charming smile. "But I must ask that you pay the fee
in advance."

"Yes, of course." She opened her reticule.

The business transaction was completed with stunning efficiency.
When it was finished, the secretary escorted her up the stairs and
down a hall. He opened a door and bowed her into the chamber.

"Please be seated in the treatment chair. Dr. Darfield will be with
you shortly."

She went through the opening and found herself in a dimly lit room. Heavy drapes were drawn across the window. A single candle burned on a table. The air was scented with fragrant incense.

The door closed quietly behind her. When her eyes were adjusted to the low illumination, she saw a large, padded chair with an unusual, hinged footrest and wide arms in the center of the room. A strange-looking mechanical device with a hand crank sat on a small, wheeled cart.

She put her bonnet aside and went forward to sit down on the padded chair. It proved to be quite comfortable, even with the footrest down.

The door opened just as she was bending over to see how the footrest worked.

"Mrs. Lake? I am Dr. Darfield."

"Oh." She sat up quickly at the sound of the deep, resonant voice.

A tall, broad-shouldered man dressed in exotically patterned blue robes stood in the doorway. The attire marked him as a true student of Mesmer, she thought. She had read accounts written by persons who had been privileged to observe the great man at work. According to them, Mesmer had favored flowing robes, subdued lighting, and background music played by handsome young men. Several of the observers had also taken note of the large numbers of women who had flocked to Mesmer's rooms for treatments, she recalled.

Darfield's brown hair was cut in a fashionable style that set off his deep, penetrating eyes and showed his excellent profile to perfection. He was not quite so handsome as his assistants, she decided, but he was a good deal more interesting, probably because he was not as young as his employees. It occurred to her that she had reached the age when a gentleman with some crinkles at the corners of his eyes and some experience of the world on his face was vastly more intriguing than a smooth-faced younger man.

She gave him what she hoped was a suitably grateful smile, the sort of smile a lady on the brink of a fit of female hysteria might give her medical practitioner.

"It was kind of you to see me on such short notice," she said.

Dr. Darfield walked into the chamber and closed the door. "My secretary tells me that your nerves are in very bad condition. Something of an emergency, I collect."

"Yes, I have been under considerable strain lately and I fear my nerves have not borne up well. I do hope you will be able to relieve me of some of my tension and anxiety."

"I will be happy to do what I can." Darfield picked up the single taper and carried it across the room to where she sat. "May I ask how you learned of my practice?"

"I saw your advertisement in a newspaper," she said, not wanting to mention Mrs. Rushton's name.

"I see." He sat down in a wooden chair across from her, his knees very close to her own. He looked at her across the flame of the candle. In the shadows his eyes were even more penetrating. "You were not referred by one of my other clients, then?"

"No."

"Very well. In that case perhaps I should explain a bit about my therapy. It is necessary that you relax and gaze directly at the flame."

She had no intention of allowing him to hypnotize her. In point of fact, she was not a good subject, according to her parents, who had run some experiments. But she had been an expert practitioner at one time and she certainly knew what a trance looked like in others.

A feigned trance would provide her with an opportunity to observe Dr. Darfield at work. Even if it transpired that it provided no particular insight into her investigation, it was always interesting to observe another professional in the field.

"A lady's nerves are delicate, in keeping with the gentle, refined sensibilities that nature has bestowed upon her." Dr. Darfield's voice was low and deep, with a melodious quality that could have taken him far in the theater. "This is especially true in widows such as yourself, who are deprived of the normal attentions of a husband."

She nodded politely and tried to conceal her impatience. The assumption that nervous disorders in women, together with myriad other vague symptoms classified under the label of *female hysteria*, were due to a lack of regular, energetic sexual congress was common among members of the medical profession. It was, she knew, a very ancient and well-documented tenet.

"The symptoms of anxiety, agitation, melancholia, and other nervous conditions in ladies are expelled from the body when the patient undergoes a crisis in the course of a treatment," Darfield explained.

"Crisis?"

"Yes. In medical terms it is known as an hysterical paroxysm."

"I have heard the term," she said.

That much was true, but for the first time she wondered if her scheme to feign an entranced state might have some drawbacks. She had never actually witnessed a subject in the throes of an hysterical paroxysm and therefore was uncertain how to simulate a realistic crisis.

The problem was that there were vast differences among practitioners of mesmerism when it came to styles and methods. She had learned her techniques from her parents, who had not put much stock in the business of inducing paroxysms. Her father had often said that the response, while dramatic, was generally a short-lived cure at best.

"The hysterical paroxysm relieves the congestion in the flow of the waves of the body's natural magnetic fluids," Dr. Darfield continued in his deep voice. "There is no cause for concern. It produces what my patients assure me is a very pleasant convulsion followed by an extremely tranquil effect on the senses. Mesmer and many learned doctors believe the crisis to be highly efficacious."

"I see."

"Now, then, to obtain the full effect of the process, you must be as comfortable as possible."

He leaned toward her and grasped a small lever she had not noticed in the side of the chair. When he pulled it forward, the footrest promptly elevated. She was marveling at that clever result when she noticed that Darfield had risen and moved to stand behind her.

She heard another lever shift and simultaneously the rear section of the chair went back by several degrees.

She suddenly found herself in a partially reclining position. It was somewhat disconcerting, she decided, but on the whole, quite comfortable. It also altered the angle of her gaze to show her the ceiling. For the first time she noticed that it had been decorated with a scene depicting a twilight sky complete with wispy pink clouds and a scattering of stars.

"A most unusual chair," she said.

"I designed it myself."

Dr. Darfield came back around to the side of the chair. He droned on pleasantly in her ear as he continued to discuss the delicate nature of the female constitution and how unnatural it was for an adult lady to be unable to experience healthy, invigorating marital relations on a regular basis. He explained that many married women also suffered from similar symptoms due to a lack of proper attention from their husbands. She recognized the quiet, authoritative tone that was used to induce a light trance and tried to compose her expression appropriately.

"Please watch the flame now," he said in a soft but very firm voice.

He held the candle so that she could see it and began to inscribe a slow circle in the air with it.

"Think of that most delicate and tender region of the female form," Darfield murmured. "That is where the congestion that causes nervous disorders occurs in ladies. I must relieve that tight, full feeling in order for you to find relief."

She knew that the little blaze was meant to concentrate her attention. Politely, she followed it with her eyes.

Darfield moved the taper in a slow, steady pattern. Behind the glow of the flame he watched her with riveting intensity.

"You will abandon yourself to my healing touch, Mrs. Lake." His voice, still mellifluous, grew more authoritative. He leaned over the chair, the folds of his robes sweeping lightly against her arm.

"I am going to put down the candle now." He did not take his eyes off her as he set the taper on a nearby stand. "You will close your eyes and be guided by my voice and my touch."

Obediently, she lowered her lashes. But she could not resist peeking.

"Do not think about anything else except the unrelieved congestion in that delicate, exquisitely sensitive portion of your body." Darfield reached out and drew the cart on which the mechanical apparatus stood toward Lavinia's chair. "Feel the blockage and the resulting tension that has gathered there. Do not repress it. Allow it to swell and build. Soon I will release you from the tight, hot sensation that is enfeebling your nerves."

Through her lashes she watched him pick up a small unguent jar and remove the stopper. A delightful fragrance wafted through the air. Some sort of flower-scented oil, she decided.

"I have invented an ingenious device that has allowed me to improve greatly upon the traditional techniques of mesmeric therapy for the treatment of female hysteria," Darfield said. "It is a highly effective and extremely efficient aid for relieving the congestion in the lower body, as you will discover."

I'm getting a bad feeling about this, Lavinia thought.

Darfield reached down and tugged on yet another chair lever. The footrest promptly divided into two sections and drew apart. She froze when she realized that the device had separated her legs by a space of several inches. It was almost as if she was astride a horse.

Alarm shot through her. She knew that her limbs were still modestly covered to her ankles by the skirts of her gown, but the position left her feeling decidedly awkward.

He's a trained practitioner, she reminded herself. A professional who gives these treatments to ladies on a regular basis. His clients think very highly of him.

For the first time she wondered just how far she wanted to take her role of patient.

Dr. Darfield rolled the narrow cart forward and positioned it between her feet. Through the veil of her lashes she saw that there was a soft-looking little brush attached to the end of a long metal arm that extended from the mechanical device. Darfield turned the hand crank a few times, apparently testing to ensure that it moved smoothly.

The long metal arm with the small brush spun rapidly when he worked the crank.

"I will now employ my invention to control the waves of animal magnetism in your body," Darfield said. "Think of those magnetic waves as a cascade of rushing water that must burst through a dam before falling into a calm, tranquil pool. Think of this medical device as the tool that will release that inner flood. Abandon yourself to the therapy, madam. You are in the hands of a doctor."

He grasped the hem of her skirts with one hand and started to ease them up toward her knees. With his other hand he pushed the little cart with the mechanical device forward between her legs. She understood now just where he intended to apply the whirling brush in order to relieve her so-called congestion.

"*Dr. Darfield.* Stop at once." She sat bolt upright, snapped her legs together, and bounded up out of the chair. "That is quite enough."

She whirled around to face him and found him watching her with an expression of grave concern.

"Calm yourself, madam. Your nerves are, indeed, very highly strung."

"They shall have to remain that way, I'm afraid. I do not care for your methods, sir. I have no intention of allowing you to treat me with that odd mechanical device."

"Madam, I assure you that my methods are firmly rooted in sound modern science and centuries of medical practice. Why, every notable man of medicine from the great Galen of Pergamum to the esteemed Culpeper himself has advised vigorous massage of that region of the female anatomy for the relief of hysteria and nervous disorders."

"A rather *intimate* form of massage, in my opinion."

He was clearly affronted. "I will have you know that there is absolutely nothing controversial about my therapies. The only thing I have done is to improve upon the old-fashioned manual techniques that have long been in use by doctors. This modern mechanical device affords my patients a far more efficient form of treatment."

"Efficiency is hardly the point here."

"It bloody well is the point if you're trying to make a decent living in this business." His mouth thinned. "I'll have you know that before I perfected my device, some of my patients took damned near an hour to reach the paroxysm. Do you have any notion of how much manual labor that required on my part? That sort of thing is bloody hard work, madam."

"*Work.*" She swept out a hand to indicate the hinged chair and his machine. "You call this work, sir?"

"Yes, I most certainly do call it work. Do you think it's easy to induce a paroxysm over and over again in an endless line of female patients? I tell you, madam, there were days when my arm and hand were so fatigued and so sore from my efforts that I was obliged to apply a poultice at night."

"Do not expect me to extend my sympathies." She plucked her bonnet off the table and started toward the door. "It appears that you are doing quite well for yourself with your therapeutic treatments."

"I make a decent living, but I am far short of making a fortune in this business. Unfortunately, to date I have been unsuccessful in attracting the attention of the fashionable members of the ton. That is where the real money is to be made, you know."

"I am well aware of that." She paused, curious in spite of herself. "Do you mean to say that your excellent advertisements in the papers fail to bring you the more exclusive sort of clientele?"

"The High Flyers always want references from others who move in rare circles," he muttered.

She could not help but sympathize. "References are always a problem, are they not?"

"Yes." He paused. "Now, then, if we might return to the subject of your delicate nerves, madam, I assure you, if you will allow me to apply my mechanical device—"

"No, thank you." She shuddered and threw open the door. "I do not think my delicate nerves would be able to withstand a treatment with your apparatus. Good day, Dr. Darfield."

She swept through the doorway and hurried toward the staircase. In her rush to escape, she nearly collided with the blond secretary in the downstairs hall. He recovered and opened the front door for her.

She tried to appear casual and nonchalant as she went down the steps to the street. She even managed a polite smile for the woman who passed her on her way to the green door. But the pose was not easy to maintain.

She was forced to concede that the decision to investigate Mrs.

Rushton's mesmerist had not been one of her more brilliant notions. How fortunate that she had not mentioned her plan to Tobias that morning at breakfast. She was at least saved the necessity of having to provide him with a report of her inquiries.

She walked briskly past the dark entrance to an alley, not noticing the man standing in the shadows until he moved out. She jumped several inches when he fell into step beside her.

"Tobias."

"A pleasant day for a walk, is it not?" Tobias asked.

"Must you lurk in dark alleys? I vow, you nearly gave me an attack of the vapors. What on earth do you think you are doing?"

"You could not resist a firsthand look at the good doctor, could you?" Tobias did not trouble to hide his mocking smile. "Did you let Darfield put you into a trance?"

"No. As it happens, I am not a suitable subject."

"That does not surprise me. You would not find it easy to surrender your will to another."

"No more than you would," she shot back. "Only consider how stubborn you have been whenever I have offered to see if I could give you some relief from your wound."

"You have provided me with exquisite relief of another sort on a number of occasions, madam. I am very satisfied with your therapeutic treatments."

"That is less amusing than you can possibly imagine," she muttered. "What are you doing here? Good grief, sir, you followed me, did you not?"

"I will admit that I was somewhat curious. Well? Did you learn anything useful?"

"Our primary client is a mesmerist, and the murder victim had some skills in the science," she said stiffly. "I admit that the fact that another one of our clients, Mrs. Rushton, happens to be seeing a mesmerist bothered me. You are the one who taught me to be wary of coincidences."

"Given the number of people who consult mesmerists about poor nerves, it would be more astonishing if it transpired that Mrs. Rushton had *not* sought therapy for hers," he said dryly. "Well? Were you satisfied with your inquiries in that direction?"

She cleared her throat. "Quite satisfied."

"You are convinced that Darfield is a legitimate practitioner?"

"Indeed."

Tobias glanced thoughtfully back over his shoulder toward the green door. "Judging from the patients I saw going into his establishment while I waited for you, he appears to specialize in the treatment of ladies."

"Yes. Yes, he does, as a matter of fact. He is an expert in the treatment of female hysteria."

"What the devil is female hysteria, anyway? I've often wondered."

"It is somewhat difficult to describe to an untrained person," she said very coolly. "Suffice it to say that it is an extremely profitable complaint so far as those in the medical and mesmeric professions are concerned because the patient neither dies nor recovers from her disease. One gets a great deal of repeat business."

"As is the case with Mrs. Rushton."

"Yes."

"Something to be said for a profession that encourages repeat business." He took her arm and started across the street. "How does Dr. Darfield treat female hysterics?"

"Why are you suddenly so curious about such an arcane medical subject?"

"I could not help but notice that the ladies who were admitted to his rooms seemed to go up those steps with a great deal of enthusiasm. I also recall that Mrs. Rushton spoke glowingly about his treatments. I assume Darfield's mode of therapy is not only effective but painless."

"Indeed."

He drew her to a halt and stood looking past her toward the green door on the opposite side of the street. She did not care for the dangerously thoughtful expression in his eyes.

"I also could not help but notice that you very nearly flew down those front steps a moment ago. You appeared quite eager to leave."

"I am in a hurry. I have a number of things I wish to accomplish this afternoon."

"Did something happen in Darfield's rooms, Lavinia?"

"Nothing of any significance," she said airily. "As you surmised, Mrs. Rushton's visits to him are entirely unremarkable and in no way connected to our case."

"You're quite certain that there is nothing in this that I should know about?"

"Tobias, I vow, on occasion you are like a dog with a bone." She made a show of checking the time on the little watch pinned to her pelisse. "Gracious, where has the day gone? I wanted to do some shopping on the way home."

"About Darfield's therapeutic techniques—"

"Do not concern yourself, sir. I assure you that Dr. Darfield's method of treating nervous disorders in ladies falls within the accepted boundaries of traditional and well-established medical and mesmeric practice."

Sixteen

EMELINE WATCHED THE GARDENER CAREFULLY WHILE ANTHONY questioned him. She felt a good deal of sympathy for the poor man. He stood in the middle of the kitchen, nervously twisting his cap, and gave short, unhelpful answers. He was clearly uncomfortable, although Anthony had gone out of his way to be polite and soothing in his approach, just as he had with the other servants.

"Have you ever witnessed anyone going into his lordship's dressing chamber at an unusual time? Late at night, perhaps?" Anthony asked.

"Never even seen his lordship's dressing chamber. Never seen his bedchamber, for that matter. Never been upstairs." The gardener cast his eyes toward the ceiling as though peering toward an invisible metaphysical realm. "Worked 'ere for seventeen years. Kitchen's the only room I've ever seen inside the house."

"Of course it is." Mrs. Rushton, seated at the head of the long wooden table, spoke with conviction. "Gardeners have no business beyond the kitchens."

Anthony's jaw tightened. Emeline sensed his impatience. This was not the first time Mrs. Rushton had interrupted.

This morning's investigation, which she and Anthony had begun with such great enthusiasm, had not gone well. None of the staff had been forthcoming. All had been ill at ease, and Emeline was quite certain she knew why. It was not guilt that made the maids, gardeners, and housekeeper so anxious. It was the fact that Mrs. Rushton had insisted upon being present during the questioning.

Anthony thanked the gardener, who was only too eager to escape. He caught Emeline's eye and shook his head very slightly. She closed her notebook with a sigh.

"Well, then," Mrs. Rushton said, "that is the last of the lot. Did you learn anything helpful, Mr. Sinclair?"

Anthony gave her a winning smile that, in Emeline's opinion, did nothing to conceal the irritation in his eyes. But Mrs. Rushton did not seem to notice. She was clearly quite taken with him. She had, in fact, paid virtually no attention whatsoever to Emeline from the moment she had been introduced to Anthony. There was a peculiar expression in her eyes whenever she looked in his direction, which was rather often.

Emeline decided that if she had seen that expression when a gentleman eyed a lady, she would have accounted the man an out-and-out libertine and debaucher of the worst sort.

"We won't know the answer to that until we compare notes with Mr. March and Mrs. Lake," Anthony said. "Thank you very much for your time this morning, Mrs. Rushton."

"Not at all." Mrs. Rushton got to her feet. She kept her attention on Anthony. "You will contact me immediately if you learn anything concerning the bracelet, will you not?"

"Of course."

"I would appreciate a personal report from you, Mr. Sinclair," Mrs. Rushton said, lowering her voice to an intimate tone. "I feel that I can speak comfortably with you, sir. Indeed, I find it very reassuring to know that a gentleman possessed of such an obviously vigorous physique is assisting in this investigation."

"Thank you for placing your confidence in me, madam." Anthony gave Emeline an urgent look and edged toward the kitchen door. "We will keep you informed of our progress, one way or another. Now, my associate and I must be on our way."

"A cup of tea before you leave?" Mrs. Rushton said quickly.

Anthony's mouth opened. Emeline knew that he was about to refuse. She leaped to her feet, frantically trying to signal him with her eyes.

He hesitated, caught her silent message, and reluctantly subsided.

Emeline turned swiftly to Mrs. Rushton. "Madam, before we leave, would it be too much to ask if I might borrow your gardener for a quick tour of your gardens before we depart? I could not help but note that they are quite extensive. Gardening is a passion of mine."

Mrs. Rushton hesitated.

"Mr. Sinclair could join you in a cup of tea while I examine your plants and herbs," Emeline added smoothly.

Mrs. Rushton smiled. "Yes, of course. An excellent suggestion. Enjoy your little tour."

"Thank you." Emeline slipped her notebook and pencil into her reticule and jumped to her feet. "I won't be long."

Anthony gave her a hapless look as she sped out the door. She pretended not to notice.

TWENTY MINUTES LATER THEY FINALLY ESCAPED FROM THE gloomy mansion. Anthony wore a decidedly grim expression.

It was clear to Emeline that his bad temper was only partially connected to the failure of their inquiries.

"I trust you had a very sound reason for leaving me alone with that dreadful woman for such an extended period of time," he growled.

"Dreadful? How can you say that? Mrs. Rushton was obviously charmed by you. She did not care a jot about me, mind you, but I believe she would like to write a sonnet or an ode to your *obviously vigorous physique*."

"I am in no mood for your teasing." He took her arm in an unexpectedly forceful manner and steered her toward the park.

It occurred to her that this was the first time she had ever seen Anthony in a temper. It was a new and intriguing side of him.

"Good heavens, sir," she murmured, "you really are out of sorts, are you not?"

"What was that business of touring the gardens all about?" He opened the iron gate and hauled her into the small, overgrown park. "You know very well that we did not go to that house today so that you could view a bunch of plants and posies."

"I know precisely why we went there." He was marching her so quickly now that her bonnet had started to bob and wobble in a precarious manner. She reached up to steady it. "And we failed miserably."

"Because of that dreadful woman." Anthony chose a path that cut diagonally across the park. "None of the servants was willing to be forthcoming in front of her. They know very well that, with Banks on his deathbed, she is their real employer. She could let any one of them go without any notice or references."

"Indeed." She was obliged to skip a bit to keep up with him. "And that is why I took my little impromptu tour of the gardens with that poor, terrified gardener."

Anthony spared her a brief, searching glance. She could tell that he was still fuming, but he also knew her well enough to be sure she had not acted entirely on whim.

"What did you and the poor, terrified gardener discuss?" he asked.

She smiled, more than a little pleased with herself. "We discussed finances."

"Bloody hell." But he slowed his pace a little at that news. "You offered him a bribe?"

"A fee," she corrected. "I was inspired by my aunt. Apparently she and Mr. March consider information a commodity like any other, and therefore they are on occasion willing to pay for it."

"True." Anthony paused to open the gate on the far side of the garden. "Tobias grumbles about the practice, but there is no doubt that it is effective. Was the gardener receptive to your offer?"

"I don't know."

"You mean he didn't tell you anything?" Anthony drew her through the opening and turned back to close the gate. "I hope you didn't give him money for nothing."

"He was obviously too nervous to speak with me in a direct fashion. He was well aware that Mrs. Rushton was not far away. But I sensed he knew more than he had told us and I assured him that the offer I had made would stand for a full twenty-four hours."

"I see." Anthony took her arm again. He said nothing until they turned down a narrow street on the far side of the square.

"Not a bad scheme," he finally allowed grudgingly.

"Thank you. I thought it was rather clever myself."

"But was it absolutely necessary to sacrifice me to Mrs. Rushton just so that you could offer a bribe to the gardener?"

"I told you, it was a fee, not a bribe. And as for sacrificing you, I'm afraid I had little choice. I would remind you that I was forced to act swiftly."

"That strikes me as an excuse."

"Come now," she said. "Tea with Mrs. Rushton wasn't that bad, was it?"

"The worst twenty minutes of my life, if you must know. The woman tried to persuade me to pay another call on her at a later time. Alone, mind you." Anthony gave a visible shudder. "She suggested an evening visit."

"It must have been a somewhat harrowing experience. I vow, I have never seen you quite so shaken, sir."

"When I asked Tobias to take me on as his assistant, he neglected to mention that there were clients such as Mrs. Rushton."

"You must admit, we have embarked upon interesting careers."

He cheered a little at that observation. "Yes, very interesting, indeed. Tobias is still not altogether pleased with my decision to follow in his footsteps, but I believe he has accepted it."

"Aunt Lavinia shares similar reservations about me. But I think she understands."

Anthony frowned slightly. "Speaking of Tobias and your aunt, there is something I wish to discuss with you."

"You are concerned about their personal relationship, are you not?"

"I collect that you have similar concerns?"

"I have become a trifle worried of late," she admitted.

"It is obvious that they have become quite, uh, close. And not just in the business sense, if you take my meaning."

She fixed her attention on the far end of the street. "What you are trying to say is that you believe that they have become intimate."

"Yes. Forgive me, I realize that this is certainly not the sort of topic one generally discusses with a lady of your years and station, but I feel I must talk to you about the situation."

"Do not concern yourself with the proprieties," she said gently. "You and I, Anthony, have not had traditional, sheltered upbringings. We have certainly had far more experience of the world than most people our age. You may speak freely with me."

"If you must know, I am troubled by the fact that Tobias and Mrs. Lake seem to be growing more quarrelsome of late."

"Yes, I know what you mean. The nature of their association appears to be quite nettlesome, to say the least."

"I thought, following the success of their investigation into the affair of the waxwork murders, that they had both sailed into more harmonious waters. Indeed, I would have said that they were falling in love. If nothing else, it was clear that they had conceived a passion for each other."

Emeline thought of Lavinia's flushed cheeks and sparkling eyes on those occasions when she returned from one of her long walks in the park with Tobias. "Quite clear."

"I have no doubt but that the problem stems from Tobias's singular lack of interest in romantical matters. He simply does not know how to woo a lady. I have tried to give him some advice, but I fear the lessons are not taking."

"I really don't think that is the difficulty," Emeline said thoughtfully. "It is true that my aunt loves romantical poetry, but I don't believe that she expects Mr. March to conform to the standards of one of Byron's heroes."

"I am relieved to hear that, because I fear he lacks that sort of polish and has no intention of acquiring it. But if that is not the problem, what the devil is going on between those two?"

"Something Aunt Lavinia said recently leads me to believe that she thinks Mr. March is attempting to, uh, limit the competition, as it were."

Anthony's brows knotted. "Bloody hell. Why would she think that?"

"In part because Mr. March refuses to introduce her to some of his connections."

"Yes, I know, but he has what he feels is a perfectly sound reason for refusing. Some of his connections have links to the criminal class. He does not think that it would be proper to introduce Mrs. Lake to that sort, and I must admit, I can see his point of view."

"It is not just that Mr. March will not introduce her to some of his more useful associates," Emeline continued. "I fear that lately he has begun issuing instructions almost daily and giving unwanted advice at every turn. She finds him quite overbearing. My aunt is not accustomed to taking orders from anyone, you know."

Anthony contemplated that for a moment. "It is clear that we are dealing with two exceptionally independent, strong-minded people. What is more, they are both quite set in their ways, are they not? I wonder what—"

A child's voice broke into his musings. It came from behind them.

"Sir. Ma'am. Please wait. My pa wants me to give ye a message."

"What's this?" Anthony halted and swung around.

Emeline stopped and glanced back over her shoulder. She saw a young boy of eight or nine years, clad in rumpled clothes and a cap, waving to them from the entrance to the narrow street. Excitement swept through her.

"That is the gardener's son," she said to Anthony. "I met him in the course of my tour. He assists his father at the Banks mansion."

"What can he want with us?"

"I'll wager his papa sent him after us with some news. He probably hopes to collect the fee I promised. I *knew* my scheme would work."

The boy saw that he had their attention. He hurried toward them.

The sudden loud clatter of carriage wheels and horses' hooves rumbled behind the lad. Emeline looked past the boy and saw a black hackney rounding the corner. The two-horse team was moving at a swift trot. When the vehicle turned into the street, the coachman cracked his whip loudly over the rumps of the horses. The beasts lunged forward at full gallop.

The gardener's son was directly in their path.

Emeline realized that the boy was in danger of being trampled beneath the hooves and wheels.

"Look out," she shouted.

She did not know if the lad heard her warning, but in that instant he seemed to become aware of the din behind him. He stopped and turned. For an instant he seemed to be paralyzed by the sight of the onrushing carriage.

"Move, boy, *move*," Anthony shouted. He started forward at a run.

"Dear heaven." Emeline seized fistfuls of her skirts and went after him.

The boy finally became aware of his dire situation. With a sudden, convulsive jerk, he made to dash for safety.

The breeze caught his cap and sent it skittering back into the path of the horses.

"Me cap." The lad whirled and raced back out into the middle of the street, obviously determined to rescue the cap.

"No," Emeline called. "No, don't go back."

But the boy paid no attention.

The carriage never slowed. Obviously the coachman did not see the lad dash back into his path. Anguished, helpless terror swept through Emeline. She could never reach him in time.

"Get into a doorway," Anthony shouted to her over his shoulder. He was several paces ahead of her.

She flung herself toward the nearest entrance and watched, unable to breathe, as Anthony and the carriage bore down on the boy from opposite directions.

Incredibly, Anthony reached the lad seconds ahead of the flying hooves. He flung out an arm, scooped up the boy, and kept going toward the side of the street.

A moment later the carriage thundered past Emeline. Out of the corner of her eye she saw the coachman hurl an object at her. It thudded against the wall beside her and dropped to the pavement. She ignored it, too intent on reaching Anthony and the boy.

The vehicle rumbled on at breakneck speed, swaying dangerously. It rounded the corner at the end of the street and vanished.

Emeline ran toward the pair where they lay sprawled together on the stones at the foot of a short flight of steps. The boy had landed on top. His green cap lay on the ground next to Anthony's shoulder. He stirred, raised his head, and started to lever himself to his feet. She saw that he was dazed but unhurt.

"Anthony." She flung herself to the pavement beside him. "Anthony. For God's sake, answer me."

For an eternity of mindless, numbing terror, she feared the worst. The elegant knot in Anthony's cravat had come undone, baring his throat. Ripping off one glove, she touched his skin with her fingertips, seeking a pulse.

He opened one eye and gave her a bemused grin. "I must be dead. I am obviously in the hands of an angel."

She snatched her fingers back. "Are you injured, sir? Is anything broken?"

"No, I don't think so." He sat up and looked at the lad. "What about you, young man? Are you all right?"

"Aye, sir." The lad held his cap in both hands, examining it with close attention. He looked up with a relieved grin. "Thank ye for saving me cap. My ma gave it to me for me birthday last week. She would have been right put out with me if I'd gone and ruined it."

"It's a very fine-looking cap." Anthony got to his feet, absently brushing the dust from his trousers. He reached down for Emeline's hand and hauled her lightly up from the pavement.

She turned to the boy. "Now, what was it that you wanted to tell us?"

The boy's expression turned serious. He concentrated hard. "My pa said to tell ye that ye'll want to speak with the valet."

"Your master's valet?" Anthony frowned. "He was not there today. I noticed the absence. Where is he?"

"Mrs. Rushton let him go a while back. Turned Mr. Fitch off without his wages or references, Pa said. Mr. Fitch was very, very angry."

Emeline exchanged a glance with Anthony. "That is very interesting," she said softly.

Anthony looked down at the boy. "Go on."

"Pa said to tell ye that Nan, one of the chambermaids, says that she noticed Mr. Fitch acting very odd the day he got turned off. She was working in the linen closet that afternoon. Fitch never noticed her, but she saw him come out of the master's dressing chamber with a small object all wrapped up in a neckcloth. He put it into his bags when he thought no one was looking, and left the house with it."

"Why didn't Nan say anything?" Anthony asked.

The boy shrugged. "We all knew Fitch had been let go with no references nor extra wages to see him through to another position. Reckon Nan figured he was entitled to help himself to a little something by way of a retirement pension."

"Would Fitch have had access to the keys Mrs. Rushton carries?" Emeline asked. "Could he have made a duplicate?"

The lad thought about that and then shrugged. "Don't see why not. He had plenty of chances to use a bit of wax to make a copy."

"What do you mean by saying he had plenty of chances?" Anthony asked.

The lad looked surprised by the question. "During one of their afternoon meetings upstairs."

Emeline frowned. "What afternoon meetings?"

The boy looked at her. "Soon after Mrs. Rushton arrived, she told Fitch that he was to make regular reports to her concernin' the health and mental condition of the master. They used to meet two or three times a week in the afternoon in one of the upstairs bedchambers."

Emeline felt herself turning pink. She dared not meet Anthony's eyes. "I see."

The boy's brow puckered in some confusion. "I once overheard Fitch tell Pa that Mrs. Rushton was in . . . in . . . *inedible.*"

Anthony looked at him. "Inedible?"

The boy frowned. "Don't think that's the right word. It was in-something, though, I'm sure of that much."

"*Insatiable?*" Anthony offered in a very neutral voice.

"Aye, sir." The lad cheered. "That was the word. Mr. Fitch said that

Mrs. Rushton was *insatiable*. 'Wears a man out and that's a fact,' he said."

"Did your pa give you Fitch's address?" Emeline asked quickly.

"Pa said he had a little house in White Street." The lad looked anxious for the first time. "Will you be paying me now, sir? My pa said I was to be sure to collect the fee ye promised."

"No need for alarm." Emeline gave Anthony a brilliant smile. "Mr. Sinclair will be happy to pay you."

Anthony gave her a wry look, but obligingly pulled out some money to give to the lad.

The boy seized his fee, grinned happily, and raced off. Anthony watched him disappear around the corner.

"I seem to recall Tobias mentioning on one or two occasions that whenever Mrs. Lake offers a fee for information, he somehow ends up paying it." He raised his brows. "It appears that particular skill runs in your family."

"Keep an accurate account, sir. We shall settle the finances at the conclusion of the case when our clients pay us."

She started to pull on the glove she had removed a few minutes earlier to check for Anthony's pulse. She paused when she noticed that her fingertips were trembling. *Anthony had nearly been run down.* She was still shaky with relief. She had to work hard to adjust the glove.

"Emeline, are you all right?"

It was too much. He acted as if nothing untoward had occurred. She rounded on him.

"*You could have been killed,*" she said loudly.

The words seemed to echo against the looming walls that framed the street.

"I'm all right," Anthony said.

"Yes, I know. You saved that boy's life, *but you could have been killed.*"

"Emeline, I don't think—"

"What would I have done if you had been crushed beneath that bloody carriage?" Her voice threatened to rise to a shout. "I cannot bear to think about it, do you hear me?"

"I expect they can hear you two streets over," Anthony said.

"Oh, Anthony, I was so terrified."

With a small cry, she threw herself at him, wrapping her arms around his neck.

A small shock of surprise went through him, but he recovered instantly, holding her so close that she could scarcely catch her breath.

"Emeline." His voice was low and hoarse. *"Emeline."*

He yanked at the strings of her bonnet with one hand and pushed the obstructing hat back off her head. He raised her face and kissed her with a wild, reckless passion that stunned her senses.

What was left of her outrage evaporated in a rush of thrilling heat. She had dreamed of this moment for weeks, tried to imagine what it would be like when Anthony finally kissed her. But the experience was unlike anything she had envisioned.

Anthony's mouth was urgent, hot, demanding. When he opened it against hers, she felt the edge of his tongue. She shuddered, utterly astounded by the intense intimacy. His arms tightened around her, molding her to the length of his body in such an intimate manner that she was aware of every contour of his strong frame.

He shifted slightly, one hand sliding down her spine to curve around her hip. She could feel him pressing against her thigh.

Two years ago she had prevailed upon Lavinia to provide some specific information on the nature of physical passion between a man and a woman. She had also given serious attention to the erotic decorations on some of the Greek and Roman vases she had seen in Rome. But nothing she had learned had prepared her for this raging excitement, let alone the size of the unyielding bulge behind Anthony's trousers.

He dragged his mouth off hers, tipped her head, and kissed her throat. She was trembling now, utterly transported. The very pavement on which she stood threatened to dissolve beneath her feet.

"Anthony."

"Good God." Anthony abruptly broke off the kiss and raised his head. He was breathing hard. "Forgive me, Emeline. I don't know what came over me. I can only apologize—"

"No." She clapped a hand over his mouth to silence him. "I vow, sir, if you say that you are sorry, I shall never forgive you."

He studied her over the edge of her fingers. Then a warm light appeared in his eyes. She felt his mouth curve into a smile beneath her palm. Cautiously, she lowered her hand.

For a few seconds they just stood there in the middle of the street, gazing into each other's eyes.

"Anthony?" She was having difficulty breathing properly, she realized.

"Come." Anthony grasped her elbow and propelled her forward toward the end of the lane. "We must hurry. Tobias and Mrs. Lake will want to know about Fitch."

"Yes, of course." She wondered if all gentlemen were so adept at switching moods in moments of great passion.

Then again, perhaps Anthony had not felt the same intensity of emotion that she had just experienced in his arms. This was, after all, the first time she had ever been embraced in what one could call a serious fashion. Granted, while in Rome she had indulged in a stolen kiss or two in a garden or on a terrace, but she had considered the small incidents more or less as experiments. The results had been interesting, but not particularly inspiring, in her opinion. Certainly they had not set fire to her senses as this kiss had just done.

Anthony, on the other hand, was two years older, a man of the world. He had no doubt kissed any number of women in such a fiery manner.

It was an appalling thought.

She was mulling over the dark vision of another woman in Anthony's arms when she glimpsed the object that the coachman had hurled toward her.

"I almost forgot." She came to a halt. "He threw something at me as he went past."

"Who? The bloody coachman?" Anthony followed her gaze. His expression hardened. "Looks like a rock. Rot the bastard's eyes. He could have hurt you."

"There is something tied to it."

She hurried across the pavement to where the rock lay on the ground. There was a string tied around it. Attached to the string was a piece of paper.

"It's a note." She removed the paper and unfolded it.

Anthony came to stand behind her. He read aloud over her shoulder.

> *Stay out of this affair. Where there has been*
> *one murder, there may well be another.*

Seventeen

"WE ASSUMED THAT THE COACHMAN WAS ATTEMPTING TO RUN down the gardener's son, perhaps to prevent him from talking to us." Anthony looked at the others gathered in Lavinia's small study. "But now it appears that the man likely never even noticed the boy. He was intent only on delivering his message. Must have been following us, saw his opportunity, and took it."

"A warning." Tobias lounged on a corner of the desk and contemplated the note that lay on the polished surface. "It could have been sent by almost anyone involved in this affair."

"Well, it certainly isn't going to stop us from pursuing our investigations," Lavinia said from her post behind her desk.

"Absolutely not," Emeline declared with equal force.

"I agree." Joan Dove absently arranged the folds of her elegant gray skirts. "In fact, it only whets one's appetite to solve the case, if you ask me."

"Indeed." Lavinia plucked a leather-bound volume from the shelf beside the desk, flipped it open, and picked up a quill. "I have begun a journal of events that are directly related to this affair so that we may keep track of all the information and observations that come our way. I shall enter this bit about the note while it is fresh. Emeline, tell me everything you noticed regarding the coach and the driver."

Emeline launched into a detailed description. Lavinia wrote swiftly. Joan rose and went to stand beside the desk, listening intently and offering occasional comments.

Tobias glanced at Anthony, who was watching Emeline with a grim expression. The incident in the street near Banks's mansion had left its mark, he thought. This was no longer merely an exciting adventure so far as his new assistant was concerned.

It was perfectly natural that Anthony would be alarmed by Emeline's close encounter with danger. But he sensed something else going on between the two young people, something beyond a gentleman's normal concern for a lady's safety. It seemed to him that there were some storm clouds gathering in Emeline's and Anthony's heretofore sunny relationship. What the devil was going on here? He made a note to discuss the matter later with Lavinia. She was far more perceptive about this sort of thing.

"From what you have told us," Lavinia said, scribbling madly, "it would appear that, until recently, Mrs. Rushton was having an affair with Banks's valet. For some reason she decided to let him go."

"A lover's quarrel?" Mrs. Dove suggested. "They argued so she turned him off without references or wages?"

Lavinia pursed her lips. "Whatever the reasons, Fitch was furious and had a motive for theft. He was later seen sneaking out of the dressing chamber with a small object wrapped in a cravat."

Tobias clasped his hands behind his back. "If Fitch elected to take the Blue Medusa instead of some other valuable that would have been much easier to sell to a fence or a pawnshop proprietor, he may have had a particular buyer in mind. Someone he was certain would pay well for the cameo."

Lavinia met his eyes. "Celeste Hudson."

A charged silence settled on the room.

"Obviously we must speak to Fitch as soon as possible," Tobias said after a moment. "Anthony, you will look for him. He probably won't be hard to find. When you discover his whereabouts, notify me at once. I will handle the interview."

Lavinia put down her quill. "I wish we knew more about the Blue Medusa. It might help us identify other people who have a particular interest in it."

Joan smiled slightly. "I know of one person who could answer most of your questions about the Medusa, assuming he is willing to do so."

LAVINIA, TOGETHER WITH JOAN AND TOBIAS, WAS USHERED INTO Lord Vale's impressive library the following morning.

The chamber was long and vast and crammed with books. It was illuminated by tall, classically proportioned windows. A circular staircase led to the upper level where yet more bookshelves were filled with leather-bound tomes. There was an air of scholarly elegance about the room that caused one to speak in hushed tones.

Unable to sit in the midst of such splendor, Lavinia began to prowl the room, examining some of the books with wonder and fascination.

Lord Vale waited until the housekeeper had poured the tea and departed. Then he leaned back in his chair and surveyed his guests with polite speculation.

"Mrs. Dove tells me that you wish to interview me in a matter that involves murder," he said.

"I hope you are not offended." Lavinia looked up from the study of a large volume that lay open on a table. She had been a bit anxious on this point. A gentleman of Vale's status had every right to be extremely annoyed at the prospect of being dragged into a situation that involved something so distasteful as murder.

"Not at all." A glint of acute interest flickered in Vale's eyes. "As much as I enjoy my scholarly researches into antiquities, I must admit that I occasionally find myself in a mood for other, equally stimulating diversions."

"A stimulating diversion," Tobias repeated neutrally from his position at a window. "Well, that is certainly one way to describe an inquiry into murder."

Vale arched one elegant brow. "I deal with the artifacts of the ancient dead most of my waking hours. A modern murder offers a pleasant change of pace."

"It was good of you to see us," Lavinia said.

Vale glanced at Joan. "Mrs. Dove is my friend. I am happy to oblige her in any way I can." He turned back to Lavinia. "I see you are interested in my copy of Mr. Lysons's *Reliquiae Britannico-Romanae*."

"This is the first opportunity I have had to examine it. The volume is very expensive, you know."

Vale smiled. "Yes, I know."

She felt herself turn pink. A man of his wealth was no doubt quite oblivious to the cost of a beautiful book.

"Mr. Lysons's unusual interest in British-Roman antiquities parallels my own," Vale continued. "You are welcome to browse through the *Reliquiae*, Mrs. Lake."

Lavinia studied the plate displayed in front of her. It showed several meticulously rendered drawings of British-Roman antiquities that Samuel Lysons had uncovered in his explorations of old ruins in his native Gloucestershire. A curious, U-shaped iron blade and portions of a pottery strainer were illustrated. Small, detailed works of art in themselves, the drawings had been colored in light, translucent washes.

Lysons was unusual not only because of his keen interest in British antiquities, she thought, but also because he paid close attention to the oddly fascinating, if somewhat mundane, relics of daily life. She turned to another one of the colored plates and smiled at the carefully rendered drawings of several elegantly shaped pottery bowls.

Tobias looked at Vale. "I'm certain that you are already aware that we are searching for the man who murdered Celeste Hudson. We believe that she stole the Blue Medusa shortly before her death."

"So you are, in effect, looking for the Medusa on the assumption that the killer now has it," Vale concluded.

"It is our hope that the bracelet will lead us to the murderer," Lavinia explained. "It is an odd relic, by all accounts. We thought it would be useful to know more about it."

"And about those who might have an interest in obtaining it," Tobias added. "Mr. Nightingale implied that there are some collectors who would pay dearly for it in order to use it to apply for admission to the Connoisseurs Club."

"Ah, yes, Nightingale. A very enterprising gentleman." Vale sipped tea and slowly lowered his cup. "Serious collectors interested in gaining admission to the club would know that, as the founder and keeper of the museum, I have a preference for antiquities discovered on English soil. Indeed, I would be strongly disposed to look approvingly on whoever presented such an object to the club's private collection."

Lavinia turned away from the beautiful book on the table. "What can you tell us, sir?"

Vale put aside his cup and saucer and got to his feet. "Before I discuss the Blue Medusa, I believe I will show you the club's private museum."

They rose and followed him to a door set into the paneled wall on the other side of the library. Vale opened it and revealed a staircase. He led the way up the steps.

At the landing he opened another door and ushered them into a long gallery.

Lavinia saw at once that the shadowy chamber extended the entire length of the great house. The gallery was lined with glass-enclosed cases, tall wooden cabinets, and massive chests of drawers.

Statuary stood in the corners. Ancient vases, urns, and broken bits of columns littered the floor. Half a dozen stone sarcophagi were stacked against one wall.

"This is wonderful." Lavinia moved to the nearest display case and saw row upon row of silver and gold coins bearing the portraits of ancient Roman emperors, neatly arrayed on black fabric.

Joan went to stand at a case and studied an exquisitely worked gold necklace set with a number of emeralds. "This is a new acquisition, is it not, Vale? I do not recall seeing it the last time I was here."

"You have not paid me a visit since Fielding's death," Vale said softly. "As it happens, I have been away a good deal of the time this past year. I spent several months exploring the ruins of an ancient

Roman villa not far from Bath. The mosaics were quite astonishing. I made some colored drawings."

Joan turned away from the necklace. "I should like to see them."

Vale smiled. "I would be delighted to show them to you."

Lavinia saw the silent invitation in his eyes and knew from the way Joan moved quickly to another display case that she had seen it too.

Tobias appeared oblivious to the small exchange. He examined a vase with casual interest and then looked at Vale. "This is the club's private museum, I assume?"

"Yes." Vale stroked the carved stone of an ancient altar with a lover's caress. "Much of what you see in this chamber was found right here in England. It is fashionable to send young men on the Grand Tour to view the glorious ruins of ancient Rome and Greece, but as Mr. Lysons has demonstrated, we have our own rich classical history to explore, do we not? The Connoisseurs are devoted to preserving British antiquities."

"England was a Roman province for several centuries," Joan said. "It is reasonable to assume that the ancients left many interesting relics."

"Indeed. The Romans left us an inheritance in the form of the remains of magnificent villas, public baths, and temples." He indicated the case of gleaming objects next to her. "And who knows how many hoards of ancient jewelry and coins are yet to be discovered buried in the ground."

"Few of those hoards are likely to be reported by their discoverers, given the law of treasure trove," Tobias said dryly. "It is asking a great deal to expect a poor farmer to turn over a cache of ancient gold and silver valuables to the Crown without payment, all so that the objects can be melted down."

"Indeed." Vale chuckled. "But rest assured that a good many undeclared discoveries are made on a regular basis, and they go far to ensure a lively market in antiquities for the likes of Mr. Nightingale and other dealers."

Lavinia examined a series of little enameled bronze brooches twisted into fanciful shapes that made her think of tiny dragons. Then she moved to look at some rings set with engraved stones.

The first featured a red carnelian decorated with the tiny figure of a draped woman. The little cornucopia and steering oar identified her as Fortuna, the goddess of good fortune. The red jasper stone in the neighboring ring depicted another draped goddess, this one winged. She was shown with a small scourge. Lavinia recognized her as Nemesis, the goddess in charge of preserving the balance of good and ill in human affairs and with the task of exacting vengeance.

Tobias lounged against an elaborately carved sarcophagus and looked at Vale. "This is an interesting collection, but I believe you were going to tell us about the Blue Medusa."

Vale nodded and walked slowly through the gallery. "The bracelet itself is said to be a particularly exquisite example of the ancient goldsmith's craft. But of even greater interest is the cameo set into it."

"So we have been told," Tobias said.

"From what I can determine, the antiquity was found sometime early in the last century. It was handed down through a family that gradually thinned out until only a maiden aunt and her nephew, a boy of about fifteen, were left in the line. One morning many years ago, the aunt's body was discovered by a maid. The kitchen knife that had been used to kill her was still in her back."

"Dear heaven," Lavinia whispered.

"There was no sign of the nephew, and a number of valuables were missing, including the Blue Medusa," Vale continued. "It seems to have been sold and resold a number of times before Banks eventually found it in a small antiquities shop here in London a year and a half ago."

"What of the nephew?" Tobias asked.

"As far as I know, he vanished for good. Perhaps he changed his name. Perhaps he died. Perhaps he made his way to America or the Continent. I doubt if anyone searched for him."

"Even though he was the most likely suspect in his aunt's murder?" Joan asked.

Vale moved one hand in a flat line. "The boy was not well liked. The neighbors feared him. Evidently there had been some nasty incidents with dead animals and some small fires that were attributed to him.

In any event, there was no one who cared greatly about justice for the aunt."

"We have heard that the cameo is an unusual depiction of the Gorgon," Tobias said.

"It is not an ordinary representation of Medusa." Vale paused at the end of the row of gravestones and looked at him from the shadows. "Sometime back I came across an old book that made reference to a peculiar cult that flourished for a time here in England in the fourth century. Arcane societies and secret temples were not unusual in the Roman Empire, especially in the more remote provinces such as England. My studies indicate that a number of them existed here. But this one was quite unique."

"In what way?" Lavinia asked.

"The cameo includes, in addition to the Medusa figure, a wand or rod. It appears to have been the emblem or seal of the cult's master, who was both feared and dreaded."

"Why?" Joan asked curiously.

Vale hesitated and then shrugged. "You will not credit this, but the old volume indicated that the master practiced an ancient form of mesmerism."

Lavinia stopped halfway to another display case and spun around. "Mesmerism? In ancient times? But it is a modern science."

Vale looked amused. "If animal magnetism is, indeed, a real force in the human body, why should it strike you as strange that techniques for controlling it might have been discovered and lost and rediscovered many times over the course of the centuries? Do you really believe that we who live in this enlightened era are the only ones who manage to stumble onto ancient truths? That we are any more intelligent, insightful, or intuitive than those who came before us?"

Lavinia winced. "I take your point, sir. But you must admit, it is odd to consider that some ancient pagan cult here in England may have practiced a science as advanced as mesmerism."

"Always assuming that it is a science," Tobias muttered.

Vale laughed softly and turned back to Lavinia. "Odd and deeply fascinating. And, in this case, more than a little disturbing."

"Why do you say that?" Joan asked sharply.

Vale resumed his stroll through the relics of the past. "According to the book, the master used his mesmeric powers, which were said to be drawn directly from the stone itself, in dark ways. From what I have been able to discern, the cult was founded on fear, secrecy, and great mystery."

"Medusa was an obvious choice as a symbol of such an unusual cult, in that case," Joan observed. "After all, in the legend, she could turn a man to stone with her gaze."

"More than a symbol." Vale paused meaningfully. "As I said, the cameo in the bracelet was considered the actual source of the priest's power. The members believed that the only person who could control it was the one who was imbued with a natural talent for drawing the energy from the stone."

A solemn silence fell on the gallery.

Tobias shattered the uneasy quiet with a humorless smile. "I trust that your interest in the Blue Medusa is purely scholarly in nature, Vale. I would not like to believe that a man of your education and experience of the world places any credence in the supposed mystical powers of an ancient cameo."

Lavinia saw Joan frown and glance quickly at their host.

But Vale looked amused. "I assure you, March, I have no use for metaphysics, especially those of a rather unpleasant, long-dead cult. But it never ceases to amaze me how often seemingly intelligent, educated people do fall under the spell of old legends and strange beliefs."

"And the Blue Medusa offers that enticement?" Tobias asked.

"To some, yes." Vale walked to a nearby cabinet and removed the iron ring on his left hand. He fitted the small key to the lock and opened the door. "Take this piece of ancient Roman glass, for instance. It is said that men have died because of it."

He reached inside and removed an intricately carved glass bowl. The object caught the light and glowed a dozen shades of fiery amber in his fingers. Lavinia was riveted. She moved closer to get a better look.

"It's incredible," she said. "Was it, too, found here in England?"

"No. I believe that it was brought here from Italy many years ago."

Joan came to stand beside Lavinia. "Beautiful."

Vale watched them both with an enigmatic smile.

Lavinia took a closer look at the large cup. Figures had been carved around the vessel in such a way that they stood out from the surface as though attempting to escape the bonds of the delicate net of glass that anchored them.

Lavinia recognized the scene that the artist had caught and frozen in the glass.

"Persephone fleeing Hades," she whispered. "The Lord of the Underworld pursues her."

The desperation on the face of the woman and the anguish and loss etched in the god's features sent a shiver through her.

"It is called the Hades Cup, and some say that it is a dangerous object to own." Vale smiled wryly. "Not that I believe in such nonsense. Nevertheless, I maintain that I do not actually own the thing. I am merely keeping it safe here in the club's museum."

He closed and locked the cabinet door with the tiny ring key.

"I think we have all taken your point," Tobias said. "Legends develop a strength of their own, and collectors are an odd lot."

"Indeed." Vale smiled. "They like nothing better than a good story attached to an antiquity. Some will kill to possess a rare object with a sufficiently compelling legend attached to it."

Lavinia threw up her hands. "Wonderful. Yet another motive for murder. At this rate, half of London will soon be on our suspect list."

$\mathcal{E}$ighteen

Tobias sank into the chair across from Crackenburne and reached for the bottle of brandy that sat on the table between them.

"Leg bothering you again today?" Crackenburne asked without looking up from his newspaper.

"It's not the leg so much as the conversation I just had with a possible suspect." Tobias tipped the bottle and poured. The clink of glass against glass brought to mind a fleeting image of the Hades Cup. "What can you tell me about Vale?"

Crackenburne hesitated and then slowly lowered the paper far enough to peer at Tobias over the top. "Wealthy. Widowed. Secretive. He's the head of a very small, exclusive little club of collectors. Writes scholarly papers for the journals. Has a habit of disappearing for weeks at a time to dig up old Roman ruins in the country."

"I know that much. I also know that he was a close friend of Fielding Dove." Tobias took a swallow of the brandy and relaxed into the chair. "Which means that he probably was aware that Dove was the head of the Blue Chamber. Think Vale might have been involved in some of its activities?"

"Never heard anything to indicate that he was connected to that criminal organization." Crackenburne folded his paper and put it aside. "Which is not to say that he wasn't, of course. In his own way Vale is just as clever and possibly just as dangerous as Dove was in his time. But I think his interests lie elsewhere."

"Antiquities."

"Yes."

"Do you think he would commit murder to obtain a very special Roman artifact associated with an ancient cult here in England?"

Crackenburne grew thoughtful. "I cannot say for certain. I've heard he is somewhat obsessive on the subject of such British-Roman relics. But I will give you my opinion, for what it's worth."

"And that is?"

"If Vale did commit murder for it, I very much doubt that you'd ever be able to trace the deed to him. He's no fool. He would cover his tracks well."

Tobias turned the brandy glass between his palms. "The murderer we're after did leave something personal behind. His cravat."

Crackenburne snorted. "Can't see Vale being that careless."

"Unless, of course, he knew that the damned neckcloth would lead us to a dead end. After all, it told us nothing except that Celeste Hudson was probably murdered by a gentleman rather than a poorly dressed footpad."

Crackenburne shook his head with grave authority. "If Vale had taken pains to leave behind a false clue, you can be certain it would have led you to whoever he wished you to think was the killer. You just said the cravat led you to no one in particular."

"It led me nowhere and therefore we must assume that Vale is probably not the killer." Tobias smiled wryly. "The logic is somewhat convoluted, to say the least, but I am inclined to agree. In truth, I never placed too much hope in the possibility that his lordship was guilty. The entire affair is far too murky for such a convenient explanation."

"Not Vale's style at all." Crackenburne picked up the brandy bottle and poured himself a glass. "But there is another reason why I think you can exclude him."

"What is that?"

Crackenburne sipped brandy with a meditative air. "Can't see Vale murdering a woman in cold blood. The man's no saint, of course. I think it's safe to say that under certain conditions he could be quite dangerous. Not unlike you, to be blunt. But I do not believe that he would strangle a woman to death. Not for a bloody antiquity."

Tobias recalled the reverential way in which Vale had cradled the Hades Cup in his hands. "Not even if he placed a very high value on that particular antiquity?"

"He's a shrewd, clever player who generally gets what he wants in the end. But in this sort of situation, I'm quite certain that he would have found other means to his ends." Crackenburne smiled slightly before taking another swallow of brandy. "Just as you would have done under similar circumstances."

Tobias watched the flames on the hearth for a time, contemplating what Crackenburne had said.

"Any other news for me?" he asked after a while.

"I did come up with a couple of interesting rumors concerning Gunning and Northampton."

Tobias cocked a brow. "Yes?"

Crackenburne paused for effect, clearly relishing his moment. "Word has it that the households of both gentlemen may have been burglarized at some point in the past several months."

Tobias put down his glass with such force that it sounded as if it had cracked on the tabletop. "*May* have been burglarized?"

"There was no evidence of a housebreaker. No smashed windows or broken locks. Nor is there any way to know precisely when the objects disappeared. Some feel the owners, who are both in their dotage, may simply have misplaced the items in question."

"What sort of items are we talking about?"

"In the case of Lord Gunning, a pair of diamond earrings that belonged to his late wife. Northampton's household is missing a very fine pearl-and-emerald necklace that was supposed to have gone to his daughter."

"Bloody hell. The lady was, indeed, a jewel thief. And I'll wager her recently widowed husband is in the same line."

———————

"Howard, do come in and sit down." Lavinia put down the pen she had been using to make notes in the journal and motioned her visitor to a chair. "I believe there is some tea left in the pot. Allow me to pour you a cup."

"Thank you, my dear." Howard closed the study door behind him, but he did not sit down. Instead, he came to a halt in front of her desk and stood looking at her. "I was feeling quite restless this afternoon so I decided to take a walk." He spread his hands. "The next thing I knew, I was standing at your front door."

"I understand," she said gently. "I expect you are anxious to know if Mr. March and I have made any progress in our inquiries."

"I must admit the subject is foremost in my mind these days." He removed his watch from his pocket and began to toy with it in an absent fashion. The gold fobs dangled and danced. "Tell me the truth, Lavinia. Do you really think you can find the bastard who murdered my Celeste?"

Tobias had told her that it was important to reassure the client as often as necessary, she reminded herself.

"We are making progress," she said firmly. "Mr. March and I feel certain that we shall find her killer."

"My dear Lavinia." The watch fobs swayed in a steady rhythm. "What would I do without you?" Howard's voice deepened and grew heavy. "My dear, dear friend. You and I have so much in common. So much to talk about. So much that we can explore together, my dear friend."

The intent quality of his gaze and the gold fobs disturbed her. Surely he was not attempting to put her into a mesmeric trance in such a sly fashion. This was her dear friend Howard, after all. He would not seek to take advantage of her with his skills. The steady, relentless movement of the fobs was simply happenstance, not deliberate. This was her dear old family friend.

"Such a dear friend . . ."

Quite suddenly she knew that she needed to look away. The urge was strong, but when she tried to avert her eyes from the gold watch fobs, it proved surprisingly difficult. She raised her fingers to touch the silver pendant that she wore at her throat, and the unpleasant sensation eased.

Relieved, she studied the page of the journal that was open in front of her. "As it happens, I am glad you came by this afternoon, Howard. I have been going over some notes and I find I have a few more questions."

"I will tell you anything I can, of course, my dear, dear friend." His voice was as resonant as a large bell. "What is it you wish to know?"

"Forgive me for such a personal inquiry, but I must ask how you came to be aware that Celeste was having an affair."

"How does a man know such a thing? I suppose it was a matter of small clues, most of which I chose to ignore at first. She began to go shopping more frequently and returned late, sometimes without any purchases to show for her efforts. There were days when she seemed too cheerful or excited or impatient for no apparent cause. What can I say? She acted the way a young woman in love acts."

Lavinia looked up at that and found herself staring at the dangling watch fobs again. The effort required to look away this time left her feeling rather breathless.

"Does that answer your question, my dear, dear friend?"

She was imagining this, she thought. Howard was not trying to induce a trance. Perhaps she was becoming a victim of bad nerves.

Returning her attention to her notes, she pressed on determinedly. There was another question she wanted to ask. She had to work hard to remember it.

"The antiquity Celeste stole belonged to Lord Banks," she said. "Have you ever met him?"

"No, my dear friend."

The gold seals bobbed gently.

"Do you think that Celeste may have somehow contrived to meet him?"

"I don't see how that would have been possible." Howard frowned. "Unless she was acquainted with him before I met her."

"I had not thought of that possibility." She tapped the quill on the edge of the ink bottle a few times. "I wonder if that is how she came to know about the bracelet."

Tap ... tap ... tap ...

"I cannot answer that, my dear, dear friend. . . ."

She suddenly realized that the tip of the quill was striking the bottle in a pattern that matched the swaying movements of the dangling watch fobs. She stopped and hastily put down the pen.

"You are trying to establish the manner in which Celeste learned of the antiquity," Howard said.

"Yes." Lavinia closed the journal. This time when she raised her eyes, she avoided his gaze by focusing on a picture that hung on the wall across the room. She tried to appear pensive rather than rude.

There was a short pause. Then, with an almost inaudible sigh, Howard dropped the watch back into his pocket. He began to pace the study.

"I think that the most likely explanation is that her lover informed her of the whereabouts of the bracelet and its value," he said.

"But if he knew those facts, why did he not steal it himself? Theft is a dangerous business. Why send her to do the deed?"

"I'll tell you why. The bloody bastard was too cowardly to take the risk of entering the mansion." Howard's voice throbbed with fierce emotion. He closed one hand into a fist at his side. "He preferred to force my Celeste to take such risks. He used her and then he murdered her."

"I'm sorry, Howard. I know this is difficult for you."

"Forgive me. You are only attempting to help, but when I think about the monster who strangled her I cannot contain my feelings."

"I understand."

"Please give me a moment to compose myself." Howard turned away abruptly and went to look at the spines of the books on a nearby shelf.

After a few seconds he smiled wistfully. "You have not lost your taste for poetry, I see. You were always very fond of it, as I recall."

It was a great relief not to have to avoid his eyes, she thought. "Emeline says it is a sign that I am a romantic at heart."

"You have not had much opportunity for romance in your life, have you, my dear?" His voice was low, freighted with understanding and deep sympathy.

"I would not say that." She tried to keep her own voice light. "My husband was a poet, if you will recall. I thought him wonderfully romantic."

"I remember meeting him at your wedding." Howard turned around unexpectedly, trapping her with his eyes. "I did not think that he was the right man for you, but it was not my place to speak of such matters. You seemed so happy at the time."

"I was happy. For a while." Instinctively, she touched the silver pendant again. The trapped feeling dissipated once more.

"I was sorry to learn of his untimely death from fever. I know it must have been very difficult for you, following, as it did, so soon in the wake of the loss of your parents."

"Howard, I think it would be best if we returned to the subject of Celeste's murder. We really do not have time to reminisce."

"Do you miss your career as a mesmerist, my dear?" he asked in a strangely gentle tone. "You displayed such a gift for the science while still in the schoolroom. Quite astounding, actually. I cannot but assume that your talents have only grown stronger with the years. May I ask what made you abandon the profession?"

"I really don't think this is the time or place to—"

She broke off at the sound of familiar bootsteps in the hall. A few seconds later the study door opened abruptly. Tobias glanced at her briefly and then immediately switched his attention to Howard.

"I beg your pardon if I am interrupting a private conversation," he said.

His tone of voice made it quite clear that he was not the least bit sorry, Lavinia thought. In fact, unless she was sorely mistaken, he was furious.

"Not at all," Howard said smoothly. "We were discussing the inquiry."

"I see." Tobias looked at Lavinia. "I believe we have an appointment."

"Really? I do not seem to recall—" Something in his expression made her swallow the rest of her words. She summoned what she hoped was a professional sort of smile. It was never a good idea to let the client know that there might be some friction between oneself and one's partner. "Yes, of course. An appointment. It slipped my mind, sir. Howard, if you will excuse us, Mr. March and I must deal with some pressing issues involving your case."

Howard hesitated, his gaze switching from Tobias to her and back again. For a second she thought he might prove stubborn. But in the end he inclined his head in a graceful nod.

"Yes, of course." He gave Tobias an unreadable stare as he went through the opening into the hall. "I shall hope for a report of positive results at your earliest convenience."

Tobias said nothing until the door in the front hall opened and closed. Only then did he turn back to Lavinia. He crossed the study, planted his hands on top of her desk, and fixed her with an expression that sent a shiver clear to her bones.

"I want your word," he said in a voice that was as chilling as his expression, "that you will never again allow yourself to be closeted alone with Hudson."

"I beg your pardon? What on earth—" She broke off on a shocked gasp when he rounded the desk and plucked her out of her chair. "How dare you, sir. Put me down at once."

"Your word, Lavinia."

"Why should I make such an outlandish promise?" she sputtered. "You know very well that Howard is an old friend." *An old, dear friend.*

"I do not trust him alone with you."

"I assure you, he is a gentleman."

"He may be a killer."

"I do not believe that for one moment."

"Even if he did not murder his wife, I do not like the way he looks at you."

She parted her lips to offer another defense of Howard. But the memory of how strangely uneasy she had felt a few minutes earlier when Howard had pinned her with his fathomless gaze stopped the words in her throat. Truth be told, she thought, she did not particularly want to be alone with Howard again, even though she was not sure why.

"Promise me, Lavinia."

"Oh, very well," she muttered ungraciously. "If it will make you set me down on my feet and cease acting in this ridiculous fashion, I shall give you my word. Any future conversations with Howard will be conducted with someone else present. Does that satisfy you?"

"Not entirely. The only thing that would truly satisfy me would be for you to drop this case and never come in contact with Hudson again. But I know that is not going to happen, so, for now, I will accept your word that you will not be private with him."

"Yes, yes, you have it."

He lowered her to her feet.

"Enough of this nonsense." She fussed with her skirts and patted her hair. "We have work to do."

He watched her with a dark, brooding expression.

"I learned some very interesting facts this afternoon from Crackenburne," he said. "It seems that those two gentlemen in Bath whose names Celeste gave us as references are both missing valuable items of jewelry."

Lavinia frowned. "Antiquities?"

"No. At least there was nothing to indicate that they were old. Merely expensive. A pair of diamond earrings and a gemstone necklace."

"Good heavens." She sank slowly back down onto her chair. "Celeste really was a jewel thief. For some reason she was inspired to try her hand at stealing antiquities. I wonder why."

"An excellent question since, in my experience, the more professional class of thieves tends to specialize in particular types of valuables. But that is not important at the moment. What is crucial is that this information gives us another way of looking at the matter."

"What do you mean?"

"I suspect that Hudson and his wife worked as partners in the family business, as it were."

She was outraged. "What's this? Are you accusing Howard of being a jewel thief?"

"I think it very likely, yes."

"First you label him a murderer and now you call him a thief. It is quite outrageous. Allow me to tell you, sir, that you are allowing your personal feelings in this matter to influence your judgment."

"But if I am right," he said softly, "if Celeste and Howard Hudson were partners in theft, we have yet another motive for murder here."

"A falling-out among thieves? You think Howard killed her not because she betrayed him with another man but because she attempted to make off with the antiquity? Rubbish." Lavinia gave a ladylike sniff. "I refuse to countenance the possibility that Howard murdered his wife."

Tobias said nothing. He just looked at her for a long moment.

"Well?" She frowned. "What is it?"

"I cannot help but notice that you are not rushing to defend Hudson from the charge of theft."

She sighed and sank deeper into her chair. "You're certain about the stolen jewelry in Bath?"

"As certain as I can be without proof. But Crackenburne's information is almost always reliable."

She picked up her pen and fiddled with it absently while she forced herself to contemplate the facts from a dispassionate distance. "I will admit that if Celeste was such an active thief, it is highly unlikely that Howard did not, at the very least, suspect something."

"I think it far more probable that he was involved in the thefts."

"If that is so, why would he take the risk of hiring us?"

"He did not want to hire *us*. He wanted to hire *you*. And he did so because the Medusa bracelet is missing and he wants to find it." Tobias frowned. "In any event, he may not believe that he is taking much of a risk."

"What do you mean?"

"Think about it, Lavinia. He didn't go to Bow Street to find a detective, did he? He came to you, an old acquaintance who remembers him fondly, a *dear friend* from the past who would never for a moment consider the possibility that he might be guilty of either murder or theft."

She winced and placed the pen very precisely down on the blotter. "I'm still not convinced. It is entirely possible that there are other explanations for the murder and the theft. Poor Howard."

"Poor Howard, indeed." Tobias looked amused. "Just his bloody luck that when he hired you, he got me in the bargain."

Nineteen

❧

His dark mood did not lift when Tobias walked into his own house a short while later and found Anthony sprawled on a chair in the study. On the table beside his brother-in-law sat three quarters of a cold salmon-and-potato pie, which was rapidly disappearing into Anthony's mouth.

"I trust you are here because you have some useful information for me." Tobias went around the corner of his desk and lowered himself into the chair. "Did you find the valet?"

"Not yet." Anthony swallowed a large bite of the pie and put aside the dish and fork. He regarded the tips of his gleaming boots. "One of the neighbors said Fitch has been spending a lot of time in the hells since he was let go from his post. I'll try again in the morning."

"Time is of the essence here, in case you haven't noticed." Tobias tapped one finger against the blotter. "I want him found as soon as possible."

"It's not that easy. He never seems to go home, and I don't even know what the man looks like."

"Use some initiative. Ask one of his acquaintances for a description. Make inquiries of the street boys. Discover which hells he favors. Damnation, Tony, you're the one who demanded to play assistant detective. I suggest you start practicing your new craft."

"You know I've been busy interviewing the prostitutes who work near the inn where Oscar Pelling is staying."

Tobias frowned. "Any luck there?"

"No."

"In other words, you haven't made any progress at all on either front, have you? I suggest you return to your inquiries. It would no doubt be more productive than helping yourself to the contents of Whitby's pantry."

"I just stopped by for a quick bite." Anthony glared at him morosely from the depths of the chair. "What the devil is the matter with you? Have another one of your lively little quarrels with Mrs. Lake?"

"My relationship with Lavinia is none of your bloody business."

"Of course it isn't. I don't know what came over me."

Tobias slammed the flat of his hand against the blotter. "I walked into her study a short time ago and found her alone with Hudson."

"Ah."

"What is that supposed to mean?"

"Nothing in particular. Just that I now comprehend the reason for your foul temper." Anthony raised his brows. "You don't much care for your client, do you?"

"I do not trust the man. He's a practicing mesmerist who may well have murdered his own wife. I'm certain that he's hatching some dark scheme that involves Lavinia. And she refuses to see the danger."

"Want some advice?"

"No, thank you. Your advice on how to charm a lady with compliments has proven a resounding failure."

Anthony cleared his throat. "Very well, then, how about giving me some advice?"

"What are you talking about?"

"I came here this afternoon because I wanted to consult with an older, wiser man who has had some experience of the world and who can assist me in resolving a particularly confounding problem that I now find myself confronting."

"Damnation, you gave me your word you would not go into the hells. If you have got yourself into dun territory, you can bloody well finance your own way out."

"Calm yourself, sir. I haven't lost any money at the gaming tables. In the event that it has escaped your attention, I've been too busy pursuing inquiries for my new employer to spare any time for cards or dice."

It dawned on Tobias that he had never heard this particular edge in Anthony's voice.

"What is it?" he asked quietly.

"Emeline."

"Damn, I was afraid of this." Tobias leaned back in his chair, stacked the heels of his boots on the corner of the desk, and steepled his fingers. "Something happened yesterday after you left Banks's mansion, did it not?"

"Of course something bloody well happened. I told you what occurred." Anthony shot to his feet and started to stalk the room. "Emeline was very nearly run down by that carriage. She could have been hurt. Perhaps seriously."

"I got the impression she felt that you and the boy were the ones in danger."

"She was in peril too, but she seemed oblivious of that fact."

Tobias contemplated his fingertips. "Thought we agreed that the driver's intention was to deliver a message, not to murder anyone."

"How the hell can we be sure of anything, least of all the coachman's intentions?" Anthony's jaw was so rigid it could have been forged from steel. "I tell you, Tobias, I'd give a fortune to get my hands on the bastard for even five minutes."

"I understand."

"I must confess that it wasn't until I went to bed last night that the full implications of the incident finally struck me. The possibilities kept me awake almost until dawn. I stared at the ceiling and kept thinking about what might have happened." Anthony waved one hand. "What if the coachman had lost control of his horses? What if Emeline had panicked the way the boy did? What if she had just stood there, frozen, in the path of the vehicle? She would have been trampled."

"Luckily Miss Emeline appears to share her aunt's tendency not to panic at awkward moments."

"When I did manage to fall asleep last night, I had nightmares," Anthony muttered. "The dreams all involved scenes in which I could not get to Emeline in time to pull her out of the path of a rushing carriage."

Tobias thought about the occasional nightmares he had experienced since making Lavinia's acquaintance. "I've had a few unpleasant dreams of that sort myself."

"This morning while you and Mrs. Lake and Mrs. Dove went to consult with Vale, I had a conversation with Emeline. I told her that I thought she should give up this notion of following in her aunt's footsteps."

"Did you, indeed?" Tobias took his boots off the corner of his desk and got to his feet. He went to the small table to inspect the remaining portion of the salmon-and-potato pie. "I expect I can hazard a guess as to the nature of her response to your suggestion."

"She got very angry with me. Refused to even consider my advice. As good as told me that I had no right to make decisions for her or to interfere with her life."

"You don't say?" Tobias picked up the knife and cut himself a hefty wedge of pie. "Now, there's a stunning surprise."

Anthony came to a halt and watched with a dark frown as Tobias took a bite of the savory pastry. "Are you mocking me?"

"I assure you, you have my complete sympathy," Tobias said around the mouthful of pie.

"Bloody hell." Anthony shoved his fingers through his hair. "I daresay you find my predicament vastly amusing, do you not? No doubt you believe that it is a fitting comeuppance for all the times that I have advised you not to behave in a dictatorial, overbearing manner toward Mrs. Lake."

Tobias said nothing. He took another bite of pie. Whitby was an excellent cook. But, then, Whitby was good at almost everything. The man who served him as a combination of butler, cook, valet, and occasional doctor even managed to appear more elegant in his clothes than most gentlemen of the ton, including himself, Tobias reflected.

"If it's any consolation," Anthony muttered, "I confess that I now possess a much clearer appreciation of the depth of your own sensibilities on the matter of Mrs. Lake's inclination to take risks."

"Always nice to know that one's sensibilities are understood and appreciated."

"I don't suppose you have any useful advice for me?"

"Certainly, I have some advice." Tobias handed him the plate. "Have some more of Whitby's salmon pie. It is very good. The leeks add a nice touch, I think. When you have finished you can go back to the business of tracking down Banks's valet and chatting with streetwalkers."

Anthony took the plate reluctantly. He looked down at the pie as though it were an alchemist's crucible. "I'm doomed to be driven mad by Miss Emeline, am I not?"

"Most likely. But I'm certain that you will find it reassuring to know that you are not the only incipient crackbrain in the vicinity. I appear to be doomed to a similar fate, thanks to Mrs. Lake."

"Is there something wrong, Emeline?" Lavinia put down her pen and studied her niece's somber face. "I vow, we are accomplishing very little here. You have been in an exceedingly low mood since yesterday. Was it the incident with the carriage?"

Emeline put aside the paper on which she had been refining her impressions of the responses of the servants whom she and Anthony had interviewed at the Banks mansion. She gave Lavinia a troubled look.

"In a manner of speaking," she admitted.

"I knew it. You did not sleep well, did you? I noticed at breakfast that you appeared a bit wan."

Emeline's mouth curved ruefully. "Is that a polite way of saying that I am not looking my best today?"

"I blame myself. I should have insisted that you take a drop or two of sherry before you went to bed."

"Anthony called upon me while you and Mrs. Dove and Mr. March interviewed Lord Vale today."

Lavinia frowned. "Anthony was here? He came into the house? I trust Mrs. Chilton was present?"

"She was here. But as it happens, Anthony did not come into the house. He invited me to walk with him in the park."

Alarm shot through Lavinia. Visions of what happened on the occasions when Tobias took her for a walk in the park made her blanch.

"How dare that young man even suggest such a thing? What on earth does he think he is about? Is that what has upset you today? I shall demand that Tobias have a stern talk with him."

Emeline made a face. "You need not concern yourself with the proprieties. We merely took a short stroll in a very public section of the park. We certainly did not disappear for an hour or more the way you and Mr. March are inclined to do when you two take your little walks in the park."

Lavinia felt herself turning pink now. She cleared her throat. "Mr. March and I have discovered that long walks are extremely invigorating for persons of our age."

"Indeed."

Lavinia narrowed her eyes. "What was it about your conversation with Anthony that disturbed you?"

"He is starting to sound altogether too much like Mr. March, if you must know."

"I beg your pardon? In what way?"

"He told me that, in his opinion, I should reconsider my decision to follow you into the private-inquiries business."

"I see." Lavinia pondered that information. "What on earth made him say that, do you suppose? He seems such a sensible, modern-thinking young man."

"I believe he was somewhat shaken by the incident with the carriage."

"Interesting. I would not have guessed that he possessed such delicate nerves. Judging from his demeanor yesterday afternoon when you both returned, I would have said that Anthony gave every appearance of being just as cool in a crisis as Tobias."

"It was not his own brush with danger that unsettled him, although it certainly gave me a terrible jolt," Emeline said. "Last night he evidently allowed his imagination to get the better of his common sense. He managed to convince himself that I had been in the path of danger and that were it not for a bit of luck I might have been hurt."

"I see."

"The entire affair has rattled his nerves and he has concluded that I should, therefore, pursue another career."

"I see," Lavinia said again, very neutrally this time.

"I was obliged to endure an extremely tiresome lecture on the subject of how I ought not to put my person in danger. There was also a good bit of boring twaddle on the nature of suitable careers for ladies. In the end I fear I lost my patience and told him exactly what I thought of his overbearing manner. I bid him good afternoon and left him standing there in the middle of the park."

"I see." Lavinia planted her hands on the desk and pushed herself to her feet. "What do you say we have a little nip of sherry?"

Emeline frowned. "I expected something more inspirational from such a clever and resourceful lady. You are a woman of the world, after all. You have had some experience of men. Is this the best you can do? A drop of sherry?"

"If it is inspiration you seek, I suggest you consult Shakespeare, Wollstonecraft, or a religious tract. I fear that when it comes to advice on the subject of gentlemen such as Mr. March and Mr. Sinclair, a drop of sherry is the most I can offer."

"Oh."

Lavinia opened the sherry cupboard. She removed the decanter, poured two small measures, and handed one of the glasses to Emeline. "They mean well, you know."

"Yes." Emeline took a tiny sip of the sherry and immediately assumed a more philosophical air. "Yes, I suppose they do."

Lavinia sampled the contents of her own glass and sought to organize her thoughts on the subject of men.

"In my experience," she said slowly, "gentlemen are inclined to become tense and occasionally extremely overwrought whenever they feel that they are not in full control of a situation. This is especially so if the situation involves a lady toward whom they feel a certain responsibility."

"I understand."

"They compensate for these attacks of nerves by giving stern lectures, issuing orders, and generally making nuisances of themselves."

Emeline took a little more sherry and nodded wisely. "It is a most irritating habit."

"Indeed, but I fear it is the nature of the beast. Perhaps you can now see why I find Mr. March so exasperating on occasion."

"I confess my eyes have been opened." Emeline shook her head. "No wonder you are given to frequent quarrels with him. I can already foresee any number of rows with Anthony on the horizon."

Lavinia raised her glass. "A toast."

"To what?"

"To exasperating gentlemen. You must admit that they are, at the very least, quite stimulating."

Twenty

THE WEAK SUN DISSOLVED RAPIDLY IN THE FOG THAT CREPT OVER the city the following afternoon. The mist had nearly succeeded in bringing a hasty end to the pleasant day by the time Lavinia arrived at the premises of Tredlow's antiquities shop. She came to a halt at the front door and peered through the windows, surprised to see that no lamp had been lit. The interior lay in heavy shadow.

She took a couple of steps back and looked up to examine the windows above the shop. A quick survey showed that the drapes were pulled closed. No light glowed around the edges of the heavy curtains.

She tried the door. It was unlocked. She stepped inside the unnaturally silent shop.

"Mr. Tredlow?" Her voice echoed hollowly among the shadowed ranks of dusty statuary and display cases. "I got your message and came immediately."

Tredlow's brief, cryptic note had arrived at the kitchen door less than an hour ago: *I have news on the subject of a certain relic of mutual interest.*

She had been alone in the house at the time. Mrs. Chilton had taken herself off to purchase some fish. Emeline had gone shopping to purchase gloves to wear to Mrs. Dove's ball.

Lavinia had wasted no time. She'd seized her cloak and bonnet and set out at once. Hackneys were scarce at that hour, but she had managed to find one. Unfortunately, the traffic had been heavy. It seemed to take forever to arrive in the cramped street outside Tredlow's.

She hoped he had not given up on her, closed his shop for the evening, and taken himself off to a nearby coffeehouse.

"Mr. Tredlow? Are you about?"

The stillness of the place was disconcerting. Surely Tredlow would not have failed to lock his front door if he had left or retired to his rooms above the shop.

Edmund Tredlow was not a young man, she thought uneasily. And as far as she knew, he lived alone. Although he had seemed to be in good health the last time she saw him, there were any number of dire things that could happen to a gentleman of his years. She had a sudden vision of the shopkeeper lying senseless on the floor after having been felled by an attack of apoplexy. Or perhaps he had taken a tumble on the stairs. Mayhap his heart had failed him.

A chill of dread flickered down her spine. Something was wrong. She could feel it in every fiber of her being now.

The logical place to search first was the shop's cavernous back room. It was three times the size of the space allotted to the display area, and it housed the vault where Tredlow kept his most valuable antiquities.

She hurried toward the long counter at the rear of the showroom, rounded the far end, and grasped the edge of the heavy dark drapery that concealed the entrance to the back room.

Pulling the curtain aside, she found herself gazing into the deep gloom of the unlit storage area. A single narrow window high in the wall provided barely enough illumination to reveal the jumble of statuary, artfully broken columns, and the occasional outline of a stone sarcophagus.

"Mr. Tredlow?"

There was no response. She glanced around for a candle, spotted one stuck upright on a small, metal stand on the counter, and hurriedly lit it.

Holding the taper in front of her, she went through the doorway into the back room. Icy fingers touched the sensitive spot between her shoulders, and she shivered.

A well of intense shadow just beyond the curtain marked the steep staircase that led to the rooms upstairs. She would investigate that portion of the premises after she had made certain that Tredlow was not down here.

A seemingly impenetrable wall of crates, boxes, and chunks of stone monuments confronted her. She forced herself to move deeper into the shadows, eerily aware of the stern, inhuman gazes of the ancient gods and goddesses that surrounded her. Several broken, heavily carved gravestones blocked her path. She stepped aside to avoid them and found herself face-to-face with the figure of a crouching, armless Aphrodite.

She went past a pair of large statues of Roman emperors, their aging, unhandsome faces incongruously affixed to the elegantly modeled, extremely well-endowed bodies of young Greek athletes, and found her way barred by a massive stone frieze. The flaring candlelight fell on a cluster of mounted warriors locked forever in a scene of bloodshed and savage death. The desperation and ferocity on the faces of the men were echoed in the twisted bodies and slashing hooves of the horses they rode.

She turned away from the frieze and wove a path among a maze of urns and vases decorated with scenes from orgies. Just beyond, a sleeping hermaphrodite reclined languidly. To her left a large centaur pranced in the shadows.

She caught a glimpse of an open door and drew a sharp breath. Tredlow had proudly pointed out his strong room when he had taken her on a tour of his establishment. It was a specially fortified stone chamber that had been part of the original medieval building that once stood on this site.

Tredlow had been thrilled to discover it when he moved into the space, she recalled. He had converted it into a large safe and used it to store his smaller artifacts and those that he considered most precious. Presumably, since it was fitted with a bolt on the inside, it had originally been designed as the entrance to a secret tunnel constructed for the purpose of allowing the homeowner to escape his enemies. But the underground pathway had been sealed shut with stone blocks a long time ago.

Tredlow had installed a heavy iron lock on the outside of the door. He always carried the key on his person.

The strong room should have been locked, she thought. Tredlow would never have left it open. Certainly not willingly.

She started toward the strong room. Her toe collided with one of the three bronze legs that supported an ornately carved Roman brazier.

Swallowing a gasp of pain, she glanced down. The light fell on several dark spots on the floor. The slight glistening of the patches indicated that they were still damp.

Water, she told herself. Or perhaps some tea or ale that Tredlow had spilled recently.

But she knew, even as she stooped to take a closer look, that it was not water or tea or ale that stained the floor. She was staring at half-dried drops of blood.

The small splashes made a ghastly trail that ended abruptly at the edge of a stone sarcophagus. The lid of the coffin was in place, sealing shut the interior and whatever lay inside.

She reached out uneasily to test the spots with the tip of her gloved finger. At that instant she heard the unmistakable squeak of the wooden timbers that formed the ceiling overhead.

Fear as sharp as a shock of electricity singed her senses. She straightened so swiftly and awkwardly that she lost her balance. Frantically, she reached out to brace herself on the closest object, a life-size male figure. The statue held a sword in one hand. In his other fist he grasped a repellent object.

Perseus holding the severed head of Medusa.

For a terrifying instant she was unable to move. It was as if she had been frozen in place by the Gorgon's gaze. The creature's unrelenting stare was truly mesmeric in its intensity. The snaky locks that writhed around the creature's stone face appeared horrifyingly realistic in the wavering light of the candle.

Wood creaked again in the terrible stillness. Footsteps. Directly overhead. Someone was up there, crossing the floor toward the staircase that descended to this level. Not Edmund Tredlow. She was very sure of that.

More squeaks.

The intruder was moving purposefully now. The footsteps came more rapidly. The person upstairs was aware of her presence. He had no doubt heard her call out to Tredlow.

Another sizzling shot of electricity freed her from the stare of the stone Medusa. She had to get out of this place quickly. The intruder would soon be on the stairs. It would take mere seconds for him to reach this room. She could not possibly get through the curtained opening that divided the shop in time to escape through the front door.

That left only the back entrance, the one Tredlow used to receive his stock of artifacts and antiquities. She whirled around, candle held on high, and searched the shadows. Through the forest of looming bronze and stone figures and the canyons of crates and boxes stacked to the ceiling, she caught glimpses of the back wall.

She went along a narrow alley formed by several impressive gravestones. Halfway to her objective, she glanced back over her shoulder and saw the glow of candlelight dancing on the ceiling near the staircase. Despair tore through her. The intruder was already in this room. If she could see his candle flame, he could almost certainly detect hers.

She would never be able to make it to the back entrance in time.

Her only hope was the strong room. If she could get inside and bolt the heavy door behind her, she would be safe.

She rushed toward the small chamber, not bothering to mask the sound of her movements. She halted on the threshold of the stone room, her courage nearly failing her when she realized just how small the space was.

She did not like close, confined places. In point of fact, she hated them.

The sound of booted footsteps coming relentlessly toward her was incentive enough to stiffen her resolve. She glanced back one last time. The figure of her pursuer was concealed by the stacks of statues and crates, but the glow of his candle was all too visible. It bounced and flared off the faces of monsters and gods as he came nearer.

She took a deep breath, stepped inside the cramped strong room, grasped the iron handle of the door, and pulled with all her strength.

It seemed to take forever for the heavy wooden panel to close. For a dreadful moment she thought that it must be stuck and that all was lost.

Then, with a ghostly whine, the door slammed closed. The candle flame jerked wildly one last time, glinting briefly on rows of ancient metal and glass objects, and then winked out of existence.

She was instantly plunged into a darkness as thick and heavy as that of a tomb. With trembling hands she managed to fumble the ancient iron bolt home by sense of touch. It seated itself with an ominous clang.

She shut her eyes and pressed her ear to the thick wooden door panel, straining to listen. The best she could hope for was that the intruder would soon realize that he could not get at her and would elect to leave the premises as quickly as possible. Then she could let herself out of this dreadful little chamber.

She heard the muffled scrape of iron on iron.

It took her a few seconds to understand the full horror of what had just occurred. With a terrible sinking sensation, she comprehended that the intruder had just turned Tredlow's key in the lock.

He was not even going to try to wrest her from her hiding place, she thought. Instead, he had effectively sealed her into this small, dark space that was not much larger than an ancient Roman sarcophagus.

THE TWO MEN CAME TOWARD HIM OUT OF THE FOG, LONG BLACK greatcoats unfastened so that the folds of the heavy garments swept the tops of their gleaming boots. Their faces were obscured by the brims of their hats and the rapidly deepening shadows.

"We've been waiting for you, Mr. Fitch," the older one said softly. He moved with a slight catch to his stride, but for some reason the evidence of past injury only made him appear all the more menacing.

The other man did not speak. He stayed a few steps back and to the side, watching events unfold, waiting for instructions. Fitch was reminded of a young leopard taking lessons from a more experienced hunter.

The older man was the one to fear.

The valet was stricken with a wave of deep dread. He stopped suddenly and glanced wildly around, seeking an escape route. None presented itself. The lights of the coffeehouse he had left a few minutes ago were at the end of the lane, too far away to afford any refuge. There were naught but empty, darkened doorways lining both sides of the pavement.

"What d'ya want with me?" He tried to sound firm and forceful. He'd had some experience in that line, he reminded himself. A good valet was expected to develop an air of grave authority.

Mayhap *grave* was not quite the appropriate word here.

"We wish to speak with you," the more dangerous man said.

Fitch swallowed. They were too well dressed to be footpads, he told himself. But somehow that deduction did nothing to reassure him. The expression in the older man's eyes made him want to take to his heels. But he knew that he would not get far. Even if he managed to outrun this hunter, he would never escape the young leopard-in-training.

"Who are you?" he asked. He heard the anxiousness in his own voice and cringed.

"My name is March. That is all you need to know. As I said, my companion and I wish to ask you a few questions."

"What sort of questions?" Fitch whispered.

"You were employed as valet to Lord Banks until quite recently. According to our information, you were turned off with no notice."

Real fear struck him then. *They knew what he had done.* The Creature had discovered the theft and sent these two after him.

Fitch's mouth went dry. He had been so certain that no one would ever miss the damned thing, but he had been found out. Visions of calamity sent shudder after shudder through him. He could be transported or even sent to the gallows for this.

"We would like to know if you helped yourself to a certain valuable on your way out the door," March said.

He was lost, Fitch thought. There was no hope for him. No point trying to deny his guilt. March was the sort who would hound a man to the ends of the earth. The promise was there in the bastard's eyes.

His only hope was to throw himself on the leopard's mercy and hope that he might be able to buy his way out of the disaster.

"She let me go without even paying me my quarterly wages. And she gave me no references." Fitch slumped against an iron railing. "After all my hard work. I did my best, I tell you, but it wasn't easy servicing the Creature."

"You refer to Mrs. Rushton?" March asked.

"Indeed. Twice a week it was, sometimes more often if she happened to be feeling particularly spirited. For nearly three long months." Fitch straightened a little at the memory of his heroic efforts. "The Creature was the most demanding employer I've ever had. And then she turns me off with no notice, no references, and *no bloody pension.* Where's the justice in that, I ask you?"

The younger man spoke for the first time. "Why did Mrs. Rushton let you go?"

"She started taking regular therapeutic treatments with a bloody mesmerist." Fitch grimaced. "Claimed he did more for her nerves than I did. She came back from an appointment one day and casually announced that she wouldn't be requiring my services anymore."

"So she let you go and you decided you were owed a little something by way of compensation, is that it?" March asked.

Fitch opened one hand, palm up, silently beseeching the hunter's understanding. "It wasn't fair, I tell you. That's why I took the damned snuffbox. Never thought it would be missed, to tell you the truth. Banks hasn't taken snuff for nearly a year and not bloody likely to ever use the stuff again."

March's eyes narrowed. "You took a snuffbox?"

"The thing had been sitting there at the back of a drawer in his lordship's dressing room for longer than anyone can remember. Who'd have thought she'd even know about it, let alone care if it went missing?"

March closed the distance between them. "You took a *snuffbox*?"

"Thought everyone in the household had forgotten about it long ago." Fitch gazed dolefully down at the pavement, wondering at the unkindness of fate. "Can't see how the Creature ever came to discover that it was gone."

"What of the bracelet?" March said.

"Bracelet?" Fitch raised his head, bewildered now. "What bracelet are you talking about?"

"The ancient gold bracelet that Banks kept in his locked safe," March said. "The one set with an unusual cameo."

"That old thing?" Fitch grunted in disgust. "Why the devil would I take it? One would have to deal with someone in the antiquities market in order to make a profit on a relic like that. I'd learned enough working for Banks all those years to know that I did not want to get involved with that lot. They're a strange breed, they are."

March exchanged an unreadable look with his companion and then turned back to Fitch. "What did you do with the snuffbox?"

Fitch shrugged morosely. "Sold it to a fence in Field Lane. I suppose he might be persuaded to tell you who bought it, but—"

March reached out and gripped the lapels of Fitch's coat. "Do you know what happened to the Medusa bracelet?"

"No." A glimmer of hope rose in Fitch. The hunter did not appear the least concerned with the snuffbox. All he cared about was the antiquity. "The bloody thing's gone missing, then, has it?"

"Yes." March did not release him. "I and my friend here are looking for it."

Fitch cleared his throat. "Can I assume that if I tell you what little I know about the matter, you'll have no further interest in me?"

"That would be a reasonable assumption on your part, yes."

"I don't know where it is, but I'll tell you this much. I very much doubt that anyone in the household stole it, for the same reasons that I did not bother with it."

"Too difficult to sell?"

"Precisely. None of the staff would have any notion of how to make a profit on such a relic."

"Do you have any idea of who might have taken it?"

"No—"

March gave him a slight shake.

"But I'll tell you this much," Fitch said quickly. "The day the Creature moved into the mansion, she took charge of all the keys, including the one to his lordship's safe. Unless an intruder broke into the house, made his way unseen upstairs to Banks's bedchamber, found the dressing room, located the hidden safe, picked the lock, and then managed to sneak out undetected, all of which seems a bit unlikely, I'd say there's only one person in the whole world who might have helped herself to the artifact."

"Mrs. Rushton? Why would she steal a valuable that she was due to inherit shortly? Indeed, one that she could have taken at any time, unquestioned, had she wished to do so?"

"I have no clue, Mr. March. But I'll give you some advice. Don't underestimate the Creature or be so foolish as to presume that her actions conform to your logic."

The hunter held him in his clutches for a moment longer, as if thinking over the matter of what to do with his captive. Fitch realized he was holding his breath.

Then quite suddenly March released him. Fitch lost his balance, stumbled back, and came up hard against the railing.

March inclined his head with mocking formality. "My companion and I are obliged to you for your assistance, sir."

He turned and walked away into the fog without a backward glance. The young leopard gave Fitch an icy smile and then fell into step beside his mentor.

Fitch held himself very still until the pair disappeared into the swirling mist. When he was certain that he was once again alone in the street, he risked a deep breath.

He had escaped the hunter's teeth by the merest shred of good fortune. He did not envy March's real quarry.

Twenty-one

❧

SHE WOULD NOT GIVE IN TO THE MADNESS THAT NIBBLED AT THE edge of her sanity. She fought it with all of her will, calling on every scrap of mesmeric training that her parents had bequeathed to her in order to do battle with the darkness that threatened to overwhelm her senses.

She wondered if this was the true meaning of female hysteria.

Time passed. She had no way to measure it. Perhaps it was just as well. Counting the seconds, the minutes, and the hours would only make it so much worse.

She sat on the cold stone floor of the coffinlike chamber, clutching the silver pendant in both hands and focusing her concentration. With painstaking effort she built a fragile fortress of calm in the deepest reaches of her mind, a place of peace and tranquillity. When it was prepared, she stepped inside, pulling her besieged nerves in with her.

And then she shut the metaphysical door against the weight of the crushing, breath-stealing night that surrounded her.

She clung to the single certainty that was the foundation upon which she had constructed her inner refuge. That one sure fact was the knowledge that sooner or later Tobias would come to free her.

"Bloody hell, where did she go?" Tobias strode down the hallway to Lavinia's cozy study, threw open the door, and swept the room with a raking glance. "She has no business disappearing like this."

Anthony came to a halt beside him. "Perhaps she is merely late returning from some shopping."

Tobias looked at Mrs. Chilton, who hovered in the hallway. "Did Mrs. Lake go shopping this afternoon?"

"I don't know, sir." Mrs. Chilton sighed. "All I can tell ye is that when I got back from the fishmonger's, she was gone."

Tobias went to the desk and surveyed the cluttered surface. "From now on there are going to be some new rules around here. When we are in the middle of a case, Mrs. Lake will not go anywhere without first informing someone of her destination and the precise time she expects to return home."

"Oh, dear." Mrs. Chilton watched unhappily as Tobias methodically sifted through the items and papers scattered atop the desk. "I really don't think Mrs. Lake will take well to the notion of more rules, if you'll pardon me saying so, sir. She's already a trifle put out by all the instructions and orders that seem to be floating about these days."

"*A trifle put out* is nothing compared to my own mood at the moment." Tobias glanced at the notes on one of the sheets of foolscap. "What's this? *Complete discretion is assured for those clients concerned with matters of privacy and secrecy.*"

"I believe Mrs. Lake is still working on the wording of the notice she intends to put into the newspapers," Mrs. Chilton said.

"She plans to advertise her services in the newspapers?" Anthony's expression lit with interest. "I say, that is an excellent notion. Should have thought of it ourselves, Tobias. A very modern approach to the business, eh?"

"I told her to abandon the entire idea. She is too stubborn to listen to sound advice." With a flick of his hand, Tobias sent the sheet of paper sailing into the small wooden trash bin behind the desk. "I warned her of the sort of clients she would attract with that method. She would do better to—" He broke off at the sight of a wadded-up bit of paper in the basket. "Hmm."

He reached down, scooped up the crumpled note, and smoothed it out carefully on top of the desk.

"What is it?" Anthony asked, moving toward the desk.

"What we in the profession like to call a clue," Tobias muttered.

Mrs. Chilton was suitably impressed. "Ye know where Mrs. Lake went this afternoon?"

"I suspect that she went out in response to this note from Edmund Tredlow. Obviously she lacked the common courtesy to leave a message telling anyone where she was going." He crumpled the note in his hand. She was all right. Nothing was wrong. Just his damned nerves playing up. "Of all the thoughtless, graceless, careless things to do. I shall have a word with her about such behavior."

Mrs. Chilton gave him an uneasy look. "Sir, I feel I ought to point out that Mrs. Lake has been in the habit of coming and going as she pleases for some time now. Indeed, she is the mistress around here and she makes her own rules for this household. I don't recommend that ye continue to issue commands and orders about all manner of things the way ye've been doing of late."

"I disagree, Mrs. Chilton." He went toward the door. "Strict new rules are precisely what is needed around here. It is high time that someone took charge of this household."

Mrs. Chilton fell back out of his path. "Where are ye going, sir?"

"To find Mrs. Lake and inform her of the new rules."

BUT WHEN HE OPENED THE DOOR OF TREDLOW'S SHOP A SHORT time later, he put aside all thoughts of the stern lecture he intended to deliver. The faint dread that had been chewing up his innards for the past hour or so had not been merely an attack of weak nerves, after all.

"Lavinia." He hoisted the small lantern he had brought with him and watched the light flare on the stone and bronze statuary. "Damn it, where the devil are you?"

There was no response from the deep shadows.

Anthony stopped in the middle of the crowded showroom and looked around with a baffled frown. "Tredlow must have closed for the night. Surprised he forgot to lock his door, though. Cannot imagine a shopkeeper overlooking such a simple precaution."

"Neither can I," Tobias said grimly.

"Perhaps she left before we arrived," Anthony said. "We may have gone straight past her without knowing it on our way here. She is no doubt home having a cup of tea as we speak."

"No."

Tobias did not know how he could be so certain of that, but he was very sure of it. The sense of wrongness here at Tredlow's was palpable now.

He went behind the counter, intending to take the stairs to the rooms overhead. But he paused when he noticed the heavy curtain that divided the front and rear portions of the shop.

He shoved aside the thick drapery and held the lantern aloft to illuminate a maze of crates, boxes, chests, and statuary.

"Lavinia."

There was a terrible hush. And then a muffled pounding sounded from somewhere at the back of the cluttered room. The noise echoed in the chamber in such a manner that it was difficult to tell where it was coming from.

"Hell's teeth." Tobias started forward, seeking a path through the looming antiquities. "She's in here somewhere. There are some candles on that table. Take one and search the far side of the room. I'll take this side."

Anthony scooped up a taper, lit it, and forged a path through the nearest aisle of crates.

The heavy thuds reverberated again through the storage room.

"I'm here, Lavinia." Tobias wove a trail through a herd of centaurs. "Keep pounding, damn it."

He went past a hideous statue of Perseus holding the severed head of Medusa and saw an ancient iron-and-oak door. Some sort of small storeroom, he thought.

Another flood of pounding thudded through the heavy wooden panels.

"I've found her," he called to Anthony.

He set the lantern down amid a cluster of broken pots on a cracked stone altar and examined the iron lock on the door.

"*Let me out of here,*" Lavinia shouted through the wood.

"Got any notion of what happened to the key?" he called back.

"*No.*"

Anthony crashed through a row of vases and stopped in front of the door. "Locked?"

"Of course." Tobias reached into the pocket of his greatcoat and took out the selection of picks he always carried whenever he was pursuing a case. "She wouldn't be trapped inside if it were unlocked, would she?"

Anthony raised his brows at the brusque words, but he kept his own tone even, almost mild. "Wonder how she came to be inside in the first place?"

"An excellent question." Tobias went to work with one of the picks. The iron lock was imposing in size, but it was old-fashioned and uncomplicated in design. He prodded the tumblers very gently. "One I intend to ask at the earliest opportunity."

The lock gave a moment later. The heavy door opened with a rusty groan that could have come from the depths of a tomb.

"*Tobias.*"

Lavinia exploded out of the darkness. He scooped her up into his arms and cradled her close and tight against his chest. She pressed her face into the fabric of his greatcoat. He felt her shudder in his arms.

"Are you all right? Lavinia, answer me. Are you all right?"

"Yes." The word was muffled against his coat. "I knew you'd come. I knew it."

Anthony gazed into the small chamber with a grim expression. "It must have been quite dreadful for you in there, Mrs. Lake."

Lavinia said nothing. Tobias felt shiver after shiver sweep through her. He stroked the length of her spine with his palm and looked past her into the tiny room. It reminded him of an upright coffin. Anger knifed through him.

"What happened?" he asked. "Who imprisoned you in that place?"

"Someone was here when I arrived. Searching the rooms upstairs. I hid in there when he came down the steps. He saw me. Locked the door." She suddenly stiffened, gasped, and pushed herself slightly away from him. "Dear God, Mr. Tredlow."

"What about him?"

Clutching his shoulders, she turned partway around in his arms, searching the gloom with anxious eyes. "I found bloodstains on the floor over there. I think the intruder murdered him and hid the body in one of the sarcophagi. Poor Mr. Tredlow. And it is all my fault, Tobias. I should never have asked him to assist in the investigation. I cannot bear to contemplate—"

"Hush." He eased her slowly to her feet. "Let us see precisely what we are dealing with here before we concern ourselves with responsibility and recriminations." He picked up the lantern. "Show me the bloodstains."

She walked to the figure of Perseus holding the Medusa head and pointed toward the floor. "There. See? They lead straight to that coffin."

Tobias assessed the carved stone sarcophagus. "Fortunately, it is not one of the more ornate types decorated with a heavy stone carving. We should have no trouble with the lid. Clearly, whoever stuck Tredlow inside managed to move it easily enough."

"I'll help you," Anthony said.

Together they leaned into the task. The heavy stone shifted readily enough under their combined weight. One man could, indeed, have managed the business, assuming that the lid had originally been sitting crosswise atop the box, Tobias thought.

Stone scraped on stone, a grinding protest that set his teeth on edge. Out of the corner of his eye he saw Lavinia flinch at the sound. But she did not retreat from whatever was about to be revealed. He had not expected that she would. In the entire time he had known her, he had never seen her back away from anything, no matter how unpleasant. Some would say that she lacked the sort of delicate sensibilities Society deemed appropriate to a lady. But he knew the truth. She was a lot like him when it came to dealing with problems and challenges. She faced them head-on.

The stone lid shrieked hollowly again and finally moved far enough across the top of the box to reveal a section of the dark interior.

The body of a man loomed in the opening. He lay facedown, crumpled in a horrifyingly careless manner. It looked as though someone had simply dumped him into the sarcophagus.

The lantern light flared on scraggly gray hair matted with blood. There was more blood on Tredlow's coat. A small pool of the stuff had formed on the bottom of the coffin.

Tobias reached into the box to search for a pulse.

"Poor Mr. Tredlow." Lavinia stepped closer. "Dear heaven. It is just as I feared. The intruder murdered him. And all because I asked him to keep me informed."

Anthony watched Tobias feel for signs of life. He swallowed heavily. "Must have struck him on the back of his head and stuck him in here to hide the body."

"The killer obviously wanted to conceal the crime, and he almost succeeded," Lavinia whispered. "It could have been weeks or even months before the body was found. Indeed, if I hadn't received Mr. Tredlow's message this afternoon, I would never have thought to look for him back here in this storeroom. If only I had arrived earlier, I might have—"

"Enough." Tobias took his fingers off the victim's throat. "For better or worse, you did receive the message." He gripped the edge of the sarcophagus lid again and shoved hard to angle it farther out of the way. "From Tredlow's point of view, it is just as well that you got here when you did."

"Why do you say that?" Anthony asked.

"Because he is still alive."

Twenty-two

TOBIAS STRODE INTO THE PARLOR LATER THAT EVENING, BRINGING with him the essence of the fog and the night. He came to a halt at the foot of the sofa and surveyed Lavinia with an assessing expression.

She lay propped against a stack of fringed pillows, covered from head to toe by the pile of warm blankets that Emeline had arranged. The large pot of very hot, very strong tea that Mrs. Chilton had brewed sat on the table beside her.

She gave Tobias a wan smile.

He turned directly to Emeline.

"How is she?" he asked.

Emeline looked up from the cup of tea she had just poured. "Somewhat better, I think. Her nerves are still quite overwrought, of course. Lavinia has great difficulty with small, enclosed spaces, you know. They make her very anxious. And she was in that dreadful little room for a long while."

"Yes, I know." Tobias shifted his attention back to Lavinia. "But she will soon return to normal, will she not?"

"Oh, yes," Emeline assured him. "What she needs now is peace and rest. She is certainly in no condition to withstand any more sharp shocks at the moment."

"How is Mr. Tredlow?" Lavinia asked softly.

"Whitby is looking after him," Tobias said. "He'll stay with him tonight. Says that Tredlow will no doubt recover, but he warned me that blows to the head are unpredictable. Tredlow may not remember anything of what occurred in the moments prior to his encounter with the intruder."

"I see." Lavinia closed her eyes. "In other words, we may learn nothing useful from him when we do manage to interview him."

"We can only hope that he will at least recall why he sent the message to you," Tobias said.

"Yes." She lifted her lashes very slowly. "Well, we must worry about that tomorrow. There is nothing more we can do tonight. I cannot thank you enough for rescuing me from that horrid chamber."

"Are you certain that you're all right, Lavinia?" he asked.

"Yes." She closed her eyes again and reclined weakly against the stack of pillows. "But I must admit I am more weary and shaken than I had first realized. Perhaps I shall ask Mrs. Chilton to prepare a vinaigrette."

"I shall call at breakfast to see how you are getting along," Tobias said.

She nodded without opening her eyes.

He hesitated a moment longer at the foot of the sofa. She sensed him looming there and knew that he was reluctant to take his leave.

"See to it that she gets a good night's sleep," he said to Emeline.

"I will," Emeline promised.

"Very well." He still lingered at the foot of the sofa. "I will bid you both good night."

"Good night, sir," Emeline said.

"Good night," Lavinia whispered, eyes still closed.

She heard him turn and walk away toward the parlor door. He stepped out into the hall and spoke to Mrs. Chilton in low, muffled tones. The front door opened and closed.

Lavinia breathed a sigh of relief. She snapped open her eyes, shoved aside the heavy blankets, sat up, and swung her feet to the floor.

"Really, I had begun to fear that he would never leave," she said. "Where's that sherry I was drinking before he arrived?"

"I've got it right here."

Emeline went to the mantel and raised the top of the decorative urn that stood on the far end. She reached inside and removed the glass of sherry Lavinia had ordered her to conceal moments ago when she had spotted Tobias coming up the steps.

"Thank you." Lavinia took the glass and swallowed a goodly portion of the contents. She waited for the warmth of the spirits to hit her and then she exhaled deeply. "I think I handled that rather well, don't you?"

"Your acting was nothing short of professional," Emeline said.

"Yes, I thought so. I must say, I am quite grateful to Mr. March. He is excellent in a crisis, and I was exceedingly happy to see him earlier when he opened the door of that dreadful little chamber."

Emeline shuddered. "I do not doubt that."

"Unfortunately he cannot resist the urge to deliver exceedingly tiresome lectures after the dramatic moment has passed." Lavinia made a face. "I knew when I saw him coming up the steps that he had come back to see if I was in any condition to listen to one."

"I suspect you are right. Luckily you managed to appear far too delicate to engage in one of your more spirited discussions with him."

"I wouldn't be the least surprised to discover that he has drawn up a new list of rules for me."

"How did you guess, madam?" Tobias asked from the parlor doorway.

"*Tobias.*" She started, very nearly spilling the remaining sherry, and turned quickly about on the sofa.

He lounged in the opening, arms crossed, shoulder propped against the wooden jamb, and regarded her with cool consideration.

"As it happens, I have taken the trouble to make up just such a list," he said. "I think you will find it very handy. I am delighted to see that you have made such a swift recovery. No need to wait until morning after all. We can go over the new rules this very evening."

"Bloody hell." She consoled herself with the last of the sherry.

Emeline went briskly toward the door. "If you will both excuse me,

I believe I shall retire for the evening. I find I am really quite exhausted from all the excitement."

"I understand," Tobias said. "Delicate sensibilities do appear to run in your family." He straightened, moved aside, and inclined his head gracefully as she swept past him into the hall. "Good night again, Miss Emeline."

"Good night, Mr. March."

Lavinia watched warily as Tobias closed the door very deliberately behind Emeline.

"What made you come back?" she asked.

"I believe it was the line about asking Mrs. Chilton to prepare a vinaigrette."

"I thought it was a nice touch."

"On the contrary," he said. "It was a bit much."

HE WAS STILL SIMMERING THE NEXT MORNING WHEN HE AND Lavinia walked into Edmund Tredlow's tiny upstairs parlor. But he was so relieved to see that his partner appeared none the worse for her ordeal that he decided to forgo further lectures.

He consoled himself with the thought that he'd succeeded in extracting the one vital concession he wanted most from her last night: She had reluctantly promised to keep her household informed of her whereabouts when she went out. That would do for now, he thought. With Lavinia, one had to be content with small victories.

Whitby looked up from the pot of porridge he was preparing. Even garbed in an apron with a dish towel draped over one shoulder, he somehow managed to look quite dapper, Tobias thought with just a touch of envy.

Whitby gave Lavinia a bow that would have made any dandy proud.

"Good morning, madam." He straightened and nodded at Tobias. "Sir."

"Whitby," Tobias said. "How is your patient today?"

"I think you will find him well on the road to recovery, although he will no doubt suffer the headache for a while." Whitby set aside the pot, wiped his hands on a drying cloth, and led the way toward the bedchamber. "But I warn you, he cannot recall much of what occurred. I fear that is only to be expected after such a blow to the head."

They followed him into the invalid's room and found Tredlow, dressed in an aging, badly yellowed nightshirt, propped up in bed. A large white bandage covered a good portion of his head. He put down the cup of chocolate he had been drinking and peered at Lavinia through his spectacles.

"I say, Mrs. Lake, are you all right? Whitby told me about your nasty experience at the hands of the intruder."

"You suffered far worse than I did." She went to the side of the bed. "How is your head?"

"Sore, but I am assured I shall recover." Tredlow looked at Tobias. "Very kind of you to lend me your man, Whitby, for the night, sir."

"You're welcome," Tobias said from the doorway. "He tells me that you cannot remember much about what happened, however. I suppose that means you cannot provide a description of the intruder?"

"I don't believe I ever even saw him," Tredlow said. "I do recall that after sending word to Mrs. Lake, I closed my shop and went out to get a bite to eat. I expected to return before she arrived, you see. I may have left the door unlocked."

"The intruder must have thought you had left for the evening," Tobias said. "He entered the shop while you were gone and was still there when you returned a short time later."

"I think I heard some noise in the back room," Tredlow said. "I must have gone to investigate. The next thing I knew, I was waking up here in my bed with you and Whitby standing over me."

Lavinia's mouth tightened. "Just as well you were unconscious while you were in that sarcophagus. I cannot imagine anything worse than waking up inside a coffin."

"Not a pleasant notion," Tredlow agreed somberly.

"Do you remember why you sent me a message saying that you wished to speak with me?" Lavinia asked.

Tredlow grimaced. "I intended to inform you that I had heard that two of my competitors had their shops broken into during the past two days. Rumor has it that someone is searching for the Blue Medusa."

Lavinia exchanged a look with Tobias and then turned back to Tredlow. "Had anyone seen or heard anything that might help us identify the intruder?"

"Not that I've heard," Tredlow said.

Twenty-three

❧

THE MESMERIST OPENED THE DOOR HIMSELF. HE DID NOT LOOK pleased to see Tobias on the step.

"March. This is a surprise. What are you doing here?" Hudson searched his face warily. "Have you some news about the killer?"

"I want to talk to you." Tobias moved forward, giving Hudson no choice but to fall back into the hall. "Do you mind if I come in?"

Hudson scowled. "You're already inside, are you not? Come with me."

He closed the door and turned to lead the way down a short corridor.

Tobias followed him toward a room at the end of the hall. He surveyed the interior of the house as he moved through it. The door of the parlor stood open. He noticed that it was dark inside. All of the drapes were pulled closed. There appeared to be very little furniture. He glimpsed only a chair and a single table. The Hudsons had not bothered to completely furnish their rented house. Either Celeste had been killed before she could choose fabrics and purchase furnishings or else the Hudsons had never intended to stay here for long.

Hudson ushered Tobias into a spare study. "Sit, if it pleases you. I'd offer you tea, but my housekeeper has left for the day."

Tobias ignored the invitation. He went to stand at the window instead, his back to the cloudy skies. He did a quick inventory of the room. There were only a handful of books on the shelves, one of which appeared to be very old. The leather binding was cracked and worn. No pictures or drawings adorned the walls. There were no personal effects on the desk.

"Can I assume that you planned a rather short stay in Town?" he asked.

If Hudson was startled by the question, he gave no indication. He went to stand behind his desk. By chance or by choice, he had chosen the one place in the room that the light from the window did not reach. He looked at Tobias from a pool of shadows, eyes deep wells of night.

"You refer to the lack of furniture in the house." With a casual movement of his hand he removed his watch from his pocket. The gold fobs danced lightly. "The house is rented. Celeste and I never got a chance to unpack properly, let alone select sofas and tables and fabrics. And then she was murdered and naturally I lost all interest in such things."

"Naturally."

"May I ask what this is about, March?" Hudson's voice took on a rich, sonorous quality. The gold watch seals swayed gently. "Surely you have not come here to discuss interior decoration."

"You are quite correct. I came here to talk about Gunning and Northampton."

The fobs jangled a little, but Hudson's shadowed features gave no hint of any reaction other than polite confusion. His eyes never wavered.

"What about them?" he asked.

The watch fobs went back to their steady, rhythmic arcs.

"They were clients of yours in Bath, I believe."

"Yes. Gunning visited me for a time because he experienced difficulty sleeping. Northampton's problem centered on his inability to sustain an erection." Howard's voice grew more resonant. The watch fobs continued to swing. "Both are common complaints among men of their years. I fail to see how either of those two cases affects this situation."

The motion of the watch fobs was becoming annoying, Tobias thought.

"Both men were victims of a jewel thief sometime after they came to you for treatments," he said.

"I don't understand. Surely you are not implying that my Celeste had anything to do with their losses? How dare you, sir?" Howard's voice did not tighten with outrage as he came to the defense of his wife's reputation. If anything, it only reverberated more strongly and deeply. "I told you, she was a beautiful, impulsive woman, but she was no thief, sir."

"Perhaps. Perhaps not. It doesn't matter now, does it?"

"A beautiful, impulsive woman," Howard repeated gently. The gleaming fobs swung like pendulums. "Not a thief. Eyes as bright as gold. As golden in the light as these little balls dangling from my watch. Look at the balls, March. Golden and bright and lovely in the light. It is very easy to look at them. Very hard to look away."

"Save your energy, Hudson." He smiled thinly. "I am in no mood to be put into a trance."

"I don't know what you're talking about."

"Celeste's criminal talents do not interest me. What does interest me, Hudson, is the fact that it is quite probable that you are also a thief."

"*Me.*" Howard's voice abruptly hardened. The watch fobs ceased swinging. "How dare you accuse me of having committed theft?"

"I cannot prove it, of course."

"You certainly cannot."

"But here is what I think happened." Tobias clasped his hands behind his back and started to prowl the room. "You worked alone for years. However, I suspect you had one or two close brushes with the law at some point and decided it might be wise to disappear for a while. So you sailed to America. You did rather well for yourself there and remained for some time. But eventually you chose to come back to England. You returned and settled in Bath."

"This is utter conjecture on your part."

"Indeed. Utter conjecture is something that I do very well. As I was saying, you set up in business in Bath. And there you met Celeste, a lady whose principles mirrored your own."

"What is that supposed to mean?"

"Merely that neither of you had any difficulty with the notion of pursuing a life of crime."

"I could call you out for that, sir."

"You could, but you won't," Tobias said. He halted at the far end of the room and looked at Howard. "You know very well that I am likely the better shot, and in any event, the gossip would be bad for your business."

"How dare you."

"As I was saying, you and Celeste formed a team. You selected the victims, no doubt favoring wealthy, aging gentlemen well into their dotage, who would be especially vulnerable to Celeste's charms. She used her wiles to convince them to consult you for therapy. Once you had them in your treatment room, you employed your mesmeric skills to manipulate them into giving you some valuable from their personal collections. Afterward they remembered nothing of the experience, of course, thanks to the instructions you gave them while they were entranced."

Howard composed himself. He stood, unmoving, behind his desk and watched Tobias with a stare that would have done credit to Medusa.

"You can prove none of this," he said.

"What went wrong this time?"

"You must be mad, sir. Perhaps you should seek professional help."

"This business with the artifact was different from the start," Tobias said. "The decision to steal Banks's relic was a change of pace for you. At first glance, it makes no sense. Your specialty is valuable jewelry, not antiquities. Artifacts such as the Medusa bracelet have a limited market. It certainly wouldn't be as easy to get rid of as a pair of diamond earrings or a pearl-and-emerald necklace."

Howard said nothing. He just stood there in the shadows, an angry snake watching for an opening.

Tobias casually picked up the aged, leather-bound book he had noticed earlier.

"I can think of only two possible reasons why you would have elected to steal the Medusa bracelet," he continued. "The first is that you knew for certain that you could sell it to a particular collector; someone whom you had good reason to believe would pay well for it."

"You are lost in your own fantasies, March."

Tobias opened the cracked leather binding of the book he had taken down from the shelf and read the title page.

Discourse on Certain Secret Rituals and Practices of the Ancients in British-Roman Times

"There is a second possibility." He closed the book and put it back on the shelf. "And, while I admit it lacks the merit of sound logic, in some ways it strikes me as even more likely than the notion of a commissioned theft."

Hudson's mouth twisted in disdain. "What is the second possibility?"

"That you are the one who has gone mad," Tobias said softly. "The second possibility is that you actually put some credence in the legend of the Medusa bracelet. Is that why you set out to steal the damned thing? Because you convinced yourself that the Medusa head cameo could augment your own mesmeric powers?"

Hudson did not move so much as an eyelash.

"I have no notion of what you are talking about."

Tobias motioned in the direction of the ancient book. "You stumbled across some mention of the Blue Medusa and its supposed powers, perhaps in that very volume. In any event, you became obsessed with the damned thing. You told Celeste that it would be your next acquisition, and the two of you removed to London and concocted a plan to obtain it."

"You are a fool, March."

"But Celeste was a woman of the world who long ago learned to look after her own interests. She no doubt sensed that this theft you now planned held only risk and no profit. Perhaps she feared that you were slipping into madness."

"Leave Celeste out of this."

"Unfortunately, I cannot do that. What really happened between the two of you the night she died, Hudson? At first I assumed that you killed her because she betrayed you with another man. Then I began to wonder if the murder was simply the result of a falling-out among thieves. But now I'm starting to think that you murdered her because she believed you were no longer quite sane and wanted to end the partnership."

Howard gripped the back of his desk chair so fiercely that his knuckles whitened. "Damn your eyes, March, *I did not murder Celeste.*"

Tobias shrugged. "I will admit that there are still a number of unanswered questions. I haven't yet deduced what happened to the bracelet, for instance. Obviously you don't know where it is either. That is the real reason you hired Lavinia, isn't it? Not to find the killer. You wanted her to find the damned bracelet."

"You amaze me, sir." Howard's laugh was harsh, completely lacking in its former mellifluous tones. "I thought you had all the answers."

"Only some of them at the moment." Tobias started toward the door. "But rest assured, I will soon have the rest."

"Wait, damn you. Is Lavinia aware of your wild speculations?"

"Not all of them." Tobias opened the door. "Not yet."

"You would do well not to tell her your crazed notions. She will never believe you. She has known me far longer than she has known you, March. I am an old friend of the family. If you force her to choose between us, she will side with me. You may depend upon it."

"Speaking of Lavinia," Tobias said, "this is probably as convenient an opportunity as any to give you some advice."

"I don't want any of your damned advice."

"Then consider this a warning, instead. Do not think for one moment that I will allow you to use Lavinia to replace Celeste."

"Do you believe that she is so enamored of you that she would never cast you aside in favor of me?"

"No," Tobias said. "But I do know this much: If you were to succeed in taking Lavinia away, you may be certain that you would not live long enough to savor your victory."

He walked out the door and closed it very gently and deliberately.

Twenty-four

He did not pause to consider his destination. There was only one place he wanted to be at that moment. He hailed a passing hackney and ordered the coachman to take him to the little house in Claremont Lane.

His leg gave a few protesting twinges when he alighted, but he ignored them and went up the steps to bang the brass knocker.

There was no response.

He was not in the best of moods, and the silence did nothing to enhance his temper. On his way out after breakfast he had informed Mrs. Chilton that he would return this afternoon around three.

It occurred to him that lately he had begun to think of Lavinia's little house as his home away from home. Rather like his club. He had even taken to issuing instructions to Mrs. Chilton just as he did to Whitby.

He knew that he had no right to be annoyed when those instructions were not carried out. Nevertheless, Mrs. Chilton had implied that Lavinia would be home this afternoon. Yet no one came to answer the door.

He went back down the steps into the street and studied the upstairs windows. The drapes were pulled shut. In his experience, Lavinia kept all of the household curtains open during the day. She liked the light.

A chill of unease drifted through him. It did not seem right that the house should be entirely empty at this hour. Perhaps some last-minute shopping had taken Emeline and Lavinia out, but where was Mrs. Chilton?

This was more than a little odd. He spent so much time in this house these days that he knew Mrs. Chilton's schedule as well as he knew Whitby's. This was not the day she took the afternoon off to see her sister.

The sense of unease darkened in him. He tried the front doorknob, expecting to find it locked.

It twisted easily in his hand.

Memories of how the door at Tredlow's shop had opened just as smoothly yesterday chilled him.

Quietly, he let himself into the front hall and closed the door. He stood for a moment, testing the quality of the silence. It told him nothing.

He reached down into his boot and found the small knife he kept in the hidden sheath. Gripping it in his right hand, he went to the door of the parlor. The room was empty.

He continued down the hall to Lavinia's study.

It, too, was empty.

So was the kitchen.

He suppressed the fear that threatened to claw at his insides and started up the stairs, careful to make no sound on the treads.

At the top of the staircase he paused. This was the first time he had ever been up here, he realized. He did not know his way around on this floor.

He studied the doors that opened off the hallway and recalled that Lavinia had once mentioned that her bedchamber had windows that faced the street.

He approached it cautiously, glancing into the other rooms he passed along the way. There was no sign of a disturbance, he noted with some relief, nothing to indicate that an intruder had been here.

A soft rustling came from the bedchamber he had decided belonged to Lavinia. He moved to the wall and flattened himself against it, listening intently.

The slight noise came again. Someone was moving about in that chamber.

Stealthily, he made his way to the edge of the door and looked into the room at an angle. A handsome screen covered in panels decorated with scenes of Roman gardens stood in his line of sight. It concealed whoever was on the other side, but he could hear the soft crackle of a fire on the hearth and a soft splash.

An elegantly arched bare foot appeared beneath the bottom edge of one of the screen panels. It settled on a towel that had been spread on the floor. There was another little splash and a second foot materialized.

The cold tension inside him evaporated. It was immediately replaced by another kind of awareness. He bent slightly to sheath the knife, straightened, and went through the partially open door.

"I would be delighted to assist you with your bath, madam," he said.

There was a soft gasp from the other side of the screen.

"Tobias?" Lavinia peeked around the edge of one of the panels, a thick towel clutched to her breasts. Her eyes widened at the sight of him standing in her bedchamber. "Good heavens. What are you doing here?"

He looked at her and felt his blood heat. Her hair was pinned up into a knot on top of her head. Wispy tendrils trailed down the length of her bare neck. Her face was flushed and rosy from the combination of the warm water and the flames of the fire. The voluminous folds of the towel she grasped draped gracefully to her small ankles.

"I'm certain that there is something poetic and romantical that I ought to say at this moment," he muttered. "But I'm damned if I know what it is."

He left the doorway and crossed the room to where she stood at the edge of the screen. She smiled at him, her eyes as brilliant as the flames on the hearth.

"I'm wet," she warned him when he reached for her.

"That is extremely fortunate for both of us." He picked her up and started toward the bed. "Because I am aching to sink myself into you."

Her husky laugh was the most alluring music he had ever heard.

He put her down on the bed and took hold of the towel that veiled her body. Gently, he tugged it aside and tossed it onto the floor. He had thought himself already fully aroused, but the heavy excitement he was feeling became almost painful at the sight of her gently curved breasts and the triangle of tight curls at the apex of her thighs.

He reached down and curved his hand around her hip. She shivered at his touch and his mouth went dry. This was, he realized, the first time he had ever experienced the luxury of seeing her entirely nude. The very nature of their affair limited such opportunities. All of their previous trysts had been hurried encounters conducted in locales that did not allow for complete disrobing.

He knew from the way she watched him strip off his shirt, trousers, and boots that she was thinking the same thing.

"Do you realize," he whispered thickly when he came down on top of her, "that this is the first time we have ever shared a bed together?"

"That thought did occur to me, yes."

"I trust you will not find the experience too dull or boring. I know how fond you are of exotic locales and a touch of novelty when it comes to this sort of thing."

She smiled up at him and put her arms around his neck. "I must admit that there are certain advantages to having a bed. It is considerably more comfortable than a stone bench or a coach seat or the top of my desk."

"Comfort is not my primary concern when I am with you," he whispered against her throat. "But there is something to be said for it."

He raised his head, found her mouth, and kissed her deeply. She returned the embrace with a sweet hunger that ravished his senses. The knowledge that she wanted him as badly as he wanted her was the most intoxicating drug imaginable. Need pounded through him, a driving urgency that was far more intense than mere passion. The hot brew flooded his veins and tightened every muscle.

He would never let her go, he vowed silently, not to Hudson or any other man.

He stroked the length of her body from bare breast to bare thigh. Her skin was soft, sleek, and wonderfully resilient to the touch. She arched beneath him. He plunged his fingers into her warmth.

"You are, indeed, very wet," he said into her mouth. "Perfect."

She moaned and twisted against him, closing her thighs around him. He could feel the fullness of the small button at the top of her cleft. He stroked lightly until she sank her nails into him.

He could wait no longer.

He eased slowly, deliberately into her snug, warm passage and groaned aloud at the raw satisfaction.

He felt the edge of her teeth on the skin of his shoulder. She clung to him so tightly that he thought they surely must be bound together for all time.

ANTHONY FELT THE TINY JOLT OF ELECTRICITY ACROSS THE BACK of his neck again. No doubt about it, the flower-seller was following him. He caught sight of the now-familiar shape of the massive gray bonnet at the edge of his vision. It disappeared quickly behind a farmer's cart, but he was sure it was the same flower-seller he had spotted a few minutes ago in the square.

A tingle of anticipation, a heightening of all his senses arced through him. He suddenly felt more alert. Objects, buildings, and the people around him appeared to be more sharply focused.

He wondered if this odd excitement was one of the lures that drew Tobias to the business of conducting private inquiries. The sensations were certainly vastly more stimulating than those that came with placing a wager or watching a boxing match, he thought.

There was no time to contemplate the philosophy of his new profession. The goal now was to identify the person who was spying on him.

"Thank you for your assistance, miss." He handed the streetwalker a few coins. She was the youngest woman he had talked to today. He guessed her age to be fifteen or sixteen at the most. "Something for your trouble."

"No trouble at all, sir." She giggled and made the money disappear into the front of her shabby gown. "Glad to help."

Her laughter made him uneasy. For a moment or two she sounded like an innocent young chit who ought to be in the schoolroom, looking forward to being launched into Society, not a hardened prostitute with no hope of a future. He wondered what sad fate had brought her here to this corner.

He touched the brim of his hat politely in farewell. The girl broke into another gale of giggles. Evidently the notion of a man offering her a small gesture of gallantry struck her as vastly entertaining.

He shook off the depressing ruminations that had been brought on by the interview and turned his attention to thinking of ways to get a closer look at the flower-seller. This could be a turning point in the case, he thought. If he handled this situation carefully, he might turn up a nugget of useful information.

The thought of proving that he had a real talent for this profession was an added incentive. If he came back with a clue, Tobias might even stop dropping hints about the advantages of pursuing a career as a man of business.

He moved quickly through the maze of twisted lanes and walks. The task of interviewing the prostitutes had drawn him into this mean neighborhood an hour ago. It was a place where the principal businesses were gambling hells, dingy taverns, and establishments run by fences who dealt in stolen goods.

He turned a corner and saw the shadowy opening of a small alley. The smell—a mix of urine, foul refuse, and some decaying animal parts—hit him with the force of a slap. He held his breath and slipped into the narrow passage.

Two boys ambled past the entrance, intent on a conversation concerning the best way to steal hot pies from the pie cart across the street. They were followed by an elderly man who leaned heavily on a walking stick.

Just as he was about to give up hope, the flower-seller drifted slowly into view. The huge gray bonnet hid her face. A tattered cloak fell around her in voluminous folds, concealing her figure. The flowers in the basket on her arm drooped.

The woman's shoulders were bent, but something about the way she moved told Anthony that she was not as old as her garments and demeanor indicated.

The flower-seller came to a halt at the entrance of the alley, obviously bewildered by the sudden disappearance of her quarry. She started to turn slowly in a circle, searching her surroundings.

Anthony moved forward, encircled her waist with one arm, and hauled her sharply into the alley. He spun her around and pinned her against the brick wall.

"Bloody hell. I should have known," he said.

There was a shocked gasp. The oversize bonnet lifted abruptly, catching Anthony under the chin. He leaned back slightly to avoid the obstacle and then scowled at Emeline.

"What the devil do you think you're doing?" he demanded.

His pulse was still racing, he realized. He was breathing hard, in spite of the unpleasant odors in the alley. Suddenly the only thing he could think about was the one time he had kissed her. Very carefully he released her.

"I was following you, of course." She straightened and shook out the cloak. "What did you think I was doing?"

"Are you mad? This is an extremely dangerous neighborhood."

"You behaved very secretively this morning when I asked you about your plans for the day." She righted the bonnet. "I knew you were up to something."

"So you followed me? Of all the nonsensical, idiotic—"

"Why were you talking to that girl on the corner? And that woman who was hanging about the tavern at the far end of the street, why did you speak to her?"

"I can explain." He took her arm and hauled her briskly out of the alley. "But first we must get you away from here. Ladies do not come to this part of town."

She glanced back at the prostitute he had just interviewed. "Some do," she said quietly. "But not by choice, I think."

"No, not by choice."

He whisked her down the street to a small square. He heard the clatter of hooves on stone and turned to see a hackney coming toward them. Relief shot through him. He raised a hand to hail the vehicle.

"Anthony, I demand to know what you were doing. I think I have the right."

The hackney rattled to a halt. He yanked open the door and very nearly tossed Emeline inside. She bounced a little when she landed on the seat. He paused to give the Claremont Lane address to the coachman and then vaulted up into the cab.

"You owe me an explanation," Emeline announced.

"Tobias asked me to make a few inquiries." He sat down and slammed the door.

"That girl on the corner. She was a prostitute, wasn't she?"

"Yes."

"And so was the woman outside the tavern." Emeline's voice was very tight.

"Yes."

"I trust you are not going to fob off some Banbury tale on me about these *interviews* being connected to the Medusa bracelet case."

"No."

"Well?" She removed the gray bonnet and placed it very precisely on the seat beside her. When she looked at him her gaze was somber and wary. "Why are you chatting with prostitutes, Anthony? Is this a regular habit of yours?"

He cursed softly and lounged back into the corner of the seat, considering how much to say. But this was Emeline. He could not bring himself to lie to her.

"If I tell you the truth, you must promise not to mention it to your aunt."

"Why should I promise?" she asked.

"Because Tobias does not want her to know how deeply concerned he is about Oscar Pelling's presence here in Town, that's why."

Her eyes widened, and then comprehension mingled with something that might have been relief appeared in their depths.

"Oh," she said. "I see. Mr. March is keeping an eye on that dreadful man?"

"Yes. And I am assisting him."

"Keeping watch on Pelling is an excellent notion," Emeline said slowly. "He is not a man to be trusted. But what do those women have to do with him?"

"Pelling is staying at an inn near here. According to one of the stable lads, he has been seeing a local prostitute. Tobias wants me to find her so that he can talk to her."

"I don't understand. What can a streetwalker tell him about Pelling?"

Anthony cleared his throat and fixed his gaze on the view of the street. "Tobias says that in his professional experience he has discovered that such women are in a position to learn things about a man that no one else knows."

"Indeed."

Anthony looked back at her. "You should not have followed me. It was a dangerous thing to do."

"If you had told me what you were about, there would have been no need for me to spy upon you."

"Damn it, Emeline, where is it written in stone that I must advise you of every move I make?"

She stiffened. "I beg your pardon, sir. I don't know what I was thinking. Of course you do not owe me any explanations. You are perfectly free to go about your own affairs. It is not as though we were married."

An appalling silence descended.

Anthony struggled to pull himself together.

"No," he said in a very low tone. "It is not as though we were, uh, married."

They sat there staring at each other for what seemed forever. A heavy sensation settled on Anthony.

Emeline moved abruptly, reaching forward with an impulsive gesture to put her hand on his. "Good heavens, what is happening to us, Tony? All this quarreling and snapping and so forth. It is not like us. I vow, we are starting to sound like Aunt Lavinia and Mr. March, are we not?"

He turned his hand palm up and gripped her fingers very tightly. "Yes, we are, and you are right. It is not like us."

"I believe it is their nature to do things the hard way." She gave him a tremulous smile. "But surely we can find our own path."

He tightened his hand around hers. "Yes."

The heavy weight lifted. His spirits rose.

He pulled her gently onto his lap. She came to him without a struggle, smiling her glowing smile. He kissed her slowly, deeply. She softened against him.

When he raised his head he was breathing quickly. Her eyes were slumberous and inviting.

It took every ounce of will he possessed to ease her back onto the opposite seat.

They finished the journey to Claremont Lane hand in hand, neither of them speaking until the hackney rumbled to a halt. With a last squeeze, Anthony released Emeline's fingers and opened the door.

Emeline paused in the opening. "Look, here comes Mrs. Chilton."

He turned his head and saw the housekeeper hurrying toward them across the paving stones. Mrs. Chilton waved madly to get their attention. Even from this distance he could see that she was flushed and breathless from her exertion.

Emeline descended from the coach, frowning in concern.

"Is something wrong, Mrs. Chilton?"

"No, no, it's just that ye mustn't go inside yet." Mrs. Chilton came to a halt, panting. "Thought it would be finished by now but they're takin' their time about it, I'm afraid. Nothing to do but come with me and wait. There's a nice little bench in the park at the end of the lane."

"Wait for what?" Emeline asked. "I don't understand."

"I just told ye, Miss Emeline, the two of 'em are in there together."

Emeline looked at the front door, baffled. "Who is in there together?"

"Mrs. Lake and Mr. March. Thought they'd be done with it by the time ye got back." Mrs. Chilton shook her head and started off toward the end of the lane. "Lord only knows what's keepin' 'em so long. Not that much to the business, if ye ask me. Leastways, there wasn't in my day."

"Not that much to *what* business?" Emeline sounded exasperated now.

Mrs. Chilton gave Anthony a speaking glance.

Comprehension struck him.

"Mrs. Chilton is right." He seized Emeline's arm and hurried her along in the housekeeper's wake. "It's a nice day for sitting in the park."

"What is this all about?" Emeline allowed herself to be swept off, but she did not look happy about it. "What is going on, Mrs. Chilton?"

"It's my own fault, I suppose. Felt sorry for 'em, ye see. Always havin' to make do with parks and gardens and carriages and such. Can't be comfortable what with his bad leg and all, and the weather is so unpredictable at this time of year."

"What on earth does the weather have to do with this?" Emeline demanded.

"Mr. March told me this morning that he would be back around three. I saw an opportunity to give the pair of them a few minutes to themselves in a warm house with a nice bed," Mrs. Chilton huffed. "It was an act of charity. How was I to know they'd take a good bit more than a few minutes?"

Anthony struggled to suppress a grin.

"A bed? Mr. March and Aunt Lavinia?" Understanding dawned in Emeline's eyes. She blushed a very bright pink and did not meet Anthony's gaze. Then she started to laugh. "Mrs. Chilton, that is outrageous. Did Lavinia know what you intended?"

"No. After she got into the tub I told her I had to go out to fetch some currants for jam. I knew Mr. March would be along shortly, so I left the door open for him. Saw him arrive nearly an hour ago and thought he'd be done by now."

"Perhaps you made things a little too comfortable for them," Anthony said dryly.

"Aye." Mrs. Chilton studied the late-afternoon sky. "Luckily it's not raining."

"True, although there is a nip in the air, isn't there?" Emeline drew the folds of the raggedy cloak around herself. "I'm certainly glad to have this."

Mrs. Chilton noticed her attire for the first time and frowned. "Where on earth did ye get that old thing?"

Emeline sat down on the bench. "It's a long story."

Mrs. Chilton sank down beside her and gazed morosely toward the closed front door of the little house. "Ye may as well tell it. It appears we've got plenty of time."

Tobias settled back against the pillows, one arm behind his head, and cradled Lavinia against his side. He knew it was getting late, but the last thing on earth that he wanted to do was leave the tumbled bed and the woman in his arms. This was the way it should be, he thought. Perhaps someday . . .

"I paid a call on Hudson this afternoon," he said.

For a few seconds Lavinia did not respond. Then she propped herself up on one elbow and looked at him. The drowsy sensuality faded from her eyes. Concern replaced it.

"You did not tell me that you intended to speak with Howard today," she said. "What did you discuss?"

"You."

"Me?" She sat up straighter, anchoring the sheet across her breasts. Her brows nipped together above her nose. "What about me?"

He touched the silver pendant she wore around her neck.

"I told you that he wants you," he said. "He's searching for a replacement for Celeste."

"And I told you that's outrageous."

"Trust me on this matter."

"How humiliating. I cannot believe that you actually embarrassed me to such a degree." She scowled ferociously. "What, precisely, did you say to him?"

He pulled her back down onto the pillows and rolled on top of her. Sliding one leg between her soft, warm thighs, he cradled her face between his hands and lowered his mouth to hers.

"I told him that he could not have you," he said.

TWENTY MINUTES LATER LAVINIA PUT ON A DRESSING GOWN TO see him out the front door. She kissed him one last time in the shadows of the hall.

"Hurry," she said. "Mrs. Chilton will return at any moment. We are extremely fortunate that neither she nor Emeline chose to come back before this. I cannot imagine what is keeping them."

He smiled to himself. He was of the opinion that the unlocked door and the housekeeper's convenient absence told a different story, but he thought it best not to question his good fortune.

"Until tonight," he said. "I take it all is in readiness for the grand event?"

"Yes. The gowns are to be delivered in an hour's time. Joan sent a note around this morning to say that her personal hairdresser will come at five and that she has arranged for the carriage to call for us at eight-thirty."

He nodded. "Anthony will no doubt show up promptly at nine. I'll put in my appearance around ten. Will that do?"

"Perfectly." She practically shoved him down the steps. "Off with you now."

She shut the door in his face.

Reluctantly, he went down the steps and started toward the end of the lane in search of a hackney.

He saw the small group of familiar faces when he was halfway to the corner. Emeline, Anthony, and Mrs. Chilton strolled toward him with a studied nonchalance. Anthony made a small show of pulling his watch out of his pocket and checking the time.

Tobias ignored him to greet Emeline and Mrs. Chilton.

"Mr. March." Emeline gave him a gracious smile. "How nice to see you. What an unexpected surprise."

"A pleasure, Miss Emeline." He stopped and inclined his head. "Good day, Mrs. Chilton. I understand you went out for currants."

"I know how much you like currant jam," she muttered.

"I am certainly very fond of yours," he agreed. "Indeed, it was very kind of you to dash out for more currants this afternoon just to make a new batch for me. I can only hope that you will feel the urge to make a lot more jam in the future."

"Depends upon the weather."

"The weather?"

She gave him a reproving look. "Can't buy good currants when it's cold or when it rains. Ye might want to bear that in mind."

"I'll remember that."

Twenty-five

AT NINE-THIRTY THAT EVENING CRACKENBURNE SLOWLY LOWERED his newspaper and looked at Tobias. "Things are not going well with your newest case, I take it?"

Tobias lounged against the mantel of the clubroom fireplace and regarded the flames. "I would happily consign the bloody case to the pit if it were not for the fact that Lavinia is desperate to solve it."

"What do you intend to do?"

"There's not much I can do except solve the damned case, prove Hudson is a murderer, and let her see him for what he is."

"She may not thank you for proving her old family friend a villain."

Tobias noticed Vale walking toward them across the crowded clubroom. "Probably not."

"How goes the situation with Pelling?" Crackenburne asked.

"Nothing new there either. Anthony is still trying to find the prostitute Pelling is bedding. She seems to have dropped out of sight. But from what we can determine by talking to the stable lad at the inn, Pelling is merely in Town to see to his business affairs."

"Nevertheless, you are concerned about his presence here."

Tobias did not take his eyes off Vale. "I find the fact that two men from Lavinia's past chose the same month to visit London something of a disturbing coincidence."

"All coincidences disturb you," Crackenburne pointed out dryly. "And I must say, one cannot feel comfortable about the man. But let us try for a degree of logic. Has Pelling actually said or done anything to indicate that he has an interest in Lavinia?"

Tobias flexed the hand on top of the mantel. "No."

"He has not contacted her?"

"No."

"She has not encountered him since that one casual sighting in Pall Mall?"

"No."

"Then very likely his business in London is nothing out of the ordinary." Crackenburne's brows jiggled. "Mayhap he is shopping for a new wife."

Tobias frowned. "Hadn't thought of that possibility."

Vale came to a halt on the other side of the fireplace. He nodded at Crackenburne and then gave Tobias a look of polite inquiry. "I'm about to leave for Mrs. Dove's ball. Can I offer you a ride in my carriage?"

Tobias managed to conceal his surprise. "Thank you." He took his arm off the mantel. "I would appreciate it. I was not looking forward to finding a hackney in this fog."

"Enjoy yourselves." Crackenburne adjusted his spectacles. "Please convey my regards to your ladies."

"I don't seem to have a lady at the moment," Vale murmured.

"And you've never met Lavinia," Tobias said.

"Doesn't matter," Crackenburne said. "From what you've told me, Mrs. Dove and Mrs. Lake both sound extremely interesting females."

Vale was amused. "*Interesting* is an odd way to describe a lady."

"At my age interesting ladies are the most attractive sort." Crackenburne shook out his newspaper. "Good evening, gentlemen."

Tobias walked back through the club with Vale and out into the fog-bound night, where a sleek carriage and an elegantly matched team waited.

"Crackenburne always seems to know the latest rumors before

anyone else." Vale got into the vehicle and sat down. "Astonishing, really. You must find him a great source of information."

Tobias grasped the edge of the door and hauled himself up into the carriage, grimly ignoring the twinge in his thigh. He settled into the comfortable cushions with a sense of relief and entertained a pleasant little fantasy of owning his own carriage and team. He could take Lavinia for long drives in the country, close the curtains for privacy, and make love to her for hours on well-sprung cushions.

"Crackenburne is quite helpful on occasion," he admitted.

The carriage rolled off into the fog.

Vale leaned back against the brown velvet squabs. "The man has a point. There is something to be said for an interesting lady."

"I agree. But in my experience, *interesting* generally implies stubborn, strong-willed, and unpredictable."

Vale nodded amiably. "Something to be said for those qualities too."

Tobias examined him in the light of the carriage lamp. "Do not mistake me, sir, I am indeed grateful for the ride in your carriage. But curiosity compels me to ask if it is the Blue Medusa or Mrs. Dove that persuaded you to attend Joan's ball tonight."

"I am a patient man, March." Vale looked out the window into the mist-shrouded night. "I have waited a year. I think that is long enough, don't you?"

"It depends what you are waiting for," Tobias said.

Twenty minutes later he paused with Vale at the top of the grand staircase. He looked down at the crowd of elegantly garbed guests, searching for Lavinia's flame-red head. It was not a simple task to find her in the throng. But wherever she was down there, he thought, she was no doubt feeling quite pleased with herself. The ball was another grand social coup.

Joan's ballroom glowed with the massed lights of three huge chandeliers. The gowns of the ladies were sprinkled about in the crowd like so many brilliant jewels. Musicians situated on the gilded balcony that surrounded the interior of the chamber poured music down on the scene.

He caught sight of Emeline on the dance floor. She was in the arms of a young man he did not recognize. Anthony would not be pleased.

That observation made him wonder where Anthony was at that moment. Fetching lemonade, no doubt.

"Our hostess is waiting for us." Vale looked toward the foot of the gilded staircase, where Joan waited to receive her guests. "Shall we go down?"

Tobias glanced at Joan. It struck him that there was something different about her tonight. Before he could decide what it was that seemed out of the ordinary, he heard his name called softly behind him.

"Tobias."

He turned and saw Anthony hurrying toward him along the balcony.

"Tobias, wait, I must speak with you."

Vale cocked an inquiring brow.

"Go down," Tobias said. "Joan is waiting. I will join you later."

Vale nodded and slowly descended the staircase, never looking away from Joan.

Anthony arrived at Tobias's side. He was properly attired for the ball, but he had a rushed air about him. His hair was damp from the fog. Excitement glittered in his eyes.

"Are you just now arriving?" Tobias frowned. "Thought you planned to come early in order to intimidate as many of Emeline's admirers as possible."

"I found her," Anthony said, excitement and triumph reverberating in the words.

"I just saw her myself, a moment ago. She is on the dance floor. Anthony, is there something odd about Mrs. Dove tonight?"

Anthony looked briefly distracted. "In what way?"

"I'm not certain. She appears different to me for some reason."

Anthony glanced past him to the foot of the steps. "She is wearing a blue gown."

"Yes, I can see that. What does that have to do with my question?"

Anthony grinned. "This is the first time she has not appeared in mourning."

"Ah, yes. Vale looks quite pleased, does he not?" He turned around. "What was it you were saying?"

"The streetwalker. The one Pelling has been amusing himself with here in Town. I found her."

"Why the devil didn't you say so?" Tobias felt all his senses sharpen. "Did you speak with her?"

"No. I was just about to leave my club to come here tonight when I found a boy waiting for me in the street. He had a message from one of the prostitutes I questioned. I'm late because I had a hard time finding her."

"On a night like this the women don't like to be out on the street unless they have no choice."

"She met me in a tavern. Said the name of the woman we're looking for is Maggie, and she gave me an address." Anthony grimaced. "For a price, of course."

"Where does Maggie live?"

"She has a room in Cutt Lane. Do you know it?"

"I know it." Tobias could feel the old, familiar sense of certainty running through him, a pulse of energy just beneath the surface. He clapped Anthony's shoulder. "Well done. Enjoy yourself with Miss Emeline. I'm off."

Some of Anthony's enthusiasm dimmed. "You're going to talk to the woman now?"

"Yes."

"Can't you wait until later?" Anthony started to look uneasy. "Mrs. Lake is expecting you to put in an appearance here at Mrs. Dove's ball. When she sees me, she will ask about you. What do you suggest I tell her?"

"Tell her that I was delayed at my club."

"But—"

"Don't worry," Tobias said. "She will not question you. Being delayed at one's club is a gentleman's universal excuse. It is appropriate to all occasions and all circumstances."

"I'm not sure Mrs. Lake will agree."

"You fret too much."

Tobias turned and made for the door before Anthony could come up with more objections.

Outside, he discovered that the fog was thickening rapidly. The heavy stuff seemed to absorb the bright lights of the house and reflect them back in an impenetrable wall of glowing mist. He could no longer make out the small park in the square.

A line of hackneys waited at the end of the row of expensive private carriages, the drivers hopeful of picking up stray business. He chose one and gave the coachman instructions to take him to Cutt Lane as quickly as possible.

His leg protested sharply when he got into the carriage. The damp night was taking its usual toll, he reflected. He dropped down onto the seat, closed the door, and absently rubbed his aching thigh.

Annoyed that the coach was not yet in motion, he reached up to rap on the roof to signal his impatience.

The vehicle's door slammed open without warning. He looked down and saw Lavinia, dressed in a deeply cut purple gown. She looked like an avenging goddess. His own personal Nemesis, he thought.

"Hand me up, if you please, March. Wherever you are going, rest assured that you are not going there alone. You seem to make a habit of forgetting that we are partners."

Twenty-six

SHE COULD SEE AT ONCE THAT HE WAS NOT PLEASED, BUT SHE chose to ignore his opinions. She was not in the best of moods herself.

She sat down and watched him shut the carriage door. The vehicle rumbled forward. Tobias unfolded the blanket that lay on the seat and tossed it to her.

"You'd better use this to keep warm," he muttered. "That gown was obviously not designed to be worn outside an overheated ballroom."

"If you had not been in such a hurry, I would have taken a moment to fetch my cloak."

She was relieved to discover that the blanket was relatively clean. Quickly, she pulled it around her shoulders and was immediately grateful for the warmth. Tobias lounged in the corner, watching her with narrowed eyes.

"I was waiting for you on the balcony," she said in response to his unspoken question. "I saw you and Vale enter and then I saw Anthony stop you. A moment later you turned and left. I knew at once that you were leaving to follow some clue. Where are we going?"

"I am on my way to meet a streetwalker named Maggie," he said without inflection. "For your information, she has nothing whatsoever to do with the Medusa affair."

"Rubbish. Do not expect me to believe that bit of nonsense. Why else would you go chasing off on a night like this to talk to a street-walker, if not to pursue—"

She broke off abruptly, her jaw dropping in shock when it occurred to her that there certainly *was* a reason why a gentleman might take a hackney to visit a prostitute. A terrible pain uncurled like a serpent deep inside her. It was followed by a hollow, utterly numb sensation. She sat there, staring at Tobias, unable to speak.

"No, my sweet, that is *not* why I am off to visit the light-skirts. Surely you know me well enough by now to be certain of that much, at least."

Relief flooded through her. Of course Tobias would not resort to a prostitute. He would not betray her. What was the matter with her? She reined in her scattered senses with an effort of will. Still feeling flustered, she tightened her grip on the blanket.

"Tell me what this is about, Tobias. I have every right to know."

He contemplated her in silence for such a long time that she began to think he might not answer her.

"You are correct," he said at last. "You do have a right to know. The long and the short of it is that I have been told that this woman named Maggie has been entertaining Pelling during his stay here in Town."

She was so surprised she could only look at him rather blankly. Not an attractive expression, she reminded herself.

"This is about Oscar Pelling?" she finally managed.

"Yes."

"I don't understand."

He rested an arm on the window ledge. "I thought it best to keep an eye on him while he was here in Town. Anthony asked some questions at the inn where Pelling is staying and learned that he has been visiting a prostitute in the area. I want to interview her."

"But why? What do you hope to discover?"

He shrugged. "Nothing, probably. But I was never comfortable with the fact that both Pelling and Hudson showed up here in London at the same time."

"I thought we agreed it was nothing more than chance."

"*You* were certain of that. I was not entirely convinced."

"So you made some inquiries into Pelling's activities?"

"Yes."

"I see." She was not certain what to say to that. She thought she ought to berate him for not telling her that he was conducting inquiries in that direction. On the other hand, he had been concerned on her behalf. She would save the lecture for later, she decided. "I assume that you learned nothing that was alarming."

"I must admit I have begun to worry a bit about Maggie. Women who get close to Pelling seem to meet with bad ends, and Anthony had a deal of trouble locating her."

She shuddered. "I understand."

"I want to satisfy myself that she is unharmed. I also want to ask her a few questions about Pelling's activities here in Town."

She gave him a quizzical look. "But he has made no move to seek me out. Indeed, why would he? I told you, at the time he found it convenient to blame me for his wife's supposed suicide. He cannot possibly have any interest in me now. Indeed, he has every reason to avoid me."

"I know. But I do not like the situation."

She smiled slightly. "I can see that."

Tobias looked out at the fog-bound street. "That is the damnable thing about this business of conducting investigations, you see. One must keep blundering about, asking questions, until one finally gets some answers."

"Not unlike our own relationship, if you ask me," she said under her breath.

He turned his head. "What did you say?"

"Nothing important. Just some personal musings."

She managed a bright little smile, but inwardly she was not feeling nearly so blasé. Their relationship was such a strange affair, she thought. Neither of them was a coward, yet in this matter they both walked as gingerly as if they were trying to cross a perilous landscape, a world in which unseen dangers lurked in every shadow.

Then again, perhaps that was only her view of the situation, she thought. For all she knew, Tobias saw nothing complicated or worrisome about their arrangement. He was a man, after all. In her experience, men tended to assess matters involving emotion in a more straightforward fashion than women did. When all was said and done, although he occasionally complained of the venue, Tobias *was* getting a certain amount of physical satisfaction on a regular basis. Mayhap that was enough for him.

They traveled the remainder of the distance to Cutt Lane in silence. When the hackney finally halted, Lavinia looked out and saw a solitary gas lamp glowing in front of a darkened doorway. Candles burned in some of the windows. Here and there a figure moved behind a thin curtain.

Tobias opened the door and got out. He reached up, gripped Lavinia around the waist, and lifted her out of the cab. Then he turned to toss a few coins to the coachman.

"We will not be long," he said. "Be so good as to wait for us."

"Aye." The coachman checked the coins in the lantern light. Evidently satisfied, he pocketed them swiftly. "I'll be here when yer ready to leave, sir."

"Come." Tobias took Lavinia's arm and steered her toward the dark mouth of a small lane. "The sooner we find Maggie, the sooner we can return to the ball."

She did not argue. She draped the blanket around her shoulders as if it were a fine Indian shawl and went forward at his side.

More candles and the occasional lantern burned in the windows of the tiny lane. Tobias stepped into the shelter of a stone doorway and clanged the knocker. The sound echoed eerily in the darkness.

There was no response, but Lavinia heard a window open on the floor above. She looked up and saw a woman leaning out, a candle set in a heavy iron candlestick in her hand. The light from the small flame illuminated sharp features and eyes that appeared to be sunk in deep wells.

The woman wore a dressing gown that was only loosely tied. The garment gaped, exposing her bony shoulders and thin breasts to the damp night and the casual view of passersby in the lane below.

"You down there," the prostitute called in a drunken voice, "are ye lookin' for some sport tonight?"

Tobias took a step back out of the doorway.

"We're looking for Maggie," he said.

"Well, now, yer in luck, then, because you've found her." Maggie leaned precariously out over the sill. "But I see there's two of ye, and yer friend is a lady. I take it yer one of those what likes to watch two women enjoyin' themselves, eh? That'll be extra."

"We just want to talk to you," Lavinia said quickly. "And, of course, we'll pay you for your time."

"Talk, eh?" Maggie considered that for a moment and then shrugged. "Well, so long as yer willin' to pay, it don't make much difference to me. Come on up. First room at the top of the stairs."

Tobias tried the door. It opened readily. Lavinia peered around his shoulder and saw a narrow hall and a cramped staircase lit by a single, smoky candle set in a wall sconce.

"Try to resist the temptation to overpay her," Tobias said. "Especially since we will no doubt be using my money."

"Of course we must use your money. I did not bring any of my own with me tonight. A lady never takes money to a grand ball."

"Somehow that does not surprise me."

He ushered her into the hall and followed on her heels, pausing only to shut the door.

Lavinia started up the staircase, Tobias two steps behind her. She was on the fourth tread when she heard the hall door slam open behind her with a jolting crash.

Two men dressed in rough clothing rushed into the hall.

They went directly for Tobias. The light of the wall sconce gleamed evilly on the blades of their knives.

"*Tobias.* Behind you."

He did not reply. He was too busy responding to the attack. She saw him grip the banister with one hand and use it to brace himself. He lashed out with one booted foot.

The blow struck home, catching the first man squarely in the chest. The villain sucked in air and staggered back, colliding with his companion.

"Get out of my way, ye bloody fool." The second man shoved his companion aside and flung himself at Tobias. His arm moved in a short, vicious arc. The blade slashed through the air.

Tobias kicked out again. The second man hissed like a snake and darted backward to avoid the boot. He had to catch himself on the banister.

"Go into Maggie's room," Tobias ordered without taking his attention off the two men. "Bolt the door."

He launched himself toward the closest villain. The two came together with a sickening thud and landed at the foot of the staircase. They rolled across the floor and slammed into the wall.

The door at the top of the stairs banged open. Maggie appeared, the iron candlestick in her hand.

"What's going on down there?" she demanded in a slurred voice. "See here, I don't want any trouble."

Lavinia flung aside the blanket, collected her skirts, and dashed up the stairs to the landing.

"Give me that candlestick." She yanked it out of Maggie's hand.

"What are ye doin?" Maggie demanded.

"Oh, for pity's sake." Lavinia pulled the dripping tallow candle off the prong and shoved it into Maggie's fingers.

"Ouch," Maggie muttered. She held her finger to her mouth. "That burns, it does."

Lavinia ignored her and flew back down the stairs, the iron candlestick clutched in her right hand.

She could see Tobias and the second villain writhing on the floor of the hall. Light danced on the blade.

The first man heaved himself up into a sitting position at the foot of the stairs. He appeared dazed, but it was obvious that he was recovering rapidly from the stunning blow he had taken from Tobias's booted foot. He scooped up the knife that had fallen from his hand and gripped one of the banister supports. He started to haul himself to his feet.

He studied the two men locked together in silent, deadly combat on the hall floor. It was clear that he was seeking the right moment to go to his companion's assistance.

Lavinia raised the iron candlestick aloft, praying that the man at the bottom of the staircase would not look back.

Down below, Tobias and his assailant heaved and rolled violently once more. One of them grunted hoarsely. Lavinia could not tell which man had cried out in pain. Rage and fear flashed through her.

She reached the second step from the bottom and swung the iron candlestick with all of her strength.

At the last instant, the man sensed the threat behind him. He started to turn and put up an arm to protect himself.

But he was too late. The candlestick glanced heavily against the side of his head and struck his shoulder with a jolting force that Lavinia felt through her entire body. The villain staggered back against the wall. The knife clattered on the bottom step.

For a shocked second Lavinia and the man stared at each other. Then she saw the blood flow from the gash on the side of his head.

"*Bitch.*"

Enraged, he lunged at her with both hands, but his movements were awkward and unsteady.

Lavinia grabbed the banister and used it to lever herself up several steps. She raised the candlestick on high again, preparing to deliver another blow. The man saw the weapon and hesitated, swaying in the light.

Tobias appeared at the bottom of the stairs, looming in the shadows, his face an icy mask. He grasped the first man's shoulder, spun him around, and slammed a fist into his jaw.

The man yelled, reeled around, and lurched blindly toward the door. The second man had it open and was already outside.

The pair fled into the fog. Their boots rang hollowly on the paving stones for a moment and then they were gone.

Heart pounding, Lavinia examined Tobias from head to toe. His neckcloth had come undone in the scuffle. There was blood on it and on the front of his greatcoat.

"You're bleeding." She picked up her skirts and hurried down the steps.

"The blood isn't mine." With a gesture of distaste he snagged the trailing end of the cravat and tossed it aside. "Are you all right?"

"Yes." She stopped on the step above him and touched his face anxiously. "Are you certain you're not hurt?"

"Quite certain." He frowned. "I told you to bolt yourself in Maggie's room."

"Those two men were trying to kill you. Surely you didn't expect me to just wait quietly in another room while they went about their business. I would remind you yet again, sir, that we are partners in this venture."

"Damn it, Lavinia, you could have been seriously injured."

Maggie chuckled above them. "Appeared as how the lady did ye a favor, if ye ask me."

"I didn't ask you," Tobias said.

Maggie cackled.

"I suggest that we conduct this quarrel at some other time," Lavinia said crisply. "We have business here, in case you have forgotten."

He rubbed his jaw somewhat gingerly. "I have not forgotten." He looked up at Maggie. "Do you know those two men?"

Maggie shook her head. "Never saw 'em before. A couple of foot-pads that spotted ye in the lane and decided to follow ye into the hall, I expect." She gestured grandly toward the open door behind her. "Come on up, if yer still in a mood to ask questions."

"Yes." Tobias climbed the steps behind Lavinia. "I'm very much in a mood to ask questions."

They followed Maggie into a dingy little room furnished with a cot, a washstand, and a small trunk. An open bottle of gin stood on a table.

Lavinia handed the iron candlestick back to Maggie and sat down on a stool near the cold hearth. Tobias went to the window and looked down into the lane. She wondered if he was hoping to spot the two men who had attacked him. There was little chance of that, she thought.

"We wish to ask you about a man named Oscar Pelling," he said without turning around. "We understand that he purchased your services during the past few days."

"Pelling. That bastard." Maggie speared the candle on the stick and set it on the table. She lowered her thin frame onto the bench and poured herself a glass of gin. "Aye, I took him on as a client for a time, but never again. Not after what he did the last time."

"What, precisely, did he do?" Lavinia asked.

"He did this, that's what." Maggie turned her head so that her face was fully illuminated by the glow of the candle. "Haven't been able to work for the past few days because of him."

Lavinia saw for the first time that the area around Maggie's eyes was badly discolored and bruised. "Dear God, he struck you?"

"Aye." Maggie gulped some gin and put down the glass. "A girl has to be flexible in this business, but there's some things I won't put up with and that's a fact. No man who raises his fists to me is allowed back in this room, I don't care how fine a gennelman he is."

Tobias had turned away from the window. He watched Maggie with a riveted expression, eyes narrowed and cold. "When did Pelling strike you?"

"The last time he came to see me." She screwed up her face with the effort of trying to remember. "Think it was Wednesday last. No, it was Thursday. He'd behaved himself right enough on his first few visits. A little rough, but nothin' out of the ordinary. But that last time he had himself a rare fit of rage."

"A fit?" Lavinia repeated carefully.

"Aye. I thought he'd gone mad. And all because I teased him a bit." Maggie poured more gin into the glass.

"Why did you tease him?" Tobias asked.

"Well, he'd come here later than usual, ye see. Almost dawn, it was. I'd just gone to bed. I looked out the window when he knocked and I could tell straightaway that he was in a foul temper. Almost didn't let him in. But he'd been a good client. Always payin' a little extra by way of a thank you. Rich as a nabob, he is."

She paused to swallow more gin.

"You said you teased him," Lavinia reminded her gently.

"Just tryin' to put him in a better temper. But it only made things worse. He beat me somethin' dreadful, he did. And all the while, he kept saying all sorts of terrible things about women. How they had snakes in their hair and how they turned men to stone with their eyes." Maggie shuddered. "Like I said, he went mad. Don't know what would have happened to me if my friend upstairs hadn't come down to see what all the commotion was about. When she pounded on the door, he stopped hitting me."

Lavinia recalled the terrifying ordeals Pelling's wife, Jessica, had revealed while in a trance. "Thank God your friend came downstairs when she did."

"Aye. The bastard like to have killed me."

"What did Pelling do after your friend interrupted the beating?" Tobias asked.

"Just turned and walked out the door as casual as ye please. Like he'd done nothing more than have some of the usual sport. To tell ye the truth, he seemed in a better mood afterward. Not cheerful, but more calm. Hasn't come back since, thank the Lord."

Tobias looked thoughtful. "You didn't say exactly what you teased him about."

"It was nothin', y'know? Just a little thing." Maggie wrinkled her nose. "Still can't understand why it set him off."

"What was the little thing?" Lavinia asked.

"His cravat," Maggie said.

Lavinia felt her blood run cold in her veins.

At the window, Tobias did not move. She sensed the hunter in him catching the scent of the quarry.

"What about Pelling's cravat?" he asked very softly.

"Well, he wasn't wearin' it that last time, y'see," Maggie said in her gin-thickened voice. "Properly dressed, he was, like he'd just come from his club or a fancy ball, but no cravat."

Lavinia met Tobias's eyes. *Impossible*, she thought.

"It looked odd," Maggie said. "Like his valet hadn't dressed him properly. So I teased him about being so eager to visit me that he had started to undress before he arrived. Asked him if he'd lost his bloody neckcloth somewhere along the way. That's when he went mad with his rage."

Twenty-seven

"I *KNEW* THERE HAD TO BE A CONNECTION." TOBIAS PULLED HIM-self up into the hackney behind Lavinia and slammed the door. "There had to be a link between Hudson and Pelling. It was just too much of a coincidence that both men linked to you showed up in London at the same time."

The fierce, hawklike anticipation in his eyes was unsettling. It was at times like this that she was most keenly aware of the dangerous edge that was always just beneath the surface of the man. She did not fear him at these moments; she feared for his safety. When his blood was up he was inclined to take risks.

The new revelations called for logic, she thought. Not immediate action.

"We must proceed slowly and carefully," she said. "I admit that the fact that Pelling lost his cravat the night that Celeste was strangled with one is an exceedingly strange coincidence. But what possible connection could there be between Pelling and Celeste?"

"I suspect that for some reason Pelling, too, is after the Medusa bracelet. It would appear that he hired the Hudsons to steal it for him.

Perhaps he became Celeste's lover. Regardless, she went to meet him that night and he murdered her, either because they quarreled or because he believed that he no longer needed her to help him get the bracelet."

"And realized too late that she had hidden the artifact before she met him at the warehouse?"

"The logic holds," Tobias said with satisfaction.

She held up her hand. "Not entirely. Only think for a moment, Tobias. If Howard knew about Pelling's involvement, then he must know that Pelling is the killer. Why would he hire us to find Celeste's murderer if he already knew his identity?"

"Because Hudson is after the bracelet, not justice for his dead wife. He must have realized the fact that Pelling doesn't have it, so he set us on the trail, hoping that if we turn over enough rocks, we'll find the bloody antiquity before Pelling does."

She spread her hands. "But why would Pelling want the bracelet in the first place?"

"Is he a collector?"

She thought back to the handful of conversations she'd had with Jessica Pelling. "To be honest, I do not know. The subject never arose. All I can say with any certainty is that he is wealthy enough to afford to collect rare antiquities."

"I think I know someone who can answer the question for us."

TWENTY MINUTES LATER, VALE AND JOAN DOVE WALKED OUT OF the mansion onto the terrace where Tobias and Lavinia waited together with Emeline and Anthony. Emeline had fetched Lavinia's cloak a few minutes earlier and brought it out to her.

Vale took in Tobias's disheveled appearance in a single cool glance. His brows climbed. "Anthony informed me that you wished to consult with me but that you were in no condition to enter the ballroom. I see what he meant. Do you mind if I ask what happened?"

"It's a long and somewhat boring story," Tobias said.

Lavinia gripped his arm very tightly. "Actually, two men tried to murder him."

"Obviously they did not succeed," Vale said. "My congratulations, sir."

Tobias glanced at Lavinia. "I had some help from my partner."

Vale inclined his head. "The two of you clearly make an excellent team."

"Indeed," Lavinia said firmly.

Vale turned back to Tobias. "What can I do for you?"

"Tell me if you know whether or not Pelling is a collector of antiquities," Tobias said.

Vale did not answer immediately. Lavinia got the impression that he was running through some private logic of his own.

"Not to my knowledge," he finally said very slowly. "It is possible, of course. I certainly do not claim to be acquainted with every serious collector in England. But I am not aware of Pelling having a scholarly interest in relics. He has made no bid to join the Connoisseurs."

Lavinia's spirits plummeted. She realized that she had been holding her breath. So much for Tobias's brilliant theory, she thought. She glanced at him to see how he was taking the bad news.

To her surprise, he appeared undaunted.

"Hudson wants the Medusa bracelet for reasons that have nothing to do with a scholarly interest in antiquities," Tobias said. "Perhaps Pelling is also obsessed with it for some unknown reason."

Lavinia frowned. "Maggie said that Pelling went mad for a while the night he came to her room after the murder. If he is not entirely sane, he may want the necklace for reasons that no one can comprehend."

"Unfortunately, we have no evidence," Tobias said. "I doubt that there is much we can do about Hudson at this juncture, but Pelling is a killer and must be stopped. If you're willing to help, Vale, it may be possible to lure him into a trap. Perhaps he can be persuaded to incriminate himself in front of two men whose oath would be unquestioned."

"I assume I am to be one of the witnesses," Vale said. "Who is the other?"

"Crackenburne."

Vale looked thoughtful. "It might work. How do you intend to set your stage?"

Tobias smiled slowly. "With the assistance of Mr. Nightingale."

Vale and Tobias exchanged glances.

"With luck we have time to bait and set the trap tonight," Tobias said.

Even in the shadows there on the terrace, Lavinia could make out the cold pleasure of the hunt in the eyes of both men.

But Tobias's predatory anticipation dissolved a short time later when he sent a carefully crafted message regarding a very private auction to the inn where Pelling was staying.

The response came back immediately. Oscar Pelling had packed his bags and departed sometime after midnight. No one knew where he had gone.

"One of the more annoying aspects of this matter," Lavinia observed over a glass of sherry just before dawn, "is that Mr. Nightingale demands to be paid for his time, in spite of the fact that the scheme was unsuccessful. And we seem to be running short of clients to cover our expenses."

Twenty-eight

Tobias arrived for a late breakfast the following morning in a mood that boded ill for everyone around him.

Anthony, looking no happier, followed him into the breakfast room.

Emeline's initial start of pleasure at seeing him faded to a look of deep concern. "Oh, dear, something else has gone wrong."

Lavinia lowered her cup back down onto the saucer.

"What happened?" she asked.

Tobias took his customary chair and reached for the coffeepot. "They have both vanished."

"Both?" Lavinia searched his face and then glanced at Anthony for assistance.

"It is not just Pelling who has disappeared. We called at Dr. Hudson's rooms a short while ago. He is gone also." Anthony hesitated politely, one hand on the back of a chair. "May I sit down?"

"Yes, of course," Emeline said quickly.

Lavinia raised her brows. "Forgive us for our little lapse in manners, Anthony. It is just that we have grown so accustomed to Tobias's charming way of making himself at home. He no longer waits upon an invitation, as you can see."

Tobias ignored the pointed remark. He poured coffee for himself and handed the pot to Anthony. "I have concluded that those two footpads we encountered last night must have reported their failure to Pelling. He no doubt realized that if we knew enough to interview Maggie, we were getting too close. He may have passed the warning along to Hudson. Or perhaps the damned mesmerist came to the conclusion on his own that it was time to leave."

Emeline looked at him. "Where do you think they went?"

"No way to know yet." Tobias surveyed the dishes on the table, an irritable Minotaur eyeing sacrificial offerings. He settled upon the tray of eggs. "I doubt if either of them would dare return to their former residences. Wouldn't be surprised to learn that they are on their way to the Continent. Perhaps Hudson will elect to return to America."

"They certainly will not be showing their faces in London in the near future," Anthony said with some satisfaction.

"The fact that both men decamped together proves once and for all that they were, indeed, associates in this affair," Tobias said.

"Not necessarily." Lavinia took a bite of egg and gave him a quelling look. "Howard may well have left Town because he was intimidated by your attitude when you called upon him the other day. After all, you more or less threatened him, did you not?"

Tobias shrugged. "More, not less."

Anthony glanced at him. "You did not mention that you had talked to Hudson. What did you say to him?"

"It was a private matter." Tobias caught Lavinia's eye while he piled eggs on his plate. "Nothing that need concern us this morning."

Mrs. Chilton bustled in with a fresh plate of eggs. "Getting to be quite a crowd out here in the mornings. We'll have to see about increasing our order with the dairymaid."

Lavinia cleared her throat. "Large quantities of eggs and milk are costly."

"I'm sure we can afford a few extra eggs," Emeline said quickly.

"Whitby mentioned this morning that he is not using the usual number of eggs lately," Tobias put in helpfully. "I'll instruct him to send some to you, Mrs. Chilton."

"Very well, sir." Mrs. Chilton started back through the door. "I'll go and fetch some more toast."

"And jam," Tobias added. "We've run out again."

"Aye, sir. More jam."

"Speaking of your excellent jam," Tobias said, "how is your supply of currants?"

It was really too much, Lavinia thought. Now he was presuming to take charge of her kitchen. The next thing she knew, he would be inspecting the linens and dictating the choice of herbs to be planted in the garden.

"There is no need to concern yourself with our supply of currants, sir," she said forcefully. "I'm quite sure we have a sufficient quantity on hand."

"But we wouldn't want to take the chance of running out altogether." Tobias smiled at Mrs. Chilton. "You're certain you don't need to shop for some this afternoon, Mrs. Chilton? It promises to be a fine day."

Mrs. Chilton heaved a sigh. "I expect it wouldn't hurt to purchase a few more." She went through the door.

Emeline and Anthony exchanged looks. Lavinia could have sworn they were both struggling to conceal smiles.

Tobias drank some coffee and looked a good deal more pleased than he had when he had walked into the breakfast room a few minutes ago.

Lavinia wondered if the subject of currants always had such an uplifting effect on his spirits. Perhaps it wouldn't hurt to keep an ample quantity on hand.

SHORTLY AFTER TWO O'CLOCK, EMELINE LOOKED AROUND THE door of the study, her bonnet dangling from her fingers. "Priscilla has just arrived in her mama's carriage. We are off to meet up with

Anthony and one of his friends to view the new exhibition of paintings at that little gallery in Bond Street."

"Very well." Lavinia did not look up from her notes on the Medusa
bracelet affair. "Enjoy yourself."

"We probably will not return much before six. Priscilla wants to
shop for a new fan, and then Anthony and his friend are going to take
us driving in the park in Lady Wortham's carriage."

"Mmm."

"Mrs. Chilton just left to shop for currants."

"Yes, I know." Lavinia dipped her quill in the ink and started a new
sentence.

"I can see you are deep into your journal. I will bid you farewell."

"Good-bye."

The front door closed behind Emeline a moment later. A curious silence descended on the house. Lavinia completed another sentence
and paused to read what she had written.

> . . . a most unsatisfactory conclusion to the affair. It is evident
> that Oscar Pelling murdered Celeste Hudson, but it is clear
> that he will never pay for his crime. The Blue Medusa has dis-
> appeared and with it any hope of collecting a fee for our
> services from anyone involved in this matter.
>
> Several questions remain unanswered. I cannot bring my-
> self to believe that my good friend Dr. Hudson is a thief, but
> Mr. March strongly disagrees with that conclusion.
>
> Where did Celeste conceal the relic before she went to
> meet Pelling on the night of her death? I cannot forget the
> valet's assurance that the only person who could have taken
> the bracelet undetected was Mrs. Rushton. But she had no
> motive.

She put down the quill and looked out into the garden. The spidery
threads of melancholia were drifting around her, threatening to entan-
gle her in one of her rare moods. She considered putting aside her
journal and turning to some poetry.

No, she thought, given the unfortunate ending to the Medusa affair, it would behoove her to return to work on writing an advertisement for the papers. New business must be found as soon as possible. There was some refining yet to be done on her notice. She was rather taken with the notion of adding a line or two about references being available upon request.

Perhaps what she really needed at that moment was some fresh air to raise her spirits, she decided. She should have gone with Emeline and the others to view the paintings and shop for fans.

References.

Fans.

The familiar snap and sizzle of intuition crackled through her, leaving her very nearly breathless. Very deliberately, she reached for her pen and wrote down her conclusion to see if it still made sense when viewed as a statement of fact.

She stared at what she had written for a long time, searching for flaws. She saw none. But there was only one way to be certain.

THE BANKS MANSION LOOMED ABOVE THE SMALL, OVERGROWN park, as bleak and cheerless as ever. When the housekeeper opened the door, she seemed surprised to see a live person on the front step.

"Is Mrs. Rushton home?" Lavinia asked.

"Aye."

"Please inform her that Mrs. Lake wishes to speak with her concerning her missing bracelet."

The housekeeper did not look overly optimistic about the prospects of an interview, but she went off to inform her mistress that she had a caller.

Mrs. Rushton received her in the gloomy drawing room. She frowned in disappointment when she saw that Lavinia was alone.

"I had rather hoped that Mr. March would accompany you," she said. "Or that nice young man Mr. Sinclair."

"They are both occupied with pressing matters of business this afternoon," Lavinia said, taking the seat across from Mrs. Rushton. "I have come to give you a full report."

Mrs. Rushton brightened somewhat at that news. "You recovered my relic?"

"Not yet."

"Now, see here, I made it quite clear that I am not about to pay you unless you find it."

"I think I may know where it is." Lavinia touched the silver pendant that she wore at her throat. "Or perhaps I should say that I think you know where it is."

"Me? That's ridiculous. If I knew the whereabouts of the bracelet, I would never have agreed to pay you to retrieve it."

"I believe that you were put into a trance by a mesmerist and instructed to take the bracelet to a secret location. There is every reason to hope that the relic is still there and that it may be recovered. But I will need your cooperation."

"Good Lord." Mrs. Rushton's eyes widened in horrified amazement. She put her hand to her bosom. "Are you saying that I may have been unwittingly entranced?"

"Yes." Lavinia unfastened the silver chain around her neck. She held it in front of her so that the pendant caught the light. "Mrs. Rushton, please trust me. I want your permission to induce another mesmeric trance. While you are in it, I will ask you some questions concerning what happened the day the bracelet disappeared."

Mrs. Rushton looked bemused at the sight of the dangling pendant. "It is not easy to put me into a mesmeric trance, you know. I am a woman of extremely strong will."

"I understand."

Mrs. Rushton did not look away from the gently swinging necklace. "See here, are you an expert at this sort of thing?"

"Yes, Mrs. Rushton. I am really rather good at this sort of thing."

SHE LEFT THE UGLY MANSION TEN MINUTES LATER, INTENT ONLY on her next destination. Luck was with her. There was a hackney standing quietly in the square almost directly in front of her.

She raised a hand and waved madly to get the coachman's attention. He made no move to get down from his box to assist her up into the carriage. She was in too much of a hurry to be offended.

She opened her mouth to give the man the address at the same time she opened the door of the vehicle.

It was then that she realized the hackney was already occupied.

Maggie was inside. Her hands were bound with rope. Her eyes were huge and stark with fear above the gag that had been tied around her mouth.

She was not alone in the vehicle. Oscar Pelling sat beside her. He held a knife to her throat.

"Get in," he said to Lavinia, "or I will kill her right here. Right now. In front of you."

Twenty-nine

❦

"I WATCHED YOUR HOUSE FOR HOURS, MRS. LAKE, WAITING TO SEE if you would make any move that would indicate that you might have been successful in your quest to find the bracelet. You were my last, best hope, and I thank you for confirming my faith in your deceitful and cunning ways."

"I do not know what you are talking about," Lavinia whispered.

"Really, you are so very typical of your sex, madam. Lying, cheating, potentially deadly Medusas, every last one of you. But knowing the nature of women as I do was what persuaded me to follow you rather than Mr. March today. It is clear he is your lover and no doubt completely under your control. *Get in.*"

Lavinia climbed slowly into the closed cab of the hackney and sat down on the seat across from Pelling and Maggie. Pelling gave her an approving smile. She caught a glimpse of the monster lurking just beneath the surface of his eyes and shivered.

"What made you conclude that I know the location of the Blue Medusa?" she asked warily.

"There is no other reason why you would pay another visit to the

Banks mansion today, is there?" He smiled with satisfaction. "Obviously you came here to conduct business with Mrs. Rushton, and the only business that involves the two of you is the Blue Medusa. I trust that you have not yet concluded your bargain and turned over the bracelet. Because if that is the case, I no longer need you, do I?"

"You must let Maggie go," she said quietly.

"Oh, I don't think I'll do that." Pelling prodded Maggie's throat with the tip of the knife. A drop of blood appeared. "She is a cheap whore who must be punished for betraying me. Is that not right, my sweet?"

Maggie closed her eyes and whimpered behind the gag.

Lavinia touched the silver pendant, in what she hoped looked like a nervous gesture. "You must let her go. You no longer need her, and killing her would be too risky."

Pelling looked at her with blood-freezing eyes. "Do not presume to tell me what to do. I knew that you were trouble on the first occasion when we met. Probably should have got rid of you then."

"That would have been foolish. After all, you had just lost your wife under tragic and mysterious circumstances. The murder of the mesmerist who had been treating her would have been a bit much for the local authorities, don't you think? They might have started asking embarrassing and exceedingly awkward questions."

"Bah. The authorities did not worry me in the least. The reason I did not punish you then was because you were not worth the time and trouble. You had, in point of fact, done me a favor. You contrived to rid me of an increasingly troublesome wife, and I was left with her inheritance. Under the circumstances, it would have been churlish to kill you."

"Churlish." Lavinia swallowed. "Yes. Quite. But now there is the problem of Maggie."

"Maggie is no problem, as you can see." Pelling tapped the knife against the woman's shoulder. "I shall slit her throat when it suits me. Until then, she will remain quiet and obedient. Isn't that right, Maggie?"

Tears leaked from Maggie's eyes.

"I'm afraid it will not be as simple as that," Lavinia said. "You see, as long as Maggie is sitting there with a knife at her throat, I will not tell you the location of the Medusa bracelet. And the bracelet is what you are after, is it not?"

"You will tell me," Pelling said. "Or you will first watch Maggie die very slowly. If you manage to resist the urge to tell me where the bracelet is during that process, I'm sure you will talk when it is your turn."

"The risk of killing both of us is too great." Lavinia toyed with the silver pendant, twisting it so that it caught the light that seeped in around the edges of the window curtain. "Much too great. Better to let Maggie go. She cannot hurt you. You are too strong and too powerful to worry about a prostitute who drinks too much gin. No one pays any attention to women like Maggie."

"Stop it." Pelling took the point of the knife away from Maggie's throat and jabbed it at Lavinia. "Stop it right now."

She flinched and flattened her back against the cushions. But there was little room to maneuver in the close confines of the carriage. Pelling could easily gut her like a fish before she could reach the door if he took a notion to do so.

Maggie opened her eyes and looked at her with an expression of resignation and dread.

"I know what you are trying to do," Pelling said to Lavinia. "You are trying to put me in a mesmeric trance. But it will not work. My mind is too strong."

"Yes, you are strong," she whispered. "Much too strong."

Pelling was amused. "It's true. Celeste and Hudson both tried their skills on me. Both failed. If they could not entrance me, you have no chance of doing so, do you?"

"No." Lavinia watched him steadily and fiddled with the silver at her throat. "My skills are poor, indeed, compared to theirs. And you are too strong. So very, very strong. But the night is coming on. Soon it will be dark. It will be difficult to keep track of two prisoners in the dark. Better to let Maggie go. She can do you no harm."

Pelling said nothing.

"You are too strong. You do not need her. She is a nuisance. Better to toss her out onto the street. She can do you no harm. You are too strong."

He was not in a deep trance, Lavinia realized. But there was an odd calm about him now, as if he had come to some conclusion and had formed a plan. She could only pray that he had not decided to slit Maggie's throat immediately and be done with the matter. The expression in Maggie's eyes told her that she feared that was precisely what was about to happen.

Without any warning, Pelling reached up and rapped on the roof of the vehicle with the hilt of the knife.

The hackney clattered to a halt.

Pelling opened the door.

Lavinia looked out and saw a portion of a fog-bound street. For an instant she feared the worst, that Pelling had chosen an isolated location where he could dump a dead body without fear of being seen.

But the rumble of cart wheels nearby reassured her. A moment later, a farmer's wagon rattled past and came to a halt in front of a door.

"I don't need you any longer," Pelling said to Maggie. He raised the knife.

Maggie cringed and whimpered behind the gag.

Lavinia's breath stopped in her throat. Her hands felt as though they had been plunged into ice. But she managed to keep her voice low and steady.

"Too strong," she said in soft, low, soothing tones. "You are too strong. There is no need to kill her. Too strong. No need to take the risk. Better not to risk killing her. You are too strong. No need to take the risk."

Pelling moved the knife again and sliced through the gag. With the practiced ease of a man who has cleaned his own fish and game, he slashed the knife downward a second time, cutting through the ropes that bound Maggie's hands.

"Get out, whore. You cannot cause me any trouble. I am too strong." He pushed Maggie out the door as though she were a bundle of laundry.

Maggie stumbled and crumpled to the paving stones.

Pelling slammed the door and signaled the coachman. The hackney rumbled forward.

"Tell me about Celeste," Lavinia said quickly. "Tell me what went wrong."

Pelling held the knife in his hand, the tip of the blade pointed at her midsection. "She tried to manipulate me. Tried to cheat me."

"You hired her to steal the Medusa bracelet?"

"I had no choice." Fury leaped in Pelling's eyes. "I wanted to hire Hudson for the task, not a woman. Word had reached me that, for a price, he would arrange to procure certain valuable items for discreet clients. Gems and jewels and the like."

He was wrong about Howard, she thought. Surely Celeste had been the thief. But this was not the time to correct his false impression.

"You needed someone to steal the Medusa bracelet?" she asked carefully.

"Yes. I was willing to pay Hudson well for his work. He listened to my proposal and seemed quite interested at first. He told me that he would research the project and give me his decision. But when I returned to conclude the bargain, he informed me that he lacked the nerve to carry out the theft. It was too difficult and dangerous, he said."

"But Celeste had a different opinion, did she not?"

Pelling snorted softly. "She came to see me a few days later. Alone. She told me that Hudson had turned me down because, after researching the bracelet in an old book he had found, he was suddenly consumed with a desire to gain possession of it himself."

She caught her breath. Perhaps Tobias had been right when he claimed that Howard had convinced himself that the legend was true. Howard was, after all, very intent on his research. It was just barely possible that in his zeal to pursue his investigations into mesmerism, he might have been tempted to help himself to the Blue Medusa.

"The fool thought that the cameo had powers that he could control." Pelling moved the knife in a gesture of disgust. "Powers of animal magnetism that would augment his own mesmeric talents."

"Celeste offered to take on the commission, didn't she? She made a bargain to steal the bracelet for you."

"For a price. She was preparing to leave Hudson. She wanted to secure her finances first."

"I see."

"I agreed to her terms because I had no choice. She and Hudson removed to London. I followed because I thought it prudent to keep an eye on my investment. One cannot trust a woman."

MAGGIE SCRAMBLED UP OFF THE ROUGH STONES, HEEDLESS OF her bruised knees and the cuts on her palms. She picked up her skirts and ran blindly, her only goal to put as much distance as possible between herself and the rapidly departing hackney.

She would tell Mr. March, she decided. She would find a way to send word to him. It would likely do no good, because it was clear that Pelling intended to slit Mrs. Lake's throat. Any fool could see that he was a cold-blooded murderer.

But March could kill, too, if necessary, she thought. She knew that in her bones. She had seen it in his eyes that night after the fight in the downstairs hall. He was no monster like Pelling, but he would be ruthless when it came to protecting Mrs. Lake. She was certain of that.

The problem was that by the time she managed to find him and tell him what had happened, Mrs. Lake would probably be dead.

It was hopeless. But she had to try. It was all she could do for the lady who had just saved her life.

Intent on her mission, she never saw the man who had alighted from the farmer's cart until she collided with him. He caught her by the shoulders and held her still in front of him. Dazed by the impact, she blinked and then found herself gazing into ice-cold, implacable eyes.

"What is happening inside that hackney?" Tobias demanded. "Tell me everything you can. Be quick about it."

"CELESTE STOLE THE BRACELET AND MET YOU AT THE EMPTY warehouse." Lavinia touched the silver pendant. She knew now that Pelling was not entirely impervious to mesmeric suggestion, as he claimed. But he was certainly not an easy subject, especially under these extremely difficult circumstances. The best she could hope to do was distract him and, with luck, perhaps influence his logic to some degree. She was buying time. "Did you murder her because you thought you no longer needed her?"

Pelling's eyes darted briefly toward the twisting silver. He appeared confused by it. He looked away and back again.

He had not heard her, she realized.

"Why did you murder Celeste?" she whispered.

He stared at her. "I killed her because she informed me that she wished to alter our bargain." A mad rage flared once again in his eyes. "The stupid bitch sent word that she wanted twice as much money for the damned bracelet. I agreed to meet her at the warehouse and hand over her fee in exchange for the Medusa."

"That's when you strangled her."

"She deserved it. She struggled, of course. Waved that damned fan at me. Tried to put me in a trance. But I killed her before she could utter another word."

"And then you realized that she had not brought the bracelet with her to the warehouse that night. You had miscalculated. Murdered her too soon. What a problem you faced. You had no notion where she had hidden the relic."

"I tried making a few discreet inquiries the morning after the murder."

"But you only succeeded in starting rumors about the missing Medusa," she said, thinking of Nightingale's late-night visit to Howard and Lord Vale's sudden interest in the search. "That was how the rumors concerning the theft of the Medusa got started so speedily."

"Yes. And then Hudson hired March to look into the matter. I must admit, it was a rather ingenious move."

"Actually, Dr. Hudson employed me to look into it."

He ignored the small correction, lost in his tale now. "I searched several of the antiquities shops, thinking that Celeste might have made a more profitable bargain with one of the dealers."

Clearly he did not know about Mrs. Rushton's inadvertent theft of her own relic, Lavinia thought. All he knew was that Celeste had obtained the Medusa, but she evidently had not told him how she got hold of it. Perhaps she had considered such details to be professional secrets.

Lavinia paused in the act of turning the pendant. "It was you I surprised that day in Mr. Tredlow's shop."

"Yes. I thought at the time that it was fortunate that you did not see me. I did not want to kill you at that point. I wanted you to continue your search. Indeed, I thought it quite possible that with March's connections the two of you might well find the thing." Pelling smiled again and raised the point of the knife. "And that is just what happened, is it not?"

"Yes."

"Where is the Medusa bracelet, Mrs. Lake?"

She drew a breath. "You don't really expect me to tell you, do you? I know that you will kill me the moment the bracelet is in your possession."

"You will tell me," Pelling promised. Something snakelike slithered just beneath the surface of his eyes. "In the end, you will be only too happy to tell me the location of the bracelet."

THE HACKNEY RATTLED TO A HALT A SHORT TIME LATER. LAVINIA could smell the river. When Pelling opened the door, she saw sagging docks and shabby outbuildings swathed in fog. She heard the creak of dock timbers, but the water itself was invisible in the gray mist. There was no indication that anyone else was about.

She tried to think of what to do next.

Pelling used the tip of the knife to motion her out of the cab. She jumped down cautiously and looked up at the coachman. One glimpse of his rough features destroyed her small hope of help from that quarter: The man on the box was one of the two men who had attacked Tobias in Maggie's front hall.

He did not meet her eyes, his entire attention on Pelling. "This is the end of the matter as far as I'm concerned. Where's the rest of my money?"

"Here." Pelling tossed a small sack at him. "You'll find that it is all there. Take it and be off."

The villain loosened the string that secured the sack, glanced inside, and then nodded, satisfied. He picked up the whip and gave the horses the signal.

The hackney clattered off and was soon lost in the fog.

The thickening mist might provide some concealment, Lavinia thought. If she could run fast enough, she might be able to escape Pelling's knife and lose herself in the gathering darkness. She collected her skirts.

"Do not think that you can escape me, Mrs. Lake." Pelling reached into the pocket of his greatcoat and produced a pistol. He smiled again. "You may be able to outrun a knife, but you cannot outrun a bullet. I am an excellent shot."

"I do not doubt that for a moment. But if you kill me now, you will never learn where Celeste hid the bracelet."

"Rest assured that the bullet I lodge in you will not kill you. Not immediately. There will be ample time for you to tell me everything you know. Now, then, we are going through that door over there." He pointed with the knife. "Move quickly, Mrs. Lake. I am growing extremely impatient."

She touched the pendant again. "You told me that you were a strong man. I believe you, sir. I have great respect for a man of your power."

He glanced at the pendant. "Stop fiddling with that damned necklace."

"Your power makes me anxious."

"As well it should."

"It makes me feel small. As if I were far away from you at the end of a very long, very dark hall."

"Stop talking." He jerked his gaze away from the pendant with obvious effort. "Go through that door, Mrs. Lake. Be quick about it."

"I know where the bracelet is," she said gently. "Shall I tell you now?"

He shifted restlessly and looked away from the pendant. "Where is it?"

"Celeste hid it well." She took a step back toward the quay that edged the river. "It is at the end of a very long hall. Can you see the hall in your mind? It is the same hall in which I am standing. I look so small there at the very end of the hall. You will have to come closer to see me." She fell back another step. "I have the Medusa here with me at the end of the hall. You must come down this long hall to find me and the bracelet—"

"Bloody hell, cease prattling on about hallways." But he took a hesitant step, following her as she edged back through the mists toward the river. "I do not want to hear about the long hall."

"But you must go down this long, long hall if you wish to find the Medusa." She continued gliding slowly toward the gray wall of fog that cloaked the river. From the corner of her eye, she watched for an alley or passageway between buildings that might provide cover for a few seconds. "Come with me down this hall. You know it well."

"No. No, I don't know what you're talking about."

But he followed, as if drawn by a string. Unfortunately, the pistol in his hand never wavered.

"It is the hall you go down whenever you find it necessary to beat a woman. It is the place where you are in control. The place where you are powerful. When you are in this hallway no one is stronger than you."

"Yes." He continued walking toward her, moving more quickly now. "I am the strong one."

"Women cannot control you when you are in this place."

"No. Here I am in command." His voice altered slightly, rising in pitch. "She cannot hurt me here."

"Who cannot hurt you?"

"Aunt Medusa."

Lavinia nearly missed her footing. "Aunt *Medusa*?"

Pelling smirked, the giggle of a young boy, not a full-grown man. "That's what I call Aunt Miranda behind her back. She thinks she can make me stop doing the bad things if she beats me often enough and hard enough. But I won't stop. Because she's right, you see. There is a demon in me and he makes me strong. One of these days I'm going to hurt Aunt Medusa so bad she'll never be able to beat me again. I'm going to kill her."

She could not retreat any farther. The river was directly behind her. She could hear it lapping softly, hungrily. The only choice was to walk backward along the stone quay. She edged in that direction. The row of empty warehouses formed a seemingly solid wall facing the river.

"You are halfway along the long, long hall..."

She moved slowly and carefully, terrified of stumbling over a stone and breaking the fragile trance. She glanced quickly at the closed doors and blank windows to her right, searching for an escape route.

"I followed her into the kitchen that night after we were alone in the house. None of the servants would live in it anymore, you see. They were all frightened of me..."

The narrow passage between two buildings loomed suddenly. It was the only opening she had seen. She stopped, preparing to run.

"...I stabbed Medusa with the carving knife. There was a great deal of blood..."

The action of taking flight would shatter the crystalline trance that bound Pelling. She would get no second chances.

"I took everything I could carry and later sold all of it, including the damned stone. She had always told me that the stone possessed certain forces, but I didn't believe her. I did not realize until many years later when my spells started to get worse that she had told the truth. She came to see me in my dreams. She laughed at me. That was when she told me that I had got rid of the one thing that had the power to banish her ghost."

"The Blue Medusa. You set out to find it."

"I must find it. She is trying to drive me mad, you see. The bracelet is the only thing that can stop her. You will tell me where it is, damn you."

She was preparing herself for the effort when there was a sudden, wild fluttering of wings to her left. A water bird squawked its displeasure and took off, soaring low across the water.

Pelling came to his senses instantly. He blinked once and then seemed to comprehend immediately that something had gone badly wrong.

"Where am I? What do you think you're doing?" He raised the pistol. "Did you think you could trick me?"

"*Pelling.*" Tobias's voice rang ominously in the fog, echoing eerily among the empty buildings. "Stop or I will shoot you where you stand."

The threat cast a mesmeric spell over the entire scene. The world around Lavinia went still and hushed.

And then Pelling whirled around, seeking the voice in the fog. "*March.* Where are you, damn your eyes? Show yourself. I'll kill her if you don't."

Lavinia ran for her life, making for the limited shelter of the lane and the protective cloak of the heavy fog. A few feet could make all the difference in determining whether she lived or died. Pistols were notoriously unreliable beyond a short distance.

"No." Pelling started to turn back toward her. "You cannot escape me, Medusa."

"*Pelling,*" Tobias called again. The voice of doom.

Pelling's pistol roared. For a terrifying eternity Lavinia expected to feel the impact of the bullet in her back. Then she comprehended that Pelling had fired at Tobias, not her.

"Dear God."

But the shot had gone wild, she realized. Pelling could not possibly see Tobias in the heavy mist.

"Forget her, Pelling," Tobias commanded in that eerie voice that seemed to come from nowhere and everywhere at once. "You must kill me first if you are to have any chance of escape."

Lavinia flattened herself against the nearest wall and peeked around the corner. Pelling had dropped the empty pistol and was fumbling frantically to pull a second one from the pocket of his greatcoat.

"Show yourself, March," Pelling shouted. Pistol in hand, he turned on his heel, seeking Tobias in the mists. "Where are you, you bloody bastard?"

"Behind you, Pelling."

Tobias emerged at last from the fog, striding deliberately along the quay toward his target. He held a pistol in one hand. The wings of his black greatcoat snapped above the tops of his boots. An invisible aura of power seemed to coil around him, deepening and growing more intense as he neared his victim.

To Lavinia it appeared as though he gathered energy from the dark mists of the oncoming night and wielded it the way a man wielded a sword.

She felt the breath squeeze out of her lungs. She had seen him in dangerous moods before, but never one such as this.

For the first time she sensed the raw, untrained talent in him and shivered. It was just as well that he had never pursued a career as a mesmerist, she thought.

In that short, dazzling moment of intuitive vision, she knew the shattering truth: Tobias's wild talents called to whatever it was within her that gave her the ability to practice mesmerism with such power. It was as though the forces of animal magnetism that flowed through him resonated with those that flowed through her.

Tobias was, indeed, dangerous, and some part of him must have sensed it years ago, she thought, even if he had never consciously acknowledged it. That was why he had taught himself such a degree of self-mastery. She wondered if he would ever come to the realization that his ability to control and suppress the forces at work within him only made him all the more of a sorcerer.

"Stay back," Pelling shouted, voice rising. He sounded completely unhinged now. "Stay back, damn you."

He raised the pistol and fired.

"No," Lavinia screamed.

Almost simultaneously, a second shot thundered out of the mists.

Pelling jerked and toppled over the edge of the quay. Lavinia heard a muffled splash.

"Tobias." She ran forward. "Are you all right?"

Tobias looked at her from the heart of the invisible storm that appeared to seethe around him. He held the pistol at his side. For an instant she was sure she glimpsed dangerous currents of energy in his eyes.

Just your imagination. Get hold of yourself.

"Yes," Tobias said softly. "I am all right. His aim was off. I think you shook his nerve."

She looked down and saw Pelling floating facedown in the river. She knew why his aim had been off. It had not been her doing. He had been terrified by the sight of Tobias sweeping toward him out of the fog.

Without another word she went straight into Tobias's arms. He caught her close and held her against him for a very long time.

It was later, after Tobias had pulled Pelling's body from the water and lashed it to the back of the cart, that Lavinia thought about the warehouse.

"I want to have a quick look inside," she said.

Tobias walked toward the front of the cart to untie the horse. "Why?"

"He tried to make me go in there." She looked at the closed door. "I need to know what is behind that door."

He hesitated and then retied the reins.

Without further argument, he went to the door of the warehouse and opened it. She walked in slowly, giving her eyes a chance to adjust to the dim light.

The interior was crowded with a number of coiled ropes, empty crates, and shipping casks.

Howard Hudson lay, bound and gagged, in the corner.

Lavinia hurried forward and removed the strip of cloth that sealed his lips. He groaned and sat up so that Tobias could cut the ropes around his wrists.

"Thought you two would never get here," he said.

$\mathcal{T}$hirty

THAT NIGHT, AFTER TOBIAS HAD DEALT WITH THE AUTHORITIES as only he could, thanks to his many connections, they gathered in the parlor together with Emeline, Anthony, Joan, and Vale.

Her study, Lavinia had quickly realized, was much too small for such a crowd, and it certainly was not impressive enough for the likes of Lord Vale. Not that the parlor was much grander, she thought uneasily. But at least there was more space.

In spite of not yet having received any fees to cover the expenses of the affair, she poured everyone an extralarge glass of her precious sherry. Surviving a close brush with a murderer inspired one to be generous, she thought.

"All three of them wanted the Blue Medusa," she said, sinking down onto the sofa alongside Joan. "Each for a different reason. Howard, I regret to say, actually put some credence in the legends surrounding it. He wanted it for his experiments. Celeste hoped to sell it in order to purchase another rung on the social ladder. And Pelling, who had become quite demented, had concluded that it would give him power over the ghost of the aunt he had murdered in his youth."

Joan shuddered. "It was a near thing. How fortunate that Mr. March arrived at the Banks mansion just as you were forced into Pelling's closed hackney."

"Indeed." Emeline took a fortifying sip of sherry. "I cannot bear to think about what might have happened had he not seen you and managed to follow you."

Vale contemplated Tobias, who occupied the chair across from him. "After this incident you will be obliged to concede that there is such a thing as coincidence, eh, March? Joan is right: If you had not happened to call at the Banks mansion this afternoon, you would never have seen Mrs. Lake getting into the hackney."

There was a short pause during which everyone took a swallow of sherry.

Tobias turned his glass between his palms and looked at Lavinia. He smiled slightly.

"It was not luck or coincidence that took me to the Banks house this afternoon," he said quietly. "I followed Lavinia because she had left a note informing me of where she had gone. Just as she had promised."

She met his eyes and saw a reflection of the same absolute certainty of knowledge that had coalesced deep inside her. Regardless of the clashes of will that lay ahead—clashes that were inevitable, given their strong temperaments—a bond had formed between them. Tobias was far more than her lover and occasional partner. The metaphysical link was now so strong that she knew it could never be severed.

"How unfortunate that you are left with no client," Joan said with a good deal of sympathy. "I understand that Mr. Hudson has postponed payment indefinitely due to a lack of funds, and Mr. Nightingale, of course, has canceled his arrangement with you."

Lavinia looked up from her musings. "Oh, I have every hope of salvaging at least one of our clients. Mrs. Rushton, to be precise."

Emeline frowned. "But she will pay you only if you return the relic and arrange a profitable sale."

"I hope to take care of that little outstanding matter first thing in the morning," Lavinia said.

They all looked at her.

Vale's eyes glittered in the firelight. "Are you telling us that you know where Celeste Hudson hid the bracelet?"

"Yes," Lavinia said. "As it happens, I was on my way to collect it this afternoon when Pelling got in my way."

Thirty-one

Dr. Darfield looked up from a journal of accounts when Lavinia and Tobias were ushered into his office. He was not wearing his exotic blue robes, Lavinia noticed. Instead, he was attired in a manner more appropriate to a successful man of business: fashionably pleated trousers, a well-cut coat, and an intricately knotted cravat.

He studied his visitors for a long moment and then he closed the leather-bound volume and rose slowly to his feet. He gestured toward two chairs.

"You have come for the bracelet, I assume," he said to Lavinia.

"Yes." She sat down and arranged her skirts. "This is my partner, Mr. March. He has been involved in this affair from the start."

She was not surprised when Tobias ignored the offer of a chair. He moved to his favorite location in any room that contained a person whom he did not know or trust. He stood with his back to the window, watching Darfield.

Darfield nodded, his expression somber, quietly resigned. "I have been expecting you since I heard about Pelling's death."

He crossed the room to a bookcase, removed several volumes from the middle shelf, and opened a small safe set into the paneled wall. He removed an object wrapped in black velvet and went back to his desk.

Without a word, he untied the cord that bound the small pouch and spread the folds flat on the desk. A large, intricately worked gold bracelet of curious design gleamed softly against the black velvet. A strange blue cameo was set into the center of the band.

Lavinia got to her feet and went to the desk, impelled by the sheer wonder of such an ancient object. The pierced work had been done with exquisite artistry. The repeating pattern of entwined snakes was so finely detailed that the bracelet appeared to have been fashioned of gold lace rather than cut and shaped from metal.

She picked it up carefully. It had looked so delicate and airy sitting on the velvet that she was somewhat surprised by the substantial weight of it in her hand. The gold was warm against her palm.

The cameo of Medusa was masterfully carved in the stone's alternating shades of blue. The tiny snakes writhed in the Gorgon's hair, her eyes stared with chilling intensity. The small, distinctive wand beneath the severed throat was precisely rendered. There was a sense of menacing power about the miniature sculpture that made her aware of icy fingers on her spine.

"Celeste arranged to encounter Mrs. Rushton while she was out shopping one afternoon." Lavinia did not raise her eyes from the bracelet. "She put her into a mesmeric trance."

"Mrs. Rushton is quite susceptible to mesmerism," Darfield said. "An excellent client."

"While she held Mrs. Rushton in the trance, Celeste instructed her to make an appointment with you for therapeutic treatments. She also ordered her to take the bracelet from Banks's safe and bring it to you."

"Which is precisely what Mrs. Rushton did." Darfield watched Lavinia handle the bracelet. "Afterward she recalled nothing about the incident, of course. Celeste was actually quite skilled at mesmerism, although she was careful to conceal the full extent of her abilities from Hudson. She trusted no man. She always said that a woman did well to keep as many secrets as possible. She did not want Hudson to worry that she might be a threat to his business."

Tobias folded his arms. "I presume you taught her the art of mesmerism?"

"Yes. I studied with a practitioner who took instruction from Dr. Mesmer himself."

Tobias cocked a brow. "Why did Celeste join with Hudson? Why not work with you?"

Darfield sat down on the edge of his desk. He was quiet for a moment, obviously sorting through his thoughts.

"Celeste was born on the wrong side of the blanket, the illegitimate daughter of a shop girl and the wastrel son of a member of the country gentry," he said eventually. "Her father never acknowledged her. He was already married to a neighbor's daughter, whose family's land adjoined his. Unfortunately, he had no aptitude for farming. He managed to drive himself into bankruptcy."

Lavinia closed her fingers very gently around the bracelet. "Celeste fought her way up in the world, didn't she?"

"Yes. Her sole ambition was to acquire sufficient money to allow her to bury her past and take up a position in Society. To that end, she used any man she thought capable of assisting her toward her goal."

"Last year she met Hudson in Bath," Tobias said.

Darfield glanced at him and then looked away. "Celeste was a very clever woman. She formed a connection with Hudson after she grew suspicious of certain jewelry thefts that had occurred among some of his wealthier clients. Her own training in mesmerism and some careful observation allowed her to conclude that he was likely the thief."

"Oh, I really don't think that Howard had anything to do—"

"Bloody hell," Tobias interrupted forcefully. "She seduced Hudson because she wanted him to teach her to become an accomplished jewel thief."

Darfield smiled wryly. "She also wanted access to his wealthy clients. As I said, she was a decent mesmerist, but she lacked the social connections required to attract a truly exclusive clientele." He moved a hand, palm up. "I could not offer her access to clients in wealthy circles. My own business is flourishing nicely, but I do not cater to the High Flyers. The right references make all the difference, you see."

Tobias caught Lavinia's eye. "So I've been told."

"Even if I had been able to offer a more refined list of clients, I would not have been inclined to become a thief. I never had Celeste's raw nerve, you see. Stealing valuable jewelry is an excellent way to wind up on the gallows, in my opinion."

"It is certainly a risky profession," Tobias agreed.

"One day Pelling walked into Hudson's office and offered him a commission to steal the Blue Medusa." Darfield paused. "I expect that you know the rest."

"Pelling was mistaken in believing that Dr. Hudson was a professional thief," Lavinia said quickly. "But Howard was researching mesmerism, and he no doubt became obsessed with the notion of obtaining the Medusa for his experiments. He turned down Pelling's offer, but he decided to try to acquire the stone himself. Celeste, however, was ready to move on and needed a financial stake. She decided to take things into her own hands and made her own bargain with Pelling."

Darfield inclined his head. "That was Celeste. Always willing to take a gamble." He paused. "Do you know, in the beginning, when I first learned that she had been murdered, I was certain that it was Hudson who had killed her. I was hatching my own notions of revenge, imagining various ways to kill Hudson without getting caught, when you two undertook your investigation. My first inclination was to try to frighten you off."

"You sent the coachman with the note to scare Anthony and Emeline," Lavinia said.

"Yes. But that same day you came to my rooms pretending to seek a treatment. I pretended not to know who you were. I decided to see what came of your inquiries."

"Thank heavens you did decide to wait," Lavinia said fervently. "You might have murdered the wrong man and risked the noose for nothing."

"You and Mr. March saved me that fate and exacted justice for Celeste." Darfield met her eyes. "For that I will always be in your debt. If there is ever anything I can do to repay you, Mrs. Lake, I hope you will come to me. I can offer free therapeutic treatments—"

"No, no, that is quite all right, sir," she said hastily. "The return of the Medusa is sufficient compensation, I assure you."

She was uncomfortably aware of another unpleasant trickle of cold energy along her spine. Imagination, she thought. Or maybe my nerves. She reminded herself that she had been under something of a strain lately.

Nevertheless, she quickly put the bracelet back down on the velvet. To her enormous relief, the uneasy sensation vanished.

"There is one thing I do not comprehend," she said, rewrapping the relic.

"What is that?" he asked.

"You said yourself that Celeste did not trust men. Yet she obviously entrusted this bracelet to you for safekeeping." She picked up the velvet pouch. "What made you different in her eyes from other men?"

"Oh, yes, I forgot that part, didn't I?" Darfield's smile was sad, almost wistful. "You will recall that I mentioned that her father was married to the daughter of a neighbor landholder. The pair had a son, who was obliged to go into trade for financial reasons."

"I understand now," Lavinia said gently. "She was your sister."

Thirty-two

TOBIAS STRODE INTO LAVINIA'S STUDY THREE DAYS LATER, LOOK-ing exceedingly pleased. "The bargain has been struck and we have been paid our fee."

Lavinia put down her pen. "Bargain?"

"Mrs. Rushton arranged to sell the Blue Medusa to an anonymous collector through the auspices of Mr. Nightingale."

"She certainly did not delay that business long, did she? Banks expired only yesterday."

"Mrs. Rushton is a businesswoman." He settled into one of the chairs in front of the fire and smiled. "In any event, she received her money this morning, and she was so delighted with the transaction that she paid us immediately."

"That is excellent news. I had no notion the sale would take place so quickly." She chuckled. "I think I can wager a guess as to the identity of the anonymous collector."

"Go ahead, try your hand at it."

"Lord Vale bought it, I assume."

He smiled. "You assume wrong. Joan Dove is the name of the mysterious collector."

Lavinia stared at him, astonished. "I was aware that she inherited her husband's collection, but I did not know that she herself had a personal interest in antiquities."

"I suspect it is a rather new hobby," Tobias said dryly.

She recalled the blue gown Joan had chosen to wear the night of her ball. And the mystery of her connection to the Blue Chamber.

"Joan is rather fond of blue," she said very carefully. "You don't suppose she wants to use the Medusa as some sort of personal emblem or seal, do you?"

"I prefer not to speculate on the notion of a possible new master of a criminal organization or on her choice of an appropriate seal."

"Does Lord Vale know that he is not going to obtain the bracelet?"

"I think it is safe to assume that Vale knows precisely what happened to the Medusa."

The door opened before Lavinia could ask any more questions. Mrs. Chilton appeared. She wore a disapproving expression.

"Dr. Hudson to see you, Mrs. Lake."

"Bloody hell," Tobias muttered. "Tell him Mrs. Lake is not receiving callers, Mrs. Chilton."

Lavinia frowned at him. "Really, sir, I will thank you not to give the instructions around here."

Howard walked into the study at that moment, his attention focused entirely on Lavinia. If he noticed Tobias rising slowly from the chair, he did not give any indication.

Lavinia jumped up quickly, grateful for the interruption. "Good afternoon, Howard. I collect that you are quite recovered from your ordeal?"

"Thanks to you, my dear Lavinia." He crossed the room to kiss both her hands.

"And thanks to Mr. March as well," she reminded him quickly.

She tried to retrieve her hands. Howard did not seem to notice the small effort. He clung to her fingers.

"Yes, of course," Howard said. He flicked a glance in Tobias's direction and then gave him his shoulder in a well-executed direct cut. "I have come to say good-bye for a while, my dear."

She tugged a little on her captive hands, aware that Howard's eyes had taken on a fathomless quality. He did not release her. She had a small moment of social panic, aware now that the only way to get free would be an ignominious struggle. She kept smiling, hoping that Tobias did not notice what was happening. The last thing she wanted was a quarrel between these two men here in her study.

"You are leaving Town?" she asked very brightly.

"Yes." Howard looked deep into her eyes. "I need time to recover from the loss of my dear Celeste. Time to come to terms with the extent of her betrayal. The knowledge that she was a professional thief is absolutely staggering. Indeed, I am undone by the news. It is best that I go off to the country to rusticate for a time."

"I agree, Hudson." Tobias crossed the room and gripped Howard's shoulder in a man-to-man fashion. "Leaving Town is an excellent notion. Give the gossip a chance to fade, eh?"

He squeezed Howard's shoulder in what appeared to be a friendly gesture. But Lavinia saw the flash of pain and astonishment in Howard's eyes. He released her hands abruptly. The interesting, bottom-of-the-sea quality disappeared immediately from his gaze.

"Indeed," Howard said through gritted teeth. The sonorous ring was gone from his voice. He gave Tobias a withering look. "Although my dear Celeste was the jewel thief, I fear that there are some unfortunate rumors circulating to the effect that I was involved in her schemes."

"Yes, I know. I heard some of those rumors myself, just this morning in my club." Tobias released his victim. "No one can prove anything, of course."

"Of course they cannot prove anything," Howard said heatedly. "Because there is nothing to be proven. I was entirely unaware of Celeste's criminal activities."

"Nevertheless," Tobias continued, "rumors of your proclivities in that direction will be damned hard to squelch, I'm afraid. Hard to attract an exclusive clientele while that sort of gossip is swirling through Society."

His smile did not look at all sympathetic, Lavinia thought. There was, in point of fact, a distinctly wolfish quality to it. She turned quickly back to Howard.

"Where will you go?" she asked gently.

"I haven't decided yet. Someplace where I can continue my researches and experiments."

"I wish you the best of luck with your investigations into mesmerism," she said.

"Thank you." He went to the door, paused, turned, and gave her a long, lingering look. "But never fear, my dear, we shall meet again. We are, after all, old friends, are we not? I have always felt that there was a connection between us. It is a link that cannot be broken by the whims of fortune or"—he glanced coldly at Tobias—"the opinions of other people who may come and go in our lives."

Tobias looked as if he was thinking very seriously about wrapping his hands around Howard's throat. Lavinia moved swiftly to get between the two men.

"Good-bye, Howard." She did not offer him her hand. "I wish you well."

"Farewell for now, my dear."

He smiled at her one last time and went out the door.

There was a short silence in the wake of his departure. Neither Lavinia nor Tobias spoke as Mrs. Chilton ushered Howard out the front door.

When he was gone from the house, Lavinia looked at Tobias.

"Those rumors concerning Howard that you mentioned were circulating in the clubs," she said without inflection. "The ones implying that he might have used his skills as a mesmerist to steal valuables from his clients."

Tobias gave her a look of polite inquiry. "What of them?"

"You wouldn't happen to know who started them, would you?"

He contrived to appear hurt by the thinly veiled accusation. "My sweet, are you accusing me of indulging in the lowest sort of gossip and innuendo?"

"Yes, that is precisely what I am accusing you of doing." She fixed him with a steely glare. "Well, sir? Did you deliberately impugn Howard's character to such an extent that he is obliged to leave Town?"

"I am crushed by your poor opinion of me." He came forward,

closed his hands around her shoulders, and kissed her brow lightly. "I assure you that I never engage in false gossip and innuendo."

"But if you thought the gossip and innuendo were *not* false—"

"Then I would not be engaging in gossip and innuendo." He kissed the tip of her nose. "I would be dealing in the truth."

"Tobias, I want to know who started those rumors in the clubs."

"I thought I had made it quite clear, my sweet, I am not the sort of man who indulges in unfounded scandal broth."

She wanted to question him further, but he chose that moment to kiss her.

One of these days, she thought, her mouth softening under his, she really would have to make it clear to him that he could not expect to win every argument with this approach.

JOAN STOOD IN FRONT OF THE TALL LIBRARY WINDOW AND HELD the ancient bracelet to the light. Her new antiquity was quite extraordinary, she thought. The pattern that had been pierced into the gold was astonishing in its detail. Medusa's staring eyes were so brilliantly worked in the multilayered blue gem that one could almost believe that they had the power to turn men to stone.

The butler appeared in the doorway. "Lord Vale has arrived, madam."

A quiet excitement flowed through her. "Please show him in."

Vale walked into the library a moment later. He crossed to where she stood at the window and bent gracefully over her hand.

"I received your message and came at once," he said.

"I thought you might enjoy examining my new relic." She handed it to him with a smile. "I know that you have a deep interest in such things."

He took it from her and said nothing for a long time, content to study the piece.

At last he raised his eyes to Joan's. "I congratulate you, madam, on your purchase."

"Thank you. I am delighted with it. Do you know, I expected to have to compete with at least one other collector at the auction. But Mr. Nightingale informed me that I was the only one to place a bid. He said that his other client learned that I had made an offer for the bracelet and declined to do so, leaving the field to me."

Vale smiled and went back to studying the bracelet.

"You were Mr. Nightingale's other client, were you not, my lord?" she asked softly.

"I cannot think of anyone I would rather see take possession of such a fantastic piece than yourself, my dear." He handed her the bracelet. "It is quite remarkable. And so are you."

"Thank you." She looked at the Medusa and thought about what it must have cost him to remove himself from the secret auction. "I find I have developed a serious interest in antiquities. I would like to apply for membership in the Connoisseurs Club." She paused. "Assuming the club accepts ladies, that is."

"I am the club's founder. I make the rules." He smiled slowly. "And I have no objection whatsoever to accepting ladies."

She smiled and held the bracelet out to him. "My application fee, sir. I hereby present the Blue Medusa to the club's private museum."

"As the Keeper of the museum, I accept your application, madam." He caught her hand and brought it to his lips a second time. Then he raised his head and looked into her eyes. "If you are interested, I can arrange for a private tour this very evening."

"I would enjoy that."

Thirty-three

A FORTNIGHT LATER, ON A SUNNY THURSDAY AFTERNOON, TOBIAS motioned Mrs. Chilton aside and opened the door of the study himself. Lavinia was sitting in one of the oversize chairs in front of the hearth, a book open on her lap. The sunlight streaming through the window set fire to her hair.

"Good afternoon, my sweet," he said. "You have a visitor."

Startled by the interruption, she looked up with that abstracted expression she always wore whenever she was summoned summarily from one of her books of poetry.

Her eyes cleared when she saw him standing there in the opening. "I did not know that you intended to call this afternoon, Tobias. What brings you here? Have we a new case so soon?"

"Not a new one. Rather the conclusion to an old one."

"What on earth are you talking about?"

"There is someone here who wishes to speak with you."

He stood back and held the door for Lavinia's visitor. The tall woman walked part way into the study and stopped.

"Good day, Mrs. Lake," she said. "I cannot tell you how happy I am to see you again and under these circumstances."

Lavinia stared, eyes very wide, lips slightly parted.

Tobias savored the expression. It was not often that he was afforded the opportunity to witness such a charming mix of astonishment and delight on Lavinia's face.

"*Mrs. Pelling.* Jessica." Lavinia fairly leaped out of the chair. She dropped the book on the table and rushed forward. "You're alive."

"Thanks to you, Mrs. Lake." Jessica smiled. "Actually, I have not used the name Jessica Pelling since the day I staged the drama of my own suicide. I have been known as Judith Palmer these past two years."

"Which is one of the reasons why it was so bloody difficult to find her." Tobias went to the window. "I sent out my letters of inquiry the day after Lavinia told me her tale. You did an excellent job of covering your tracks, Mrs. Pelling."

"I did my best," she said. "I was quite certain that my life depended on it, you see. Oscar was becoming increasingly mad. The rages were occurring more often, and each time he seemed more out of control when they struck. I knew I had to get away. I took your advice, Mrs. Lake."

Lavinia released her and stepped back. "You took it so well that I myself was convinced that you were dead. The only question in my mind was whether Pelling had murdered you or if you truly had taken your own life."

"I cannot tell you how much I regret not being able to tell you the truth. I had hoped that you would reason it out for yourself."

"The fact that your body was never found gave me some small hope, but I could not be certain." She looked at Tobias. "What were these letters of inquiry you mentioned?"

He moved one hand in a negligent gesture. "I wrote letters to a number of my associates from the old days. They are scattered throughout the country."

"Ah, yes, your fellow spies," Lavinia said. "Very clever of you, sir."

"I also asked Crackenburne to tap his extensive network of friends and acquaintances. You gave me a good description that day you told me the tale. The fact that Jessica was somewhat taller than average and that she had disappeared with an unusual family ring was extremely helpful."

"Yes, of course," Lavinia said. She gave him an admiring smile. "You reasoned that Jessica must have sold the ring to support herself in her new life, so you set out to trace it, didn't you?"

"That was one of several strategies I employed. I also knew that we were looking for a single woman who would have turned up out of nowhere two years ago. Eventually, word came back that there was a person meeting all the particulars operating a school for young ladies in Dorset."

Jessica gave him a wry smile. "It is fortunate for me that Oscar did not hire you to search for me two years ago, sir."

Tobias shook his head. "I doubt that he was eager to find you. Your so-called suicide proved quite convenient in financial terms. He had your inheritance, after all."

"And shortly after that he became occupied with his quest for the Medusa bracelet," Lavinia said. "He had sold it in his youth after murdering his aunt. But as his madness grew, he came to believe that he needed to recover the bracelet to ward off her vengeful spirit."

Jessica shuddered. "I knew that he was sinking into his madness."

Lavinia smiled at her. "I cannot tell you how happy I am to see you."

"You are not the only one who is pleased to know that Mrs. Pelling is very much among the living." Tobias smiled. "Pelling's lawyer is equally delighted. Jessica is officially a widow now, and a wealthy one, at that."

"I must tell you, the money will come in handy," Jessica said. "There is not much profit in operating a school for young ladies."

"How do you come to be in London?" Lavinia asked.

"Mr. March sent me a letter introducing himself and informing me of the very good news that Oscar Pelling was dead. He offered to pay my expenses to come to London to visit you and assure you that I was alive and well. I believe he planned this reunion as a surprise for you."

Lavinia looked at Tobias. He felt the warmth of her smile throughout his entire body. Pleasure and a deep sense of certainty flowed through him.

"Mr. March feels that he has no talent for grand, romantical gestures," Lavinia said to Jessica. "But in truth, he possesses a distinct and most remarkable ability to select just the right gift for me."

Thirty-four

THE FOLLOWING AFTERNOON LAVINIA PUT THE FINISHING touches on her advertisement, sanded and blotted the foolscap, and sat back to savor her clever wording.

The door of the study opened just as she was about to read the lines aloud to herself to hear how it sounded. Tobias walked into the room.

Sometimes, she thought, his timing was uncanny.

She eyed him warily. "What are you doing here?"

"The warmth of your welcome never fails to lift my spirits and brighten my day, my sweet."

"I thought you said at breakfast that you planned to discuss another investment with Crackenburne today."

"Crackenburne can wait. He won't be going anywhere. I told you, the man never leaves his club." He looked down at the paper in front of her. "What is that?"

"I have finished my advertisement. My only regret is that I was unable to find a way to use the word *intrigue*. Nevertheless, I intend to send this off to the newspaper today. Would you care to hear it?"

"You are determined to ignore my advice on this matter, are you not?"

"Yes, of course I am." She cleared her throat and read the advertisement.

> Persons wishing to commission an expert for the purpose of conducting inquiries of a personal and private nature may send word to the address below. Exclusive references are available upon request. The utmost discretion is assured.

"Hmm," Tobias said.

She narrowed her eyes in warning. "Do not bother to criticize. I am quite satisfied that it sounds extremely professional and I am not interested in your opinion."

"It certainly sounds professional," he agreed. "But I could not help but notice that you make no mention that you work with a partner."

"You are entirely against the notion of placing a notice in the papers. Why would you want to be mentioned in it?"

"I suppose it is a matter of pride," he admitted. "We are occasional partners, after all. But that advertisement makes it sound as though you always work alone."

"Well—"

"If you are determined to advertise, I would think that you would want to draw attention to the unique nature of the services you offer. Surely anyone wishing to employ a professional for the purposes of making private inquiries would be more inclined to do so if he thought that he would be gaining the experience of not one but two experts in the field."

He had a point, she thought. "Well, I suppose I could rewrite it to bring out that aspect."

"Excellent notion." He reached out, caught hold of the page between thumb and forefinger, and twitched it out of her grasp. "I shall be happy to assist you. Tomorrow morning at breakfast we can discuss the new wording. It may take a while, but I'm sure that, together, we shall come up with a very enticing advertisement."

"Pray, do not trouble yourself, sir." She snatched the paper back from him and gave him a cool smile. "With a minor change or two, this one will work perfectly well. I shall make the modifications this afternoon and send it around to the paper today."

"Damnation, Lavinia—"

The door opened behind him. He broke off and glared at Mrs. Chilton over his shoulder.

Lavinia turned quickly toward the door. "Yes, what is it, Mrs. Chilton? A visitor?"

"No, ma'am." Mrs. Chilton fixed Tobias with an unreadable look. "Miss Emeline's gone out with Mr. Sinclair, and now I'm off to shop for currants. Just wanted to let ye know that I'll be gone for a while."

"More currants?" Lavinia frowned. "But we cannot possibly have run out so soon. I fail to comprehend why we are going through so many currants lately."

"It's the jam." Mrs. Chilton backed out into the hall. "Takes a lot of currants to make good currant jam. Well, now, I'll be off. Expect I'll be back at three." She paused, one hand on the doorknob, and gave Tobias a sharp look. "And not a minute later."

Tobias smiled slowly. "Take your time, Mrs. Chilton. No need to hurry back."

Mrs. Chilton closed the door very firmly and went down the hall. Lavinia could have sworn she heard her chuckling.

"I simply cannot comprehend how this small household can go through so much currant jam," Lavinia muttered.

Tobias took her into his arms. "Mrs. Chilton is experienced in the preparation of jam. You must allow her to make the decisions pertaining to the quantity of the ingredients needed."

"Well, I suppose so. Nevertheless—"

"You and I are expert in another line, are we not?" he asked very softly.

She started to argue, and then it struck her that he had just called her an *expert*. It was one of the few times he had paid tribute to her professional skills. The accolade gave her a glow of pleasure.

"Very true," she murmured.

"We are also partners." He brushed his mouth deliberately across hers. "And I think that now would be an excellent time to discuss some of the details of our business association."

"What details would those be, sir?"

His eyes held hers with all the power of a brilliantly accomplished mesmerist. "The most pressing matter at the moment is that I am in love with you, Mrs. Lake."

She thought at first that she had misunderstood him. Her second thought was that her imagination had run wild. And then a glorious sense of happiness blossomed deep inside her. He was, she thought, the only man she had ever met who could truly entrance her.

She slid her arms around his neck. "This is an extremely fortunate turn of events, Mr. March. Because I seem to have fallen in love with you too."

He smiled slowly, deepening the enchantment without saying a single word.

"It will not be easy, you know," she said a trifle anxiously. "I mean, we do tend to quarrel a lot and the business aspect complicates things and I expect there will be any number of problems in the future—"

He put his fingertips against her mouth, silencing her. And then he smiled again.

"You and I never do things the easy way," he said.

And then he kissed her.

The advertisement could wait, she thought. Some things were vastly more important.